OROPE

THE WHITE SNAKE

A NOVEL BY
GUENEVERE LEE

NEW YORK

LONDON • NASHVILLE • MELBOURNE • VANCOUVER

OROPE

Published in New York, New York, by Morgan James Publishing. Morgan James is a trademark of Morgan James, LLC. www.MorganJamesPublishing.com

Publisher's Note: This novel is a work of fiction. Names, characters, places, and incidents are either products of the author's imagination or used fictitiously. All characters are fictional, and any similarity to people living or dead is purely coincidental.

Maps designed by Guenevere Lee and illustrated by Sheharzad Arshad

ISBN 978-1-68350-739-0 paperback
ISBN 978-1-68350-740-6 eBook
Library of Congress Control Number: 2017913244

Cover & Interior Design by:
Megan Whitney
Creative Ninja Designs
megan@creativeninjadesigns.com

Morgan James is a proud partner of Habitat for Humanity Peninsula and Greater Williamsburg. Partners in building since 2006.

Get involved today! Visit
MorganJamesPublishing.com/giving-back

To my mom,
and not because she gave birth to me,
or raised me –
though she did that too.
But because, when I was ten,
she told me to write...

THE WHISPERERS OF THE GODS

THE OCEAN SHALL RISE UP AND SWALLOW THE LAND

"We were the first, and we will be the last." Rashma Hal'Hotem scraped the sinew away from the bone. Her sisters chimed after her: "We were the first, and we will be the last."

The three silver-eyed women sat on the ground, surrounded by sparks rising from the fire and the chanting of hundreds of women. In a small depression dug into the soft sand of the desert, the embers of the fire burned bright against the night.

The women's bronze skin was painted with dark red blood. Their wild, dreadlocked hair was tied with the symbols of their position. They had removed their Ancestral Cloaks, the only clothes they ever wore, and sat naked. The hooded cloaks of skin and bones were placed carefully behind them, the bones facing up to the stars.

They announced themselves as the ceremony began. "I am Rekra Hal'Hashap, who speaks for Life." Rekra wore a necklace of white feathers and claws, and dried water reeds were tied into her hair.

"I am Akrape Hal'Whata, who speaks for Rebirth." Akrape wore a necklace of pearls and seashells. Her hair was tied with the skin of snakes dried into circles so they were eating their own tails.

"I am Rashma Hal'Hotem, who speaks for Death." Rashma wore a necklace made from the skulls of lizards, and vulture feathers were tied into her hair.

The most prominent of the Gogepe, the Whisperers of the Gods, had layers and layers of bones strung to their Ancestral Cloaks, which would sometimes rattle together as the wind caught them. Rashma had far more bones on her cloak than either Akrape or Rekra.

The leathery skin of the Rhagepe had been tattooed with the signs of the goddesses, each one referring to a different achievement in their magic arts. They had just finished painting each other with the blood of the camel they had sacrificed, and the sticky symbols they had drawn still shined with wetness. Rashma, who spoke for Death, finished cleaning the first bone with her black stone fire knife and handed it to Akrape, who spoke for Rebirth.

Rashma looked at Akrape with satisfaction as the younger woman carved the sacred signs into the bone with a large piece of amethyst. This was Akrape's first calendar ceremony. She had only been chosen to be a Rhagepe in Rakeesh, the time before Orope. Of course she had, like all women with silver eyes, trained since birth to one day become a Rhagepe. There were only three Rhagepe to every tribe, and most women lived their entire lives without ever being chosen to speak for the gods.

She could still remember the day she had been chosen to speak for Death. She had been fairly young, but where most women had to spend years training themselves to receive visions, she had always been able to hear the gods while she slept. When Hotem, who spoke for Death, had died, Rashma had taken her place over many others, and became Rashma Hal'Hotem. Her first calendar ceremony she had been so nervous she couldn't stop her hands from shaking, but Akrape seemed calm, carving the symbols with a steady hand before passing the bones to Rekra, who spoke for Life.

"Kreesh tharlaum," Rekra muttered the words over each one as she threw them into the copper cauldron. Each symbol had a different meaning, and Rekra knew them all in her heart. Rashma felt proud of her, of both of them. She wanted to tell them so, but to say anything other than the sacred words would break the flow of the ceremony. No, her praise would have to wait until the sun rose, and the gods returned to their slumber.

They were far from the lands they usually inhabited. The meeting of the Rhagepe took place at the southern edge of the great Kerlra Hal'gepe mountain ridge, the Teeth of the Gods. The mountains began at the north edge of the desert, growing high into jagged peaks and extending farther to the north than any Whisperer had dared to travel. They saw the mountains as steps to the gods, and so meeting at the base gave the Gogepe a stronger bridge to reach them.

Perhaps the Gods themselves had built the temple at the foot of the mountain. Rashma believed it so. Three large intersecting circles were all that remained. The walls, having crumbled over the countless cycles that had passed since its creation, now only rose as high as one's waist. If there had been a roof, it had long since fallen beneath the sand. The centre of the temple, where the three circles joined, was where the calendar ceremony took place. Twelve pillars still stood around the inner temple. A large tarp made of fine leathers and exotic skins donated from every tribe had been stitched together and hung from the pillars to hide the inner temple from sight. Only the Rhagepe would be allowed to enter.

Rashma felt a great lift in her heart whenever she visited the temple. It was as though she could feel the very breath of the gods on her face as she listened for their voices. She felt a connection to this temple she had never felt with another human, not even her fellow Rhagepe. The gods were the only friend or lover she would ever need. They gave her visions to guide her, to warn her of dangers, and in return all they asked was that the old ways be preserved. They filled her with comfort and gave her a place in this barren world.

The first time she had become truly aware of the Rhagepe, when she barely measured as high as her mother's hip, was when she saw one of the Rhagepe in her tribe perform the cloak ceremony. It could only ever be performed once in someone's life. It was the only ceremony by which the Rhagepe could speak directly with the gods, to ask them any questions and receive answers. It was the only ritual more sacred than the one being performed now. The greying woman had ground the bones of her Ancestral Cloak, and the cloak itself was boiled in one of the copper cauldrons at the temple. The other two Rhagepe stood and watched, but they were not allowed to help. She sacrificed a camel, collecting its blood into the pot. The bone dust, along with the eyes of many animals, and the sacred herbs gathered from plants found in the depth of the desert were boiled in the blood and then drunk. A change came over the woman, she went into a trance. Rashma had watched wide-eyed in fear, as the woman raved long into the night, speaking words that sounded like gibberish, until finally settling into an uneasy sleep.

On the following morning when the Rhagepe finally rose she was calm and serene, and told everyone of her experience. Tears brimmed her eyes, as she spoke of how the gods had shown her wonders she could not now speak of, how the gods had given her wisdom and great secrets. The gods had even taught her a new spell, one that would curse a great enemy. From then on she was treated with great respect. It was as though she had transcended them all and become a god herself. When Rashma was chosen to be a Rhagepe for the Gopema tribe a full cycle later, she declared she would never know the touch of a man or the joys of a child. She would perform this ceremony one day. She would sacrifice her cloak and speak with the gods and hear their wisdom directly.

At the beginning of every full cycle, the time it took a babe to become an adult, and the time it took for the wandering star Zera to travel through the twelve constellations, they met there. Zera had just entered Orope, the white snake. The Whisperers brought gifts, like the skins for the tarp along with animals for sacrifice and jewels they had captured or traded for. They hoped these gifts would appease the gods into granting them a calendar free of evils. There were about two dozen groups of Rhagepe, one for each tribe, on the sand in front of the temple, each one collecting a cauldron of bones, members of their tribes standing outside the light of the fires, watching the rites being performed, the children witnessing this for the first time with wide eyes. Those who had witnessed this more than once, ground against each other, thrusting in time with the drumming that came from within the temple.

Rashma had finished scraping clean the last bone and, pulling on her Ancestral Cloak, began to chant, rocking back and forth in the sand. Other sisters who spoke for the Goddess of Death and cleaned the bones were also finishing, and each one signalled this by joining the chant. The drumming surged. The chiefs, who wore the skull of their first kill on their heads began to dance around the circle of spectators at the edge of the firelight. The chiefs' Ancestral Cloaks rattled as they moved the practiced steps, their staffs clattered, feathers and claws hanging from their ends as they were held high above and swung around.

Akrape carved the last sacred sign and joined Rekra in the chant, taking it to a higher pitch. Their words were more frenzied. In every trio of Rhagepe, those finishing their tasks got to their feet and began to gyrate their naked bodies as they circled their copper cauldrons, the chant becoming louder, more fervent. Rekra and other Rhagepe who spoke for the Goddess of Life finished saying the sacred words over the last bone and trilled their tongues, leaping to their feet. The drums became manic, children joined the chiefs dancing in a circle, and those thrusting together arched their backs as they peaked. It was said children conceived on this night were given the greatest of destinies.

The Rhagepe, all cloaked once more, picked up their cauldrons by the three rings that hung on their rims. The pot was heavy but the strength of the Goddesses flowed through them now. The cauldrons felt as light as empty baskets as they continued to dance, carrying their bones towards the open entrance of the temple. They entered not through one of the large circles, but where two of the circles connected. The walls were narrow and lined by torches but grew wider as they reached the inner sanctum. At the mouth of the inner sanctum was the broken frame of what had once been a great door, now a path opening into the covered centre. The hides of golden leopards, black jaguars and sandy mountain lions covered the floors, and in the middle of the room a pit had been dug out and lined with slabs of rocks, smoothed out so it resembled a great bowl. As each group of Rhagepe entered the tent, they overturned their cauldrons, announcing their tribe as they dropped the bones into the bowl.

"We are of the Gopema," Rashma announced proudly. "We return to the gods to hear their words."

In the larger circles outside the inner temple, and able to look in, were the drummers. They were young girls training to one day become Rhagepe. In the three corners of the inner sanctum was a torch, giving light to the large space. As each cauldron was emptied the sisters continued to encircle the temple, until every set of Rhagepe was inside and all the bones were in the pit. They sat.

The drumming, the chanting, and the dancing all ceased at once.

"We were the first," announced one woman, Karesha Hal'Harag, with sheer white hair. She was hunched over, her breasts drooping down to her belly. Her face was a labyrinth of wrinkles and swirling tattoos. Her Ancestral Cloak had three layers of rib bones, each layer tied crosswise onto the one below. Karesha and her mothers had led the Rhagepe during the calendar ceremony since they had first come to this temple. Her necklace was a snake eating its own tail, pearls in the place of its eyes, seashells hung in her dry hair. She spoke for the Goddess of Rebirth. Hers were the most sacred words.

"And we will be the last," all answered back.

"Collect the first vision," old Karesha ordered, pointing at Rashma. Rashma's cloak had the second most bones, a third layer just beginning, and the knowledge of her desire to perform the cloak ceremony had raised her in the esteem of all, giving her the right to be the collector of visions during the ceremony.

Rashma pushed herself up from the ground. She crouched at the edge of the bowl, now filled with the carved bones. Reaching into the mix she pulled out the first one she clutched. All the most important visions that the Rhagepe had had over the past twelve constellations had been carved into these bones. Now it was time to find out which one the Goddesses feared the most, and which ones they would warn their people of.

"It speaks of famine," Rashma read the finely carved symbols. There would be at least a dozen bones pulled out warning of famine. There always were. But there was always famine. Many of the Rhagepe nodded, murmuring, "I too have had this vision."

"Sister Life," the old crone pointed to another woman. Although she still had a glimmer of youth in her face, her hair was greying and one of her eyes was white and blank. She wore no necklace, but had fashioned a crown from seaweed and feathers. Her cloak had nearly two layers. "Check the blood."

The crowned Rhagepe held a round slab in her hand, twelve figures carved into it, each one representing one of the twelve constellations they used to measure the passage of time. She took a long needle carved from a charred bone and pierced her lip. Blood pooled over her teeth and she spit onto the stone slab, hitting the image of Sakabe, the red scorpion, but the blood spattered on many of the other images. "The famine shall be great. Beginning in Sakabe, and continuing on to the next coming of Orope."

The sisters murmured their worry. They did not grow crops, but they still fed from the crops of those they traded with. And so the divining continued. If Rashma pulled out a bone and none had shared the same vision it would be tossed aside. If there was uncertainty among them, Karesha would decide if the vision would be added to the calendar.

"A ram shall give birth to five queens, and they shall be suckled by fire," Rashma read, and all at once the women began to cry of their visions.

"I saw the mountain crack open and swallow five babes in fire!"

"I saw stones rain down on five mountains!"

"I saw two golden mountain lions eat five sheep!"

Karesha quieted them and began to strain through the dreams, picking up the important facts, and when the blood was checked no one was surprised that Apeko, the gold ram, was the only symbol bloodied. "In Apeko," Karesha announced, "five great or powerful figures shall be slain."

They continued, several more symbols of famine being removed, before Rashma picked one that made her pause. She looked up at Karesha and spoke with a quiet voice. "The ocean shall rise up and swallow the land." The Rhagepe went silent. Then, one at a time, they began to hiss, trying to scare the bad omen away. Rashma had had such a vision, a great wall of water standing at the edge of the land, but had decided not to have it carved onto bone. She had tried to tell herself it hadn't been a vision, but just a dream. Her mother used to tell her of the lands her people had come from before they had wandered the desert, the lands which had been swallowed up by water because the Whisperers had ceased to heed the old ways. They believed that so long as they continued to deliver the warnings of the gods, they would be spared such a fate from ever happening again. There was no use denying it now, if another Rhagepe had seen this.

"Who else has seen this?" Karesha's voice snapped like a whip and the hissing stopped.

"I have had this vision, Sister Rebirth," Rashma said slowly, hoping it would go no further than that.

"And who else?"

"I," another of the Rhagepe spoke up, then more people spoke, their voices rising to a fervent pitch until everyone in the tent was screaming "I! I! I!"

Karesha held up her hand. "Check the blood."

Another needle was procured, and the sister who held the stone, her lips swollen and red, pierced her flesh once more and spit. "Orope," she said after a pause, but it was not the only symbol struck by blood, all of the animals had become spattered in red.

The drumming began again as Karesha walked from the holy structure, her arms held high above her head, everyone outside going silent and watching her intently. The other Rhagepe slowly streamed out of the tent after her, forming a circle around Karesha as she moved into the centre. Her arms fell and the drumming ceased.

"The calendar is complete!"

The tribesmen cheered, but Karesha would not let them rejoice.

"Silence!" And the crowed listened. "The wrath of the gods is being brought down on us! We must go to the kingdoms and demand they heed the gods, or else the world shall be swallowed by water a second time!"

No one spoke.

"The Goddesses demand we send one to speak for each of them! One for each kingdom! Those of you who wear the Ancestral Cloak! Those of you born in the time of Orope! Those of you who have not a single hair of grey – step forward!"

At first no one moved, then a man and woman from either side of the circle pushed through the ring of Rhagepe. It was clear this was their second Orope; they were both tall and strong. The woman's charcoal hair was long and dreadlocked. The man had red hair and a beard cropped short. They had many tattoos, each representing a phase in their life; coming of age; making their first kill.

The woman had the tattoo of being joined with another and the sign of a mother. A man stood next to her, clutching her arm, his eyes wide with fear. She had to pull her arm away from his grip, and although he made no further move to stop her, his hand remained reaching out towards the mother of his children. She wore a cloak of arm bones and ribs, the bones going down past her hips. Her face was one carved of stone, facing towards the Rhagepe and not turning back to the man she had been with.

The red-haired man had an unimpressive cloak, with rib bones and leg bones tied to the shoulder, the rest blank, marking him as the eldest son of a youngest son. His tribe cheered for him, some slapping him on the back with encouragement as he walked forward. He looked around with a dazed expression, as though looking for someone he couldn't find.

They stood before the Rhagepe uncertainly.

"No other?" Karesha's eyes went over every face in the crowd.

Finally, a figure pushed through, much shorter than the other two, and with a shock they realized he was half their age. This was his first Orope. But he wore the Ancestral Cloak, and his was two layers of rib bones. His hair was black and his eyes were silver. His skin was clean of any tattoo.

"You are very young." Karesha smiled kindly at him.

"That is why I have no grey in my hair."

There was a nervous laughter throughout the tribes.

"Do you understand what will be asked of you?"

The boy shook his head no.

"Bring the cauldron," Karesha called out, and three of the youngest Rhagepe came before her holding one of the copper pots that had been used to carry the carved bones to the ceremony. They held it up in front of the three born in Orope. "You must reach in and pull from it a skull. The skull shall decide your fate. The youngest may choose first."

The cauldron was held at the level of his eyes. He reached his arm in, having to go up on his toes so his hand could reach down and touch the smooth skulls. His fingers found an eyehole, and using that he managed to lift the skull up. He held it and stared into the empty space where its eyes had once been. It was long and thin, a sharp triangle where a nose should have been jutted from the skull, and its front teeth had a gap between them and the rest of the jaw.

"The horse!" Karesha called out. "You have been called to the land of Mahat! You shall speak for the Goddess of Life!"

The Rhagepe who had checked the blood, red droplets still falling down her chin, stepped forward and took her crown of feathers and seaweed, placing it on the boy's head. It was slightly too large, and fell down his brow, threatening to cover his eyes. The sisters of Life cheered and the boy smiled awkwardly.

The man chose next, his hands pulling out a much smaller skull, though similar in shape. Its nose slanted not as steeply, and the front teeth curled back.

"The llama!" Karesha exclaimed. "The Great Jungle! You shall speak for the Goddess of Rebirth!" And Karesha took her own snake necklace from her neck and dropped it over the man's head, and another cheer erupted.

The woman put her hand in last, pulling out the only remaining skull. It was larger than both, its nose ending in a jagged crack instead of the smooth slope of the other two, and at the top on its head were two round dark discs where the great horns had been hewn off.

"The ram!" Karesha finished. "You will go to Matawe! High into the Kerlra Hal'gepe! You shall speak for the Goddess of Death!"

At that Rashma stepped forward, removing her necklace of lizard skulls, collected over nearly four full cycles of life, each skull a slightly different shape and size, but all carved with the symbol of three intersecting circles. The crowd was quiet. No one cheered for Death.

Provisions were made for the chosen three. The finest and largest hides were found and placed in front of each traveller. The nearly two dozen tribes lined up and walked past the three, giving words of wisdom, and placing on their hides salted and dried meat, ringlets and fine items forged from precious metals, imbued with sparkling stones – trinkets they could trade along their journey. One chief gave the tall red-haired man a falcon he used to hunt with. The youngest of them had three Rhagepe who spoke for Life surrounding him, using long needled sticks to tattoo a line piercing a circle on his shoulder blade, the sign that he had become a man. They were to be given everything the tribes could spare, so that their mission would be successful.

"You must go to these lands! You must find their chiefs! You must find what corruption ails their land! You must warn the chiefs and the people! You must tell them of the flood! You must tell them of the gods' wrath! You must tell them to heed the old ways!" Karesha's voice sounded like a drum before her people. "Ours are the old ways! We were the first!"

"And we will be the last!" Every Whisperer yelled, and their answer was like a thunderclap in the dry desert.

On the morning, the messengers would set out, and the tribes would watch as they shrunk and were swallowed by the desert's horizon.

It took Rashma and the Gopema tribe nearly two turns of the moon to reach the shores of the Hatmahe Sea, the land their tribe roamed when not at the Kerlra Hal'gepe. Hatmahe was the word they used for a burial place. When one of the Whisperers died they would carry what remained of the body after taking the bones necessary for the cloak here, dried out in salt to last the long journey, and feed it to the sea. The Gopema had not come here for a burial though. The fishing villages along the sea traded food for the predictions of the Rhagepe. They would live out the remaining cycle travelling along the shore, and return to the Kerlra Hal'gepe only when Zera entered Orope again, for the next calendar ceremony.

Rashma often thought of the three messengers who had set out on the journey the Goddesses had given them, but she would not discover their fate for a long time, perhaps not until all the tribes returned for the next calendar ceremony. She supposed the only way she would discover their fates before then was if they were to fail, for all would feel the gods' wrath.

They made camp within sight of the sea. Fires were lit and children ran around in the wet sand as their parents began cooking the lizard meat that had been caught during the day. They had no tents; the starry sky was the only shelter they needed. Akrape and Rekra laid their cloaks out next to Rashma's, the bones facing down, the soft, worn leather their bed. They always slept arm-in-arm, their closeness giving strength to the visions the gods sent them, but the three Rhagepe were uneasy, and had been for some time. None of them had spoken of it, but they hadn't received a vision from the gods since before the calendar ceremony.

It wasn't unusual for the gods to be silent for a long period of time, but placing a flood in the calendar had put them all on edge.

Dreams and visions were different. When Rashma dreamt it was a flurry of images, places and people ran together like drops of blood and it was rare that she would even remember them when she woke up. A vision announced itself like the sun peeking over the edge of the world. All would be clear, would move slowly and with purpose, more often than not the vision would present itself as a tableau carved in stone, figures unmoving, frozen in action. As she fell asleep that night, nestled in the arms of her sisters, she knew she was falling into a vision. The sky was black, rocks sped past her in the place of clouds, and the Kerlra Hal'gepe mountain range rose up. Before her stood three naked, withered women, so thin they looked like skeletons, wisps of white hair falling in their face, their breasts shrivelled up and useless, their fingers ending in pointed nails, like the stingers of scorpions. They pointed down at five children set before them upon the sand.

"They shall all die," they spoke in unison.

The children all looked alike, chubby cheeks and fat limbs, good healthy children destined for a long life, swaddled in the skin of goats. The women pointed to the second child on the left, drops of blood falling from their nails onto its forehead. "This one shall drown," and a fist of water reached up from the ground and grabbed the infant. Their fingers moved to the right, to the child in the middle, another drop of blood falling on its brow. "This one shall burn," and flames erupted from its swaddling, though not a sound came from the writhing babe. They moved again to the right. "This one shall turn to stone," and from where the drops of blood had stained its forehead a darkness began to infect the child, and it became as the mountain. Their fingers reached the last child on the right. "This one shall starve," and it withered into a skeleton.

"What of the first?" Rashma looked to the child on the left.

It was not a drop of blood that fell on the child, but a stream, eternally flowing. "It was the first, and-"

"Rashma!"

Rashma came awake, feeling fury rise in her throat. The gods had been speaking to her! Who would dare wake a sleeping Rhagepe? But the speaker had been Akrape, her hands on Rashma's shoulders, shaking her awake.

"What have you done? I was being sent a vision!"

Akrape looked down, shame on her face. "But the ground... it whispers."

"What?" Rashma sat up, noticing there was life in the camp, dawn only beginning to dye the sky amethyst. People were muttering, there was a sense of fear and agitation in the air. Then she felt it, like she was being shaken hard, but Sister Rebirth had taken her hands off the speaker of Death. Now nearly everyone in the tribe was awake, and children were crying. Rashma remembered the five children in her dream, not a single one of them crying or showing any distress at their impending demise. More than that, she remembered the calendar ceremony, and all her sisters calling out their visions involving the number five.

The ground went still again. The chief was on his feet, wearing his leopard skull, the remains of his first kill, on his head. He calmed his people with his words, but the Rhagepe were not listening. They had their hands deep in the sand, trying to feel the movement of the earth, but it did not stir anymore. Long after the others had been calmed and the sky began to redden, they stayed with their hands in the desert.

Some time later, Rashma pulled out her hands and dusted them on her robes.

"The earth rose, a sleeper shifting in discomfort, and settled once more," she decided.

"Sister, your vision," Akrape began.

"Never mind," Rashma smiled at the younger woman. "If the Goddesses deem it important, they shall send it to me again. Come, put your arms around me and help me to catch their whispers once more."

Again they settled on their cloaks, holding each other tighter than before. Sleep would not come again, and soon after the three of them nodded sadly at each other in the ember glow of dawn. The Gods had gone silent once more. The Gopema were all denied sleep, stretching out on their cloaks, babies crying for milk, children wrestling in impatience as their fathers and mother made fires and began to skin lizards.

"Did we not camp closer to the waters?" Rekra asked as she climbed to her feet.

Some of the children had begun running towards the beach, which now seemed to be half a day's walk farther away. The sand revealed by the shifting water was littered with shells and seaweed. The children were delighted to pick up the hidden treasure of the sea. The sand sloped down a good distance and dropped off where jagged rocks and coral were normally nestled under the waves. Some of the adults were neglecting their fires, puzzled over the shift. They knew the tides of this place, and they had never seen the water recede so much.

"When the earth moved, might it have moved the water?" Akrape asked.

"And not move us?" Rashma shook her head. A sudden fear had seized her heart. In the distance, glinting in the early sun, there was something on the water – no, not something *on* the water, but the water itself. A great swell had raised the sea into the air. It seemed small at first, perhaps the height of a small hill, but still it came closer and closer, growing in size all the time. In a moment, they could hear the rush of the water, and soon it seemed the height of a mountain, and still the children were running towards it, pointing up in astonishment, as others began to cry out in alarm and run away. Mothers snatched their babes, men scooped up their cloaks.

Rashma stared at the wave in horror. The sky looked normal, the wind was calm and the sun shone down. There was nothing to hint that this was not reality, save for the sudden mass of water that was about to break onto land. They had all seen it in their visions, they had been told it would take place in this, the time of Orope, but she had thought they had time to change the minds of the gods. Surely the gods had not sent them this vision unless they had been giving them a chance to save themselves. *There must be some way to stop this!*

"Quick! The fire knives! We must entreat the Gods with our blood!" Rashma sat on the sand and her sister followed, each pulling out a black stone knife, the same they used the cut the meat away from the bones. The sisters held their left arms out towards the swell, and with their right plunged the knife into their wrists, pulling it along and opening their forearms, Akrape and Rekra giving a small gasp of pain as their flesh parted and streams of dark blood began to stain the sand beneath them.

"Stop!" Rashma screamed out to the gods, the roar of the water now so loud she could barely hear herself. She got to her feet, holding her arms out wide, the greedy sand beneath her devouring her blood. The swell reached the water's edge and broke on the land, crashing down as a wave greater than any she had ever seen before. White tendrils of sea foam, like the tendrils of hair on the Goddesses' heads, rushed to meet her. Akrape and Rekra were screaming, tears running down their faces. The water reached the children, and a moment later the children were gone. Rashma called out.

"We were the–", and the wave took her.

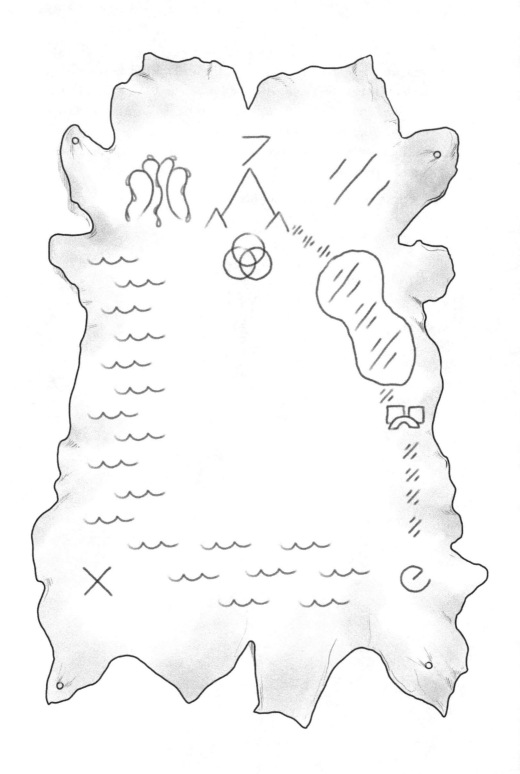

THE SEA OF SAND

GODS DO NOT NEED PROTECTION –
ONLY MEN DO

A death rattle came from the lizard's throat as it twitched and died. Tersh smiled at the lizard impaled on the end of her spear. It had been seven days since the calendar ceremony, where they had been chosen to go to the three great kingdoms and warn them of the gods' fury, and seven days since they had tasted fresh meat. Her mouth had begun to water the moment she'd spotted the lizard moving through the sand. The lizard was more than big enough to feed the two of them and save some to dry and carry on their journey.

Three had been chosen, but only two had gone east together. The man with red hair, chosen to speak for the Goddess of Rebirth, had gone west towards the Grey Mist, the Jungle. It would take at least two turns of the moon to reach the borders of Mahat. Though Tersh had no idea how much longer it would take for her to continue travelling north into the mountain kingdom of Matawe. She should have been chosen to speak for the Goddess of Life, to go to Mahat. She knew the land, knew the language. The memory of pulling out the ram's skull and being met with silence still tasted bitter in her mouth.

The sun was beginning to set behind them. Tersh picked up her prize and looked over at Kareth, the eager boy – *man*, she reminded herself with a sigh yet again – staring at the dead lizard with large, hungry silver eyes. It was difficult for

Tersh to think of him as a man though. His face was still smooth and beardless, his body mostly hairless, his limbs short and thin, but he wore the Ancestral Cloak of his father and the Rhagepe had given him the tattoo of a man. The gods had chosen him for this sacred mission. The young man still scratched his shoulder where the new tattoo itched, and he wore the crown of seaweed and feathers the Rhagepe had given him as a necklace because it was too big to fit around his head. Still, he had seen Zera complete a full cycle. Tersh knew she ought to think of him as a man.

"Skin it while I make the fire," Tersh handed the limp animal to him, and it instantly seemed larger in his small hands.

While they had tattooed the boy, some of the Rhagepe who spoke for Death had taken her aside, to teach her things no one but the Rhagepe had ever been allowed to know. They showed her secret herbs, and taught her a curse. It had been chilling to watch, and she still thought of it now, how they had mixed the dust of bones with blood dripping from cuts in their arms.

"You may not find the sacred herbs where you go, but blood is the greatest tool when making a curse, and only those who speak for Death may do so," they had explained, but it had sounded like a warning.

They had left their people in the morning after the calendar ceremony and walked through the day. Tersh could not find it in herself to speak. She kept thinking of Ka'rel standing in the sand, their son Farek clasping onto his leg, both of them freely crying as she walked away. Her daughter, Ba'rek, her oldest, stood apart, her face sullen. Ka'rel had been angry with her too, nearly too angry to speak. When he handed her spear to her, it was more like he was throwing it at her.

"Come back alive," he had told her sternly.

She had felt the cold hands of guilt clasping her heart. His dark eyes spoke louder than his voice, telling her that she shouldn't have stepped forward. She almost hadn't. When they had asked those born in Orope who wore the cloak to step forward Ka'rel had clutched her so tightly her arm still had the marks where his nails had dug in. But the others in his tribe were looking at her with awe, and she knew she would lose their respect if she stayed still. Worse still, if she hadn't gone forward when Kareth, who was only half her age, had been brave enough to, she would have lost respect for herself.

She knew she might never see them again. Ka'rel, who made everything he cooked taste like fire and passion. She knew this journey would take her far out of their reach. Farek, calling out the names of the stars as the three of them nestled together at night. Ba'rek, not able to look her in the eyes as she had said goodbye. But she also knew she had to go. The gods had chosen her. Farek and Ba'rek would grow up and be honoured in their tribe because their mother had spoken for the Goddess of Death – and she would not fail. Failure did not only mean her death; it meant the death of everyone.

The gods were angry. The gods needed to be appeased.

Tersh crouched in the sand, piling up the few branches and dried plants they had managed to collect over the last few days. She unfolded the large skin she carried with the many things the tribes had given her spread out. There were jewelled bracelets, leather pouches full of dried meat and fruits, and extra skins to keep them warm at night. She took a small black pouch containing the charcoal she was always careful to collect after every fire they made.

The first night the boy had shivered, his eyes covered by the hood of his cloak, his face creased with the strain from not crying, and finally Tersh had forced herself to speak. "We will make a fire. You will feel better."

"I don't need a stupid fire," Kareth had pouted. "I'm not afraid of the dark."

"It's not the dark you should fear, but the cold," Tersh had sighed. She had been given a few good logs by one of the tribesmen. They were too heavy to keep carrying, so it made sense to use them right away and save the charcoal.

"Then make one," Kareth sounded very much like the son of a chief, and Tersh found it hard to not pick up one of the logs and throw it at the small angry face that stared at her.

"Why don't you?" Tersh suggested instead, handing over the logs and stepping back. Kareth had twisted his face up in annoyance.

"I told you I don't care about a fire."

"You can't make a fire," Tersh had muttered, then busied herself piling the logs into a point around some kindling. She took out the fire knife the Rhagepe had entrusted to her. The stone knife was black and glimmered like water when light hit it. It came from the lands of the Grey Mist, west of the Kerlra Hal'gepe, where the man with red hair had gone. Their edges were sharper than any made by hand, and rubbing the knives against a stone would create the sparks of fire. Only the Rhagepe carried them, but one had been given to each of the three chosen before setting out on their journey. Striking the fire knife off a rock she made a spark, and again and again until the kindling caught and a small flame began to grow. Kareth stared with curious eyes.

The fire burned and Tersh tried to find some comfort in its heat. She sat back and stared at the boy, realizing this was the first time they had spoken to each other.

"I am called Tersh Hal'Reekrah of the tribe Go'angrin." The well-rehearsed words were sand in her mouth.

"Kareth Al'Resh," he had whispered in return. "Of the tribe Gorikin."

"It is all right to be frightened... but you speak for the Goddess of Life. We have been honoured."

"I'm not afraid," Kareth repeated indignantly, then with a slightly weaker voice added: "Although... I don't know how we are supposed to stop what's coming. The Rhagepe said the gods would swallow the world beneath the sea."

Tersh nearly felt overwhelmed for a moment, as though she were already being dragged beneath the waves. How *could* they convince the chiefs? What corruption *were* they meant to find? "You speak for a Goddess. Your words are hers. The old ways must be preserved. The world is changing and the true gods are being forgotten, corruption grows in the land. We must draw the evil out of the lands like poison from a wound. We must give honour to the gods." She stopped short, feeling light-headed. She no longer felt the cold of the desert night. "You will not know your path, but the gods do and they will lead you. You must trust in them. You must feel them, here," she reached out and touched Kareth's chest, feeling the strong heart beating beneath the chilled flesh.

The next day Kareth did not sniffle nor struggle to hold back his tears. They walked faster and did not stop as often to take a drink of water. Neither felt the pangs of hunger. They spoke of their lives before being chosen. Kareth had indeed been the son of a chief, but his father Resh had died in Rakeesh, the time before Orope. Kareth wore the oldest cloak in his tribe, and his mother had often told him he was meant for greater things.

"I always believed her," Kareth had said in a dreamy voice, "but this was beyond anything I had ever imagined."

But that was days ago, and now Tersh felt like a strong wind could defeat her. They needed fresh meat if they were to go on any longer. Catching that lizard had been a small mercy in an uncaring desert. She looked up from the fire to see whether Kareth had finished with the lizard and she felt her jaw fall open slightly. Most of the juicy meat was in a pile next to the boy, having been stripped off with the skin and all he had left was a tangled mess of limbs and bones.

"You utter fool, did your father teach you nothing before he died!?!" Tersh shouted, rushing over and snatching what remained of the lizard. Kareth flinched as Tersh grabbed the bloody mess from his hands, and for a moment she remembered one time when her own father had stood over her, screaming at her for some childish mistake she had made. No, not one time. Too many times to remember each moment with any clarity. Tersh looked to the fire, taking a long breath. "It's fine," she cleared her throat, "we can salvage most of it."

"I..." Kareth was looking at his hands, grasping at his knife uncertainly.

"You need to learn," Tersh mumbled to herself, still unable to look back at Kareth.

Kareth was only a boy before the calendar ceremony, and had obviously never been taught to hunt or kill or skin. Tersh should have realized that from the first night when Kareth couldn't even make a fire. They would not share the same path for long. Soon Kareth would be on his own, and before that happened he ought to be able to care for himself.

"I will teach you."

"I don't need a teacher," Kareth sounded annoyed, but then he looked over to Tersh, biting his lip as though he wanted to say something more.

There were long days before Tersh found another lizard. This one was not so long or plump as the last, but it would have to do. Tersh found a flat enough stone to lay it on and Kareth leaned next to her.

"Let me do it," he said with the excitement of a child.

"First, watch me," Tersh took out her knife.

Kareth sighed loudly. "Just tell me what to do and I'll do it."

"No," Tersh stared him down. "You watch. You learn. Then you do it. First, we cut into the neck."

She pushed the blade in and dark blood began to bubble up. She leaned down to suck as much of the blood up into her mouth as she could, swallowing the warm salty liquid with satisfaction. The blood wasn't so great to drink, but in a desert anything was preferable to dehydration. And it made it easier to see what she was doing.

"The skin is tough, but that is good. You don't need to cut so much, just get hold of the skin," she dug her finger into the hole she had made, "and pull." The skin came off in a clean strip, all the way down to the tail. "See, it's easy."

"Are you going to talk the entire time?"

Tersh gave him a warning glance.

Kareth hung his head.

The boy shrugged his shoulder, mumbling. "I'm sorry... I'm hungry."

Tersh's father would have hit him for being insolent. Tersh cleared her throat and forced a smile onto her face. "Yes. I will talk. You will listen."

When they found the lake, Kareth said they must have made a wrong turn, for surely this was the Hatmahe Sea they had found. The waters were so vast they could not see the land on the other side. Kareth's tribe was from the west, and he had never seen a body of water so large that was not the sea or the ocean.

"It is the sea," Kareth said, a look of despair on his face for the first time since beginning this journey.

"No," Tersh walked towards the shore, stabbing her spear into the muddy sand and kneeling down to use her hand to scoop the clear crystal water to her mouth. "Come, taste," she smiled.

Kareth did the same, kneeling down and cupping the water, his face turned up in disgust, but when the cold liquid touched his lips he tasted no salt. This was not the sea. He smiled, taking another sip and another. "The gods must have blessed this water to keep it so pure," he said in amazement between gulps.

Along the lake were many trees, and as they continued to walk south the days seemed cooler as they stayed in the shade. Some of the trees bore fruit as well, and they picked many, filling their skins. They would rest in the midday under the foliage of the trees, and both felt at peace. For the first time, Tersh felt happy she had been sent on the journey.

Before long they found villages. There were many boats lining the shores, and low huts made from white mud bricks among the palm trees. The people would watch the Whisperers walk into their town with concern on their faces. In these parts it was well known Whisperers could speak with the gods, could see visions of the future in their dreams. Some people ran to them as they walked by, handing them fresh fish they'd caught, or vegetables from the gardens, in the hopes that they would ask the gods to bless them, but most kept a wary distance.

"I'd like to stay here," Kareth said as they walked through a second village, this one smaller, and the people friendlier. Already they carried so much fish that they could not accept any more.

"We cannot. We do not belong with them. We belong only where the gods have told us to go." Tersh spoke with an edge in her words, wishing to stay in the village for a few days as well, but knowing the gods were wilful and would not forgive disobedience. There would be time to rest when they'd reached the kingdoms. They hadn't just been chosen to speak for the gods. They had accepted. Tersh often wondered if Kareth, for all his youth, knew what a difficult task it was to accept a mission from the gods.

They continued on, purposely spending their nights far away from any villages, to avoid the temptation of bartering for a straw bed and a roof over their heads. Instead they would sleep under the stars. Each star was a god smiling down at them.

The lake narrowed as they continued south, the shore on the other side becoming visible and getting closer each day. When it became a river again, they would find the city with many bridges, the city on the border of Mahat. Kareth would sometimes talk excitedly about the wonders that he imagined awaited them, and Tersh would smile despite herself.

Tersh watched as Kareth laid the light lizard on its belly on the stony shore of the river. The body of the lizard wasn't so big, but its tail was so long that it easily ran the length from Kareth's fingertips to his elbow. Kareth took out the fire knife and, holding the lizard by its neck, began cutting into the flesh. He grabbed the tough skin with his fingers and pulled back a strip from the neck to the tail, then another one and another one, until its entire torso was bare. He turned the lizard over and found a sack of bright eggs, like the hot coals in fire, nestled in its flesh. He scooped them out and placed them on a concave slab. Then he cut off the lizard's head, about to toss it aside.

Tersh cleared her throat, and Kareth looked up annoyed, knowing he was forgetting something. Whenever Tersh told him what the next step was though, she would get a string of angry words in reply about how he knew what he was doing and Tersh's 'help' was just distracting. Kareth looked at the lizard head in his hand, biting his lips. "Oh!" he finally said, pulling out two small sacks from its cheeks. They were full of venom, but could be used for medicine. He handed them to Tersh, who would prepare them later into a salve with some herbs she had been given.

Using the knife again he began to cut the flesh off the smaller limbs, careful this time not to cut the tender meat. The lizard's tail was still twitching as Kareth began to strip the flesh off it, first cutting through the delicate membrane, then pulling it off the meat. He stopped halfway down, where the tail became too narrow, simply cutting away the rest and discarding it with the head. It flopped uselessly, slapping against the wet pebbles.

Using her own knife Tersh created a spark, igniting their small fire. The sun was nearly gone now, and the fire lit up the area around them. She tended it for a moment, until it was strong, then turned to Kareth. Kareth handed her the skinned lizard, hardly able to hide the pride on his face. He was right to be proud.

The lizard was skinned perfectly. Tersh nodded as she hung the lizard between two branches stuck into the ground, holding the meat above the fire. Then she took the slab with the eggs still on it and placed it at the base of the fire to cook.

"Tomorrow, you will begin to hunt," Tersh nodded.

Kareth smiled. "And how much longer until we reach Mahat?"

"We will be there soon. It has nearly been two turns of the moon. A few days more." Tersh turned the lizard over. The cooked side bubbled slightly and the smell rose up, making both of their stomachs growl.

Tersh reached over and grabbed a small folded pouch and from inside took four dried dates. She handed two of them to Kareth.

"To celebrate." She smiled. "It was a good skinning."

Kareth nodded with self-assuredness. "I know. I told you I knew what I was doing."

"Yes, you did, several times, and loudly. I hope it feels nice to finally be right." Tersh chuckled, taking the lizard and the eggs off the fire, and she split them into equal portions.

Kareth had a large smile on his face as he started eating.

Two days later they came to a city. Kareth had never seen one before. The buildings were made from the same white mud bricks they had seen in the villages, but here the buildings were built two – or even three – storeys high. Kareth could not stop looking up at their height. He bumped into people in the narrow streets. Surely a city this size could hold over a thousand, an impossible number for him to imagine, but there were people everywhere. The streets were lined with vendors selling foods and goods. Most of them wore simple white or sandy clothes, light cotton tunics or loincloths, but they looked like grand robes to a boy who had never seen a person wear anything other than a hooded cloak.

"I never imagined Mahat was so big!" Kareth said with wide eyes.

Tersh laughed. "This is not Mahat, just a city on its border. Mahat is, well... You'll see. This place is a shadow compared to the great cities of Mahat."

Kareth continued on in a daze, his head probably spinning trying to imagine a city even bigger than this. Tersh had told him it was impossible to explain the size of Mahat, from the grand palaces to the massive pyramids, and as Kareth looked around him he wondered if he'd be able to explain the size of this place to others.

Kareth walked right into a man. The fat merchant growled something and pushed him aside.

"What did he say?"

"Something rude," Tersh cleared her throat in discomfort.

"You can speak their tongue? Have you been here before?"

"Yes, a few times," Tersh had nodded. "My tribe comes this way often. These people honour the gods, and our Rhagepe would often sell their lords visions. This is the gateway to Mahat. Much of my youth was spent in the Sea Mahat..."

Kareth stopped listening. Here the water split into dozens of rivers, all leading towards the sea. The city was nestled between the rivers, a series of low, short stone bridges connecting one end of the city to the other.

"Mahat has taller buildings that this?"

Tersh laughed softly. "I heard they have built temples the size of mountains. This city is nothing. You will see."

They crossed four bridges. Each one had a long line of people, horses, and carts trying to get across the narrow paths. Every crossing would take a long time as they shuffled along and the excitement Kareth had first felt was slowly being replaced by annoyance at the crowds of people. The stench of human waste only grew worse. He was beginning to feel like they would be there forever, but they finally reached the fifth and last bridge. The bridge into Mahat.

The final bridge was twice as wide and longer than any of the previous bridges, and was made from sandstone so smooth it glittered in the sun. Large statues of leopards sat on either side of the bridge, and on the other size were two large columns that ended in a pointed tip, the sides covered in strange symbols. Tersh could see it would take far longer to cross this bridge. Despite its size, guards waited on the other side to check every person and what they carried with them before letting them through.

"Say nothing to them. They won't understand you and might take offense," Tersh warned Kareth as they got closer to the guards.

The guards were broad-shouldered and their well-shaped muscles were on display as they wore no shirt. They wore clean white linen skirts pleated in the front, the folds revealing a bright sky cloth underneath, and belted with a bronze buckle at the waste. On their heads they wore white linen nemes, a headdress that covered their foreheads and went back down to their shoulders, like a mane of perfect white hair. For weapons they held black spears, and curved bronze swords hung on their belts.

Most of the people crossing the border into Mahat were given little more than a glance, though those bringing over large carts of goods were sometimes taken to the side as other guards searched through what they carried. Tersh saw the guards going through one cart, carelessly throwing the merchant's belongings in the sand while the merchant watched with a distressed expression on his face.

Tersh knew that even though they carried very little, the guards might give them the same treatment. But if there were problems, what then? Coming here as a child, he chief of her tribe taught them that some men in this land had to be bribed, and that the more important the man the larger the bribe had to be. What kind of jewels or precious metals would have to be given over if there was a problem?

The guard nearest to Tersh looked them over, went to wave them through, then quickly looked back and held up his hand.

"Halt!" he spoke with force. The two Whisperers stopped short.

The entire column of people crossing came to a stop as a second guard approached, looking the two of them over with a snarl on his face. "Rattlecloaks. They're as naked as slaves under those bones," he spoke with a gruff voice, and spit into the dirt at their feet. "Witches! Cursed! We don't want you here."

"The gods do," Tersh spoke their language with an accent, but her words were perfectly clear and loud enough for the crowd around them to hear.

Kareth looked too nervous to move, his wide eyes staring at the pointed spears hovering above their heads. The people seemed just as nervous, taking steps back, forming a circle around them. They were too scared to get close, but too curious to leave. The guards lost some of their bite once Tersh spoke, and a slight unease grew in their eyes.

"The Paref is dead, we only heard the news yesterday. He was a god, not one of the desert spirits you sacrifice animals to. His spirit will wash Mahat until he is reborn in his son. Your presence during that time will poison the land."

"The Paref is dead," Tersh whispered to Kareth.

"Gods do not take the form of man," Tersh replied to the guards with narrowed eyes. "Gods are the wind, the fire, the water. Death and life and rebirth."

"Paref Rama the fifth lived. Paref Rama the fifth died. Paref Rama shall be reborn as Paref Rama the sixth. Life, death and rebirth all in the form of one man."

Tersh was silent for a moment, wondering if they should turn around. There were other ways – far longer ways – but still other ways they could cross into Mahat, but something drove her on. She spoke for the Goddess of Death, and Death could not be stopped in its path.

"If you shall not let us pass, we will curse you and this land in blood!" Her voice became louder and the people moved farther away. All had heard of the Whisperers' power to converse with the gods, and they all knew no power was greater than a gods'.

The guards started to laugh and Tersh felt her face getting warmer.

Kareth knew the Paref was chief of this land, ruler of all men and livestock, owner of the land and all with it. It was to the Paref he knew he must go to, to warn him of the gods' wrath, to help him find the corruption and overcome it, to convince him to honour the old ways and appease the gods. What sign could it mean that the Paref was dead? Who would he go to now?

His breathing was getting faster. Tersh looked angry and the guards were obviously dismissing them as a threat... No, there had to be a way to scare these men into letting them pass. Kareth immediately got on his knees, unfolding his skin and taking out the small black pouch he had filled with charcoal. He brushed some of the sand off the rocks of the bridge and began drawing three intersecting circles.

"What are you doing?" Tersh hissed down at him.

"Performing the blood ceremony," Kareth tried not to smile, wanting to look dour.

"But you-" Tersh stopped herself, understanding what the boy was doing.

Kareth did not know the true symbols for the three Goddesses, those were kept secret by the Rhagepe, but instead began drawing the three symbols the Rhagepe had given them the night they were chosen. In one circle he drew a snake eating its own tail, in another a lizard, and in the final circle he drew a feather. His drawings were crude and even he could barely tell what they were when he had finished.

Tersh turned to the guards whose laughter was quieting as they looked at Kareth in confusion. "Do you want to know what he's doing?"

The guard shrugged as though he didn't care. "He can do whatever he wants, so long as he doesn't do it in Mahat."

"He's performing the blood ceremony. You *have* heard of the blood ceremony, haven't you?" Even if they hadn't, she knew men like this would say they had just to look smarter in the eyes of their peers.

"Of course," the guard started to look uncertain and the other leaned over to whisper something uneasily in his ear.

"Maybe I could use some of the camel jerky as an animal sacrifice?" Kareth muttered to himself.

Tersh wanted to hide her face in her hands and roll her eyes, but she kept her face as serious as the stone leopards guarding the bridge. "I suppose so," her voice sounded slightly strained.

Kareth began to chant. It was a simple childhood rhyme, asking the rain to return to the desert. It was a silly song, but he sang it slowly, swaying back and forth, imitating how the Rhagepe sounded as they had performed the calendar ceremony.

"We don't want trouble; you simply cannot enter our land until the Paref has safely been reborn," one of the guards spoke quickly.

"Gods do not need protection – only men do," Tersh glared, feeling tall among these frightened faces, even though she was easily the shortest person there – besides Kareth.

Kareth took a piece of the camel jerky, with the same reverence she'd seen Rhagepe show towards animals that had been sacrificed, its meat prepared for this exact moment.

"Tell him to stop," the first guard was beginning to sound panicked, his staff halfway lowered, but Tersh did not fear him. No man in Mahat would dare kill one of the Gogepe.

Kareth picked up the fire knife as it glinted in the sun. He felt a strange dizziness as he continued to chant, barely stopping for breath. He was no longer swaying by force, but his body seemed to be moving and convulsing on its own, he held up the knife to his left forearm, not fearing the pain, feeling a strange excitement. He could hear the echo of his heart beating in his ears as he ran the knife along the edge of his skin, not cutting deep, but just deep enough for blood to begin to trickle from the wound.

He felt someone gently shaking his shoulder. Kareth looked dazed for a moment as his chanting was cut off. He looked around confused, the guards had parted the crowd to let them pass. He wondered what had overcome him, wondered if the Goddess of Life was in him then, and if the blood ceremony might have worked after all. Hadn't Tersh warned him that blood could be used to make a curse? He wondered if maybe they shouldn't be playing with such forces.

Kareth felt the pain in his arm, even for a shallow cut it was the first time he had ever run a blade across his flesh, and his skin felt like it was burning. Kareth quickly gathered his things back into the animal hide and got to his feet, the crowd silently watching as the two began to walk towards the east, no one daring to try and stop them again. The charcoal drawing remained on the bridge, but looking back, Kareth saw the column of people were careful not to step there.

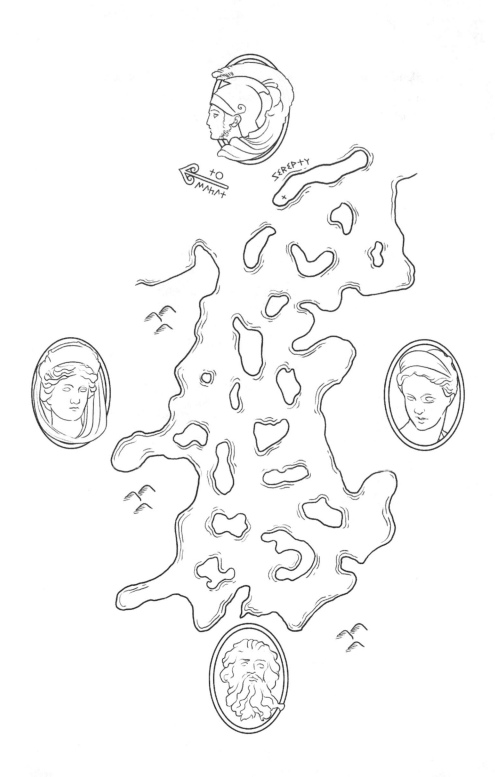

THE SEPHIAN ISLANDS

THEIR WAY IS BLOCKED
BY THE RISEN SEA

T he sun was just rising over Serepty, the sea to the east becoming shades of lavender and honey. People were waking up and beginning to move through the narrow streets, carrying woven baskets on their heads. Samaki always woke with the sun, but this morning instead of having his meal in the comforts of the villa, he quickly dressed and left the small, but richly decorated room. The villa was narrow, all the buildings here were. The rooms were above and below each other instead of next to one another because of the mountain's slant. The rooms all opened onto a balcony – the roof of the room below it – and stairs along the side led down to the street. Villas looked like staircases built for gods going up the mountain.

Samaki was from Mahat, though he had adopted the dress and manners of the many different cultures he visited. Most men of Mahat just wore thin linen tunics, a belt at the waist giving the garment some form. But Samaki wore auburn wool pants from Caemaan, with a snake belt and gold buckle he'd gotten from a Whisperer – and only the gods knew where the Whisperer had gotten it – and leather strapped sandals he had gotten here in Serepty. If he had to wear a shirt he had a silk tunic. When he could he left his toned chest open to the weather, his neck adorned with half a dozen amulets of gold, silver, and bronze. His head was bald, the only custom he kept from his people. The rich men of Mahat wore long black or sandy wigs weaved with gold on their shaved heads, but even after

33

Samaki made a small fortune from his trade routes, he couldn't bring himself to follow the customs of the higher classes. Instead he let his head and skin turn dark, kissed by the sun.

"Are you leaving us so soon, Samaki?"

Samaki turned and found a plump balding man wearing a white toga. It was Postes, one of the richest men on Serepty. He owned a vineyard on the south side of the island. He was covered in gold rings and his brooch was a golden owl with red jewels for eyes. He emerged from the bottom room, a large smile on his face as he greeted his guest. Their frequent dealings with each other had led to Postes inviting Samaki to stay with him.

Samaki had no trouble understanding their language, and could speak it as if it were his mother tongue, save for a slight accent he couldn't seem to overcome. "If the wind holds out, we leave for Mahat today."

Yesterday the winds from the south had been strong. With the winds, and the outgoing tide, they would make good time, and return to Mahat in the evening after two nights at sea. If it took any longer they would be forced to approach the land under darkness. The seabed there was shallow, and it was easy to run a ship aground if the right path wasn't taken.

"I'm going down to the dock, to see if the ship's been loaded properly and if we can launch," Samaki explained, too tired to want to chat. He loved the lush grassy island of Serepty, but he grew restless when he stayed in a place too long. They had already been here far longer than planned because of the bad winds. They had been delayed many days.

"Of course, of course," Postes never lost his smile, it was a permanent fixture on his face, and as fake as the Paref's hair. "We will all miss you dearly, and eagerly await the next time you will grace our shores."

"I will return soon, for my things, if we are indeed departing today."

"Excellent, so you'll join my family for the morning meal."

Samaki wanted to protest. He would rather get some food from one of the stalls near the dock, but he could not refuse Postes' hospitality. He was far too important a trading partner. Postes held the key to the Sephian Islands, and the

Sephian Islands had enough wealth to make a merchant like him richer than the Paref. One must have the right friends. Postes was certainly the right friend.

"Until then," Postes held out his hands and Samaki took a step forward, letting the rotund man grasp his shoulders and pull him close. In the Sephian Islands it was custom to kiss twice, once on each cheek, when meeting or saying goodbye. At first the custom had confused Samaki. Kissing was for family, or the women he led to his bed. Samaki had learned to adapt. It was his most valuable skill. Samaki dutifully gave two quick pecks, and then Postes released him.

The door led onto the narrow streets, two guards holding spears standing on either side of the entrance. They were there more for show than anything else. Samaki never heard of violence taking place here. Nothing beyond a few drunken fights. No, the guards were there simply to mark this villa as one of importance, with a man living there worthy of having his life protected.

No matter how many times Samaki walked through these streets, he always felt awed by this place. The palace of Serepty, where their King lived, was nestled high on the island. The steep incline of the land made it almost look like a wall of malachite as one approached by ship. The island was a mountain rising out of the sea, tall and jagged. There were no beaches. The rocks dropped off the steep cliffs to the water. Long wooden quays had been built at the bottom of an alcove for ships to dock. Stairs both carved in stone and made from planks nailed together crept up from the docks to the city. The city itself zigzagged up towards the gypsum walls of the palace, a jewel set in a lush land. It was those sparkling walls Samaki always saw first when he sailed there, beckoning him to their shores, promising him riches beyond imagination.

The Sephians believed that once these islands were a mountain range. After angering Neiston, the lord of the sea, he cleaved the land in two, filled it with water, and pulled the mountain range down, creating a collection of hundreds of islands. Serepty was the largest of these and the most northern. Serepty was the doorway to the Sephian Islands, and all trade from Mahat and the rest of the northern continent came here first. That is what brought Samaki there. He made the trip here four or five times a year, bringing goods back and forth between Serepty and the Sea Mahat.

The people here had long hair of various colours, from golden and earthy to black as night. Sometimes, though rarely, he even saw ruby red hair. They say Paref Rama the First had red hair. Samaki couldn't help but wonder if maybe Rama, the greatest Paref who ever lived, had some Serepty blood in his veins. The thought would be blasphemy in Mahat. The Paref was a living god, they said. His blood could never be of a lower race. But how could any man, living god or not, resist these women? They were far more voluptuous than any woman of Mahat. Their skin was like the olives that grew on so many trees on this island, their nipples like the dark pits he would spit out as he nibbled on the salty orb. Every time he visited he couldn't leave without tasting one of their exquisite women.

Sephians wore mostly silks, the fabric was sheer and they left it open down to their navels where it was secured by a belt. They were the height of impracticality, and the Sephians had to walk slowly to keep from having their fine silks from falling open. In Mahat the sand and rocks would destroy such a garment, but here the land was milder, and always a breeze or a great wind came off the Middle Sea to refresh them. The first time Samaki had come here, he thought he had found a paradise.

He soon reached the docks, and despite his promise to return for the morning meal, could not help visiting his favourite stall. The fisherman who owned it had a daughter whose beauty he tried to hide by dressing her in the shabbiest of togas, but nothing could hide her golden curls or the curves of her breasts. Samaki was disappointed that the girl was not there that morning, just the sea-weathered old man, who squinted at Samaki and smiled. He shucked two oysters for his favourite customer, not knowing Samaki had shucked his daughter's oyster with just as much skill, but perhaps less effort.

Samaki slurped on the oysters as he walked down the cut stone steps, throwing the empty shells towards the bay below. Most fishermen were still out, but many were beginning to return, the quays were filling up with the small boats, some with a short mast, but most using oars to travel. Samaki's ship, the Afeth, was by far the largest, and lay in the middle of the others like a colossus. He had named her after the Mahat god of chaos. Nothing was more chaotic than sailing on the open sea, and he hoped to garner favour with the harshest force of nature by naming the ship after the snake deity. The spine of the ship had been carved to resemble a snake, the bow carved like its hissing head rising up to strike, and the stern pointed like its tail, coiled to hold the lantern they hung there. She had two masts with a massive sail on one and a sail half the size on the other. The sails were sewn together from many pieces of cloth, giving them a checkered look when they were full of wind. Below deck they had a large hold currently stocked to the brim. The deck was large, large enough to care for the crew that slept there at night, and rowed during the day. Each oar was as long as the ship, thicker than a man's arm, and the flat blade at the end as wide as a man's chest. It took two men to pull each oar though it could be done with one who had considerable strength. There were twelve oars on each side of the ship. The oars were pulled up into the rowlocks, crisscrossed over the deck where a few dozen of his crew were still sleeping in the early hours.

His crew was fifty men strong, most of them from Mahat who had dreamed of being more than farmers like their fathers, but some came from Serepty or other Sephian islands. His first mate came from none of those lands . His first mate was a large woman, her skin dark as charcoal, who came from the golden lands far north of Mahat, a place called Kuroe. Most of the gold from Mahat came from Kuroe. Tiyharqu had come to Mahat when she was still little more than a girl, travelling with her father who had been a spice merchant. She grew fascinated with the Hiperu, the great river that connected the mountains to the sea delta, the life-blood of Mahat.

Tiyharqu left her father to apprentice under a shipwright. Samaki had met her over a decade ago when he had bought his first ship. That ship had been half the size, with only one mast, but she had been sturdy and with her he had made enough money to return to Tiyharqu and buy the Afeth. Tiyharqu had been designing the ship in her head for many years, and Samaki was the first person to appreciate her plans. The two grew a friendship as they built her together. Mostly she was Tiyharqu's design, but Samaki had added his own flare, like the snake design. When the ship was ready for sea, Tiyharqu had decided to go with him, to experience the world and make some gold.

"Harqu!" Samaki called up from the dock.

"Maki!" Tiyharqu leaned over the side of the ship, her white teeth glinting through a large smile on her face. "The hold is full and the wind moves north. We should make sail today when the tide goes out."

"I was hoping for that." Samaki smiled back at his old friend.

Their hold was filled with many things, but mostly wine from Postes' vineyard. In Mahat they made no wine, only beer made from honey and sweet to the taste. Samaki preferred wine which was rich and bold and made from grapes. The red wines were a special favourite of Paref Rama's, and he hoped to sail up the Hiperu to his palace in the Mountain Mahat, and sell him the wine for the highest profit. He had already made that trade several times. It was one of the reasons his relationship with Postes was so good.

"Do all the men know to be back before the tide changes?"

"They know," Harqu laughed, "but sometimes it is hard to leave the warmth of a woman."

Most of the men would be bedding with temple priestesses, or drunk in a bathhouse. Very few ever made it back from the voyage with all the money they had made. "Oh, I know all too well, but the warmth of Mahat is just as welcoming."

They cast off before mid-day as the tide went out. Samaki had gone back for the morning meal with Postes, already making plans for his return in a few months. Samaki would, of course, stay with him at the villa. Many of the men on deck were hungover as they set off and were barely able to hold onto their oars. Only one had failed to return. Samaki wasn't concerned. It was common enough for men to leave ship without word, either staying for family or love or having found a better job. That man had only been on the Afeth for two voyages, had come from Serepty and probably wanted to return home. It was one less share to pay when they reached Mahat, and that suited Samaki fine.

The winds were strong, the sea calm, and there were no signs of a storm coming. Samaki felt confident they would arrive in Sareeb, the capitol of the Sea Mahat, in three days. At night the rowing continued, but only in shifts so most men could sleep while others continued to man a few of the oars, just to keep them on course. Either Samaki or Tiyharqu would take the rudder, using the stars to guide their way. Heading straight north was easy, they had only to follow a cluster of stars known as the Sisters. Unlike the other stars, the Sisters barely moved in the sky, and they were always used to take bearings when going north or south.

As the second day passed the winds stayed strong, and Samaki had a good feeling they'd reach Mahat early. The men were able to relax, since the wind was pushing them faster than they would have been able to row, and Samaki allowed the men to have an extra cup of beer as they sang and laughed into the night. In the morning, as the sun began to rise, Tiyharqu woke Samaki for his shift at the rudder.

"Land ho," she said softly, nodding towards the red bow of the ship. A bright line of trees could easily be made out. The Sea Mahat was always lush with life. There were countless rivers and streams, most of it was marshlands thick with reeds. It was a line of emeralds set on the Middle Sea.

Samaki turned to the rudder, to correct their course slightly eastwardly, when he saw it. It came from the south, a great swelling of the water. It was moving so fast for a moment Samaki could only stare in shock. And then he realized it would be upon them in a moment, and he turned to his first mate urgently.

"Harqu!"

The stern of the ship rose up and they remained at an angle for a moment while the swell hit them. Tiyharqu grabbed the side of the ship for support and those still sleeping jerked awake at the strange motion. The ship evened out as they reached the top of the swell, their sails went lax but their speed stayed the same, and Samaki realized the wind wasn't pushing them anymore, but the water was pulling them along.

"What the gods?" Tiyharqu went to the edge of the ship. They were raised above the sea before and behind them. The swell was a great wall of water. "What is happening?"

"It looks like a wave before it breaks," Samaki said quietly, but a swell this big would mean a wave far larger than any he had seen before. He looked back towards the shore, now approaching faster than ever, and the breath seemed to leave him.

Then suddenly the stern of the ship lurched back as they fell off the southside of the swell. Their sails filled with wind again as the water continued on without them. Many of the men were now standing on deck, staring off at the swell as it disappeared. It took a moment for Samaki to regain himself. He felt like he had dreamed it.

"Back to work," he finally ordered, but his voice was weak.

"Pick up those oars men!" Tiyharqu's voice was stronger, and the men came to life, though some continued to whisper about what they might have just seen, all thought it was the end of the matter, just another strange story to tell while drinking with friend.

But then... They could only stare as the shore disappeared behind the swell, and then they saw the white spray of the water as it connected with the land. Palm trees swayed wildly before becoming consumed by the white foam. The men rowed faster, eager to reach land, to find out what had happened, but Samaki only felt dread.

"Another!" Tiyharqu called out, pointing to the south. Another great swell was coming at them.

"Brace yourselves!" Samaki called out, clutching at the gunwale with one hand and trying to keep the rudder steady with the other. The ship lurched more violently this time, the swell seeming to pick up power the closer it was to land. The rudder shuddered in his grip, and then they reached the top of the wave and for a moment all seemed calm.

"We'll be dashed against the shore if this continues!" Tiyharqu called out.

"Secure the sails!" Samaki order to the nearest row of men. "Make ready to turn to starboard. We must move south against the waves!"

Again they came off the backside of the wave and levelled out in the water, as a handful of men climbed like spiders up the masts to roll up and tie the sails.

"Starboard-side, oars up!" A dozen gleaming oars came out of the water and the oarsmen on the left side of the ship redoubled their efforts to turn the ship around. Just as they turned the bow of the ship south another swell was upon them. "BRACE!"

The shore was gone. The swells had kept coming that morning, though growing smaller and weaker as the day went on. When he felt they were out of danger, Samaki let the men rest, before readjusting their course back north. They reached Mahat just as the sun was beginning to hang heavy in the sky, making everything look as though it were burning, but Mahat was not there.

They began to see things beneath the churning water, trees and papyrus reeds in the muddy deluge. Then they saw the flotsam and jetsam churning in the rough seas, pieces of wood, curved slightly. They rowed quietly through the debris. There had been a large port here when they had left Mahat, but now the only evidence were the things floating by them and the shadows they could make out beneath the waves.

Samaki was not the kind of man who thought much about the gods and their business, but for the first time in a long time he felt a certainty that the gods were at work. Mahat had been punished for some evil he could not imagine.

"Boats," Tiyharqu muttered, staring at the destroyed pieces of wood in the dark waters, a feeling of dread coming over the entire crew.

The bloated bodies came next. Most were naked; their faces had a pale sheen. There were men and women, and children.

No one spoke, but every crew member was thinking the same thing. Mahat had been destroyed. The sailors who were from Mahat lost some of the colour in their faces. They were rowing over land where their villages had once been. Those bodies may very well have been the bodies of their families.

"Until we find shore," Samaki began, feeling the momentum of the ship slow, and knowing he needed to keep his men strong until they found some respite. Even he was beginning to worry that all the land had been flooded, that they would not find fresh water. Without it they would die. He could not let those thoughts enter his crew's mind, "We cannot afford to lose speed."

"But, the children-" one man began.

"First we find the shore!" Tiyharqu shouted. "Then we find the answers!"

The men looked despondent, but they continued to row, though not at the speed they would have normally gone. Many were looking out to the sea, trying to make out the faces of the dead, praying to the gods that all were strangers. Even Samaki could not help but look at the bodies. The village he had grown up in was near the shore. What had happened to it?

Time passed. The sun was nearly set. The moments seemed to freeze and Samaki felt locked in them. Then, one of the men shouted *land!* and the rower's speed increased. At first it was just a dark line on the horizon, but as they got closer they began to make out the shapes. A line of people walking along the shore, many carrying heavy burdens, and the shady palm trees they walked beneath, back in their place above the water on the strong land.

In the Sea Mahat, the Hiperu broke off into hundreds of smaller rivers to create the lush delta. They could see one of the larger rivers. A few boats were running back and forth, helping people to cross. There were lines of people trying to reach either side. It seemed there was no consensus about which side was better, people were simply trying to leave, trying to get as far away as possible from where they had begun.

"Hail!" Samaki greeted the small boats made from reeds roped together carrying the tired looking people, some wearing clothing, though just loincloths and fewer still wore tunics. "What happened here?"

The boatman nearest to them shook his bald-head. His boat was filled with so many passengers the water was threatening to overtake them. The boatmen used long poles to touch the bottom of the river and push themselves across.

"No one escaped... we were lucky to be on higher ground..." he looked dazed. He reached the shore and his passengers jumped off into the shallow waters and continued walking as a new batch of people boarded his boat. Some gave him small copper coins, others had nothing to offer but trinkets from the bundles they carried, but he took nothing, filling his boat until it threatened to sink from the weight.

"Can you tell me where we are? We've lost our bearings. This shore looks unfamiliar." The crew rowed against the current to stay in place.

"There is a village here... was..." another of the boatmen answered. "It was called Carmahat."

Carmahat. He knew the name. This was the river they had been aiming for, up the centre of the Sea Mahat. Sometimes they sojourned in Carmahat. It was a fairly large village, and sometimes they could enjoy a rest before continuing on the next day, trading some of their smaller goods for a nice warm meal after the journey. But Carmahat was halfway between the shoreline and Sareeb. It was impossible that a wave could reach this far... wasn't it? And what of Carmahat itself? Why couldn't he see the tops of any of the buildings? But... no, the buildings were made from mud bricks. Most buildings in the Sea Mahat were.

They would have been smashed and disintegrated by the force of the wave. Maybe the waters would recede, but all the villages would have to be rebuilt. Gone... they were all gone...

"Did the wave... really reach as far as this?"

"No shiplord, it reached farther," the boatman's face became dark. "The wave was meant for Sareeb. I hear the waters crashed against the great palace. Only the high lands, like this, have managed to stay above water. The fresh water has been tainted by salt. The salt will seep into the ground. The crops will die. The people try to leave, but their way is blocked by the risen sea, and only boats like mine have survived, and they can only cross rivers. The Sea Mahat is lost."

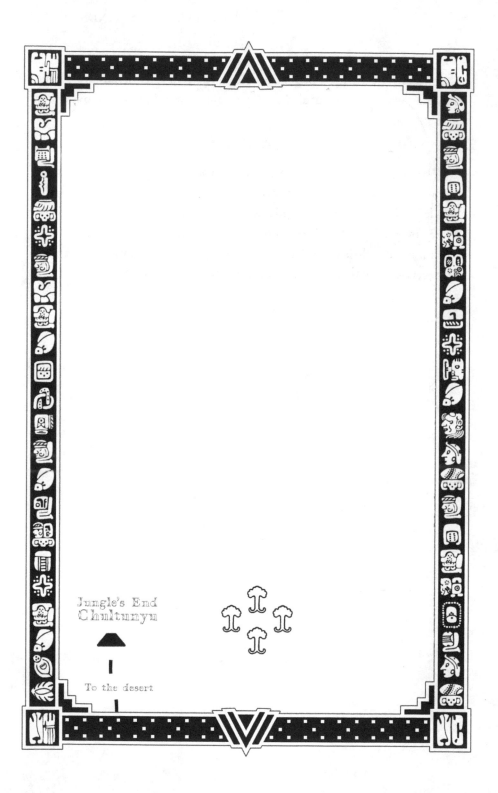

Jungle's End
Chultunyu

To the desert

THE GREY MIST

THE TEMPLE BURNED AROUND HER

Where the desert ended, the jungle began. The land east of the Kerlra Hal'gepe mountains belonged to Mahat, but the lands west belonged to the jungle. The jungle was lower than the desert. It grew out of a valley at the base of the mountain. Some called it the Grey Mist, others just the jungle. A few knew it as the land of pyramids. It was shocking to see so much colour laid against the desert. There seemed to be no end to the trees. The sounds that came from it were strange and echoed around the basin. Most days the tops of trees were covered in a mist.

Sha'di thought that maybe on a clear day he might see where the desert began again on the other side. But even on the clearest days walking along its edge, he saw no end to the jungle and worried he would never be able to find his way through the tangle of vines once he entered. He had travelled straight west from the temple of the Rhagepe where the calendar ceremony had been performed. He had gone on alone, the other two chosen to speak for the Goddesses going west towards Mahat. His only company was the falcon the chief of his tribe, the Gonnamdi, had given him.

They told him to keep the mountains to his right as he walked, and when the mountains became the jungle to continue without stopping for maybe two turns of the moon. Eventually he would find a pyre, and he must light the pyre. It was a signal fire the people of the Grey Mist had left for the Whisperers, who often traded prophecies from the gods with them. The Rhagepe would light the pyre, and people of the jungle would come. For long days he followed the stony base of the mountains, until the stones gave away to soft sand, and the mountains became the jungle.

He felt the loneliness and silence of both the desert and the mountains. He could imagine his tribe back along the west shores. Some nights he desperately wanted to be with them – to be with Nnenne. Nnenne, with fire red hair and silver eyes. Nnenne, who made his heart tight whenever he saw her. She was to be a Rhagepe one day. Already she had begun to have visions from the gods.

"You will leave me soon," she would whisper to him as they lay together in the sand, still breathing heavy, sweat glistening on their copper skin.

He thought she meant he would leave her for another woman. "I'll only leave you for as long as it takes for the night to come again." He couldn't help but turn her worries into a joke.

They had been together the night before the ceremony, safe in each other's arms until dawn. She had been solemn that night, and he had thought it had been because it was the first time she would enter the sacred temple for the calendar ceremony. Now he wondered if maybe she had known he would be chosen to speak for Rebirth, that he would be sent away the next morning. She had been in the outer circles of the temple, one of the many young women drumming. As the Whisperers lined up to give the three chosen what little could be spared, she stayed within the crumbled walls.

He knew if he didn't go to her, she would never come out to him.

The next morning, he could not find her at all. His eyes scanned the crowd gathered to watch them leave in the morning. Every time he saw red hair he hoped it was her, but it never was. She had always told him he would leave her, but she had left him first.

The falcon squawked from her perch on his shoulder. She had a tiny leather hood covering her eyes to keep her calm, but it was clear she was hungry. He had tethered her to the bones of his cloak by the small leather jesses fastened to her feet, adorned by the little bells that would chime softly every time she moved. Of the three chosen to speak for the Goddesses during the ceremony, his cloak had the least bones. He was only the second man to wear it in his line. His father had been the youngest son, and so only given the leg bones – the least important – of his father. But as the eldest son Sha'di had been given his father's rib bones to add to the cloak. Those with fewer bones on their cloaks were thought of as lesser in the tribe, so it was a shock and an honour beyond anything he'd ever expected to be called for this. He wondered if his mother had known. She had been a Rhagepe, speaking for the Goddess of Rebirth as well, though she had died in childbirth when he was still a boy. He could barely remember her, just silver eyes and a round face.

"Calm yourself, my little glutton," he scratched the falcon under her chin.

Sha'di put down his skins. He had many things bundled up there. He checked his two water skins. When available he drank lizard blood to stave his thirst, but the water was essential, and he would only spare a sip or two every day. He had only brought enough to last maybe three turns. He picked up a lure – a small piece of dried lizard meat tied to the end of a long leather cord – as he took off the hood and released the falcon from her jesses. The falcon was small and fast, darting quickly as she turned around him. He swung the lure, warming her up, she darted for it and he pulled it away, then she flew up high. From there she could see the entire desert and jungle. She could pick out a black speck and know if it was prey or not. Suddenly she turned down, folding her wings and plummeting to the earth. She glanced off the sand, catching something in her talons, and then flew up again. He swung the lure and when she caught sight of it she headed towards him, carrying her prey with her.

"Good work, Nnenne," Sha'di whispered, letting her take the lure as she dropped the large lizard she had caught. He hadn't meant to name her Nnenne, but he had begun speaking to the woman he loved even though she wasn't there, and then he had begun speaking to the falcon as though she were Nnenne. Sometimes he dreamt of the real Nnenne. He could see her standing in the outer circle of the temple, her back to him, her long dreadlocked red hair going down her bare back, her Ancestral Cloak in the sand next to her. He would reach out to her.

"You shouldn't be here," she would say, and the dream would end.

He would share some of the fresh meat with the falcon Nnenne, as well as save some of it, drying it out for more lures. They would hunt every day, sometimes more than once, and being so close to the jungle they always had fuel for fire. With the fire knife the Rhagepe had given them it was easy to cook his food every day. He couldn't remember having ever lived so easily. If it weren't for the loneliness he would have wanted to stay at the edge of the jungle forever.

The longer he was alone, the more anxious he became. As he neared the end of the second turn of the moon, the stars overtaking the night as the moon waned into darkness, he would squint his eyes in the sun, hoping to see the pyre on the horizon. When the third crescent moon rose he began to wonder if the pyre wasn't on the edge of the jungle, but within the tangle of trees. Maybe he had already passed it. His water skins were nearly dry. He wished the Goddess of Rebirth would speak to him, give him a sign, but there was nothing but silence around him.

As the sun began to lower towards the ground, he took Nnenne out to hunt. The motions had become routine to him. He swung the lure, and she flew up high to catch her prey, only this time when she landed she didn't dive to the ground with her usual speed, and instead landed on what looked like a rock in the distance. Sha'di sighed, gathering his things and walking towards her. She wasn't usually so easily distracted. Maybe there was a dead animal she had gone to investigate.

Nnenne cawed gently as he approached.

"Save your excuses, Nnenne," he glared in the distance.

What he had assumed was a stone turned out to be a manmade structure. It was a round pyramid, the base the width of a man and twice as wide as the top, which was flat. It was made of stones, painted in fading red. Bones – human bones, surrounded the base. The top, which was the same height as Sha'di, where Nnenne was happily pecking at something, had logs and wrapped bundles of dried moss, and something else that had caught Nnenne's attention. He held out his hand holding the meat from the lure, and Nnenne hopped onto his arm, taking the meat and ripping it apart.

Was this the pyre he had been looking for? The top was blackened, as though many fires had been lit there before. There was no doubt it *was* a signal fire, and Sha'di couldn't imagine there were many pyres out in the desert along the edge of the jungle.

He laid down his bundled skin, letting Nnenne walk on it and giving her a few more morsels of dried meat to content her, no longer caring about his own dinner. "You don't deserve this, you lazy lizard," he muttered softly.

He took out the fire knife, and a small rock and went to the pyre. The height made it awkward to light, so he took one of the moss bundles and made sparks over it until it began to burn, then he reached up and placed the flaming bundle under the other logs.

The moss produced an incredible amount of smoke, and he could smell burning flesh. Soon a high grey pillar reached into the sky. There were still a few hours left in the day. Someone would see the smoke. Someone would come. Sha'di laid his cloak down, tethering Nnenne to it as she ate her meat, and sat down against the pyre, facing the jungle, waiting.

He concentrated eagerly on the tree-line for a long time as the light faded, feeling his eyes become heavier, until he could no longer keep them open.

He was in the temple again. The night was nearly over. Everyone slept. He walked quietly, knowing that he might be a speaker for the Goddess of Rebirth, but that it was still forbidden for anyone but a Rhagepe to enter those walls.

A woman stood in the middle of one of the connecting circles, her back to him. Nnenne? No, she had long hair, but it was black and straight. He reached out to her.

"You shouldn't be here!" the woman screamed as she turned around, and fire erupted around them.

Sha'di awoke feeling his heart race. He tried to catch his breath, still seeing the burning woman, unable to process why or who it had been. What had he just seen? Could that have been a vision? He realized the falcon next to him was in distress. She flapped her wings, hitting his leg and nudging him back to reality. He saw nothing before the jungle in the dim morning light at first. Then his eyes focused, and he saw *them*.

He hadn't heard the men come out of the trees. The figures were so still they might have been carved from wood, though they stared at Sha'di with piercing eyes. There were five of them, each nearly indistinguishable from the other. They all had straight long black hair down to their waist. The bottom half of their faces, from the lips to the base of their necks were completely beardless and painted bright red, as were their hands and legs. Their chests were bare, and they wore only red loincloths. The men stood apart from each other, some by the tree line, others having come closer, and were so still they did not even show signs of breathing.

"No, Nnenne, I don't think we *are* dreaming..." Still, he wasn't certain. His eyes focused on the man closest to him, noting that he did not hold a weapon. None of them held any weapon, save for the man closest to the trees, who had a sling held casually in his hand by his side. There was also a bundle wrapped in black skin next to his feet. Sha'di pushed himself up, his head still drowsy from sleep. He must have spent the night sleeping against the pyre and now its fires had completely died out.

"Whisperer," the man closest to him finally spoke, taking a step forward, his companions remaining completely still. He slowly looked around. "Where are your others? Where are witches?"

His voice had such a strong accent Sha'di almost didn't understand him at first. Then he realized he was asking where the Rhagepe were. This was a pyre lit by the Rhagepe when they had a message from the gods to give the people of the Grey Mist.

"I come alone. I – the Rhagepe sent me. I speak for the Goddess of Rebirth. I am Sha'di Al'Sha'di, of the tribe Gonnamdi."

"Red," the man said, pointing to Sha'di's hair, his face unreadable.

Sha'di wondered if maybe they had never seen red hair before. It was uncommon among the Whispers as well, though many people in his tribe had the same colour. "Your hair is long," he finally replied. He was used to seeing only women keep their hair long.

The man said nothing for a moment, then his features finally changed, a smile appearing on his bi-coloured face. He laughed. "Why you call us here

Whisperer? You speak for gods? Like witches? You man." It was no question. Whisperers wore no clothes beneath their cloak.

"A great change is coming. I must speak to your chief."

The man's face became sombre again. "Chief far away, Whisperer," the other men had started coming closer, though they didn't feel threatening.

"I must go to him all the same. The gods demand it."

"I Tetchtok of Chultunyu. I take you, then fate yours," Tetchtok smiled and motioned towards the dark jungle.

Sha'di was aware that if he followed them and entered the jungle, he would be leaving everything he knew behind him. How would he hunt? How would he fight? He didn't know what dangers lay in that place; he only knew that he must go. There were no choices left for him.

After resetting the pyre, the men led him through a path they hacked away with strange swords made from wood called a yaxha. Dozens and dozens of shards made from the same stone as the fire knives lined the sides of the yaxha like teeth. With one quick slash the yaxha would cut through anything the jungle had placed in front of them. Before long they came to a wide, shallow river, and Sha'di was overcome with the sight of so much water that he jumped in, Nnenne squawking on his shoulder as he plunged his face into the cool liquid and gulped thirstily. The men with him laughed, wading through towards the other side. Sha'di was amazed that the red paint on their legs didn't wash off in the water. They passed more rivers than he could count. Most of them were small streams that he could just step over, but others were as deep as a man's waist and ran so fast they were difficult to pass without losing your footing.

Sha'di thought once in the shade of the jungle the heat would diminish, but instead he began to feel a new kind of heat. The air in here was warm and moist, and after half a day he felt completely drained of all his energy. The farther in they went, the more oppressive the heat became, and he stopped at every stream to gulp down water before moving on.

Although Sha'di wanted to rest, the men always carried on, only stopping for a brief meal once. The man who carried the bundle pulled out some large bright fruit. They would smash them against rocks, breaking them apart and unearthing the bright rose quartz-coloured juices inside. Tetchtok held one out towards Sha'di, but as the Whisperer reached out to grab it Tetchtok pulled it away.

"We brought for witches, pay witches for dreams, messages from gods. I give you, for messages from gods."

"I have none for you," Sha'di said meekly. "I don't have visions… only a message for the chief of the jungle people."

"Jungle people?" Tetchtok laughed. "We are Petzuhallpa, in your tongue Pyramid Builders."

"My apologies, but still, I was told to give me message to your chief."

"What message?"

"The gods are angry, that's all I can say. Your chief will understand more."

"Chief understand what chief want. I want know what chief know," Tetchtok shrugged and started putting the fruit away.

Sha'di felt his stomach grumble, and looked at Nnenne who sat placidly on his shoulder. He hadn't eaten all day, and he had no idea if he would be able to use the falcon to hunt in such a lush environment.

"Wait, I had a vision… maybe," Sha'di mumbled, thinking of the dream he had had the night before. He barely understood it and had no evidence that it had been a vision, but he would tell the man anything if he would give him a meal.

"Tell," Tetchtok held out the fruit tauntingly towards him, a smirk on his face. His companions gave a small chuckle, saying something in their language Sha'di couldn't understand.

"The gods sent me a vision of a woman, burning and writhing in pain. She stood in a temple, and the temple burned around her."

Tetchtok looked back at his companions, translating what he'd said to them. One of them laughed and said something.

"Kalotch say that any woman. What look like?"

"She..." he couldn't remember her face, he wasn't even sure he saw her face, just the horrible flames consuming it. "She had long black hair, completely straight. Not a single knot. Not a single curl."

Tetchtok chuckled and translated and the other men laughed. The man with the sling found it particularly funny and said something in reply.

"Tolek say that every woman," Tetchtok laughed.

Sha'di looked despondent, but Tetchtok threw him the fruit all the same, maybe in payment for being amusing. He smashed the fruit against a rock, expecting it to open after one swing like what had happened for the others, but the fruit was harder than he had realized, and he needed to use both hands to smash it repeatedly – all the while hearing the laughter of others and Nnenne's squawking as her perch became unstable – until finally it broke open. He sucked at the fruit, but it was so sweet his mouth puckered and he nearly choked. The men only laughed louder, but he didn't care, once he got over the shock of the strong taste, it was the most incredible thing he'd ever eaten, and he quickly scooped out the bright innards and left only the cacti-like skin behind.

When they got up to leave Sha'di was still thinking about the dream, wondering where it had come from. Straight long black hair, maybe in the jungle everyone had that, but for him it was beyond unusual. Long and black, perhaps, but until he met the men he travelled with now he had never seen hair so straight. They said he was describing every woman, but he wasn't describing the woman he had *actually* seen that night in the temple. Every night he relived the moment in his dreams...

He couldn't sleep after being chosen. He kept thinking about Nnenne staying in the temple, cutting herself off from him, and he couldn't resist the urge he felt to go to her. There wasn't a single sound when he crept through the sleeping figures of his tribesmen. She was still standing in the temple when he finally reached it, her back turned towards him. Had she been standing there all night? Had she been waiting for him? He felt a slight panic as he put his foot over the side of the crumbled wall, fearing the gods would strike him down, but he kept reminding himself that he had been chosen to speak for the gods, that he was worthy to enter the sacred temple, and sure enough when his foot connected with the ground the earth did not open up to swallow him. A bolt of lightning did not strike him down, nothing changed. He walked towards her, reaching out–

"You shouldn't be here," she whispered, turning around, her face streaked with tears.

"Will we see each other again?" He had asked in a quiet voice, terrified of her answer.

"Come with me," she took his hand, and began leading him towards the inner sanctum of the temple.

They followed what was left of the outer walls to the entrance the Rhagepe took to enter the temple. Where the three circles of the temple connected, the inner temple, looked like a triangle. The Rhagepe would refer to it as the womb of the gods. When Sha'di had been there before, during the last calendar ceremony last Orope, when he was still just a boy, he and his friends would giggle that if the inside was the womb, then surely the path the Rhagepe walked towards it was the god's vagina. Certainly it had the same shape. The memory came back to him and he nearly laughed, then he realized Nnenne was taking him to the inner temple, and he felt himself go cold...

The memory faded away as they walked, the jungle grabbing his attention. He felt overwhelmed by his surroundings, and he lost himself in the thick foliage. He was amazed with every strikingly bright flower they passed, shades of the setting sun and bright gemstones. Animals were everywhere, birds and small fury mammals that climbed in the trees. He barely noticed when they came upon the village.

Suddenly he noticed people coming up to him. They had a similar look to Tetchtok and his men. The red dye on the lower halves of their faces, hands and legs. Some wore loincloths. The children wore nothing at all, nor did they have the red dye on them. The women kept their distance, whispering to each other, as they looked him over. Their chests were bare as well. They had the dye on the top halves of their faces as well as on their breasts and hands. All the people looked healthy, the women curvy and the children pudgy. He felt envious of them. The Whisperers were all thin and bony, moving from one meal to the next. Some of these people, like the older men, had waists wider than their shoulders. How amazing it would be to eat enough every day to turn out like that.

The village itself was made up of huts built from leaves and thin sticks. Most of them blended in with the forest. The only reason he could tell it was a village was a wide circular space in the middle of the huts were a large fire pit was. He wasn't used to seeing so many structures together. The Whisperers hardly ever built anything. Sometimes they would use skins and sticks to make lean-tos to protect themselves from harsh sandstorms, but the only permanent structure he had ever really seen was the Rhagepe's temple. Perhaps the most noticeable structure in the village was built alongside the trees, a high tower that stuck up above the tall branches. From there, Tetchtok explained, they could see the smoke from the pyre. A man was up there now, taking turns looking in all directions.

"More than one fire we see," Tetchtok said. "Also, birds land there."

Tetchtok didn't offer more of an explanation, but told Sha'di to wait while he entered one of the large huts. It wasn't taller than any of the others but was much wider. When Tetchtok emerged a few moments later, a large robust man followed him. He was by far the roundest man Sha'di had ever seen, and the only person he had seen in the jungle wearing anything more than a loincloth. He had a red tunic on made from the pelt of a black jaguar, the belt made from silver and topaz. His hair was also braided, and the end of each braid had a precious stone or precious metal or some other shiny trinket.

Sha'di knew at once this was the chief, and bowed his head in respect. "Chief of the Pyramid Builders, I bring a warning from the gods."

Tetchtok smiled and shook his head. "Chief of Pyramid Builders? No... chief, of village," Tetchtok motioned around the small clearing. "Chief of Pyramid Builders far away, impossible to reach. I take you to Chultunyatl, chief of Jungle's End. Many days from here," Tetchtok said quickly and then began to speak with the chief.

Sha'di felt his face flush with embarrassment, and then annoyance. The chief of the Pyramid Builders was impossible to reach? What did he mean? And who was the chief Tetchtok said he'd bring him to? What was Jungle's End?

"Feast tonight!" Tetchtok announced happily, but Sha'di just felt bewilderment.

It took seven more days to reach the place Tetchtok called Chultunyu, Jungle's End. Sha'di couldn't imagine the size of the jungle if it took nearly ten days of walking *into* it in order to reach what these people considered the end. He tried to not feel daunted, but every day he felt a greater unease as the jungle darkened around him, becoming thicker and harder to cut a path through.

His first night in the jungle had been a welcome experience. Hunters had caught a few wild pigs and an assortment of birds. Sha'di had never seen any of those animals, let alone eaten them. They were roasted over an open fire, while the people of the village gathered in a great circle around it, singing songs and drinking a bitter liquid that made his head swim.

Everyone was interested in him, wanting to touch his hair or stroke Nnenne. None of them could speak his language, save for Tetchtok, so Sha'di was lost in their words. He managed to learn how to say 'hello' and 'more please' when he wanted drink or food, but that was all. He realized he would have to learn their language, as he was certain Tetchtok would not want to follow him around and be his interpreter.

The next morning, with a staggering headache, Sha'di and a group of ten men headed out. Joining him were some of the men who had brought him to the village; Tetchtok, Tolek, and Kalotch. Sha'di began asking the names for the things around them, and listened to their speech intently trying to unlock it, but by the end of their travels he had only learned a handful of words and still couldn't string a proper sentence together. Worse still, the men would laugh every time he repeated whatever they taught him.

They ate well every night, but sleeping in the jungle was nearly impossible for Sha'di. The ground was hard and uneven, the air moist and too hot, and he was constantly being bitten by insects. He would listen jealously to the sounds of sleeping men around him, wondering how they could ignore the sounds of animals that only seemed to grow louder at night. And of course, it was so dark he couldn't see the hand before his face. It filled him with a terrible fear that at arm's length would be some predator waiting to pounce. He woke up every morning sore and miserably tired.

Yet this was not the biggest surprise for him. That had been the rain. It seemed to drizzle every other day. Very few of the drops penetrated the thick jungle growth, yet he could hear the pitter-patter above him. If it wasn't raining, there was a thick mist over them. He had seen rain once, when he was a child. All the people of his tribe had danced in it, throwing their cloaks to the wet sand, opening their mouths to taste. This rain had the opposite effect on him. He hated it. He never felt dry anymore. He never knew it was possible to hate water, but a week in the jungle made him realize it was.

The last morning, when Tetchtok announced to him that they would arrive at Chultunyu that day, was the happiest he had felt since he had last been with Nnenne.

She still came to him in his dreams. Gone was the woman on fire, and now when he entered the temple, Nnenne was there to lead him to the inner sanctum, but they never made it, something would always wake him up before they could. He had to be satisfied with the waking memory he had. They *had* entered the pillars of the inner temple that night. The torches weren't lit and he could see nothing in the darkness, save for Nnenne's silver eyes.

"What if the Rhagepe find us here?" he had asked nervously, never intending to go so far into the forbidden place.

"They won't. I have seen this night a thousand times in my dreams," Nnenne's voice was smooth and soft. She kissed his neck, her hands untying his cloak and letting it fall to the ground behind him.

"And what did you see this night?" Sha'di's voice was weak, his strength all but taken away by Nnenne's lips kissing his neck again, and again.

"You will give me children tonight," she said between kisses, "in this most sacred place, on this most sacred night."

"Children?" Sha'di laughed. "I think there's only room for one in you." He reached down and his fingers stroked her curly red hairs.

"Give me a dozen," she whispered, her hand suddenly grabbing his erection, making him gasp slightly. "For you, I'll make room."

She pushed him to the ground and climbed on top of him. They saw with their hands, moving over each other's bodies, feeling each other's skin, memorizing the shapes and curves.

His body responded just thinking about it, and he pulled his cloak closed to hide any embarrassment from the Petzuhallpa as they walked through the jungle.

When he had awoken at dawn the next morning she was gone. He left the temple, the sun just beginning to turn the night sky into a gentle amethyst, but she was nowhere. He walked around the camp, checking every woman with red hair. He looked for her desperately, but she was gone, maybe hiding. There had been times since when he wondered if maybe it had all been a dream, but he could still remember her warmth, and knew it had to have happened.

"There," Tetchtok said, breaking him from his reverie.

The jungle had been growing less dense for an hour or so, and as Sha'di squinted through the branches and vines he saw a wall of dull red behind it. He couldn't imagine what kind of structure it was until they got closer. They passed by many of the same kind of huts Sha'di had seen back in the other village, but here there were many more, and far, far more people, all with the same red dye covering the same parts of their bodies.

They were all cheerful, singing and running around, grabbing each other. More dancing ensued. Sha'di had never seen happier people. Every once in a while, they would pause to notice the strangers in the midst, but then almost immediately tried to get them to join it.

"Today Sipakti," Tetchtok had explained, though Sha'di had no idea what he meant.

In the village, all the huts had been in a circle around a large fire pit, but here the huts were centred around the tall red structure. When they finally emerged from the trees they saw the large round plaza and Sha'di nearly fell backward in shock. The plaza was surrounded not by wooden huts, but ones made out of stone, maybe a hundred of them. In the middle, towering above everything else, was a pyramid, like the pyre he had seen at the desert's end, only this one was so tall and wide that its top was the same height as the trees. A ramp wound up its square body, and on the flat top was a large house made out of stone. The entire thing was coloured in the same red dye. It was a long time before Sha'di could find his voice.

"This is... This... Your chief lives here?"

"Sometimes." Tetchtok shrugged, amused by Sha'di's shocked reaction. "Come."

Tetchtok began towards the ramp and Sha'di followed, unable to look anywhere but straight up. The people around them paid them no notice, engrossed in their celebration of Sipakti. Sha'di wouldn't have even noticed them if he'd been surrounded by grabbing hands. He could not believe anyone was capable of building something so large and tall. How many men, how many *full cycles*, had it taken to build? Petzuhallpa, Pyramid Builders, was a fine name for these people.

At the top Sha'di looked at his surroundings. It was dark jungle as far as he could see. He tried to see the desert, but through the mist-topped trees it was impossible. He wasn't even certain which way the desert was. He turned towards the large square entrance. The building on top was simple, no flare or decoration, but was impressive for its size alone. It was over twice the height of a man, and the door could fit four men abreast easily. In front of the door, near the edge of the ramp was a large rectangular stone, about the height of his waist. It was painted a darker red than the rest of the pyramid. He turned his attention back towards the doorway and entered behind the other men.

It was dark inside and musty. There was something burning in the corners that gave off a strong scent. Sha'di blinked at its overpowering sweetness. There were a few squares cut out of the ceiling to let in light, and beneath each opening was a pool the same size and shape to collect water. Each pool was alive with flowering lily pads.

There were several dozen plump men crammed into the room, making it seem smaller than he thought it would be. The men there all wore tunics like the chief in the village. Their hair was braided with decorations. These men had far more jewels than the village chief though, and some had strange piercings in their lips and ears. Of those men who didn't wear headdresses, he noticed that their heads seemed strangely long and narrow, as though someone had grabbed them by the hair and stretched their heads out. A few men held fans made out of long white feathers, fanning themselves as they looked at the strangers with disinterest.

Kalotch went to the front of the room and spoke to the most ornately dressed man standing in front of a dais with a large stone chair on it. This man wore a crown of feathers and silver, and held a polished wooden staff tipped with topaz, and Sha'di was positive that he must have been seeing the chief. Then the man struck the ground with his staff three times and a hush came over the room. A young man at the back, wearing only a loincloth, ran through a door behind the dais as the man wearing a crown began speak.

"Hail Chief Tanuk," Tetchtok whispered into Sha'di's ear translating so he could understand. Tetchtok could speak these words with less of an accent. Sha'di thought he must have had much more practice in this formal setting.

Tetchtok continued. "He holds father's staff in his stead. He Chief of Old Chiefs. He Chief of Jungle's End. He guards the way. He hears Whisperers."

From the back of the room, a man slightly older than Sha'di emerged. He wore a long cloak of jaguar skin, his long braided hair had no trinkets tied at the ends. He wore a large crown of silver and topaz and white feathers. His jaw and hands were dyed red, but the rest of him seemed very plain compared to every other man in the room. Under his cloak, he only wore a simple white tunic, a silver belt buckled at his slim waist. He walked up the dais and sat on the chair, staring down at the room with a straight back and severe expression on his face. He spoke, and everyone in the room turned to look at Sha'di.

"He wants know message you bring."

"Is he the chief?" Sha'di asked, just to be safe.

"No, his father chief. He wear crown while father at Chipetzuha, Red Pyramid."

"Isn't this the Red Pyramid?" exasperation seeped into his voice.

Tetchtok laughed and translated, and others began to laugh, save for Chief Tanuk, who smiled kindly at him and said something to Tetchtok in a soft voice.

"Chief Tanuk says this *simple* red pyramid, but father at *big* red pyramid, far north, where chief of all lives. There all chief of Three Lands live."

"Then I must go there and warn them."

"Warn what?" Tetchtok asked impatiently.

"The gods are furious. A corruption, evil, has come to this land and others. A great flood will come, like the flood of old, to wash away those who do not respect the gods. The gods must be appeased. Your chiefs must follow the old ways, or all your people will die."

Tetchtok translated, and to Sha'di's surprise no one was fazed.

"Chief Tanuk says your people hear gods whisper this much."

"Yes, but, always the gods were appeased," Sha'di stammered.

Tanuk began speaking at length and Tetchtok had a hard time translating.

"Chief Tanuk say... here has badness, evil... Chief of Red Pyramid has turned from her people."

"Her?" Sha'di asked for clarification, but Tetchtok kept translating, ignoring him.

"Never has bad been more here, he say... but only Chief of the Red Pyramid can appease gods. Her you must tell."

"I will go there, I just... don't know the way."

Tanuk spoke to the older man who also wore a silver crown, and the two seemed to argue for a moment.

"Who is he?" Sha'di asked.

"Chief Tanuk's uncle."

Finally, Tanuk said something and his uncle went silent. He spoke, and Tetchtok translated.

"Chief Tanuk says... he say, he take you. Say... time is come to join father at Red Pyramid."

Tanuk stood, smiling at Sha'di, his eyes gleaming. The others all cheered and clapped, all save for his uncle. He stared up at his nephew with a dangerous look.

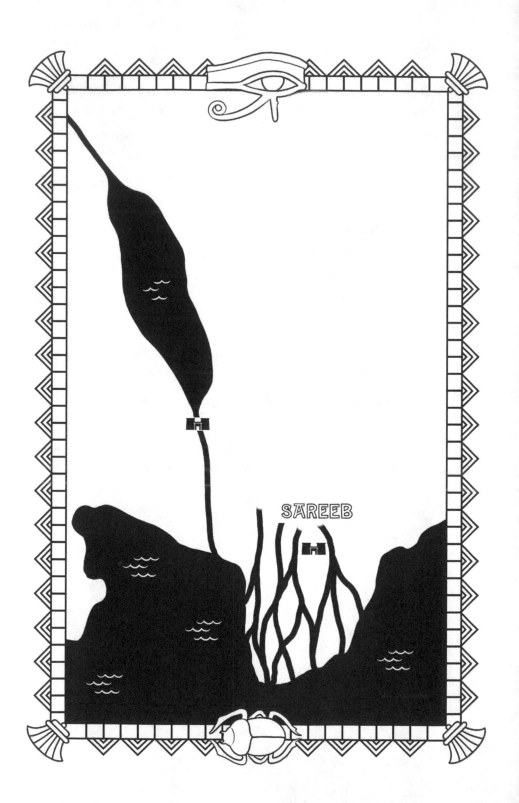

SAREEB

YOU HAVE NO CONTROL OVER YOUR PAWN. IT GOES WHERE THE STICKS TELL IT

The road from the border city to Sareeb began as a desert, and ended in a lush forest. It was a gradual change, brought on by the many rivers that forked off from the Hiperu, creating the large delta. Every day there was more life around them, more magnificent colours, more birdcalls, more encounters with local merchants who travelled along the road for trade. The closer they got to Sareeb, the more people they saw, and not just merchants. They saw entire families, seemingly carrying everything they owned, walking with empty eyes.

As a general rule they avoided speaking to anyone. Kareth and Tersh would wait along the side of the road in the trees. The Whisperers were not welcome in this part of the world. Where most places they were respected for their connection to the gods, here they were feared for it. It wasn't difficult to convince Kareth to hide. Since crossing the border he had become quieter. He always had a serious look on his face, as though he were lost in thought.

When she had been Kareth's age, Tersh's tribe had travelled to the Sea Mahat. During the calendar ceremony a plague was predicted along the fishing villages her people traded with, so their chief decided to take them across the border where he believed they would be safe. They had stayed along the shore through several constellations. Tersh learned the language and customs of these people. Tersh never forgot the beauty of this land and never stopped yearning to return. She would probably never stop being disappointed she didn't get to stay in Mahat as its messenger, but she was thankful that at least the gods sent her on a path that would take her through Mahat.

At night, they camped at the side of the road amongst the trees. Kareth had an easy time falling to sleep. Tersh would spend a long time looking up at the stars, remembering all the nights she had done the same, only lying next to Ka'rel's warm body instead. She could still smell the salt of his skin as she drifted off. One morning, Kareth woke with a start just as Tersh was making a fire.

"You look as though you still wear a cloak of dreams," Tersh had remarked, trying to make him smile, but the boy only scowled at the ground.

Tersh cooked some fish over a small fire, the entire time Kareth saying not a word. It wasn't until after they'd eaten, when Tersh was pouring dirt over the hot embers, that he made a noise.

"Could a man be sent a vision from the gods?"

"A man?" Tersh shrugged. "I think maybe that's a woman's providence. Only a woman can be Rhagepe. Only Rhagepe can hear the gods."

"But I was chosen to speak for the gods as well, and I'm a man."

Barely a man. "You were chosen to be a messenger, not a Rhagepe," the questions were beginning to make her feel uncomfortable.

"I dreamt of two great white birds, sent from the gods, to carry us on our journey," his voice seemed distant.

"I dream every night. It does not mean those dreams were sent by the gods."

They began to walk, and it was a long time before Kareth spoke again.

"Do you think... when I performed that ceremony...?"

Tersh couldn't help but laugh, but quickly stopped when she saw the hurt look in Kareth's face. "It wasn't a real ceremony."

"Yes, I know I made it up... but that doesn't mean it wasn't real. I *felt* something," Kareth pointed his silver eyes up at the sky. "I feel like something inside me... opened. Whatever I did back at the border... my mother would say it was like picking up a random rock, only to break it open and find it's full of quartz."

Tersh looked at Kareth. She wondered how much of what he was saying was nothing but a boy's imagination and how much of it could actually be true. What did she know of the Rhagepe? The boy had silver eyes. He had been chosen to speak for a god. How could she say he did or did not receive a vision from the gods? If the gods wanted them to be their voice, it was possible they might also send them visions in order to guide them.

"Two birds, you say?"

Kareth turned towards her, his face brightening. "Yes. I think the gods are trying to tell us of how to proceed next."

"None of the birds I've seen in these parts could carry us anywhere. Besides, we're nearly at Sareeb. Your journey is nearly ended."

Kareth sighed. "Maybe... maybe the gods are saying that this journey is only beginning."

After the sun had reached its zenith and begun to descend once more, they saw Sareeb for the first time. The ground slanted down, and they could see the entirety of the city before them. They both had to stop walking and stare in stunned silence. This was perhaps ten times the size of the border city, with dozens of massive pillared-temples. It was split in two, a large river going down its centre, ending in a lake on the south side of the city walls. More shocking still was when they noticed that the lake had swallowed up the southern half of the city. They could see the tops of trees and buildings, people using boats to move through narrow alleys.

A flood.

Tersh felt weak.

"It's begun," Kareth whispered.

Tersh could only shake her head. "We don't know that."

"The city is flooded!" Kareth turned to her. "Their chief is dead and the flood has already come! We're too late!"

"We are not too late," Tersh took the boy's shoulders in his hands, her stern, dark eyes staring him down, her voice calm and level. "The city still lives. The gods have given them a warning, but the flood is not complete. The Rhagepe told us the floods would touch every constellation in the full cycle. The gods would not have sent us if there wasn't any time to stop this."

Slowly Kareth nodded his head.

As they walked the rest of the way they both finally understood the lines of people they had seen heading for the border. They were escaping this, carrying what little they owned, praying that the flood would not follow them west. Tersh could only hope that was true.

Once they reached the city they could see the damage was much worse than they had though. The water had cascaded over the city walls with such force that many of the tall statues on the south side of the city had been toppled over or broken in two. They entered from the west side, the gates open and no guards anywhere to be seen. There were people milling through wrecked houses, lifting up stones as they waded ankle-deep in water. Everyone had the same tired expression on their faces. In a small square along the river bodies had been piled up. There were hundreds of them. Most of their eyes were still open, bulging out of their heads as they had gasped for breath in their final moments.

"What happened here?" Tersh asked a man who was tending to one of the bodies. The body lay on a wooden table next to the pile and the man was cleaning it while his younger assistant was stripping him of his clothes and jewellery. They both wore dirty tunics and stubble had begun to grow on their heads. She had never seen the people of Mahat looking so dishevelled.

The man shook his head, barely noticing who was speaking to him. He was indifferent, but to Tersh's surprise he did not give her the disdain she was used to experiencing with these people.

"A wave came from the south, two – no," he wiped the sweat from his face, "three days ago? Many waves, torrents of water. I honestly couldn't say how many. I've barely slept since. I've never... Half the city was drowned. The water went to the very steps of the White Palace."

The White Palace was in the centre of the city, sitting on the eastern riverbank. It was the highest building there, a massive three or four storey rectangular structure. The walls angled inward ever so slightly so that the top was narrower than the base. It was built of stone so white it shone like a beacon. At the four corners were white obelisks tipped with gold. The southeastern one had fallen. It lay shattered, discarded, as so many of the city's citizens had been. Tersh noticed the water no longer reached the palace. It had receded. The thought made her smile. It truly was only a warning. The waters were leaving. They still had time – before the flood came again.

"What does he say?" Kareth asked impatiently.

"The waters are receding," Tersh smiled at him. "Now we must go see this new chief of theirs."

They needed to find a way to cross the water. When they reached the river they realized with some shock that there were no bridges. It was not because they had been washed away, but rather no bridge had ever been built there. The river was much too wide, and the bank muddy. The water itself was filled with large boats travelling through.

"They must use ferries." Tersh looked up and down the river, but saw none of the small boats normally used for ferrying travellers. In all likelihood they were in the southern part of the city, perhaps looking for survivors, or going through drowned houses to loot whatever had been left behind.

She glanced at Kareth for a reaction. He wasn't paying attention to her. His eyes were focused on the White Palace across the river. Tersh turned to see what had captured his attention. A stone path led from the palace to the water. It was lined with dozens of statues of men holding spears. Each had one foot forward as though they had been turned to stone mid-march. At the end of the path was a wooden pier along which were four grand golden barges painted with the colour of marsh flowers. They were a multitude of sparks and hues, a thousand different birds giving flight, with the bow and stern pointed up and carved to look like bushels of wheat.

Tersh smiled at Kareth, whose mouth hung open as he stared at the glittering boats. They had golden cabins set near the back. The cabins were so large they looked like they could have housed an entire family. At each cabin's four corners stood a statue of a man, but each statue had the head of a different animal, the head of a heron, the head of a leopard, the head of a crocodile, and the head of a jackal. At the top of the ornately carved cabin was an eye facing the bow.

"They're not really made of gold," a woman spoke to them.

Tersh looked to her right and saw a bald, broad-shouldered woman, with skin like a fire knife looking at her with a smile. She wore a bright red vest and large baggy grey pants. On her chest and hands, she wore many silver and gold amulets. Tersh couldn't tell if she was a merchant or a pirate. Both looked much the same to her.

"I'm... sorry?" Tersh asked, noticing that there were actually quite a number of people lined up along the river, staring at the golden barges.

"The ships are made of wood, like any ship. They took sheets of thin gold, and used paint to stick it to the sides. Otherwise, she could not float." The woman's accent was not from these parts though her use of the tongue of Mahat was nearly perfect.

"How do you know?"

"Who is she?" Kareth asked, but Tersh ignored him.

"I build ships. It is my trade. My name is Tiyharqu."

"Tee.. yuha...?"

"You may call me Harqu, if it is easier, Go-man."

It had been a long time since she had been called Go-man. In their own tongue they called themselves Gogepe, Whisperers of the Gods, but many people either did not know the meaning, or simply enjoyed the sound of saying Go-man. Tersh didn't mind. It was certainly better than the other name people called them. Rattlecloaks.

"I am called Tersh Hal'Reekrah of the tribe Go'angrin. He is called Kareth Al'Resh, of the tribe Gorikin."

"And where are your tribes?"

"In the Sea of Sand. We have come alone... with a warning, from the gods."

"A warning for whom?" Tiyharqu asked, her smile never fading.

"We must speak to the chief, the leader of this place."

"I'm sorry, you should have come earlier," Tiyharqu pointed back towards the palace. "See, the King is leaving Sareeb."

Tersh looked back and saw a retinue of people walking down the path from the palace to the golden barges. There were a dozen or so guards. These guards dressed just as the ones at the border. The familiar pleated white linen skirts, each belted at the waste, bright amethyst being revealed in the folds, and on their heads they wore nemes of the same royal colour. Each one held a black spear tipped in bronze, and short-shorts hung from their belts. They looked like living versions of the statues they walked beside.

Behind them walked young women wearing sheer white tunics, revealing their breasts and dark nipples beneath. They wore wigs of black braided hair. They held up half a dozen awnings stitched with golden threads, making them glitter in the sun. Underneath the awnings they had to squint to see the royal family shaded in darkness. They walked with their backs straight and chins high, wearing ornate wigs and tunics that went down to the ground, with sky and golden threads. A man, Tersh assumed was the Paref, was first. He wore a strange cap on his head, it was tall and stiff and a dark river colour. Behind him walked a shimmering woman and further behind still went several children.

"They go to seek the Paref."

"The Paref? That isn't him?" Tersh pointed to the man walking under the first awning.

"No, that is Utarna, the King of the Sea Mahat. The Paref lives up north, in Nepata. My ship sails for there as well."

"Tersh, what is happening?" Kareth whined behind her.

"Your ship? You mean one you built?"

"Yes, the Afeth. She is not as beautiful as those barges, but to me she's worth a thousand such ships."

"I–" Tersh stopped herself from speaking. She was about to tell the woman how they had to travel to Nepata, to speak with the Paref and deliver their warning, but what good would that do? The Whisperers were unwelcome in these parts. She certainly wouldn't offer to take them – at least, not unless Tersh thought of a way to convince her.

"Have you captained your ship long?" Tersh finally asked.

Tiyharqu laughed pleasantly. "I have never captained her, though I have watched over the Afeth while her captain was on shore."

"You are not the captain?"

"No, I am the builder. Perhaps, I am the mother of the Afeth, but Samaki is the father. He is captain." Again she laughed, this time her voice booming across the river as the gold-tipped oars of the barge were placed into the water, and they began to pull away from the land.

Tersh pointed to the closest ship anchored in the river to them. It was a small ship, a crew of five or so manned her, and its sail was dirty and tattered. "Is that your ship? It is not grand like the King's, but it does look sturdy."

"That?" Tiyharqu pointed at the ship, a wounded look coming over her face. "That ship is nothing. The Afeth is, next to a golden barge, the grandest ship on the Hiperu!"

"Could I see her?"

She looked uneasy, maybe worried about being seen walking with a Whisperer. "Well, she isn't far, if you want to look. I don't mind showing you the way."

"I'm going to go, but I'll be back soon," Tersh turned to Kareth, explaining quickly.

"Where will you go?"

"We need a ship if we want to speak with their chiefs, and maybe I've found one, but it will be easier if you stay here."

"They have more than one chief?" Kareth asked in confusion.

"Yes, I never really understood it myself. Every city has a chief, and there is another greater chief above him. Him they call the Paref, the chief of chiefs. They think he is a god. I thought he would be here, but Harqu tells me the Sea Mahat Chief is travelling north to see the Paref," Tersh explained quickly, worried Tiyharqu would lose her patience.

"And the Paref is dead?"

"Dead, only for his son to take his place. There will always be a Paref in Mahat. Now stay here," she handed Kareth her spear, just in case. "If you move, I may never find you again with so many people."

She turned, taking her skins with her, knowing she would need to use gold or jewels to barter. She didn't really think it would be hard to find Kareth. Whisperers couldn't help standing out in a crowd, but she certainly didn't want to waste any time looking for him if this Captain Samaki decided to take them on board.

Tiyharqu led them north along the riverbed. They weaved through countless people watching the golden ships leave, each person silent and unmoving, a deep sorrow in their eyes as they watched their King abandon them. They didn't walk far. All the ships were grouped together in this one area along the bank.

"There she is." Tiyharqu stopped and pointed towards a ship anchored a short distance from the shore. There were no docks or piers here. No large ship could come closer. There were several small ships anchored in the area, but the Afeth was by far the largest. The spine of the ship resembled a red snake, its head rearing up at the front, ready to strike, its tail at the back coiled around a lantern. Unlike the other ships surrounding her that either had no mast or only one, she had two white sails. The oars were pulled up into the rowlocks, crisscrossed across the empty deck. "Maki," Tiyharqu called out to a man sitting on the shore, "Do not look at those golden ships with such longing, for surely Afeth will become jealous."

There were two men sitting there on the rubble of a building, whether it had been damaged during the flood or if it had just fallen down due to disrepair was hard to tell. They both sat on stones, and between them on a larger piece of rubble was a small, long wooden box Tersh immediately recognized as a senet box. Although the men were sitting towards each other, both of them were staring at King Utarna's ships as they rowed away.

The man closest to them, Samaki, turned towards them. He wore auburn wool pants, belted with snakeskin and a gold buckle. There was nothing on his muscular chest save half a dozen amulets of precious metals. His head was shaved, so she guessed he was from Mahat. He was tall, though to Tersh all men in Mahat seemed taller than average. He smiled at Tiyharqu, his face friendly but weathered by a long time on the open sea.

"What's this you've found? Whisperers in Sareeb? A most uncommon sight."

"I am called–" Tersh began, but Tiyharqu cut her off.

"This Go-man thought some dilapidated dingy was the Afeth, so I had to show her the error of her ways."

"I am called—"

"I don't care," Samaki cut her off this time, turning back to the game of senet.

Tiyharqu beamed at her ship, her face filled with pride. "Well, what do you think?"

"Uh, beautiful. Truly." She meant it too. She would have assumed it was a ship built for the Paref, if the golden ships weren't still glistening behind it. However, she wasn't looking at the ship. She was looking at the captain playing senet.

Tersh took a step towards them. She knew the game well, and had often played it when she had lived in Mahat. For a while she had even owned a senet box, but it had been lost or traded ages ago. The box was both what the game was played on and where the pieces were kept. The box they were playing on was a simple one, made out of aged wood. The top had a grid of thirty squares arranged in rows of three carved into it. Ten pieces, five cones and five spools, were on the grid, spread out in various positions, or next to the box. The last five squares were the only ones with any markings, hieroglyphs she didn't understand outside of their meaning in the game.

"Are you winning, captain?" Tersh asked, leaning over his shoulder.

Samaki gave her an annoyed look, "I never win against Hamota."

Hamota, a bald man with black stubble on his chin smiled wide. "I am simply a lucky man."

"How do you play?" Tersh asked.

Samaki narrowed his eyes. "You speak my tongue well enough. In all your time in Mahat, you never encountered senet?"

Tersh smiled innocently. "Oh, of course I have. I meant what rules, no one I've met can agree on them. How do *you* play?"

Samaki regarded her a moment, and then maybe because he was annoyed with losing, or maybe because he was curious about the Whisperer, he motioned towards Hamota. "Sit, I'll show you."

"We haven't finished yet," Hamota protested.

"We're finished. You won – again."

"It's always a pleasure, captain," Hamota rose from his rock. "I'll come back with a cart to collect the cask of wine you owe me."

"You can collect the beating I owe you as well," Samaki said bitterly as he began arranging the pieces on the left side of the grid in alternating positions. "I suppose I should thank him for taking that accursed wine from me," Samaki muttered under his breath.

"Come, Hamota," Tiyharqu motioned towards him. "I've lost my audience. Let me walk with you so I have someone to listen to my talk."

"Your company would be welcome. I may need a big woman like you to help me lift all that wine," Hamota clapped his hand around Tiyharqu's arm, a friendly gesture, and the two began to walk away.

Samaki grabbed four flat sticks lying on the rock, one side painted black, and handed them to Tersh. "You know the basics, yes?"

Tersh nodded, taking the sticks. "The two of you were betting on the game?"

"It does make it more fun."

Tersh studied his face. Samaki did not look like he was having fun. His mind seemed to be elsewhere. "Well, if it makes it more fun." Tersh sat on the rock, putting her things next to her. She opened the skins just enough to reach in, her fingers rummaging through the trinkets until they found one of a suitable size. She pulled out a gold ring, a large emerald set on the band, and placed it next to the board.

"Ha, I've always believed a gamble with a Go-man is a dangerous thing." He picked up the ring, letting the sunlight sparkle in the emerald, before putting the band in his mouth and biting. Satisfied, he put the ring back. "And if you win?"

"Maybe some of that wine?"

Samaki narrowed his eyes again, but then smiled. "If that is what you want, that is what I'll wager. No one will buy it from me now that the Paref is dead."

The game was simple enough, trying to get the pieces off the board by moving them around the grid until they reached the squares with the hieroglyphs on it. The first hieroglyph was three lutes, the next was three wavy lines representing water, the third was three ibis birds looking to the left, and the final hieroglyph was two figures leaning on one knee. The last square was blank. People always had different rules for what these squares meant. Samaki explained that to get the pawns off the board one had to reach the blank square, but first they had to land on the lutes. If they landed in the water, they had to return to the beginning. Landing on the ibis let you switch any two pieces on the board not on a hieroglyph, and if you landed on the kneeling man the other player couldn't capture your pawns.

"It's strange finding a Whisperer who can speak the tongue of Mahat so well," Samaki commented, but his brow furrowed as he concentrated on the game.

"My tribe travelled here when I was very young. We stayed through many constellations." Tersh was not thinking very hard about her next move. Already Samaki had gotten four pawns off the board while she had only managed two. Everyone has their own strategy for senet. If a pawn lands on a square with another pawn already on it, those pawns are switched. It was called capturing. But if two pawns of the same type are next to each other, they can't be captured. Samaki always kept two pawns next to each other unless he was forced to move them apart by an unfavourable cast of the sticks.

"I've heard Go-men go crazy if they leave the desert for too long."

Tersh laughed. "I've heard the same of merchants who are on the sea too long."

Samaki smiled. "But that's true!"

"This is my first time to Sareeb. Are you from here?" Tersh asked.

"No, I..." Samaki's face darkened. "My village is gone, wiped away as though it never existed, and all those who lived there..."

"I'm sorry," Tersh was worried his mood would sour and he'd dismiss the Whisperer before she'd had the chance to bargain with him.

Samaki let the sticks fall, one dark side up. "Three." He moved his piece from the ibis off the board. "I win," he grabbed the emerald ring, slipping it on his finger.

"It suits you," Tersh smiled but was trying to look disappointed that she had lost.

"Winning suits everyone."

"Do you want to play again?"

"Do you have any more emeralds in that bag of yours?"

Tersh opened her skins again, this time looking for something a little larger. She pulled out a thick gold bracelet, a Mahat symbol carved into the middle. "Well, it isn't an emerald, but I'm sure it will do."

Samaki didn't check it this time. "I'm sure it will. And I'll give you my finest cask of wine if you win – I certainly won't let that lizard Hamota have it."

"No."

"No?" Samaki raised his eyebrows. "Something else then?"

"Yes. I'm seeking passage north, to Nepata," Tersh tried to keep her face calm, worried the slightest change in expression would anger the man. "And you can keep the bracelet, as payment."

"Passage north? On *my* ship, you mean?" Samaki's dark garnet eyes opened in slight disbelief at the cloaked woman's gall. "I'm not certain my men would be able to stand the smell."

Tersh felt her face flush with heat. "If your men could smell anything over their own stench, I'm sure that would be true."

Samaki was silent a moment, staring very intently at Tersh. She began to feel uncomfortable. Finally, he spoke. "Very well. If you win, I'll take you."

"Me, and mine."

"Of course, you and yours. You can bring your smelly bag as well."

"Let's play," Tersh said, and Samaki let the sticks fall.

Tersh was focused this time, and began moving the first two pawns only.

Samaki smile. "I shouldn't give you advice, but I like to watch an opponent lose with dignity. You shouldn't leave so many pawns behind, they become weak."

"If I try to move them all together, they are slow."

Samaki was several paces back, trying to organize his pieces like a snake on the board. "Go-men just don't understand the importance of standing together. You're a scattered people."

Tersh smiled, her first pawn landing on the lutes. "Yes, but we come together when we need to." On her next turn she moved her second piece to the blank square next to the lutes.

Samaki laughed. "Clever, a blockade. But you'll have to move eventually."

"Eventually," Tersh began to grin. By capturing his pawns to get by them, Tersh's remaining three cones were already lined up next to each other. Then she began to leap frog two towards the hieroglyphs.

Tersh couldn't keep the blockade. In senet, if you *can* move a piece, you *must*. She got two pieces off the board, but then her third piece fell into the water and had to move back to the beginning. Samaki took over the blockade and managed to get three pieces off, but then Tersh got two more, and Samaki another. Then they were tied. Samaki's final piece was on the lutes.

"You can have all the strategies you want," Samaki quietly remarked, maybe only to himself, "but in the end you have no control over your pawn. It goes where the sticks tell it."

He dropped the sticks, three dark sides up. "Damn." He moved forward one square and into the waters. He went back to the start.

"We're at the mercy of the gods," Tersh landed on the lute. Samaki was catching up. Then, Tersh moved two spaces to the ibis, and finally tossed three. "But sometimes the gods are merciful."

Tersh thought Samaki would be angry, but he smiled at the Whisperer instead. "The gods whisper to you. You have an unfair advantage. But," he reached out and took the bracelet. "A deal is a deal. I will take you to Nepata."

"Me and mine."

"Yes, yes, I already-"

"No, I don't just mean my bag, but my son, too."

Samaki laughed out loud. "Never gamble with a Go-man! Why don't I listen to my own advice?"

"A deal's a deal."

"Yes, you and yours can come. But, this," he held the bracelet up, "is payment for one. I hope you have another bracelet in there."

"I do. Give me a price. I shall pay."

The greed in Samaki's eyes was obvious. They seemed to glitter like the gold bracelet he held. It was worth no more or less than any of the trinkets he wore, but to a man like Samaki there was never enough gold in the world. They always wanted more. They would even help someone they found distasteful if it meant their purse grew heavier.

"You and the boy can come, but we have no food to give you, you must find that yourself as well."

"We are the Whisperers of the Gods. We can feed ourselves."

"Good. We leave tomorrow, once our business is concluded here," he held out his arm and Tersh only hesitated a moment before reaching out, the two clasping each other's forearm.

"Thank you, Samaki."

"You can call me Captain, and before you get on my ship, you better both bathe."

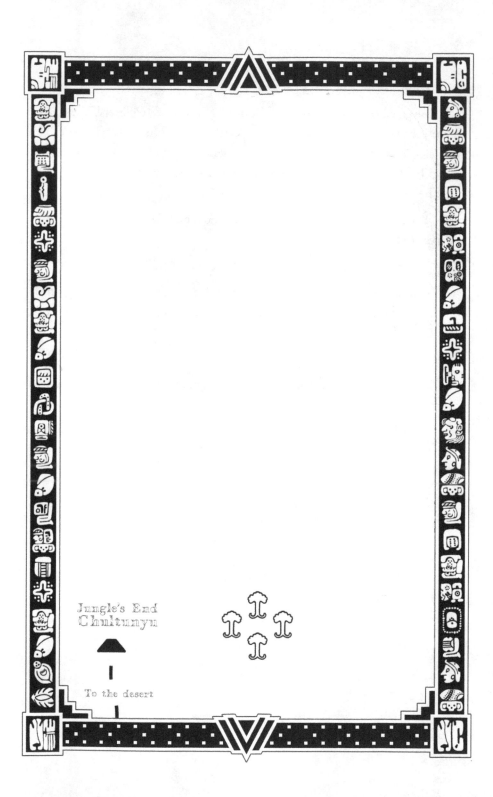

Jungle's End
Chultunyu

To the desert

CHULTUNYU

YOUR COMING MUST BE
A SIGN FROM THE GODS

The moon had waxed and waned while they made preparations to leave Chultunyu. They would travel from one end of the jungle to the other. To Sha'di the task of leaving a place was a simple affair. He wasn't used to having more things than he could carry, but these people were intent on bringing hundreds of useless objects with them; numerous cloaks, many fanciful jewels and trinkets, dozens of servants. They packed tents and tunics and furs and foods and so many things it made his head spin just looking at all the preparations they went through.

Although he felt a great urgency to reach Chipetzuha – *the* Red Pyramid – he couldn't help but feel happy to stay a little longer. There was more to this city than he had first realized. Most of it was hidden throughout the jungle. He could walk for an hour in any direction and not find the end. Instead, he would wind through huts, amused by people's curious glances at him and children giggling and wanting to touch his red hair. It was obvious to see from the red pyramid at the city's centre, and the red dye they all wore on their skin, that this was a sacred colour to them. Is that why the gods had chosen him to come to the Grey Mist, because they would be more willing to heed his words?

He didn't get that impression from the rich fat men he had seen crowded in the pyramid when he'd first arrived. He had learned they were called chakatl, and were a kind of minor chief who helped Tanuk rule. Few of the chakatl had any time to speak to him, and those who did looked down on him like they might a child. They were all tall and chubby, and honestly he felt like a child in stature next to them. The only person who seemed any different from them was their chief, Tanuk, who ruled here in his father's absence. He had agreed to take Sha'di north and join his father at the Red Pyramid, and he seemed eager for the trip.

"All chief go to Chipetzuha," Tetchtok had explained before leaving to return to his small village. "All chief live there, leave their son or brother rule. Nothing more sacred than Chipetzuha."

They had been given a small hut to share near the pyramid. It was large enough to hold all the men who had travelled with Sha'di. The ground was covered in the soft skins of jaguars. Torches lining the walls lit every corner. There was a small fire pit in the centre with a hole in the middle of the pointed roof for the smoke to escape. They slept together side-by-side for a week before leaving. Sha'di had watched them go, Nnenne perched on his shoulder, feeling a great sense of loneliness descend on him once more. Who would he have to talk to with them gone? Only one other man there spoke his language. He wasn't a chakatl, but he certainly dressed like one. His name was Xupama, and he did not give the impression that he wanted to have polite conversation with Sha'di outside the pyramid.

As it was, Sha'di tried to avoid the pyramid and Xupama as much as possible. He preferred to spend his time along the large river just north of the pyramid. There were many merchant stalls there and he enjoyed walking among them. Every day boats would arrive from upstream, carrying various fruits and animals to sell at the stalls. There was always something new for him to discover, some strange animals that looked like a human baby covered in fur with a long tail, or birds with impossibly bright plumage of every gemstone he knew. There were fruits of every shape and colour and he made it his mission to try every different one he could find.

Although it still rained an absurd amount, being able to keep himself dry in his hut made him appreciate it more. He started to enjoy the sound of the drops hitting his roof as he slept. He even enjoyed standing in it and letting the water wash the dirt away from his skin. So long as he had a fire to return to, it was quite nice. And anyway, most days were sunny and bright and full of colour.

He also greatly enjoyed attempting to speak the local language with the merchants who travelled up and down the river. He could still do very little in the way of forming sentences, but they were all cheerful and enjoyed teaching him new words. One merchant selling fish had also been kind enough to gift Sha'di a net he could take to the river and use to catch fish. With a long branch he had sharpened into a spear, he spent most mornings there catching his meals.

Sometimes he would use the fish he caught to trade for goods, but more often than not he would put on a show with Nnenne. He would swing the lure and she would swoop over the heads of the people gathered to watch. Children were especially enchanted by this and would squeal with delight whenever she came so close they could feel the wind from her wings on their faces. In return for his demonstration, they would give him food, and sometimes even trinkets, jewels carved into wood to wear as jewellery. He had no use for them, but appreciated them all the same.

One midday, after purposefully avoiding the pyramid for several days, a young boy wearing only a loincloth came up to Sha'di, tugging on his cloak to get his attention. Sha'di looked down at the boy. His black hair was cut in a way to make him look as though he wore a bowl on his head. It was the cut all young boys had here.

"Xa'ti, come," the boy said. The people here were unable to pronounce his name properly, but he had grown used to it. The boy tugged at him and pointed towards the pyramid. "Come."

'Come' was one of the few words Sha'di knew. Sha'di sighed. He was not looking forward to going back to the incense-filled room atop the pyramid. He always felt like he had difficulty breathing in that dark place, and would much rather spend the rest of the day under the hot sun. However, he knew he should not ignore being summoned by whoever wanted to see him.

He followed. The boy would run ahead, stop and wait impatiently as he waved him forward, repeating 'come' over and over again. Sha'di didn't care, he took his time, smiling at the locals as he passed, and they would give him chubby smiles back. Sha'di had noticed he too was beginning to gain weight. His cheeks felt fuller, his ribs did not stick out as much. The food here was plentiful and he often went to sleep with his stomach so full he felt like it might burst.

When they reached the pyramid they started the long climb. The view from the pyramid still had not lost its grandeur to Sha'di. The thing he liked most about the pyramid was reaching the top and looking out over the jungle. At the side of the chief's home was a ladder carved into the wall. One could climb this ladder to sit on the roof and see the whole world from that place, if not for the mist. He always hoped it would be a clear day so he might be able to see the golden desert in the distance, but the mist never seemed to leave the treetops.

At the top was also where the anteans were kept. Sha'di was surprised the first time he climbed to the top to find another small hut there. Inside were many shelves with perches for the large birds. A man there fed them and kept watch there for the birds' comings and goings. The anteans, Sha'di learned, were used to send messages between all the villages in the valley. Each antean had been trained to fly back and forth to one village, carrying a small bag tied to its back. Inside the bag were small tablets, each one carved with a different hieroglyph, which was a code for whatever message they wanted to send.

Sha'di wasn't just impressed by the ingenuity of the system. The birds themselves were amazing to behold. They were massive black birds, their wingspan nearly twice the length of Sha'di's body. They weren't especially nice to look at, with bald crested heads and a band of bright white feathers around their necks, but they had a serenity and grace about them that made them look regal and certainly worthy of living on top of the Chultunyu Pyramid.

He could hear the anteans' cries as he climbed the pyramid ramp that day. Obviously it was feeding time. A grumbling in his own stomach reminded him that he should eat too, but his mid-day meal would have to wait until after his audience.

Just as he reached the end of the ramp and the main entrance to the audience chamber, one of the chakatl walked out briskly, a look of anger in his eyes. Sha'di didn't recognize his face, all the chubby men looked similar to him, but he recognized what he was wearing. His feathered silver crown and the polished wooden staff topped with topaz identified him as Tanuk's uncle, Mayek. He gave Sha'di a brief look of disdain before pushing past him. He was followed by three young men wearing loincloths and bowing their heads in servitude.

He entered the stuffy room with hesitation. The feeling of tension in the air from the uncle's brisk departure was nearly as overpowering as the incense. Unlike most of the times he had visited, there were no chakatl standing to the side of the room waiting to speak with the Petzuhatl, the Great Chief of the Pyramid. Tanuk sat not on his chair but instead stood by one of the square pools of water. He was watching two small boys play. They had carved wooden figures they were using to battle with each other.

Sha'di was surprised to see a young man standing next to Tanuk. The man looked to be the same age as Sha'di. Tanuk, with his jaguar cloak, large silver and topaz crown with white feathers, and broad shoulders looked rather imposing next to the younger man who was lithe and only wore a tunic the shade of a dark lizard, buckled with a simple leather belt. Sha'di wondered if he was the son of a rich merchant, or some chakatl's son. Mayek's brisk departure and the informal atmosphere made him feel slightly uneasy.

The two men, as well as the children, had a very distinct look he'd noticed the day he'd arrived at Chultunyu. At first he didn't know if he was imagining the strange shape of their heads, but soon came to realize that their skulls were longer and narrower than the common people with whom he spent most of his time.

"*The look of gods*," Tetchtok had explained with a wink. He said they bound the heads of their babies to resemble gods. Sha'di didn't know if he had been teasing him when he had said that. Perhaps it was just the way they braided their long black hair.

Xupama stood by the dais where the throne was. When he saw Sha'di standing in the doorway, he gave a great flourish with his hands and announced him in a loud voice. Sha'di only understood a few words, but had heard enough formal introductions by now to know he was hearing one. Although he looked and sounded respectful towards Tanuk, Xupama seemed to be sneering at Sha'di ever so slightly. Xupama was fairly old, his skin taunt and weathered, and he was thin and tall. He was the tallest man by far in Chultunyu. He wore a large white and black feathered headdress, giving him even more height.

"Ah," Tanuk looked at Sha'di with a kind face, motioning him into the room. He turned to the old interpreter, calling him over.

Xupama came forward, giving a grand bow and scraping the ground with his headdress in front of Tanuk. Unfortunately for Xupama, his display was lost on Tanuk who had already stopped paying attention to him.

Before anyone could speak, the young man at Tanuk's side rushed forward, a large smile on his bright face. The whites of his teeth seemed to separate the natural bronze of the top of his face from the dark red of the lower half.

"Hello!" The man exclaimed happily in the Whisperer's tongue, clasping Sha'di by the arm in the same manner his people did. Nnenne squawked uncomfortably at the sudden noise. "I am called Tenok, of the tribe Jungle's End."

Sha'di tried to suppress the grin on his face, recognizing at once that while this man had learned a few sentences in his language, he had by no means mastered them, and he certainly did not want to offend him by laughing.

"I am Sha'di Al'Sha'di, of the tribe Gonnamdi," he smiled at the young man who still had not let go of his arm.

Sha'di repeated the names over and over in his head. Tanuk – Ta-*nook*. Tenok – *Teh*-nohk. They were frustratingly similar. Despite their different body types, the two had incredibly similar faces. Sha'di thought they must be brothers.

Tanuk said something, an amused expression on his face. Xupama started to translate, but before he could Tenok tried to do it himself.

"I brother. I learn your speak." From his leather belt he pulled out an old sling. "You teach speak, I teach sling?"

"Tenok," Tanuk spoke sternly, though not angrily. He gave his younger brother a look, and at once Tenok shrugged and with a disappointed face turned back to Sha'di, tucking his sling back into his belt.

"I go now, Sha'di Sha'di. Farewell."

Sha'di nodded as Tenok exited through the opening at the back of the room, leading to the royal family's private chambers. Once he was gone, Tanuk smiled anew and gestured towards the boys playing at his feet.

"These are my sons," Tanuk spoke with pride, and although Sha'di had understood him, Xupama began to translate with great relish.

"The Chultunyu-chib'–"

"Xupama," Tanuk gave the translator a dangerous look.

"My apologies, Tanuk-chib'atl."

"Wait, what did you call him? Chultun...chibnip?"

Xupama said something to Tanuk, who gave an annoyed nod, giving him permission to tell Sha'di what it meant.

"Chultunyu-chib'atl is Tanuk-chib'atl's royal name. It was given to him when he was given charge of Chultunyu. However, Tanuk-chib'atl prefers to be called by his birth name," Xupama's mastery of the language was obvious, though he spoke with the accent of the northern tribes, which Sha'di had always found to be strange to his ears.

'Atl', Sha'di remembered, was a title given to the great chiefs among the Petzuhallpa. 'Chib'atl' meant something like 'small great chief'.

"I understand. The Rhagepe in our tribes take the names of their predecessors in much the same way."

Xupama sneered at him like an insolent dog. "Sand witches are nothing like the Petzuhatl, the Pyramid Lords. They are the Pyramid Builders. Your people don't even know how to pile one stone on top of the other."

Tanuk said something harsh and Xupama straightened his back, clearing his throat and replacing his sneer with a forced smile. "Tanuk-chib'atl wishes to know how your mastery of our tongue is going."

"Slowly, chib'atl," Sha'di replied with their words, making Tanuk's face beam with amusement. He could always make someone smile by speaking in their language.

"Tanuk-chib'atl wishes to teach you the high tongue."

"The high tongue, chib'atl?" Sha'di never bothered looking at Xupama, he kept his eyes on the young prince. He much preferred to see a smiling face and pretend Xupama wasn't even there. It was fairly easy to do. Since Xupama was so adept at translating he spoke almost in unison with Tanuk, it was almost as though the words were coming out of his mouth.

"There are many pyramids, and a great distance between them all. All places have their own chaktan, low tongue, but the chakatl all speak katan, the high tongue. It is the language spoken at Chipetzuha, the Red Pyramid."

"So, if I want to speak with the great chief, I must learn the... katan? I'd be honoured for the help."

A sudden cry came from the smaller of the boys. The older one had taken his wooden doll and pushed him into the pool in the fight. Large tears began to burst from his small eyes and his mouth seemed to double in size as he began to cry uncontrollably. Tanuk got to his knees, whispering soothing words to his wet son, while at the same time two young women emerged from the back rooms. They wore long white tunics, and their hair was braided with colourful feathers. Sha'di guessed they cared for the children.

Tanuk stood back up as they swooped in and took the children.

"Boys," Tanuk grinned at Sha'di as his son's cries grew distant and then disappeared altogether. "You have... children?"

He could still feel Nnenne's soft lips kissing his neck. *"You will give me children tonight."*

He shook his head. "No, but... there was a woman."

Xupama translated and a playful look came to Tanuk's eyes. "There always is."

"Their... mother?" Sha'di managed to say in chaktan.

"Dead. Childbirth," Tanuk looked away for a moment, as though he needed to compose himself, then smiled at the Whisperer and said something else he couldn't understand.

"Tanuk-chib'atl's wife gave him two sons, just as his father had two sons, and his grandfather had two sons. Their line is blessed. Tanuk-chib'atl knows it will be difficult for his sons to grow up without his father and mother, but he is certain their uncle, Mayek-huitl, will raise them into mighty rulers."

"Food!" Tanuk called out suddenly.

The boy who had brought Sha'di to the pyramid ran into the back room. A moment later four servants came out, each carrying a basket of fruit and cured meats. They held them out and the three men walked over to them, Tanuk continuing to speak.

"Tanuk-chib'atl says he intended to stay with his children longer, until the eldest, Koyo-chib'atl, was old enough to wear the sacred colour."

Sha'di knew he meant the red dyes all the adults wore. He had learned that when a child reached the age they were considered an adult, they were allowed to wear the dye and grow their hair long. He understood the practice, though his tribe's traditions were different. When he had come of age, in the Orope before this, he had been given a tattoo of a line intersecting a circle on the back of his shoulder.

Tanuk took a large piece of fruit and bit into it, still speaking.

"Tanuk-chib'atl only changed his mind because your coming must be a sign from the gods."

"Tanuk-chi... chib'atl, you said there was some trouble with the chief of the Red Pyramid. Can you tell me what?" Xupama translated quickly and Tanuk nodded his head.

"It... is difficult," he took a piece of meat, but offered it to Sha'di instead of eating it.

Sha'di's stomach growled in approval as he took the meat, which had been sweetened in sauces, and ate it hungrily.

"She won't... make a sacrifice to save her people," Tanuk shrugged. "Perhaps that is why the gods have sent you. You must convince her to do what is right."

Sha'di began to go to the pyramid once a day and Tanuk would try to teach him something new. The high tongue katan was essentially a completely different language. Some words were very similar, but there were others that sounded nothing alike between both tongues. It also gave him a chance to learn more about how the people here lived and ate. Tanuk's food was always the best that could be offered, and Sha'di began to look more forward to the meals he would eat rather than the katan he would learn.

A few times Mayek-huitl was there as well, and it became increasingly clear that he was upset over some argument the two of them were having, but Tanuk would not speak about it and he knew it would be rude to ask. It must have had something to do with their journey to Chipetzuha. He just hoped it would not interfere with their departure. Arrangements continued as usual. The day before they were set to leave, Tanuk told Sha'di there would be a ceremony as they left.

"The journey to Chipetzuha will take a long time, nearly two tenpeiwali. The journey is perilous. Many of those who leave for Chipetzuha never reach it. The ceremony will ensure that the gods watch over us," Tanuk had explained while Xupama translated.

A tenpeiwali, Sha'di had learned, was how the Petzuhallpa kept time. They had two ways to count the passing days, though Sha'di had yet to understand either since neither used the moon. All he knew for certain was that every twenty days a great feast was held on a day they called Sipakti – which had been the day he'd first arrived at Chultunyu. Another sign from the gods? He had thought they were just celebrating his arrival, but Tetchtok had laughed and informed him they were actually celebrating a god named Tektzapotl. In fact, the celebrations had been going on all that day at different places in the village. Twenty days later they had had another feast. The food, of course, had been excellent.

The morning of their departure they met before dawn and climbed the long ramp to the top of the pyramid. All the chakatl were in attendance. Many people had begun to gather at the bottom of the pyramid to watch the ceremony. Tanuk stood in the centre of the doorway, his uncle on his right and his younger brother Tenok on his left. Before them was the dark red stone, a dark obelisk in the morning light.

Most of the chakatl stood inside the building, peering over the shoulders of the royal family to see the ceremony, but Sha'di and a dozen or so others were allowed to stay on the ramp. These were the places of honour. The ceremony began almost without Sha'di realizing it. He was expecting drumming or chanting, but instead it began with five people walking up the ramp. They were halfway up when Sha'di realized a silence had fallen over all those who watched.

Of the five men making their way, four of them were dressed the same, wearing dark red tunics and silver bands with topaz on their foreheads. Sha'di noticed they wore no dye on their skins like every other adult and their heads were shorn completely of hair. The last man, the plumpest of them, wore a large headdress of turquoise feathers. Instead of a tunic, he wore a skirt made from the same plumage.

"Who are they?" Sha'di asked Xupama, who had been allowed to stay on the ramp solely to translate for him.

"He is the high priest of the Fire God Tzuhtekatl," Xupama answered in annoyance at being disturbed, grabbing a piece of fruit from one of the nearby servants holding a basket and sucking on it loudly.

The priests reached the top and walked to the dark red stone before the doorway at the edge of the ramp. He held his arms wide, facing the crowd below and speaking words loudly enough for all gathered to hear. As he spoke, the sun began to peek over the pyramid, rising behind them.

"Hail Xipektek, god of force, patron of war, warden of farms, of growth, of disease," Xupama began to translate, bending down to whisper into Sha'di's ear. "He who controls the seasons, he who helps the hunt and fuels trade. He who speaks for Rebirth."

Sha'di felt a tingle run down his spine as the high priest turned to his right, his arms still stretched high as he continued to speak.

"Hail Hutzelpotchl, god of will and the sun, patron of war and fire." The priest turned to his right again, now facing the entrance of the pyramid and the onlookers. "Hail Ketzakoatl, god of wisdom, life, and knowledge, warden of the morning star, bringer of fertility, patron of the winds and the light." Finally, the priest turned towards the last direction. "Tektzapotl, god of providence, matter and the invisible, ruler of the night, he who is impalpable, patron of ubiquity and the twilight."

He turned back to the dark red stone – an altar, Sha'di realized. "Hear us, this day Itskwintl, in the time of Tzochikoatl. Accept our offering and protect our chib'atl as they journey towards the holiest of places, Chipetzuha."

The high priest finally lowered his arms, and his eyes still turned towards the sky held out his hand to one of the red priests, who quickly rushed forward and on bended knee handed him a small grey stone knife. It was a wide flat blade, no longer than the priests' hand, but Sha'di recognized the stone as flint and knew the flecked stone would be incredibly sharp.

"Bring the sacrifice."

Sha'di craned his head to look down the ramp, to see what animal would come up. His people normally used the camel for sacred sacrifices, but he hadn't seen any camels since coming into the jungle. What animal did they hold holy? Or did a ceremony like this even require their holiest of animals? Perhaps a small lizard or bird would suffice. He was brimming with questions and curiosity when one of the servants approached the high priest. Sha'di recognized him as the boy who had been sent to fetch him all those days ago.

Mayek muttered something angrily and Tanuk gave him a quick glance. Sha'di knew that whatever was about to happen was the source of their argument, but beyond that still couldn't understand what was upsetting either of them.

Then, much to Sha'di's confusion, one of the red priest brought forward a bowl filled with red and, with a small cloth ball, began to apply the dye onto the boy's face, first dabbing his jaw and then moving onto his quivering hands. The boy was becoming a man, though he seemed a little young to Sha'di. When they had finished applying the dye Sha'di had expected some kind of cheer, but everyone remained silent. Two of the priests grabbed the boy's wrists. Moving to the altar, they lifted him so that he could sit on it.

"What are...?" Sha'di began to ask as another of the priests crouched down by the boy's feet, holding his ankles steady, and the last one took a small curved piece of wood and held it against the boy's neck. They stretched him taunt. The boy seemed nervous, squinting his eyes tight, but he did not struggle or make a sound as the high priest raised the knife above his head.

The knife came down. The boy screamed. Blood spurted from his sternum. Sha'di felt himself take a step back, trying to put distance between himself and what he was witnessing. He came against Xupama's body who put strong bony fingers around his arms, forcing him to stay put and watch as the high priest dug his hand into the now squirming body of the boy. The small body on the altar suddenly went limp and quiet and the high priest jerked his arm out, his hand now holding a small red pulsating object.

There was a deafening roar from the watching crowd. The dawn sun made the heart glimmer as the priest began turning, offering it to every direction. The priest turned back towards Tanuk. Tanuk nodded his head to accept the sacrifice. He looked bored.

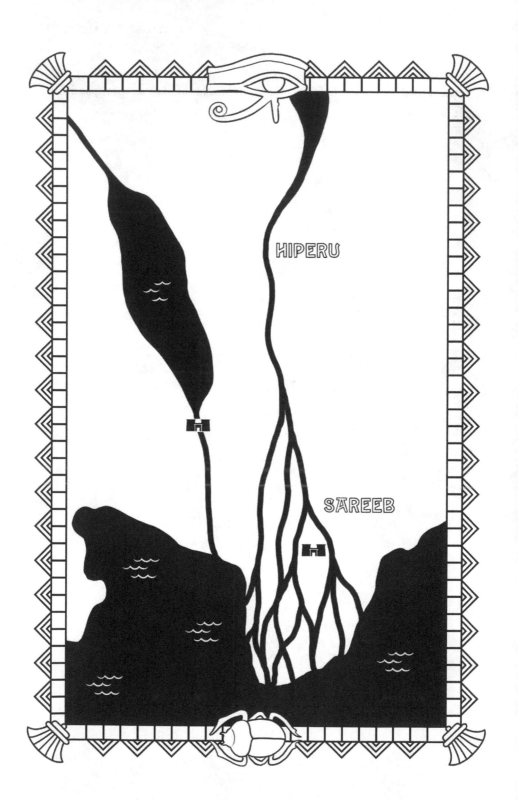

THE HIPERU

IN' THE WATER SHE GOES

The water was cool and Kareth enjoyed diving deep into it, his fists collecting lumps of soft clay and sand from the bottom and bursting back to the water's surface. He stood upright, neck-deep, a bright grin on his face. Tersh stayed nearer to the shore, not going past her knees and crouching down to scrub her face and arms. Neither knew how to swim, but Kareth wasn't apprehensive about wading out farther. The Hiperu did not have a strong current and there were so many men and boats around he felt certain if anything were to happen, there was help nearby.

The crew of the Afeth was on deck making ready to depart. Tiyharqu stood among them, making last minute checks that everything was in order – especially their cargo. Their departure had been delayed because many crew had left in an attempt to return to their villages and find out the fates of their families, but more than enough men were eager to leave Sareeb, having lost everything in the flood. Tiyharqu was still taking names down on a ledger of papyrus laid over a slab of wood.

Samaki called out something from the shore. It must have been a joke, since he started chuckling to himself.

"What's he saying?" Kareth called out to Tersh.

"He says he's an ignorant heathen who's abandoned the gods," Tersh calmly called back.

Kareth rolled his eyes. "He called us smelly again, didn't he?"

"Never mind what he says."

"He ought to try smelling himself. He smells like a damp rag!" Kareth laughed and dove underneath once more, this time opening his eyes. The waters were murky, but he could see the hulls of ships, just able to make out tiny white barnacles as light danced over them, and farther out he could see long dark strands of something green. He pushed himself back up, gasping for air.

"There's an entire world down here!" Kareth said.

Tersh did not respond as she was already walking away, stepping onto the muddy shore. Their cloaks hung on a rock next to Samaki, their folded skins sitting next to him. Tersh had insulted Samaki countless times over the past few days to Kareth, but never with malice. And when Kareth voiced concern over whether they could trust the captain to watch their things, the older Whisperer would just nod.

"He's a scoundrel, but I don't think he's a thief."

Kareth followed, rubbing his hands through his short hair. Tersh had decided they were long overdue for a cutting and had shorn Kareth's hair so short he almost felt bald. She had done the same to her own dreadlocked hair, knowing it was attracting too much attention. It annoyed her to do it, and she'd rushed the job so it had not come out very even, but she would do anything to avoid trouble while in Mahat.

"They may find it less distracting if we look more like them," Tersh had explained, but Kareth had not been willing to completely shave off his hair as the men of Mahat were so fond of doing.

Samaki said something pleasantly, holding the Whisperer's Ancestral Cloak out to Tersh.

"If he said we smell again, tell him that he smells like a camel," Kareth said, taking his own cloak from the rock, the one with three layers of rib bones on it, and gracefully wrapping it around himself.

"Tell him yourself, you ought to learn their tongue."

Samaki was still speaking with Tersh, motioning for them to follow, and the three began walking towards the Afeth.

If there had ever been a dock on the riverbed, the flood had washed it away, but the fishermen had been quick in starting to build a new one. Several narrow wooden planks had been laid out from the shore, their supports hidden beneath the water.

They were rickety and Kareth nearly lost his balance. Soon they came alongside the Afeth. The red snake at its bow looked menacing in the late afternoon sun. The deck was at the height of Tersh's head, and a small rope ladder hung from the side to help them climb up. Samaki, for his size, was nimble as a spider climbing his web, but both Whisperers struggled awkwardly to climb onto the deck.

Kareth yanked Tersh's cloak gently to get her attention, he nodded at the two large white sails with a sly grin. They were a patchwork of different shades, but white nonetheless. Kareth couldn't help but remember his dream of the two white birds carrying them to their destination.

"The gods *did* speak to me," he whispered to her.

"Speak up. These people can't understand you."

Kareth turned a sombre gaze on Tersh. "The gods understand me."

"And the gods hear you, whether you whisper or not. I, on the other hand, don't have that ability."

The crew looked wearily towards the Whisperers. Most of them did a good job of ignoring them, busy arranging their few belongings under the long benches that ran vertically across the ship. Instead of the benches being built on top of the deck, boards had been taken out to create a depression for their legs to go in. There was a crossway meeting at the largest of the masts for crewmembers to walk down without having to walk over any of the depressions or on the benches.

"We can sleep on deck," Tersh translated what Samaki was telling her. "We won't have to row, unless there's an emergency."

"What kind of emergency?"

Tersh looked uneasy. "Sometimes you need to be faster than the other ships."

They went down the walkway, towards the stern. Tiyharqu stood there, speaking with one of the young crewmembers. Most of the crewmen had clearly only recently become men. Tiyharqu barely noticed them, merely nodding and mumbling as she checked over her ledger, an arm casually slung over the tiller – a long thick piece of wood used to move the rudder and steer the ship.

"This," Tersh said as Samaki motioned towards a trapdoor, "is the cargo hold. The only people allowed down there are Tiyharqu and the captain."

"Why? What's down there?"

"Some horrible drink that robs men of their senses."

"Uh... all right."

Tersh said something to Samaki that made the captain smile. He turned to the crew and yelled something and the men stopped what they were doing and cheered.

The cheer was cold. It was an automatic response, dying quickly on the tongues of every man who had made it. Tersh looked down at him, and gave him a reassuring smile, but he couldn't find it in himself to return the sentiment.

The Hiperu was wider than any river Kareth had ever seen before. He enjoyed sitting on the deck and just staring at the passing palm trees, smiling as the graceful slender ibis cranes took flight whenever they approached. At night they would pull along the shore. Some men stayed on the ship to sleep, but most nestled underneath the trees along the shore. Kareth and Tersh would sleep a short distance away from the others.

They rose with the sun, the men eating whatever food reserves they had, or whatever fish they had managed to catch the day before when they hadn't been on rowing duty. They were quick to set off. The air was cool in the morning, and Kareth still felt drowsy as he sat down at the bow of the ship, propping his head up with his hands and feeling his heavy eyelids droop.

"Look," Tersh nudged him and Kareth sat up with a start, confused at first, then followed Tersh's gaze forward. To the right of the river, he saw what looked like triangles, the golden tips of which sparkled in the morning sun.

It was hard to tell how far from the river they were exactly. There were three of them that he could see, built out of white rock, the top third of all of them encased in gold. The one in the middle stood tallest of all. Kareth thought he could make out trees along their bases, but if those tiny things were full-grown trees, then the pyramids were... Kareth was stunned into silence. The entire crew had become still. Many had stopped rowing and just stared off at the gargantuan structures. A long time passed before Samaki's voice suddenly snapped everyone out of their daze.

There was a quick shuffle as everyone got their oars in hand again and found their rhythm once more. Obviously Samaki was not paying them to gawk at the landscape.

"What are they?" Kareth finally managed to speak.

Tersh shook her head. "I have heard of them before. They were built by their chiefs, long dead... They say these tombs can send a soul to be with their gods. I had never imagined their size..."

Kareth stared at the pyramids for as long as he could see them, going to the stern of the ship to follow them. Even after they were gone from sight he still stared at the horizon.

Samaki grunted something dismissively.

"What did he say?"

"That they're just a pile of stones," Tersh replied quietly.

After leaving the pyramids behind there were a few villages along the shore, fishing communities with small white mud huts and smaller one-man boats made from woven reeds were a common sight, and the few people living there would happily rush to the shore and wave their arms at them, calling out some greeting. The farther they got from Sareeb and the more days that passed, the fewer those sights became.

Every now and again, they would see something on the horizon. Sometimes Kareth wasn't certain if they were pyramids, or just hills. Some were close enough to the river that he could tell they were palaces or pyramids, or had been. Most of them had crumbled into piles of cut stone. In one place the river widened into a lake that must have been a great city once, but some flood had perhaps changed the path of the Hiperu so now the water ran through the ruins. They sailed through tall columns and the remains of ancient walls.

"They say this city was drowned by a vengeful Paref," Tersh translated what some of the men were talking about. "Plotters murdered her son, so she killed them – and everyone else. The wrath of a mother is truly greater than that of any gods," she said it as a joke, but she had sounded rather sad.

Although Kareth didn't try to learn their tongue as Tersh had suggested, he did take a certain fondness to trying to learn the sailor's songs. The first day of their journey had mostly been silence, with a few conversations here and there. The winds were with them, so the journey was easy, but as the winds began to decrease and the rowers' work increased, the sombre silence had turned to singing. At first there was just quiet humming, then a soft song or two, but after a few days the entire ship would erupt into a chorus that even Samaki and Tiyharqu would join in. Kareth had felt compelled to sing along with them.

Sometimes the crew would try to speak to him, or try to teach him words, pointing at something and giving the name. He'd forget most of them almost instantly, not really listening in the first place, but a few names stuck and he learned the words for boat and fish and other things he saw every day. There were also times when Kareth wasn't sure what he was being taught.

One of the crewmen, the oldest man on the ship, whose eyes would crinkle whenever he smiled, took a certain fondness towards Kareth. He was a strong man who had probably seen nearly four full cycles, well-built, though his skin looked like old leather. The stubble growing on his head and chin when he forgot to shave was peppered black and white. His name was Sef. He was patient with Kareth. Where other men got frustrated and stopped trying to speak to him, Sef would repeat himself, making gestures or pointing at the surroundings to make his meaning clear. He enjoyed pointing at animals, giving each one a name in turn. Most of the time, he wore a bright smile on his face, but one animal made his face darken.

"Maseh," he said, pointing towards a log floating in the water.

Kareth had stared at the log in confusion. Was there an animal on the log he was pointing to? Perhaps something swimming next to it? He couldn't tell, and then the log dipped under the surface and never came back. Sef had shuddered then, shaking his head and muttering to himself. Maseh, whatever it was, was something Kareth did not forget.

Days bled together, and Kareth lost count. All he knew for certain was that the journey was far from over. He was surprised to one day to see a shimmer of gold up the river from them. Kareth and Tersh had gone to the bow with

Samaki to look. He had been hoping to see more pyramids. Instead, he saw that the golden objects were floating on the water.

"The chief's golden ships," Tersh had nodded.

"I didn't think we'd see them again. I thought those ships would be the fastest on the river," Kareth said in awe.

Tersh said something to Samaki, who started laughing.

Kareth looked at her for an explanation.

"He says, nothing is faster than the Afeth."

Tersh and Samaki started talking again, the ship getting closer and closer to the barges, figures walking on the decks coming into view. The gemstone colours painted on the golden ships looked stunning sat against the muddy water of the Hiperu and the dull shades of papyrus reeds and trees along the coast. The rowers were hidden from view, blocked by the golden cabins, but Kareth could see the shining oars – also gold-leafed – dipping in and out of the water in perfect rhythm.

"Samaki thinks we should follow the barges," Tersh said.

"Follow them? Of course we're following them. Aren't we all going to Nepata?" Kareth shrugged.

"We could easily pass them, but Samaki thinks it's better to stay behind them."

"Why?"

"Bandits."

The word made Kareth's heart feel like a drum in his chest, and he turned away to hide the grin growing on his face. Bandits. He'd heard of bandits, of course. There were a few roaming gangs even in the desert, but he'd never seen one up close. They had always just been an adventure story told over the campfire. Were there really bandits along the Hiperu? Did they have a hideout near the river, hoards of gold and jewels and beautiful women?

"Do you think... we'll see bandits?" Kareth asked in a small voice.

Tersh frowned. "Let's hope not."

The Afeth kept its distance from the barges. They were close enough that they never lost sight of them, but not so close to garner attention or be seen as a threat. There were other small fishing vessels that followed behind the barges. Kareth reasoned that it must be quite common to seek protection in numbers. It seemed that as long as they kept their distance from the royal party, it was perfectly acceptable as well.

At night Kareth could see their massive bonfires and hear their raucous singing, but he never thought of trying to get close enough to see what was going on. He was more than content with the company they kept, and far too preoccupied now with imagining bandits jumping down from the palm trees, only to be fought off by Tersh and himself. Just imagining it he could feel the power of the gods surge through him. The gods would give him the strength to fight any adversary. He would fall asleep with a smile on his face.

One morning, the royal party did not get back on their ships. The crew waited patiently to set off; some men started fishing, and others just took the chance to sleep in. The afternoon came, and they realized the royal party had decided to spend a sojourn along the Hiperu. Kareth couldn't figure out why. The river here was no more or less beautiful than any other part of the river, yet something had taken their fancy, because the next day the barges still stayed moored along the shore.

Kareth took to exploring.

He found himself practicing out loud the names he had learned, but there were only a few he had taken to heart. He had learned nothing as quickly as the songs though; he sung them as he wound his way through the tall trees, enjoying the coolness of the shade. The afternoons here were hotter than what he was used to. In the desert it was hot, yes, but he had been raised along the shores of the ocean, where a cool wind would normally come off the waves. But here he felt sticky from the heat, and felt tempted to jump into the Hiperu just to cool down.

"In' the water she goes,

Dip her in, pull her out,

Row that ship faster boys, in out."

Kareth sang without even understanding the words coming out of his mouth, he just enjoyed the rhythm, matching his footsteps to it as he walked.

"The captain yells: clear deck!

Move aside and make way,

It's time to say goodnight, in out."

He pushed aside some tall grass, letting his singing get louder, when he suddenly heard someone giggling. It had been so long since he'd heard the laughter of a young girl that at first he thought it was a bird, but soon he recognized it for what it was, and began to look around wildly for the source.

"Who's there?" He asked, then added in thickly accented speech of Mahat: "Who here?"

"Who are you?" A young girl was standing at the edge of a clearing, her body half hidden by a palm tree. "What are you?"

She wore a sheer white tunic, folded and pleated, that went down just past her knees, the sleeves wide and barely reaching her elbows. Around her neck was a heavy thick gold necklaces, decorated with turquoise and jasper beads shaped into the pattern of a bird spreading its wings. Her black hair was thick and combed straight, cut at her shoulders, save for a single braid from the side of her head that went to her waist, tied with a golden cord. On one of her forearms she wore a bracelet shaped like a snake winding its way up her arm. Even her sandals were tipped with gold. Her face had been coloured with soft shades of red and bright coral, the colour of cacti lined her eyes, making them seem wider and brighter. He stared at her in disbelief. She stepped out of the shade towards him, the sun instantly making all the gold she wore sparkle. Her skin, ever so gently bronzed, looked pale compared to his.

"Are you a goddess?" He whispered. Then shook his head. He was being a fool to think that. She was just a child, maybe not that much younger than himself.

"Who are you?" She repeated, and this time he recognized her words.

"Kareth Al'Resh, of the tribe Gorikin."

She stared at him with wide dark eyes, like polished stones, not understanding a word he was saying.

He pointed towards his chest. "Kareth."

"Harami," she said, pointing towards her own chest.

She asked him a question, but he couldn't understand.

"Um... song. What song?"

She asked again, then started humming the tune.

"Oh..." he smiled, and began to sing the next verse.

"Wake them up, bang the drum,

It's time to go again,

Take your oars, let's go boys, in out."

She laughed, and Kareth couldn't help but think that her laughter really did sound like a bird's song.

"Oh!" She ran back to the tree she had been hiding behind and returned carrying a woven basket filled with large bright fruit. She picked out one of the biggest ones and held it out to him. "Here."

He smiled, putting down his skin and reaching out to take the fruit from her delicate hands. She sat down in the tall grass and he sat next to her. She took a fruit for herself, digging her nails into the skin to peel it, and he followed suit, though less gracefully and shimmering juices began to run down his hands. They laughed together as he tried to lick the sticky liquid off his fingers.

They ate in a comfortable silence. She began humming the tune of the song he had been singing, taking pieces of the fruit and carefully eating them. When they finished he wanted to ask her if she had come from the golden barges. Maybe she knew the Paref. Maybe she could help him. But he could not think of how to say any of those words. Instead, he only managed one simple word: "Thank."

She smiled. "Thank *you*," she corrected him.

"Thank *you*," he repeated.

She suddenly jumped up, holding her hand out to him.

He took her hand and she pulled him up. They began running through the trees. She started singing the song he had learned, and he quickly joined in, their voices mixing with the birdcalls all around them.

"In' the water she goes,

Dip her in, pull her out,

Row that ship faster boys, in out."

Every now and again she would stop, next to some tree or bush bearing fruit, picking the largest ones and pilling them into his arms. There were countless fruits and berries, and soon Kareth could barely hold them and as she added more they just began to roll out of his arms and onto the ground.

Harami showed no signs of stopping, until they suddenly heard someone calling out. She seemed to pale slightly, then she smiled at him. "Tomorrow, yes?"

"Uh, yes!" He struggled to keep balance of the fruit, not sure if she had asked him to meet her again tomorrow or not, but unable to clarify as she suddenly took off through the trees and was gone.

Kareth returned to the ship with some difficulty, because he was trying to keep the fruit from falling – though mostly failing – and because he was not entirely certain where the Afeth was. When he finally found her the crew started cheering when they saw what Kareth carried and instantly started feasting on his findings. Sef began to dutifully hold up whatever he was about to eat and ask Kareth to name it. Kareth had, much to his own surprise, started to like his little lessons from the older seaman, and could not help but think he might be able to impress Harami tomorrow.

The next day Kareth was up with the sun, eager to set out and meet with Harami again. The sun was barely above the trees before he grew too impatient and took off. This time he grabbed one of his skins to carry the fruit with. He wandered through the trees, unsure of where he had met her last time, and not even certain she would be in the same spot. He started singing loudly, hoping that, wherever she was, she would hear him and come.

He could not say how much time passed, but the sun was nearly overhead when he heard her sweet giggle coming through the trees to meet him.

"Kareth!" she called out happily. She had her basket with her again, but this time it was filled with cured meat and fish, dried dates and fresh fruit. She set it down between them and the two began to eat. Much to his surprise she wore an entirely new set of jewels, just as grand and colourful, but this time the wide necklace around her neck was only lines of beads, and she wore two identical bracelets on her arms, wide gold bands with a sparkling watery stone set in the middle. Her tunic, although similar, had a fold of lilac cloth in it now. For the first time in his life he felt self-conscious wearing his Ancestral Cloak and nothing else. What must she think of him? He tried to bury the thought, focusing instead on her smile.

"Today..." Kareth searched for the word, "fruit?" He held up his skin, showing her he was prepared this time.

She nodded excitedly. "Yes!"

They wandered through the trees again. Not rushing this time, but leisurely strolling. Kareth would pick a fruit and say the name, and either Harami would giggle and correct him, or nod with approval. He felt himself swell with pride every time he picked the right name.

The sun was getting low by the time Harami finally said. "I – go – back." She used small words, carefully pronouncing them, but even then Kareth was only slightly sure of what she had said.

"Tomorrow... yes?" He asked this time.

She nodded vigorously. "Yes!"

He wandered back to the ship, humming the song he had taught Harami. When he got back Tersh met him as he dropped his skin full of fruit for the crew to cheerfully begin to eat.

"Where do you go all day?" Tersh asked.

Kareth merely shrugged. "Exploring."

Tersh nodded, clearly not believing that was the entire story, but obviously seeing no point in pushing the matter either.

As they fell asleep lying next to each other, staring up at the vast expanse of stars, Kareth could not help but ask one question.

"Tersh... how do you say friend in the tongue of Mahat?"

Tersh turned to look at him, an amused expression on her face. "Why do you ask?"

Kareth shrugged again. "Just curious..."

"Kehmas."

"Kay-mahs..." Kareth repeated slowly.

Tersh propped herself up on her elbow. "Softer, *keh*-mas."

"*Keh*mas," Kareth tried again, still looking up at the stars.

"Better. Now, go to sleep," Tersh said, lying back down, but for a long time afterwards Kareth kept repeating the word softly to himself.

The next morning he set out early again, and this time did not have to wait long for Harami to appear. She brought a basket of food, a different arrangement, though equally delicious. This time though, instead of beginning to eat with her, he held out a small object for her to take.

"Kehmas?" He asked slowly. He held a golden bracelet. The band was thick, but clearly of poorer quality than anything she wore. On the bracelet was the smiling face of the sun with five sunbeams around the edges, each one lined with tiny rubies. He was almost embarrassed to hand it to her, but he wanted to give her *something*. Tersh had told him many times how the people of Mahat did not like the Whispers, but she was more than happy to sit and eat with him.

He held the bracelet out and she looked at it with confusion for a moment. "Kehmas?" he repeated again, worried that it was the wrong word, or that he was pronouncing it incorrectly.

She smiled, and giggled, and he laughed and she excitedly took it and put it on her bare arm. It was too big for her wrist, and she had to push it all the way up until her sleeve was hiding it, but she lifted her sleeve and showed it off to him. She said something quickly and excitedly, but he didn't understand. She stood up and twirled, her dress opening up like the petals of a flower, holding her arm out so the rubies caught the sunlight. Then she plopped down, laughing.

"Kehmas!" She said sweetly.

"I'm glad you like it, Harami."

"Yes," she breathed, pointing at him. "Kareth. Friend."

He held out his hand. She quickly took it in both of hers, and they stayed like that a moment, before bursting into laughter again.

All at once Harami's face went quiet. She became stiff, her eyes looking away from him, looking behind him. He turned just in time to see a hand reaching towards him, grabbing him roughly by the neck of his cloak and lifting him off the ground. Harami screamed.

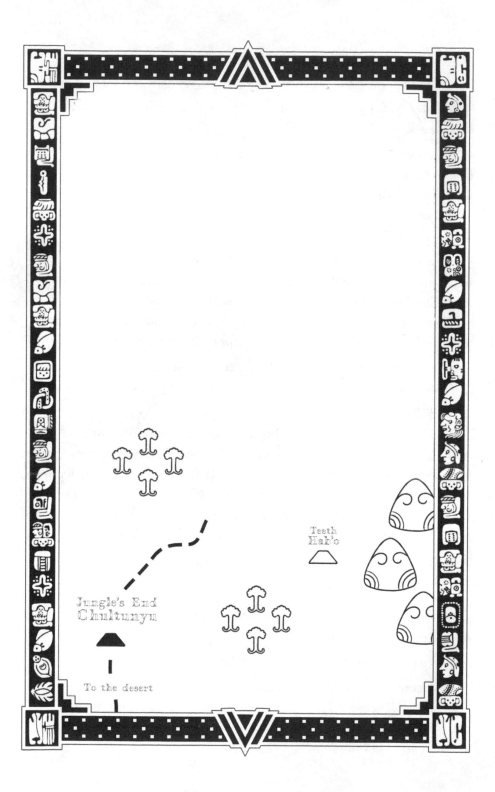

Teeth
Hab'o

Jungle's End
Chultunyu

To the desert

THE JUNGLE

SHE WILL TURN HER FIRE
KNIFE ON HERSELF

All that was left of the corpse was scattered bones, tufts of fiery fur, and red smeared on the jungle floor. Sha'di had no idea what the animal had been before, but looking at the bones he felt uneasy. The arm bones were too long, and the skull misshapen, but the size and shape of this animal would have been the same as a child. Just like–

No, he shook his head. He wouldn't think about that.

His hand reached up absentmindedly to Nnenne, perched on his shoulder. He stroked her soft feathers, feeling some amount of comfort.

"Jaguar," Belam spoke in a gruff voice, shattering the eerie silence around them.

Sha'di looked at the warrior nervously. He had only met Belam on the second day of their journey. He was one of the few people who was patient enough to try and speak with the Whisperer, and for that reason Sha'di often tried to spend time with him. Belam was young, younger than Sha'di. Although he was shorter, Belam had wide shoulders and strong muscles. His wooden yaxha, lined with jagged fire knives, was still strapped to his back, but he held his sling ready, a smooth clay ball cradled inside.

"Still here?" Sha'di asked, his eyes peering around the small clearing.

Belam slowly shook his head.

What little meat had been left on the bones of the animal was being overrun by all manner of insects. Sha'di had to conclude that the jaguar had abandoned its prey some time ago, maybe even the day before, but that didn't make him feel less uneasy.

Belam kicked the animal's skull, and through the cracked bones Sha'di could just make out white maggots swarming over what was left of its brain. He had to turn around, feeling a sudden heaving from deep down in his stomach. Nnenne, disturbed by the sudden movement, flapped her wings once, and then went still again.

Sha'di had barely been able to look at meat since... since the day they left Chultunyu. He certainly hadn't been able to eat any of it, and smelling the decaying blood and rot made him feel suddenly faint.

Nnenne squawked gently.

"I know, I know," Sha'di breathed. "What kind of a man feels queasy at a dead animal?"

"Gone," Belam said, and this time put his sling and ball back into the pouch strapped to his leg.

"Go back? Tell others?" Sha'di asked, his mastery of chaktan, the low tongue, was still extremely fragmented, but he found he had an easier time having a conversation these days.

"No. Jaguar gone," Belam smiled. He and the other Pyramid Builders tended to use what sounded like baby talk to Sha'di, but he didn't mind. When they tried to use proper sentences with him he became completely lost.

"What... animal?" Sha'di managed after sifting his mind for the right word.

"Forest person," Belam nodded.

Sha'di's eyes must have bulged, because Belam started to laugh. He had a loud, infectious laugh. His mouth would open wide and his head tilt back, no matter how small the joke or situation, Belam's laugh was always full force.

"Not people like us," he gestured back and forth between Sha'di and himself. "People like... aletz."

"Aletz?" The word was unfamiliar to him.

"Aletz..." Belam thought. "Aletz lives in the air, in the water, in the trees," he touched his chest. "In men."

"Spirit?" Sha'di asked, and Nnenne buried her beak under her wing to bite something that was bothering her.

"Aletz," Belam gave a wide motion with his hand, as though pointing at everything.

"Aletz," Sha'di nodded, thinking he could understand.

Every evening as dusk settled on the jungle they stopped and made camp. They would make a clearing and spread out to sleep for the night. Tanuk, his younger brother Tenok, and the other chakatl who had followed their master slept in the centre. Around them in a ring slept the servants and on the outside the warriors and hunters stayed. At any given time during the night at least a fourth of the warriors stayed on watch. Along with tents or lean-tos, every night most men would cover themselves in a fine mesh net designed to keep insects from biting them.

"To protect against the bad air," Belam had explained, lending Sha'di an extra net he had brought. Most men had two or three in case one ripped. 'Bad air', Sha'di learned, was a disease one got from a mosquito bite. While many insects could inject you with poison and kill you instantly, bad air lingered in your body, slowly weakening you and eroding your mind until you descended into madness.

Sha'di ate the fruit he had foraged as he walked up front with Belam. Hunters had killed many animals that day, as they did every day, and there was a feast in the centre of their camp, a large bonfire surrounded by singing and mirth and wrestling. Wrestling matches were by far their favourite pastime.

He gave his share of the meat to Nnenne, who happily picked at it next to him. "Eat up, you lazy glutton," Sha'di muttered. Nnenne hadn't been able to hunt since leaving Chultunyu, the jungle was far too thick, but still he noticed the bird becoming rounder every day.

There were small fires circling the camp, those warriors who were not on duty sat around them cooking their own meat, or simply talking and sharing stories. Those fires would be lit all night; they believed it helped keep the predators at bay. Sha'di kept close to the ring of warriors. He knew it was more dangerous on the outside of the circle, but he couldn't bear the idea of spending time with the *great* chiefs of Chultunyu. Every evening, the first few days of their travels, a servant would come to Sha'di and invite him to share the fire with Tanuk, and every evening Sha'di hid his disgust behind a forced smile and politely declined. Soon enough the invitations stopped coming.

Sha'di still found it nearly impossible to sleep in the jungle. He couldn't stop thinking of the quiet nights in the desert. Back then he had hated how cold it got at night, how families would have to curl up against each other to stay warm. It wasn't until he started sleeping next to Nnenne that he enjoyed having to resort to that. The heat in the jungle, however, never left. It was constantly humid, and the hum of insects and birdcalls was never ending. Sometimes he would hear the low growl of an animal, and no matter how distant it had sounded he would be kept up for a long time after, imagining some hideous monster bursting into their camp and tearing them to shreds.

This was the land of monsters. He had witnessed that first-hand.

He set up his mesh net, digging four sticks into the ground and resting the net on top of them. He brought Nnenne underneath with him every night, though there were nights when she would grow restless and the flapping of her wings brought the mesh down on her until she was wrapped in it and squawking so loudly she'd wake him and everyone nearby. He couldn't bring himself to leave her outside it though, not when the warriors kept sharing stories of people they had seen catch the bad air.

He fell into a restless sleep. The dream came. It had been awhile since he had had it, but it still felt all too familiar. Silently walking through the desert, his sleeping tribesmen all around him, the lone figure standing in the temple walls, waiting. He knew he was dreaming, and he stopped walking to stare at her. If he reached her, she would disappear, and he wanted to spend another moment staring at her while he could.

Her long, dreadlocked hair fell down her back, swaying in the warm desert wind. He called out to her, but his voice sounded distant, and she did not seem to hear it. He started walking again, feeling an urgency to reach her. He didn't care if she disappeared, he knew at least he would reach her, touch her, feel her for a moment before he awoke.

"Nnenne?" His hand went to her shoulder.

"You shouldn't be here," it was her voice speaking, but when she turned around it was not Nnenne standing before him. It was not even the burning woman. It was a young boy, his hair cropped short, fresh red dye on his face and arms. His eyes were open wide in shock, and his mouth hung slack. In his hand he held his still-beating heart.

Sha'di could hear screaming and came awake with a start, the scream dying on his lips as he sat up. This time he was the one tangled in the net, Nnenne squawking frantically next to him. A few warriors looked at him with their eyebrows raised. Most of the camp was sleeping, though a few men stirred at the sudden screaming, looked around a moment, then fell asleep once more.

"Are you well?" One of the warriors asked, his face was somewhere between concern and laughter.

"Fine... fine... a... bad dream."

The warrior's face became serious. "What do the gods say, dreamer?"

Sha'di felt an angry frustration building up inside him. Were the dreams from the gods? Why? There was only one thing he did know, only one thing he could say: "They say the old ways must be followed."

The next day Sha'di did not walk ahead with Belam or any of the other scouts and warriors. He waited while the party packed for another day's journey. The servants were quick in their duties, but it was still well after morning before they were ready to set off. Neither Tanuk nor any of the other chakatl surrounding him looked all that worried about making good time.

The chakatl weren't dressed as gaudily as they had been back at Chultunyu. Most of them wore simple white tunics with decorative belts; a few had simple cloaks on. Only Tanuk still dressed as he had back in his pyramid. Sha'di had almost admired Tanuk at Chultunyu, but now he couldn't look at him without seeing that bored expression as his priests had held the boy down...

When they travelled they walked in a line. Most of the warriors stayed in the centre of the column, close to the chakatl in order to protect them, the rest of the warriors and servants stretching out in front of and behind them. Xupama stayed close to Tanuk. Sha'di assumed he had been asked – or perhaps ordered – to come along to act as a translator for Sha'di, but the Whisperer wished he hadn't.

"Well, we have to speak to him eventually," Sha'di patted Nnenne on his shoulder, who just bobbed her head up and down.

Sha'di stayed near the back of the line of chakatl, wondering if he should make his way towards Tanuk. Most of the chakatl gave little sneers at him, and the warriors looked at him uneasily. It wasn't that the warriors didn't trust Sha'di. They just weren't used to seeing him walk in the middle of the group.

He could see Tanuk was laughing at something Tenok had said, and Sha'di wondered if he had the right to interrupt their conversation or if he should wait. He had already waited days, what was one more?

"So you've crawled out from your burrow, have you?" Xupama's shrill voice came from beside him.

Sha'di had been so focused on Tanuk, he hadn't noticed the tall man walking there.

Xupama, predictably, was dressed just as foolishly as he had been back at Chultunyu. Only a man who aspired to be a chakatl would dress like one while hiking through the jungle. His tall headdress made from the large white antes feathers looked heavy and uncomfortable, and Sha'di couldn't help but hope that it was.

"I wish I had a burrow," Sha'di smiled despite himself. It was nice to hear his own language, even if it was spoken in Xupama's accent, "then maybe I could escape this humidity."

"The gods blessed this land with unlimited heat and water, to ensure she would be fertile for all eternity. Surely a *man* such as yourself, who speaks to the gods and lives in a land of sand and rocks can respect the great gifts given here."

"You don't have to like the gods' actions to respect them. Much the same can be said about people too, don't you think?" Sha'di smiled.

Xupama's taut brow furrowed even further, as though he were trying to decide if he had been insulted or complimented – or neither.

Just then Sha'di noticed that someone was making their way towards them, and saw with some surprise that it was the younger brother, Tenok.

Tenok said something enthusiastically to him that he did not fully understand.

Sha'di gave a confused look.

Tenok gestured to Xupama and said something else in an exasperated voice.

"Tenok-huitl wonders where you have been all this time."

"Enjoying the wonders of the chultun," Sha'di answered, speaking half in chaktan and half in his own tongue.

Xupama translated what he said and Tenok gave a small laugh.

"The jungle has no wonders. It's a land of death and misery we spend our entire lives fighting."

Listening to Xupama's translations, Sha'di found himself mentally editing everything the translator was saying. He cut out the customary "Tenok-huitl..." and replaced the overly-flowery language Xupama liked to use.

"You haven't spoken to us in days."

"I was... distracted," Sha'di managed to reply in chaktan.

"My brother offered to teach you the language of allpas, the tongue spoken at Chipetzuha, but instead you've just been practicing with the warriors. A chib'atl offered to give you lessons. I expected to see you sooner than this."

Although Xupama translated it into his honey-sweet tone, Sha'di could hear the disappointment in Tenok's voice.

As much as he wanted to distance himself from the chib'atl who had looked on with such boredom as a child had been butchered at his command, he also knew he needed him and the chakatl if he wanted to gain audience with their chief at Chipetzuha. The gods were not being lenient with the challenges they were sending his way.

"You speak my tongue a little?" Sha'di asked.

Tenok gave a shy grin. "I wish to learn."

"Maybe we can... practice." He glanced at Xupama, not kindly. "Alone."

Xupama began a great flourish of words in protestation, most of which Sha'di could not understand, nor did he care to.

Tenok was already waving the gaudy man away. "Yes, I would like that very much," he smiled, not even looking at the translator. "Thank you Xupama. I'm sure you can find other walking companions to your liking."

Xupama sounded like a growling jaguar as he stomped off, heading towards Tanuk. Sha'di wondered if he meant to complain to him. He watched him go. He chuckled to himself when he saw Xupama reach Tanuk, only to hang back and follow like a dog at his master's heels.

"The ceremony..." Sha'di began in his own tongue, speaking slowly and waiting for Tenok to nod before he would continue. "The one the morning we left."

Tenok was quiet a moment, nodding to himself, translating Sha'di's words in his head. "Ah, yes," he finally said. "A... giving to god."

"Sacrifice..." Sha'di muttered the word darkly.

"Yes, sacrifice to god. For good... happiness."

"Good fortune."

"Hm... fortune," Tenok repeated the word a few times to himself.

"Why was it done?"

Tenok blinked, not understanding.

Sha'di tried again, using a mix of the low and high tongue he had learned. "Why it happen?"

"The gods demand sacrifice," Tenok shrugged, slipping back into chaktan. "Whisperers do the same. I have heard of the blood ceremony."

The blood ceremony. Even the words were chilling to Sha'di. He had never witnessed it, though like every Whisperer he knew what it meant. Most outside of the Rhagepe never learned how it was actually done, save that a blood sacrifice was demanded. Nnenne had given him some of the darker details once.

"She will turn her fire knife on herself," Nnenne had mimed with her soft delicate hands, holding an imaginary knife on her stomach, and pulling it across lengthwise. "Some die from the shock, others manage to reach in and pull out their own entrails. It is said she can read the gods' symbols in the twists. Others," she moved her hands up to her neck, "the ones who are too cowardly to suffer through the pain, cut their throat and die faster that way. They say the longer the Rhagepe lives and feels the pain, the more terrible the curse will be."

He found himself petting the falcon Nnenne's soft feathers, feeling uneasy. He had felt sick for days after she had told him that, and even now it managed to disturb him. The idea of killing oneself wasn't really what troubled him, it was that they felt the need to unleash such a terrible curse. Were there truly actions so heinous it demanded the blood ceremony as retribution?

"The blood ceremony is different," he spoke in the Whisperers' tongue again. He felt like no other language was appropriate to use when speaking of such a sacred thing. "A Rhagepe will kill herself, never another. We sacrifice animals, camels are the most sacred, but humans... No, never that."

Tenok looked thoughtful, then scrunched up his face as he searched for the right words. "I thought it... normal. In chultun, jungle, all important times have sacri... sacrifice."

"Why was your uncle angry?" He held his breath, not wanting to offend him, but also needing to understand what was happening around them. If he couldn't understand these people, how could he hope to save them from themselves?

"Mayek-tatcha," 'tatcha' was the katan word for uncle. "He wanted right sacrifice. Tanuk wanted..." he switched back to chaktan. "Tanuk is afraid."

"I don't understand," Sha'di spoke the sentence easily in katan; it was one of the first sentences he had learned to say in it.

"After the many waters, our land was saved by a great priest, B'uwaminetz. He spoke to the gods, like your Rhagepe."

Sha'di wasn't certain he understood, something about being saved by a male Rhagepe? He almost corrected him, saying that only women could speak to the gods. Then he remembered the dream, the dream he'd had so many nights since being chosen to speak for the Goddess of Rebirth. Maybe sometimes a man might be graced by visions from the gods. It was possible...

"He told them to save our land we must travel to Chipetzuha, and anoint it with the blood of the allpa and his family. Only the youngest son was spared."

"You killed allpa?" Sha'di was certain he had heard wrong. Allpa meant the chief of all the Petzuhallpa.

"He had failed the gods, and the gods demanded his blood. Understand?"

"I think..."

"It worked. The waters receded, and our land prospered once more. Since then, an allpa's sacrifice is needed to keep the land alive. Understand?"

"Why allpa?"

"Allpa's have the blood of gods in them. Nothing is more sacred."

"But... boy in Chultunyu... no allpa."

"No. Exactly. Mayek-tatcha wanted the son of a chakatl to be sacrificed, but my brother said no. He fears... He thinks once they start sacrificing chakatl, they will never stop. He worries every pyramid will one day be like Chipetzuha, with a huitl sitting atop, just waiting to come of age and be sacrificed."

Tanuk was right to be afraid, Sha'di thought. This was a twisted version of the old ways. No wonder the gods were angry.

When Tanuk summoned Sha'di that night, he went.

The chakatl had all brought tents on the journey, but Tanuk's was by far the largest. It was as big as the hut Sha'di had lived in at Chultunyu, made of a thick dark canvas. Inside carpets had been placed on the floor and there was bedding and chairs and bright lamps in the four corners.

Tenok sat on the floor, picking at a plate of fruits and cured meats, chuckling over some joke he must have just told. Tanuk sat on one of the wooden chairs, which during the day could be folded and carried by the servants more easily. There was a table next to it, a small wooden horse on the top, which Tanuk moved absentmindedly with his finger.

"Whisperer, you grace us with your presence, how kind," Tanuk looked up at him, but there was no joy or kindness on his face. He wore a mask of no emotion. He spoke in katan, and Sha'di was struggling to make sense of what he said when Tenok spoke up in the Whisperers' tongue.

"Thank you for coming."

"Forgive my rudeness," he answered in katan, Tenok had taught him the sentence that afternoon as they had walked.

"Can you understand without a translator?" Tanuk asked in chaktan, knowing the language was easier for Sha'di to understand.

"I... getting better," Sha'di tried to smile.

"I'll leave you two alone," Tenok jumped up. He was holding a sling, twirling it as he moved towards the entrance. "Some of the servants wanted a hunting demonstration – and I aim to please."

Tanuk gave a low sigh as his brother jaunted away from the tent, rushing through the flap, leaving them alone.

"Sit," Tanuk motioned towards the other seat.

"I want to speak of... killing ceremony," Sha'di said, annoyed that he had already forgotten the word for sacrifice. He'd asked Tenok to teach him many things that afternoon, but he realized now he had already forgotten most of them.

"My brother said you were... concerned about it."

"Concerned?"

"Bad feeling."

"Yes, very bad feeling. Tanuk-chib'atl. Killing not old way. Gods want we keep old way."

Tanuk raised an eyebrow. "I have no love for killing men, but that is the old way. Gods have always demanded the sacrifice of men."

"No, Whisperers keep old way. We are first, we are last," he tried to translate the words of his people, but they fell flat in a different tongue.

"Our people are the most ancient... oldest," Tanuk changed the word when he saw the confusion on Sha'di's face. "We crawled from the sands, and the gods, crying because of our pain, rained down their tears and the jungle grew around us. The gods gave us the secret of the pyramid, and the joy of writing. They gave us the old ways. Your people followed us from the sand, jealous of our achievements, but you turned away from the gods' pity."

Sha'di swallowed his anger at Tanuk's ignorance. "Gods speak to us."

"Yes, because they want you to listen. But you do not listen, you stay in the sand and you suffer and you do not learn the old ways."

We were the first, he chanted in his head, *and we will be the last.*

"I know killing ceremony scare you. It scare me," Sha'di changed his tactic.

Tanuk was quiet, slowly nodding his head. He picked up the wooden horse, looking at it sadly. "Killing a huitl is terrible... bad."

Sha'di wanted to ask him how killing a rich man was worse than killing any other, but he bit his tongue. He needed Tanuk on his side.

"Help me change way. Help me save here, this place" Sha'di pleaded. He wanted to explain how their sacrifice was a corruption of the old ways, a corruption the gods abhorred, but didn't even know how to begin.

"I will help you, of course, but I fear... we have different ideas of how to save my people."

No matter, Sha'di tried to smile. *It's me the gods will speak through.*

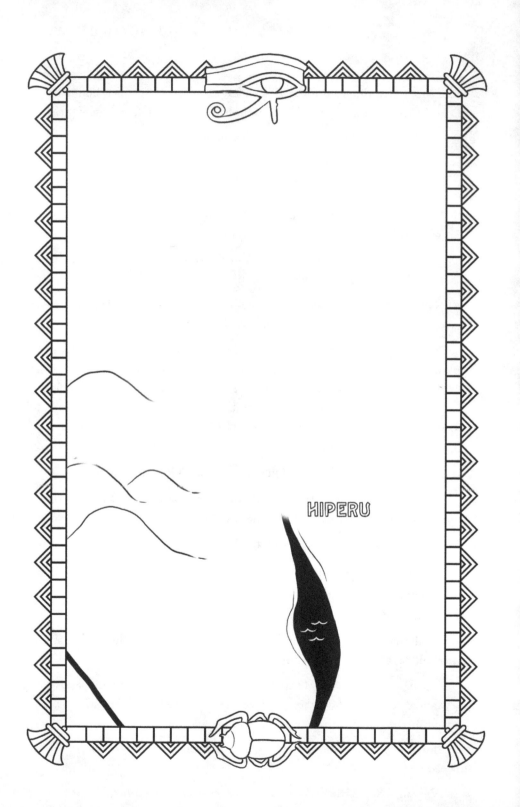

HIPERU

THE HIPERU

A CHILD NEEDS TO LEARN DISAPPOINTMENT

They heard them coming before they saw them. There was a great amount of swearing and yelling. The sailors looked around not understanding the words coming from the boy's mouth, but Tersh understood all too well and sighed in annoyance. She was not surprised to see Kareth emerge from the thick trees along the shore of the Hiperu, though she was surprised to see him being carried by two large guards, each one holding onto an arm as Kareth screamed and kicked, his legs waving ineffectually in the air.

"Is this your filth?" One of the guards asked angrily as they threw Kareth onto the grass.

Kareth jumped to his feet, ready to lunge at the guards in their white pleated skirts and nemes, but Tersh took a quick step forward.

"Kareth!" Her voice was a whip.

Kareth went as still as stone, slowly turning, his eyes opened wide. He had never heard Tersh sound that angry, and the look he saw on her face clearly unnerved him as he seemed to shrink in front of her.

"He... travels with us," Samaki stood closer to the shore. He had been filling a small reed boat with supplies to take back to the Afeth, making sure their stocks were well supplied for whenever the royal barges finally decided to set off once more.

"Filthy Go-men!" The other guard spat, the wad of saliva barely missing Kareth, and stared at Tersh like a lizard caught in an eagle's gaze.

"Come here," Tersh growled, feeling uneasy with Kareth standing so close to the angry guards. As quickly as a scorpion he skittered over to the older Whisperer, going to her side.

"He was harassing a royal princess!" Tersh and the other sailors were all too aware of the curved bronze blades hanging at the guards' sides. Only Samaki looked relaxed, a large smile on his face as she walked forward.

"He is only a boy, and not from this place, he doesn't understand our ways."

"Understand this," a guard stepped forward, and he loomed above all the other men gathered there. "If I smell his stench anywhere near the royal family again, the only part of him I'll return is his head."

"Of course, the boy won't leave sight of our ship again," Samaki smiled, but gave a sideways glace towards Tersh, and the Whisperer knew it was a command.

"Filth. I shall pray Djekuna swallows you all," the guard spat again, and then both of them turned and walked back through the trees.

All were silent, staring back and forth between the Whisperers and their captain, no one daring to say a word. Tersh expected Samaki to begin yelling, but his easy smile remained on his face.

"Finish loading the supplies and get back on the Afeth. We're leaving."

"What of the royal barges?" Tiyharqu spoke up, having not moved from her place sitting around a senet board with some of the crewmembers.

"Oh, they're leaving too, no doubt. I want to be ready to leave with them," no one moved for a moment. Samaki's smile fell away. "Do the gods need to command you? I said move!"

Everyone jumped up, collecting their sleeping rolls and belongings, almost running to the reed boats along the shore, their arms full of sweet fruits and a few had baskets of fish and bird meat they had caught while relaxing along the shore. Satisfied with his crew, Samaki turned to the Whisperers. He didn't even look at Kareth; he spoke only to Tersh.

"You keep your son on the ship. I don't care if you have to tie him to the mast. If you bring trouble to me again, I will leave you both behind."

"I understand," Tersh spoke, trying not to look angry, but her body felt like it was on fire. If Kareth had really been her son, she would have beaten him then and there.

When Samaki left she turned and looked down at Kareth. More so than even the first night they had travelled together, Kareth looked like only a small child, weak and frightened.

"What did you do?" She tried not to yell, but her voice was louder than she had meant it to be.

"We were only playing, Harami is my friend–" His hands picked at the bones of his cloak uneasily.

"A princess isn't your friend!"

Kareth looked down at the grass, and his fear seemed to melt away. He narrowed his eyes angrily, but dared not look up.

Tersh could see his eyes glossing over with tears, and felt shame, shame for yelling at him, shame that he would still be weak enough to cry when someone scolded him. He wore the mark of a man. He had the duties of a man. He was still only a child.

"Get on the ship." She managed to control her voice.

They gathered their skins and loaded them onto one of the small reed boats. The ship was close enough to the shore that they could paddle across with just their hands. Kareth sat at the front, but refused to help and kept his arms crossed. Once they reached the Afeth, Kareth grabbed hold of the rope ladder and scrambled up, not even bothering to grab his skins, so Tersh was forced to carry both of their things onboard.

The ship was ready to sail just as the royal barges began to pull away from the shore. The other ships that followed were still scrambling to make ready as the crew took to their oars and pushed away, continuing their journey upriver. There were at least a dozen ships travelling with the barges, most of them filled with haggard looking people. Tiyharqu had remarked several days ago that they were most likely heading north because they had lost their homes in the south and were searching for something better.

Something better... Tersh thought. They'll find nothing better until the gods are appeased.

◆　◆　◆　◆　◆

Kareth didn't speak for days, and Tersh didn't try to speak to him either. None of the crew could break him out of his shell, not even kindly Sef, who had easily been able to make Kareth smile before. No he too was only met with an angry stare. Tersh spent most of her time with Samaki and Tiyharqu, usually playing senet, as the other crewmen were wary of speaking to a Whisperer.

"His anger will lose its bile," Tiyharqu had said with her large toothy smile one evening.

"Let him be angry," Tersh had shrugged. "A child needs to learn disappointment."

They stopped going ashore with the crew at night, sleeping on the hard deck instead. Tersh had expected Kareth to complain, but he didn't even try to leave the ship. He had that much sense at least.

"She *was* my friend."

Tersh blinked. They were sitting next to each other, the midday sun bearing down on them. Kareth had been silent so long his voice took her by surprise. She turned towards Kareth, who had finally found the courage to stare into her eyes, glaring at her.

"Don't be a fool. The people of this land are frivolous. I'm sure she found you interesting, but she's already forgotten you."

Kareth's face became bright red. He stood up. "You don't know anything!"

Tersh stood, calm and collected, nearly a full head taller than the boy. To Kareth's credit, he did not wilt away this time, but stood all the straighter.

"Why are you so angry?" she asked.

The question seemed to stump Kareth for a moment; he opened his mouth to reply, then closed it again, and finally spoke. "You keep treating me like a child. I'm not a child!"

"Only a child needs to prove that."

Kareth brushed the comment aside. "I wasn't doing anything wrong, and you should be on my side!"

"I *am* on your side," Tersh wished Kareth would go back to being silent. The crew were all looking at them, the rowing had begun to slow down as the men began to mutter to each other, trying to figure out what the Whisperers were saying, not a single one of them understanding a word of their tongue.

"Then why didn't you defend me!?!" Kareth no longer looked angry, only hurt.

"Against royal guards? And say what? Common men are forbidden from going uninvited to the royal family."

"*She* came to *me*!" The anger returned.

To their side Tersh saw Samaki stand and begin to walk towards them, clearly having had enough of this disturbance.

"It doesn't matter, you're no royal–"

"I am the son of a chief! And he the son of a chief and so on since before our people came from the drowned lands. My cloak is three bones deep! I was chosen to speak for the Goddess of Life. How dare you call me common! HOW DARE YOU!!!" Kareth turned, stomping off, but he couldn't go far. The edge of the ship was only an arm's reach away.

Samaki had reached Tersh. "You need to control your boy," he muttered dangerously.

"Would that I could..." Tersh sighed.

"Back to work, scum!" Samaki called out and the crew began to row harder. Tiyharqu was laughing at the stern of the ship.

Tersh was angry at Kareth, but she felt for the boy. He had been taken from his mother, from his friends, far too soon. He was alone in a strange new land, and had finally found a friend. Only now he would never see that friend again. She knew she should leave him alone, let the anger bleed out of him like the vile puss it was, but she couldn't help but see her own son hurt and alone. Despite her better judgement she went towards Kareth.

"It's all right to feel angry," she said, reaching out to touch his shoulder.

Kareth whirled around, his face twisted into a snarl. "Don't touch me!" He pushed at Tersh with all his strength, but it was like pushing against a wall. Tersh barely moved and instead Kareth stumbled backwards, his foot hit the gunwale, only ankle high, and then he was falling backward, his eyes open in surprise.

Tersh reached out to grab him, but he was already gone. It took a moment for the splash to register, to realize what had happened. She felt her heart seize. She looked around at the other crew, some of them were laughing to themselves. They didn't know, she realized with panic. *They don't know.*

"He can't swim," her voice was a barely audible whisper.

Samaki was not laughing. "What?"

"He can't swim!" Tersh screamed, remembering to speak the words of Mahat this time.

It still took a moment for the crew to respond, to translate what she had said through her panicked accent. Sef was the first to react, diving over to the side of the ship. He hit the water just as Kareth's head surfaced. He had fallen near the bow, but already he was at the stern, the ship still pulling away.

"Paddle backwards!" Samaki ordered and the crew began to reverse the direction they had been pulling the oars.

Another man, Iason, jumped into the water, while Tiyharqu grabbed a length of rope and threw it towards Kareth. Kareth splashed wildly for a moment, and then went under again.

Tersh was on her knees, gripping the sides of the ship, desperate to reach out to them, to help, but what could she do?

Kareth surfaced again, this time with Sef holding him above the water. Kareth didn't seem to recognize he was being helped, he was still thrashing around wildly.

"The damn cloak's pulling him down!" Sef called out, and the two went under again as Iason reached them.

When Kareth came up again the two crewmembers yanked at the cloak's collar, ripping it apart. It fell away from Kareth's shoulders.

"NOO!!!" Kareth shrieked, and began to punch the crewmen trying to help him. He went under again. Sef's mouth was bleeding, and Iason was holding his eye in pain.

"Damn him! Let him drown!" Iason yelled, but Sef had already dived down again to get Kareth.

"Maseh. Maseh!" Someone shouted and all eyes went towards the shore where what looked like a log was drifting towards the thrashing in the water. But it wasn't a log. Tersh knew that very well. 'Maseh', their word for crocodile. She had seen one once, in the Sea Mahat long ago.

The children had been playing in the river. The muddy waters had been shallow, going no deeper than their waist. They had been throwing mud at each other, shrieking in delight. There had been no warning that time. No one saw it coming beneath the darkened waters.

She remembered the boy. One moment he was laughing, and then there was a splash of water as he was pulled under. The crocodile spun with the boy in his mouth. His head surfaced once to scream, but the next time it came up his eyes were lifeless and the blood... the blood clouded the water worse than the mud as all the children screamed and ran to their mothers, who were anxiously calling for them to run to the banks.

"The rope!" Iason called out desperately. Tiyharqu had already pulled it back in and was throwing it out towards him again.

Iason grabbed it and tugged.

"Pull me back! Pull me back!" He begged.

"Wait! WAIT!" Tersh cried, looking at Samaki, terrified they'd leave Kareth to the animal.

"Wait," Samaki ordered, though Tiyharqu had made no move to pull him back in.

The crocodile was moving fast, cutting through the water, Sef and Kareth were still nowhere to be seen.

"PULL ME BACK!!!"

It was the length of two men away, one man-

Kareth and Sef re-emerged. Kareth was unconscious, his head slumped against Sef's shoulder. Sef grabbed onto the rope with a strong arm and Tiyharqu began to pull the rope, several other men helping. They pulled fast, but the crocodile was moving faster.

They reached the edge of the ship, men reached down to grab at them, Sef lifted Kareth into the air for Tiyharqu to grab, the crocodile was an arm's length away. Someone grabbed Sef's arm, they were pulling them over the side of the ship. The crocodile burst out of the water, its jaws the same length as a man's leg, its limbs stunted and terrible. Its mouth opened. There was screaming. The splash of the water obscured Tersh's vision of them.

Tersh ran to the stern, pushing down men to reach them. The three of them lay on the deck, Kareth completely still, blood covering the deck.

"No..." Tersh felt cold.

Sef moved first. "He isn't breathing," he said gruffly, blood running down his chin from where Kareth had hit him. The blood, Tersh realized, was from Sef's mouth. There wasn't a single wound on Kareth... but Kareth wasn't breathing. His small hands clutched his cloak, but the rest of him was limp, and his lips were beginning to lose their colour.

Iason was coughing and sputtering on the deck, moaning curses at Kareth, but everyone was ignoring him, focused on the boy. Sef hit Kareth on his chest, once twice, then opened his mouth and turned him on his side. Some of the others helped to hold him while Sef pounded him on the back, and then Kareth sputtered, water coughing out of his mouth, and he took a deep raspy breath. His eyes fluttered and then went still.

Tersh felt like the world was falling away, but then she saw the gentle rise and fall of Kareth's chest. He was breathing, unconscious, but breathing. She started laughing, and the other men joined in relief. All save Iason, who was still muttering curses to himself.

When Kareth finally opened his eyes again it was night. They had put to shore the moment they found a suitable place to camp, confident that they'd be able to catch up to the royal barges the next day. Tersh had laid his own cloak on the sand for Kareth to sleep on, and then had covered him in the cloak he had nearly died trying to save. The crewmen had made jokes at Kareth's foolishness, but Tersh understood. A Whisperer's Ancestral Cloak was their soul, their legacy, their connection to the past and future.

The necklace of seaweed and feathers that the Rhagepe who spoke for Life had given Kareth had been lost in the river, probably breaking when his cloak was torn from his shoulders. It was a great loss to lose such a powerful talisman, but a small price to pay to keep his cloak and his life. She touched the necklace of lizard skulls she had been given by the speaker of Death, and wondered if it might ever save her life.

She touched Kareth's short hair as he slept, enjoying the sound of his breathing. The sun set and the others went to sleep, but Tersh lit a fire and stayed vigilant. When Kareth finally opened his eyes and looked at her, the first thing he saw was Tersh's smile.

"My cloak-" Kareth said with a sudden anxiety, though his voice was weak.

"Right there," Tersh patted his chest.

Kareth's hands reached around the sides, grabbing the soft leather and bones, making sure it was real.

"I'm sorry I yelled at you," Kareth looked away, ashamed.

"I'm sorry I yelled back... It was... wrong," Tersh couldn't find the right words. She could remember her own father yelling at her whenever she made some mistake. She remembered holding her son the first time and swearing she would not treat him the same. *Kareth is not your son*, she thought darkly.

"I had a dream. I saw a great beast under the water," Kareth muttered, his eyes staring up at the twinkling stars.

"That wasn't a dream," Tersh began, but Kareth seemed not to hear her.

"It was a monstrous thing, and it swallowed you whole. I could hear you screaming inside its stomach. The beast then turned and ate an entire city. It opened its jaws and in one bite the city was gone, and the screams were deafening..." Kareth looked Tersh in the eyes. "It made me afraid."

"You brushed against death in the river. That is all that dream was, your fear."

Kareth seemed uncertain. "I think it was a dream from the gods."

Tersh sighed. "Only the Rhagepe hear the gods."

"I dreamt two white birds would carry us on our journey, and look," his arm shot out from under the cloak, pointing at the Afeth sitting still in the water. The hull of the ship bled into the darkness, but the white of the sails was easily spotted.

Tersh looked at the sails a moment. Sometimes, when they flapped in the wind, they did remind her of the powerful wings of the ibis who lived along the shores of the Nepata, but in the end she shrugged and turned back to Kareth. "Sails are hardly birds. It is easy to interpret dreams however you want."

"I know I'm young," Kareth looked stronger, his eyes seemed determined to convince her.

Tersh sighed. "You're not-"

"I am. I'm young and... and this is new, but I am not a fool. Maybe these are just dreams, but maybe.... The gods chose me," he finished.

His glare only made Tersh's smile widen. "If you want to tell me about your dreams, please do, just... be more careful around the edge of the ship, okay?"

Kareth laughed. It was nice to hear the sound again.

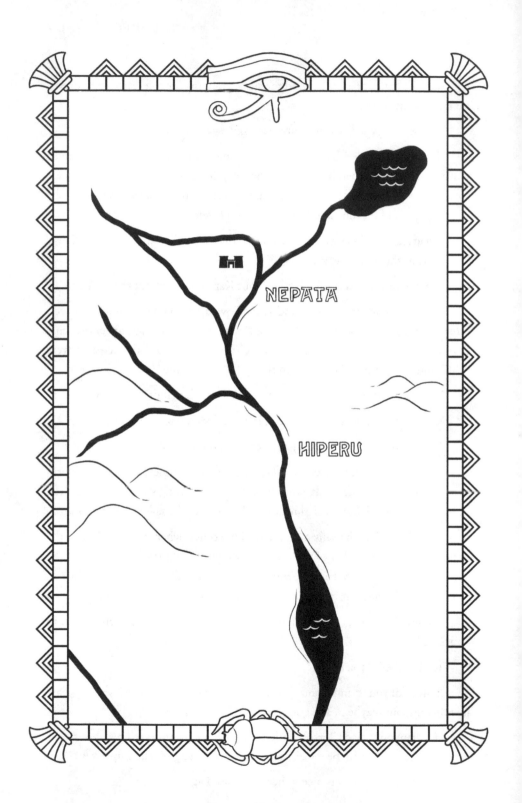

NEPATA

HIPERU

NEPATA

THE SOUL WANDERS

The city of Nepata dwarfed Kareth's memory of Sareeb. The city was surrounded by bright white limestone walls, so tall it would take a dozen or more people standing on each other's shoulders to see over it. The walls ended at the river, two massive statues of men stood vigil on either side of the water, each one with a foot taking a step forward, one arm at their side holding a crooked cane, and the other pulled across their chest, holding a stone sword. They were human in every regard, save for their heads. One had the head of an eagle, the other the head of a snake. The Afeth sailed between the behemoths, her tallest mast only reaching their knees.

Guards walked along the top of the wall, and once through the entrance they saw the massive gate. The wood and bronze gate only rose half the height of the wall.

"The gates have not been closed for over twelve full cycles," Tersh translated what Samaki said. "Not since the great Paref Rama defeated the armies of the Matawega. The mountain people."

For half their journey they had been able to see the Kerlra Hal'gepe mountains off to their left, the tops white-tipped and reaching into the clouds. Most days the grasslands between the Hiperu and the mountains were too dusty to make them out clearly, but occasionally the days were calm enough that Kareth felt like he could reach out and touch them. He hated those mountains, because soon his journey would end in Nepata, and Tersh would continue on into the mountains and Kareth knew he would never see her again.

The beast will swallow her whole, Kareth thought. He shuddered.

Through the gates they could see that while Sareeb had one large white palace, Nepata had two, twins of each other, one on either side of the river. The palaces rose above every other building in the city. Their white walls gently sloping inwards, massive round pillars bordered the castle, with another wall surrounding them, the palace grounds hidden within.

They were in the Mountain Mahat now. The lands surrounding the city were as fruitful and lively as the Sea Mahat had been. Hundreds of rivers cascaded down from the mountains, joining together to make the Hiperu. Nepata had a dozen rivers coming down through the city, and from them a series of canals had been created in the place of roads. There were so many boats inside the city, small reed boats, larger ships with dozens of oars, and a few ships near the same size as the Afeth with a great sail.

The houses here were all stone and beautiful, Kareth thought. The ones along the main river were all two or three storeys high, which had seemed massive to him in the first city he had travelled through with Tersh. Now that he stood in the shadow of those gigantic walls and palaces, he thought they seemed quite modest. He saw a few hard-packed dirt roads between the houses and canals, they were massive avenues lined with palm trees and statues of resting leopards. Few people if any walked along them, yet the river was clogged with boats, more so the closer they came to the palace.

Tersh and Samaki were speaking of something, and when they finished she walked over to Kareth.

"Samaki says we've arrived in time to see something very special." She sat down beside him.

"Oh?" Kareth couldn't pull his eyes away from the boats and buildings around him. The river widened in front of the palaces, undoubtedly shaped by the labour of man, into a massive square lake, the palaces at the north end. After the river ran between the palaces, it must have turned to the left or right because directly behind the palaces he could see another building. That building was perhaps half the height of the palaces and seemed to glitter like gold.

He was also trying to find the golden barges. They had never caught up with them after losing them on the river. Kareth was convinced they could have. He suspected that Samaki had decided they should keep their distance. He could still remember the last time they saw the barges. He thought he had seen Harami on the deck of one of them, but he couldn't be certain.

"He says it's unusual for so many boats to be out on the river. They must be here for the Paref's funeral," Tersh explained.

"Funeral?" Kareth turned to Tersh. They had learned the old Paref that had died ages ago. "Why would they wait so long?"

"Well... I can't say I know why completely, but I remember when I was a young girl, living in the Sea Mahat, some great man died. They waited a hundred and twenty days after he died to bury him."

"One hundred and twenty days?" Kareth tried to think of where he had been a hundred and twenty days ago. He had seen six turns of the moon since the calendar ceremony. He guessed he would have still been in the desert when the Paref died.

"That's how long they say the soul wanders Mahat before settling in its body again," Tersh shrugged.

Kareth remembered the guards at the border to Mahat saying something about the Paref's soul wandering. "I thought they said the Paref was to be reborn in his son."

"Well, it must be different for Parefs, or maybe when they say body they mean the body of the man they're reborn into. I don't know. Their ways are strange to me."

Kareth thought the entire thing was ridiculous. Didn't they all know that when you died, your body became one with the earth again? That your soul became the wind and the rain and the stars at night? You became one with the world and the gods. Kareth had been taught that as a child. Why were they taught here that you wandered lost for a hundred and twenty days before becoming trapped in another body?

Because they've forgotten the old ways, a voice whispered inside him. The gods were angry that they had forgotten. When they forgot, they allowed evil to seep into their land. He would have to teach them the old ways again.

"Samaki said we have to wait for the funeral to end. The palace won't accept any visitors until the old Paref has been seen to his final resting place."

Kareth sighed, feeling impatient. He had hoped he could just deliver his message to the Paref and then be on his way. He thought maybe once he was finished he could go to the mountains with Tersh, maybe use his dreams to keep her safe. After all, how long did it really take to tell a man that the gods were angry and that the old ways needed to be heeded? Once he did that whatever evil corruption the Rhagepe had spoken of would be taken care of by the Paref. Surely he didn't need to spend half a day in this city.

Or maybe... maybe he could take the next ship south and go back home. In a few turns of the moon he would be along the shores of the salt sea, and be with his people again.

The afternoon dragged on, the heat of the sun making Kareth feel uncomfortable. He fiddled with the silver broach at his neck. The leather straps on his Ancestral Cloak that kept it secure around his neck had snapped in the river when it had been ripped off, so Kareth had used one of the broaches given to him by his people to keep it secure. It was large, as big as his palm, and engraved with a woman's stern face. He wasn't used to its weight and sometimes it felt like it was digging into his skin.

Sef tried to speak to him as they all tried to pass the time, but he couldn't concentrate on the man's words. He could still barely string a sentence together in their tongue. After a while he walked away from everyone so he could be alone, sitting by the water, leaning against the side and staring at the opening in the palace walls, wondering what everyone was expecting to emerge.

Suddenly they could hear the sounds of drums and horns coming from inside the walls. It was faint and the tune was difficult to make out, but Kareth thought it sounded vaguely similar to one of the songs he had heard the crew singing as they rowed. It was slower though, and somehow seemed sadder.

From the walls came a small, simple ship. There were ten rowers on either side, bald men wearing plain white tunics, and between them in the centre of the boat was something long and grey he couldn't quite make out. He had been expecting a golden barge, but that was the only ship that emerged, and the other boats began to part and let it pass. He heard some of the people shout at the ship as it glided by. It sounded as though they were calling out salutes, and he thought he heard the wailing of women on the wind. Other than that, the boats had become deathly quiet.

When the boat came closer to them, Kareth could make out the shape in the middle. It was carved from stone, in the shape of a man lying down, though perhaps twice the size of a real man, the bottom flat and wide, as though it were a box. The top half had a man's face staring up at the sky, a pointed beard on his chin, and on his head he wore a nemes twice the size of any he had seen on the guards. His arms were crossed at his chest, one hand holding the same crooked cane he had seen the statues by the river gate holding, and the other hand held a stick that had tassels at the end. He thought it looked like a whip of some sort.

The salutes and crying continued until the ship finally reached the gates and left through them. Then all at once the common noises of everyday activity began again. People spoke to each other, and boats moved off, returning down the canals back to their homes. It seemed as though the Paref's funeral boat was already a distant memory to them.

"I thought it would be his body," Kareth said, moving back to Tersh, who was speaking to Tiyharqu and Samaki.

"No," Tersh explained. "The bodies of Parefs are buried in a secret place. Most likely his body was spirited out of the city before his death was even announced, or perhaps there is a secret burial site for him in the city."

"Why is it so secret?" Kareth was confused. What would it matter if people knew where a body was?

Tersh laughed. "They say a Paref is buried with a treasure so great a man and his sons and grandsons could live rich for all their days."

"But... why?" Kareth tried to imagine what that much treasure would look like. He probably wouldn't be able to carry it in his skins.

Tersh asked Samaki something, and then translated his response.

"Samaki says it's so the Paref can live comfortably in the afterlife with all the things he loved during this life. It seems Parefs are fickle, and like to split their time living in their son's body, and living in their grand tomb."

Tersh and the others laughed, but Kareth couldn't see what was funny. He didn't like the idea of fickle Parefs, not when it was a Paref he needed to convince of the gods' wrath.

Samaki said there was no point in them trying to enter the palace that day, so rowed towards a place to spend the night. They went to the east side of the city, away from the mountains. Here the canals were narrower and fewer, and the buildings not as tall and made from cruder stone. The water level was a little low. Kareth could see by markings on the walls what its normal level was, but at this time of year it was about the length of his arm lower. Stairs were cut into the stone to reach the ground level.

Before they docked the ship, Tiyharqu took them aside.

"Samaki intends to spend the night at an inn," Tersh translated. "We are welcome to join them, but..." Tersh looked at Kareth's cloak and the look made him feel uneasy. "Whisperers are not well-loved in this land. We could offer an innkeeper all the gold we carry and they still wouldn't take us."

"What are you suggesting?"

"Tiyharqu thinks it's a simple matter of wearing one of their tunics."

Kareth had often looked at the tunics a few of the crew wore and wondered how they could stand covering their bodies in that itchy fabric. He loved to be free, to feel the wind and sun on his body. Wearing a tunic just seemed uncomfortable, but what truly bothered him was what Tersh had left unsaid. They would be known as Whisperers *if* they wore their cloaks.

"You mean us to take off our cloaks, to hide our identities in shame?" Kareth felt angry. Why should they be ashamed? "I'd rather sleep on the boat."

"That wouldn't be wise," Tersh looked slightly exasperated. "Men might hesitate to rob a guarded ship, but they might not hesitate to harass a ship carrying Whisperers on it. It would not be good for Samaki."

Kareth wanted to remark that he didn't care what was good for the merchant, but he knew that was a cruel thought. Samaki had carried them this far, when he knew others would never dare. They owed Samaki more than the gold they had already paid him.

"You don't need to take off your cloak," Tersh said, untying her own cloak and swinging it around so the leather was on the outside and the bones inside.

Tiyharqu laughed and said something. Kareth didn't understand it entirely, but caught something about 'looking civilized'.

Kareth fumed, but bit his cheek to keep quiet. They were not in a friendly land, and in such a place Kareth realized they would need to adjust if they wanted to stay safe and complete the mission the goddesses had given to them. Compromise was necessary for everyone's sake. Maybe Tiyharqu did not understand what was at stake, but Kareth did.

Tiyharqu found some tunics for them to wear with leather belts, shabby itchy things and Kareth almost immediately started scratching his covered skin and couldn't seem to stop no matter how many times Tersh slapped his hand. When they turned their cloaks around Kareth could feel his ancestor's bones digging into his shoulders, and as they dug into his skin he felt shame at needing to hide that which in the desert made him so proud.

They docked next to some stairs that led to the courtyard of a public house. The only thing that distinguished it from the buildings around it that also opened onto the canal, aside from its size, was the image of wheat next to a jug carved into the canal wall. Sef had told him it meant beer – whatever that was. The inn was three walls around a courtyard, the canal standing in for the fourth. In the middle of the courtyard was a well and around it a few wooden benches. Guards stood at the top of the stairs. They did not wear the nemes or pleated skirts of the royal guards, but rather dark muddy tunics, curved bronze swords in their belts.

They spoke with Samaki a while. Samaki handed one of the guards a heavy looking small wooden box. The guard smiled widely and motioned for them to disembark, nodding to each of them in turn as they hopped from the rope ladder to the base of the stairs. Most of the crew would stay for a meal, Kareth knew, but most would not stay the night, and many would probably not return to the ship.

Kareth, Tersh and Sef walked to the main building, across the courtyard from the stairs. Opening the door, they found a large rectangular room filled with benches and tables and men of various ages. From the look of their clothes, they were from many social classes, but underneath this roof all acted equal. In one corner musicians with stringed instruments and drums were playing. From the high ceilings lamps hung down, but even so the room seemed strangely dark and stuffy. There were two doors in the common room, one which led to the courtyard, and another which led to a road outside. The wings of the building, accessible only from the courtyard, were where the rooms were.

Sef ordered them beer as they walked in, and as they took a seat at a small table in the corner, clay cups filled with the frothy liquid were deposited before them. Kareth sniffed the drink cautiously. He had never had beer before, and didn't know what to make of it. The first sip was mostly the white froth on the top, which had a vague bitter taste, but a welcome texture. The second sip he got the actual beer. It was thick, and had a faint honey taste, but mostly bitter and warm. His face scrunched up in distaste. Tersh and Sef both laughed at him. Feeling embarrassed, he kept drinking all the same, noticing to his surprise that each sip seemed to taste better than the last. By the time he finished his cup and Sef was ordering more, and he felt light-headed and dizzy.

More of the drinks came, there was loud singing throughout the room. At one point, Kareth seemed to remember standing on the table, singing loudly as the men around him cheered and hollered. Then he seemed to recall being in the courtyard, feeling like he was floating, vaguely aware that someone was carrying him.

When he awoke the next morning his mouth tasted rancid, and as he moved it felt like a knife was thrust into skull. He could feel the hay beneath him, and knew that he was in a small room. There was enough light from the small high window to see a figure sleeping on a pile of hay on the other side of the room. As he tried to push himself up he felt the sickness come over him all at once and his stomach heaved. The noise woke Tersh up, who at first made a face of disgust, then sighed. She left and when she returned she carried a wooden bucket, a water skin and sawdust to cover the vomit.

"Next time, use the bucket," was all she said as she went back to sleep.

Kareth tried to say something, but all that came out was more sickness – this time, into the bucket.

◆　◆　◆　◆　◆

When Kareth awoke again the taste in his mouth was even worse, and although his mind still felt like senet sticks being shaken in a cup, he managed to push himself up. The smell of vomit seemed to choke him and he nearly leaned over the bucket to empty his stomach again, but he managed to keep it down, reaching for the skin of water and drinking greedily. He noticed that Tersh was no longer there, and pushed himself up.

He felt like he was swaying as he opened the door and walked out, but amazingly he managed to keep from falling down. In the courtyard he saw the sun was near to reaching its zenith. He was amazed that he had managed to sleep for so long. A few men were talking in the courtyard. Tersh stood with Samaki, and Tiyharqu was directing a few of the crew who were unloading some stock, while loading up some new barrels. It seemed Samaki had traded with the innkeeper. Sef, Iason, and most of the crew were nowhere to be seen. Kareth figured they were already on board.

Tersh saw Kareth and waved him over. A few of the crewmembers laughed and patted him on the back, but every touch felt like blow to him and he nearly stumbled. Kareth managed to notice that Samaki and the others had shaved off the stubble that had grown on their heads and faces. Samaki and Tiyharqu wore their nicest breaches and vests, and had adorned their necks and arms with rich medallions and bracelets.

"So, you've survived," Tersh and Samaki were also laughing, and Kareth wanted to glare at them, but suddenly felt sick again. He took deep breaths to calm his stomach.

Tersh sighed. "I'm glad you woke up. Samaki wasn't going to wait for you, and without him I'm not sure how good our chances of getting into the palace are."

"Are we leaving now?" Kareth finally found his voice. It sounded haggard.

"As soon as they're finished."

"You want more beer, while we wait?" Samaki spoke slow enough for Kareth to understand what he said.

The word 'beer' sent a wave of nausea through him. "Water," Kareth croaked, pointing towards the well.

Samaki shook his head kindly. "The water isn't clean in the city. The only thing to drink here *is* beer."

Kareth waited for them by the side of the canal, intermittently vomiting and turning on his side grasping his head in pain. At one point Sef came down to him, handing him a skin of 'safe' water. Sef was one of the few crew who didn't disappear overnight.

"The men have been paid what they were promised. The rest are waiting for their cut of the sales. Most don't want to stay for another journey. They want to go home, see their families," Tersh explained as they climbed back onto the ship, a sadness in her eyes.

Kareth could understand. The thought of seeing his mother again filled him with... he couldn't explain it in words. Sadness and longing and excitement and... and...

The Afeth left and made its way through the canals back to the main river, now turning towards the water gate to the palace. Maybe a tenth of the ships Kareth had seen the other day were in the great lake before the palaces. It seemed empty compared to yesterday, but the noise made up for it. Boats called out to each other, people on ships threw each other things in bags, while others held out fruit and fish, calling out to others to buy them. Kareth realized it was a floating market.

They went through the gates. Inside the palace grounds, there were long alleys filled with brightly coloured flowers and bushes next to the massive columns. Kareth could see women wearing wigs sparkling from the gold woven into them and sheer gowns walking along stone paths, followed by young men in white tunics or loincloths holding shade over their heads. Guards in splendid golden nemes walked close by them. A few men walking through the gardens wore long white gowns, with golden belts and rings with large cut stones on them. They wore dark wigs or nemes and most of them had long black beards jutting from their chins. Great rulers of Mahat, he realized in awe. Could one of them be the Paref?

Along the side of the river were statues like the massive ones they had sailed between, but these were only twice the height of men, and there was more than just an eagle and snake head, he also saw a jackal and an ibis and a crocodile and a leopard and countless animals he had never seen or heard of. Each one was different, and each one looked down at the passing ship with a stern look.

There were two docks made from stone, the sides gilded with gold, one on either side of the river for each palace. They pulled up to the one on the right, the crewmen throwing ropes down to waiting guards. Samaki called down to the guards happily, but they only stared back with wary looks. They spoke a long time, Samaki's smile getting smaller and smaller as the conversation dragged on. Finally, just as Samaki seemed on the verge of anger one of the men Kareth had seen walking through the garden approached them. He walked with two young female companions, each one covered in silks and jewels, tight golden collars around their necks. There were so many jewels dripping off them, Kareth thought it must be heavy and uncomfortable. Strangest of all, wore some half-melted lumps on the tops of their heads. Four small boys in loincloths held onto one pole each which held up a large awning that covered the three of them.

"What's on their heads?" Kareth whispered to Tersh.

She looked just as puzzled as he felt when she shrugged to shoulders.

The man smiled when he saw Samaki, and Samaki's smile returned. It seemed obvious the two of them knew each other. The man who stood on the dock must have been important, but his clothes seemed very simple compared to the women he walked with. He wore beautiful shining white linen, but his silver belt was small and understated. He wore only a few rings. His copper wig didn't have any gold woven into the strands.

Samaki turned to Tersh and said some rushed words.

Tersh looked like she was about to argue, but Samaki had already lowered the wooden plank Tiyharqu in charge of the ship.

"What's happening?" Kareth asked, wondering why they weren't following.

"Samaki says the new Paref is... weary of strangers. Samaki has been invited in by the man, but we have to wait. Samaki says he'll be back before long and then..."

"Then we'll see the Paref?" Kareth asked hopefully.

Tersh nodded, but there was no certainty in her eyes.

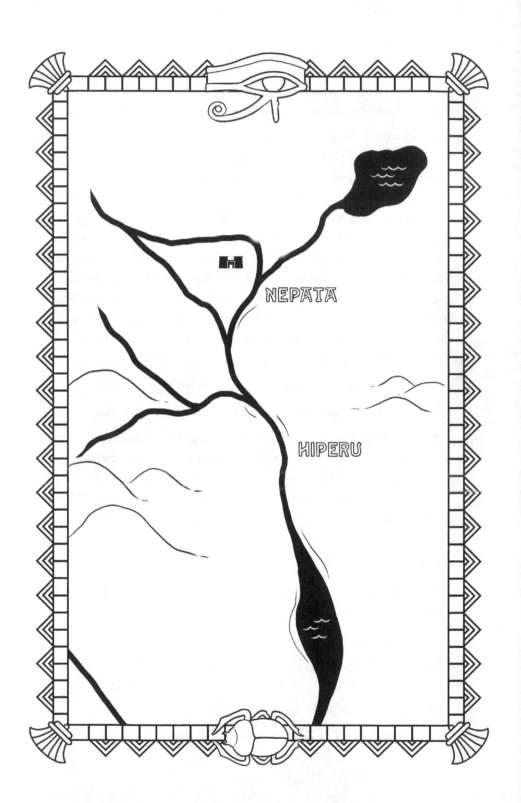

NEPATA

HIPERU

THE PALACE OF THE RISING SUN

NO ONE WILL BELIEVE A LIAR'S WARNINGS

Samaki was smiling so wide his cheeks hurt, but he dare not let his face drop. He was furious, and he would have loved nothing more than to have lashed out at the guards who had spoken to him as though he were some common peasant. He had been coming to the Paref's palace for years, trading and enjoying the Paref's favour. But, he thought darkly, the old Paref was dead.

Paref Rama was the fifth of his name, an old man nearly fifty-years-old, who had grown robust and drunk. He had reigned for nearly twenty years, Samaki realized, and perhaps his death shouldn't have shocked him as much as it did. The truth was when he had heard the news in Sareeb he had felt as though a bee had stung him in the eye. Samaki had made a large fortune from trading the savoury grape wine of the Sephian Islands to the Paref. Most in Mahat loved beer, or perhaps the honey wines from the lands north of Mahat. Most of his stock was wine, and he was not entirely certain he could sell it now.

He could still remember the first time he had come to the palace. It had been around three years ago. He had been selling wine to the Paref long before that, but always through one of his agents. He had taken his ship to the same golden quay it lay at now, meaning to unload his casks of wine. He had never dared step onto the plaza, though he would often stare enviously at the lords and ladies walking by, laughing to themselves, lounging in the gardens while musicians played delicate instruments.

"A merchant can be as rich as a Paref, if he's smart enough," he could remember telling his father that the day he had told him he would no longer go out and collect papyrus reeds or fish or hunt with him, that he was going to leave the village of marshmen and strike out on his own.

His father had laughed at him.

"A smart man wouldn't leave a good home and a good life. You're a fool, just like your mother. She always dreamed of silks and silver," he said bitterly.

Samaki had never known his mother. She had caught fever after giving birth to him and died shortly thereafter. Whether or not she ever truly had those dreams, he didn't know, but his father despised such talk.

"When you're sick of starving, you can come back," he had nodded, going back to gutting and cleaning the fish he'd caught that day. He hadn't even bothered to look up as Samaki had left.

He wouldn't go back poor and starving. He refused to. He did starve, and he was poor – at first. There were many times he did think of going home in defeat, but his father's cold laughter rang in his head. The next time he returned home he wore a gold medallion around his neck, and around his waist he had tied a blush silk belt. He thought he would see pride in his father's eyes, or the realization that Samaki had made the right choice.

His father only laughed again. "Rich as a Paref, eh? I can waste what I earn on silk too, but I'd rather eat."

Samaki had never pleased his father.

With a pain he remembered again how he never would. There was no village, there was no reed boat. It was all washed away. The little mud hut he had slept in, his childhood friends, his father... He pushed the thoughts away, swallowed them deep. He had no time to mourn, not when his position hung so precariously. The only thing that mattered was selling the wine. If he couldn't, he was in trouble. He would need to go to silver-lenders to fund his next voyage, and he knew once he fell into debt, he would never climb out of it. The silver-lenders were skilled at making sure no one did.

Every night since learning the news he had prayed to the gods Afeth and Baph that this new Paref Rama had the same tastes as the Paref before him. In Sareeb he had even visited a temple dedicated to Afeth and left an offering of some of the wine he meant to sell – giving it away seemed a trivial matter if the new Paref rejected him.

"Tell me of our new Paref," Samaki said pleasantly, still straining to look happy through his anxiety. They walked across the massive stone plaza towards the entrance of the palace. It was called the Palace of the Rising Sun, and had been home to the Parefs since the city at the base of the mountains now called Hattute was abandoned by the people of Mahat. The entrance of the palace was massive, with two black obelisks on either side inscribed with golden hieroglyphs. The palace behind them was called the Palace of the Setting Sun, and the only difference on the exterior was that their obelisks were red. It was home to the King of the Mountain Mahat, though Samaki had never traded nor met with him.

The man who had come to them on the docks was named Imotah, the tzati of the Palace of the Setting Sun, and so in charge of everything that happened within its walls. The tzatis were only second to the Paref in true power. They received their positions not only from their intelligence and wisdom, but their knowledge of spells and potions. More importantly, they received the positions by being related to the Paref. Imotah was the youngest brother of the fourth Paref Rama, and he was a few years younger than his nephew the fifth Paref Rama had been.

Imotah had the features Samaki now associated with the royal family, the weak chin and elongated head. He could still remember the shock and disappointment he had felt when he first met a member of the royal family. He had imagined shining men and women of indescribable beauty. Fishermen's daughters looked more pleasing to his eyes than the ladies of the palace.

Tzati Imotah was tall and chubby, but his eyes were too close together and his nose too big. He wore a plain wig, the hair cut to shoulder-length with straight bangs, as was the usual style, and on his chin he wore a braided beard that stuck out like a horn. The old Paref had looked much the same, except for a larger girth. The only time he had ever seen an attractive royal was when the bride came from outside the palace walls, but even then beauty was not assured.

"The young god is a splendour to behold. He is the sun and beacon of hope in Mahat," Imotah extolled, his voice dripping with sarcasm as he smiled at Samaki. The jest made some of Samaki's anger fade away and he smiled more easily.

The women, who had moved to walk behind them, giggled. The melting lumps on their wigs were only worn of the hottest of days. As they melted they released incense to mask the smell of sweat from walking in the heat all afternoon. It was sickeningly strong. Samaki wondered if they were Imotah's daughters. What he knew for certain was that they were related to the man somehow, their weak chins and buck-teeth gave it away. The palace was a tangled spider-web of inter-family relations.

"Young... A boy then?" Samaki could not remember having met him before. The old Paref had sired many sons, but only one by his High Wife, and Samaki had no doubt she had ensured her son's succession would be swift. He had only seen the High Wife Djeperu a few times, always at the Paref's side. She always had an air of command about her, and Samaki felt it would be wise to stay in her graces. Samaki knew her first child had been a girl, and had one of the sons of lesser wives who were older and stronger than her own marry that daughter. Those other sons might have been able to wrestle the throne from the current Paref, if Djeperu wasn't standing in their way.

"Not in swaddling clothes, thank the gods. He has seen fourteen years, so he is a *man*," Imotah stretched the word out, as though he didn't quite believe it was a true fact.

They entered the palace. Guards looked at them wearily, but allowed them to enter. The massive palace walls were just that, only walls. Inside the true size of the palace was revealed. It was only two storeys high. It was not the height of the palace that was impressive though, it was how much sprawling it was. The palace spread out like a great labyrinth, beautiful engravings painted over in bright colours showed the first Paref Rama's great victory against the kingdom of Matawe. He drove a chariot, wielding a bow, hundreds of men lying dead by his feet, the massive amounts of spoils being depicted went on and on, past the point Samaki could see.

"You lovely jewels go frolic by the cool pools. It is too beautiful for you to come into the dark palace." The girls giggled once more and did just as Imotah suggested, taking their walking shade and going back the way they had come.

Samaki followed Imotah into the palace. The first chamber was filled with rows and rows of giant columns, each one so large it would take five grown men holding hands to encircle one. There was no rooftop and the sun lit up beautiful tableaus of Parefs and their wives and children enjoying the nature of their gardens. From that chamber they entered a long corridor, this one with a roof. Despite the corridor's many windows, it was much darker compared to outside, though also wonderfully cool.

"How did the Paref die?"

Imotah shrugged. Despite their constant intermarriages, there was not much love between the royal family members. "Too much wine? Too much food? The Paref did not care much for his health in his final years. My doorkeeper says he died mid-thrust in his youngest wife, Nifer. They had to carry him from the harem on a litter."

"Only a god would end life so blissfully," Samaki smiled, feeling a slight pang of jealousy.

At the end of the long corridor, a few narrow halls opened up to them. There were no markings beyond the painted frescos, but Imotah had walked these halls his entire life and knew exactly which one to go down without even thinking. The corridor they chose was narrower, and Samaki could see the light of day at the end. Samaki had been to the palace many times before, but he had always been led by someone, and wasn't sure he'd ever find his way through the halls by himself.

"It was a good day to come," Imotah explained. "The Paref was legitimized as the reincarnation of his father yesterday, so today all the tzati and djoti have come calling in order to ensure they still have their positions. Otherwise, you may not have found the Paref on his throne accepting guests."

"I appreciate finally getting a taste of luck," Samaki sighed.

They exited onto a large courtyard twice of the size of the plaza, but instead of stone, the courtyard was covered in plants and dotted with cool pools of water where ibises rested and small pink flowers floated. Along the sides of the courtyard were more columns painted bright gold and red, and between them countless doors leadings into the many chambers of the palace. They went to a door on the far side of the courtyard, passing by pageboys and other lords who gave courteous nods. Samaki stared at their wigged heads. He could understand their desire to shave off their hair. Hair was a dirty thing in such heat. Why they bothered to then wear decorated and styled wigs was something he simply did not understand. He found the fake beards the lords all wore particularly amusing.

The door to the throne room was no larger than any of the others, but inside there were long steps leading up and the frame was golden. Up the steps they went, into a high roofed hall. There were massive tall windows, rose silk draped over them, gently blowing in the wind. The room was cool and inviting, and it was packed with lords and ladies. On a high dais of golden steps was the throne. The chair was so large the boy who sat in it looked like a tiny doll.

He may have been fourteen-years-old, but Samaki would have sworn he was only ten. He looked sickly thin. He barely had a chin, and even the pointed black beard tied to his face with golden string could not hide that fact. His pointy face and tiny eyes made him look more like a mouse than a man. The top row of his teeth jutted out of his lips. He was dressed in an extravagant golden silk robe, wrapped around his body and over his shoulder, and on his head he wore the Paref's golden nemes. The brow of the nemes was embossed with both the golden head of an eagle and a man wearing a feathered hat. It was so large it threatened to consume his tiny head.

On either side of him were tiny wooden benches. On his right was the familiar face of Djeperu. She wore a simple pure white linen dress, adorned with a thin red beaded belt, and on her black wig sat a thin golden band. She wore the clothes of the Paref's Mother. Despite the simplicity of the dress, with her piercing black eyes and high cheekbones, she still looked far more regal than the young girl less than half her age on the left of the Paref.

The young girl looked to be about fourteen as well. She had a beautiful round face with wide dark eyes, and beneath her sheer white dress he could make out the dark circles of her nipples. She was covered in more jewels than the giggling girls who had been following Imotah. At her neck was a thick necklace in the shape of a bird made entirely out of rubies, and her wig was made from golden thread.

Next to the seated figures were young girls wearing tunics and plain black wigs, holding long fans shaped like palm fronds, dutifully moving them in rhythm with each other. At the foot of the dais stairs, and indeed all around the room, stood broad-shouldered guards. Moving through the crowd of lords were tunic-clad girls holding golden trays topped with fruit. There were many waiting to speak to the Paref, but Imotah cut to the front of them, interrupting a portly fat man who was grovelling before the throne.

"My lord Paref and dearest nephew," Imotah said loudly, a lovely smile on his narrow face.

"Uncle," Rama smiled, and it was an ugly sight to see his large teeth emerge from his mouth. The beautiful woman to his side looked straight ahead, seemingly not wanting to acknowledge anyone in the room, but Djeperu held Samaki's gaze. "Have you come with more gifts?"

"Always, beloved nephew," Imotah bowed low. "And my lady, the Paref's High Wife. My lords, I present to you the glorious merchant Samaki, who was loved by your father. Samaki, behold the opulent Paref Rama and his High Wife, the southern Princess, eldest daughter of King Utarna of the Sea Mahat, Merneith."

"My lords," Samaki put on his most charming smile, bowing as low as his body could bend.

"Rise, merchant," Rama commanded. He had a weak voice, Samaki realized. It seemed the gods hadn't been willing to offer the boy any gifts when he was born, save for his father's name. "I fear my father's memory died with him, but his spirit resides in me now, and I'm sure the love he felt for you dwells in me now."

Djeperu leaned over and whispered something into her son's ear before he continued. "Yes... Samaki. I have heard the name. It was said you could produce the finest wine in all the world from the hold of your ship."

"Of that I know not, but the Paref Rama before you loved well the wine I brought for him."

"Yes, that is good..." Rama looked bored, and his eyes turned away from him to stare at the Princess Merneith at his side with longing. Samaki was losing his attention. Imotah gave him a look that said he could not, or would not, help him beyond this point.

"I was most grieved to learn of Paref Rama's death when I arrived in Sareeb. The gods, it seemed, were horrified as well, for they sent a great wave throughout the Sea Mahat, no doubt it was their endless tears at his loss," he tried to sound light-hearted, but his voice twinged as he spoke. *They loved your father so much, they had to take mine in his stead.*

"Yes," Rama turned back to him, his face troubled. "I have heard of the flood. It was unfortunate of the gods to do that. But when the Paref's soul wanders, Afeth runs freely."

Afeth. His ship was named for the god of chaos, but Samaki did not bother saying so aloud.

"As it happened, I was in Sareeb because I was returning from Serepty with my ship's hold filled with the grape wine Paref Rama loved so dearly. If you are soon to be crowned, I would be honoured to sell you all I have for your great feast."

"Sell?" The Paref's Mother looked annoyed and Rama followed suit. Obviously having been given gifts all day, the boy was expecting the same from Samaki.

"It loathes me to sell and not give, aye, but I fear I cannot afford to give it freely, as much as I wish to. The most I can do is offer it at a lower price than the glorious Paref Rama offered me, for I must hire new men and, indeed, must feed my family," his voice seemed to lower at the last word. What family? His family was gone...

Djeperu leaned over and whispered something else to her son. She had never been so bold with her husband in front of his subjects.

"I am not interested in special favours," Rama said, and Samaki felt his heart drop in his chest. "I will buy your wine, and pay the price same as my father, to honour him at my wedding feast. Instead, you may give me another gift."

Samaki looked at Imotah uncertainly, but the tzati seemed to have no idea what the boy meant either. "Oh, and what gift may a lowly merchant such as I give to a great Paref?"

"I have decreed one of my duties as a new Paref is to show my enemies and allies alike my grace and power. I wish to send tribute to the great kings of the lesser kingdoms. I would have use of your ship."

He couldn't refuse, he knew that. If he refused the boy wouldn't buy the wine, and if he didn't sell the wine, he might as well sell his ship. He forced his smile. "And where would you have my ship sail?"

"I would have you sail north to Hattute, the city nestled at the base of the mountains. I wish to honour King Hatturigus, apparently the sixth king of that name to rule there. They call him King Under the Mountain."

Samaki had heard some of the tales about the wars in the mountains, where there ruled two kings, the King Under the Mountain in Hattute, and the King Over the Mountain who lived in the high peaks of the city Nesate. There were also stories of five Queens or, some said, five witches, who wished the tear the kingdom asunder. The constant wars in the mountains had kept him from ever sailing there before. There was not much profit for a merchant who did not peddle weapons in war-mongering countries.

"Nothing would please me more than doing this for you, my Paref," Samaki bowed again, this bow decidedly not as low as his first.

"Imotah, see to the arrangements," Rama waved them away and they stepped aside.

The fat lord they had cut off earlier glared at them, but turned to the Paref with a smile. "As I was saying..."

They left the throne room and went back out into the courtyard.

"Did you know he would ask me to do that?" Samaki turned to Imotah.

"I honestly had no idea," Imotah smiled, and Samaki couldn't tell if he was lying, or what the man would have to gain from being dishonest. These people bathed in lies. Samaki thought they often forgot they could tell the truth.

"Why even ask a merchant to carry tribute to a king?" Samaki was already beginning to calculate how long it would take and how much it would cost. Would he have enough space in his cargo to carry goods to trade? Otherwise he would lose too much on the trip.

"I suppose, like all the Parefs before him, he would rather spend his gold on jewels and feasts instead of state matters. He is only sending the tributes because his mother insisted he do it. New rulers are always seen as being weak until they prove themselves, either in friendship, or through warfare. My noblest nephew is not a warrior."

Samaki was glad at least to have solved the problem of selling the wine. Now he would just have to make the exchange and hire new crew for the journey north. And what of the Whisperers?

"That reminds me," Samaki said as they left behind the courtyard for the dim hallways that led to the palace entrance. "I travel with two... people. They wish to speak to the Paref. They are holy messengers, and they believe they have an important message to share with him."

"We get more holy men than we can count. They are a bore, and I doubt my shining nephew wants to be bothered by them."

He knew he owed the Whisperers nothing, but he had grown a fondness for Tersh. They had often played senet and talked during their journey north, and he wanted to help her and her son if he could.

"Come back to my ship and meet them. Decide for yourself if they're worthy to go before the Paref."

Imotah shrugged. "Very well, I had no other plans this afternoon. I have often thought of you as a friend. It would be my pleasure to help you."

Samaki knew it would also be Imotah's pleasure to be owed a favour.

When they returned to the ship, the Whisperers were instantly on their feet, anxious looks on their faces, while the other crewmembers only looked on with mild interest. Samaki and Imotah walked up the gangplank.

Tiyharqu greeted them at the top. "Captain," she nodded, then turned to Imotah and bowed. "Gracious tzati. You honour us with your presence."

Samaki pointed to the Whisperers. "These are the holy messengers."

"I thought they'd be men, not a woman and a child. This one's younger than the Paref," Imotah almost laughed. Looking Kareth up and down.

"But he certainly looks older," Samaki muttered.

"Can we go before the Paref?" Tersh asked.

Kareth looked at Imotah, his silver eyes shining, and Imotah was taken aback. He grabbed Kareth's chin, looking long and deep into his eyes. "Never in my entire life..." he whispered to himself.

Samaki could understand Imotah's reaction. Him and his crew had often talked about the strange silver eyes. He had never seen eyes like those on the men of Mahat, or even in Serepty, where eyes could be the pigment of water or a cloudy sky. Once he had seen a woman with the shades of leaves behind her lashes, but never silver. No, the only time he had seen eyes like those was when he had met a Rhagepe once. He heard all Rhagepe had silver eyes like those. He had imagined only the sand witches had them. Most of the crewmen were weary of Kareth because of those eyes.

Kareth jerked his head away, turning towards Tersh with an annoyed expression.

"Dage ki karlai thenu morikah tomech mo hothomeiru?" He muttered angrily, and Samaki could only imagine he hadn't made a kind comment.

Imotah's eyes narrowed. "Just where do you two come from?"

Tersh looked at Samaki uncertainly.

"No one will believe a liar's warnings," Samaki cautioned.

"We come from the desert," Tersh answered slowly.

Imotah's eyes widened. "Go-men?" He turned to Samaki incredulously. "You sailed all this way with Go-men on board?" He sniffed the air. "I thought they all smelled like blood and decaying corpses."

Tersh looked angry, but Samaki tried to smile. "I made them bathe," though in truth he sometimes thought they smelled better than most of his crew. "These are good people. Though the young one is slightly troublesome at times..." he laughed, and Tersh was forced to smile.

"The Paref will never agree to see Whisperers," Imotah said simply.

Kareth looked eager to know what was being said, and when he saw the disappointment on Tersh's face, he began to tug on her cloak and ask her a question in their tongue. Tersh pushed him away.

"We speak for the gods. He will see us," Tersh insisted.

Imotah laughed. "Paref Rama *is* a god," though Samaki knew the man did not believe his own words. "He can speak for himself."

"The flood in Sareeb is only the beginning. Terrible things will come to pass unless we can warn the Paref," Tersh spoke carefully, her voice lowered; her eyes seemed darker.

Samaki knew Imotah was not a superstitious man. Nevertheless, there were too many stories of terrible things happening to men who had been cursed by the Whisperers to be ignored. Curses sent by Whisperers had brought down some of the mightiest Parefs. The city of Hattute had been built by the sixth and last Paref Amotefen, who had hunted down and slaughtered every Whisperer he found within the border of Mahat. Amotefen was killed by his own cousin, and his great city fell to a prince from the kingdom of Matawe. Since then the people of Matawe had constantly been at war with each other because of that city, because it had been tainted by Whisperer blood.

"I honestly don't know how I can help you. If I bring you two before the Paref, he'll strip me of my position – or even my life. And, he'll ignore whatever you have to say. It would take years of convincing before he'd ever consent to be in the same room as you."

"The flood is not proof enough?" Tersh asked incredulously.

"A hundred floods would not be proof enough your gods held any power in Mahat," Imotah waved a hand at her dismissively.

"Perhaps you can convince the Paref to see you in time," Samaki said, feeling strangely guilty that he could not stay and help them longer. "I need to leave soon and head north to Hattute, the city at the base of the mountain. I won't be able to help you from there."

"The mountains?" Tersh looked surprised. "I need to go there, and speak with their king."

"It seems you need to speak to every king..."

"No, he needs to speak to the Paref, my mission is to speak to the ruler of the mountain. We only travelled together because our paths were the same."

"What do you mean that's the only reason you travelled here together? What are you saying?" Samaki narrowed his eyes at him.

"I must follow the river north," Tersh hesitated only a moment before her face became resolved. "Take me with you," she looked at Kareth with a pained expression. "I cannot waste time here in Nepata."

"You'd leave your son here?" Samaki was surprised. Were Whisperers really so cold?

"He's not..." Tersh trailed off.

"He's not your son, is he?" Samaki chuckled. "*You and yours* indeed. I swear, the more you fool me the more I like you. You Whisperers are as slippery as fish."

"What was that you said about liars, Samaki?" Imotah asked in an amused voice.

"He'll find no help here," Samaki looked at the boy piteously.

"He cannot come with me... He must follow the gods. We all must. The sticks fall, and the pawn moves. Isn't that so?" Tersh looked at Samaki with the face of a defeated woman.

Imotah smiled sweetly. "He need not starve. Any house is always in need of a servant. I think my stables could use another boy."

Samaki eyed him warily. He was uneasy of making any deals with the tzati. He seemed as trustworthy as a money-lender.

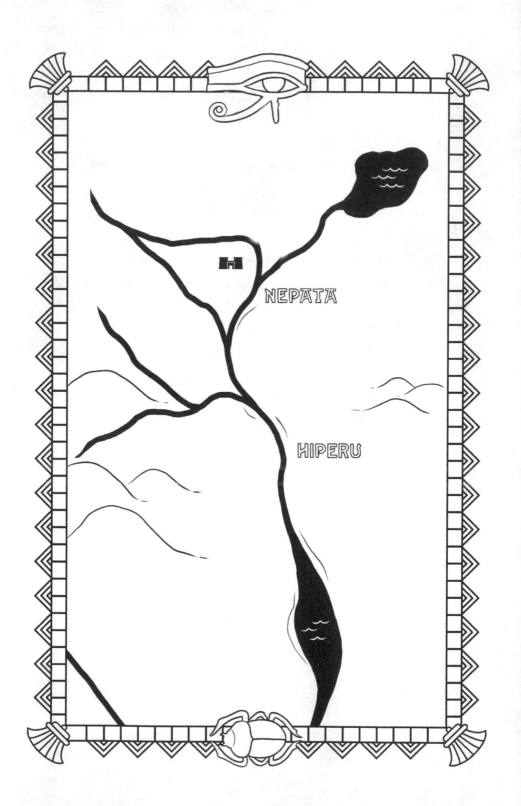

NEPATA

NOTHING IN THE FUTURE CAN EVER CHANGE YOUR PAST

"Tomorrow," Tersh said as she entered the room, and Kareth understood what she meant well enough. He'd been spending every night for the past dozen or so days falling asleep in anxiety, knowing that soon Tersh and the others would sail away and Kareth would be left alone with the men of Mahat and his mission.

Tomorrow.

It was too soon. Kareth had been trying to learn their language earnestly since coming to Imotah's home. He had finally accepted the fact that soont he wouldn't have Tersh to interpret for him, but it wasn't enough time. He was getting better at speaking, asking for simple things like food or directions, but he was still struggling to understand the replies he got. Without Tersh, he would become no better than a deaf mute in a stranger's home.

Imotah had invited them to stay in his estate while Samaki made preparations to set sail for Matawe. The tall tzati had a massive house, a palace in its own right, though miniscule compared to the Paref's. Surrounded by gardens and ponds was the house, a large rectangular building made from white stone, covered in painted with frescoes of wars and gods and the strange hieroglyphs neither Kareth nor Tersh could understand.

"Who was going to teach a Whisperer to read?" Tersh shrugged when Kareth had asked her why she had never learned to understand the hieroglyphs. "And what child wants to learn to read? I was more interested in climbing trees."

Although the canals wound around the estate, the entrance led to one of the few roads in the city, a grand boulevard lined with statues and fruit trees. The stables were next to the gates, but Kareth avoided going there. There were many such homes in Nepata to the west of the palaces, where the rich djoti and tzati lived.

Although Imotah allowed the Whisperers to stay in his home, he did not extend the courtesy of giving them a room to sleep in. Instead they slept in the same room as Tiyharqu. The room was so large it could have accommodated fifty men. When Kareth first walked into it, he couldn't understand why anyone would need so much space. What was the point of having a massive palace and giant rooms?

Silks hung from the windows, there were marble tables with gold bowls filled with fresh dates, olives, pomegranates, and other fruits Kareth hadn't learned the words for yet. There was a massive bed in the centre of the room, with posts on each corner and an awning of silver silk covered it. There were living plants as well, in the corners and hanging from the walls and ceilings. The walls had carvings inlaid with gold. Kareth was taken with them, tracing the lines of faces with his fingers, wondering who could carve stone so perfectly.

"His name is Paref Neema," Tiyharqu said, suddenly at his side, and Tersh translated. "He was the first Paref. He united the Sea Mahat to the Lake Mahat."

There were several images of Neema on the wall, and Kareth realized they told a story. The first image was of a boy, in one hand a sword, the other a staff. The next picture he was grown, and lines of a hundred tiny men were carved next to him, making Neema look like a colossus standing among them. In another picture he held the hand of a woman and the two were staring into each other's eyes. In the next the woman was gone, and in her place Neema held the heads of a dozen dead men by the hair, and on his own head he not wore a tall hat, the same one he had seen the Sea Mahat King wear. *A crown*, Kareth realized.

"He won his crown in battle, but afterwards there was peace in the Mahats."

"What happened to him?"

Tiyharqu laughed. "He died. All men die, even Parefs. He died three thousand years ago."

Three thousand years? Kareth scrunched his face trying to wonder how many turns of the moon that was, how many full cycles of the constellations. He'd only lived through one. What could he do with that much time? Could he learn the tongue of Mahat? Could he convince the Paref to heed the old ways and appease the gods? How much time did he have anyway? How much time had already been wasted?

He spent most of his days in the room staring at the murals around the room while the Afeth made ready to sail. Samaki was busy finding extra cargo to take north with them to trade, and Tiyharqu was busy looking for a crew. Every day Tersh would give him an update, and it twisted Kareth's heart. She will be gone soon. Once they were gone, he would be alone. The gods were always there, but he could not hear them. Since he fell in the Hiperu, since the dream of the horrible beast devouring Tersh and an entire city, he had no dreams from them either, as far as he could tell.

He fell asleep on his pile of cushions on the floor staring at Neema's face, a voice inside his head whispering *tomorrow, tomorrow, tomorrow…*

The next morning she struggled to wake as wisps of morning light began to creep into the room. He felt exhausted. Kareth had gotten used to seeing Tersh in a tunic, but that morning she did not put the garment on, and turned her Ancestral Cloak out so the bones could plainly be seen. Kareth cracked a smile, and reached for his own cloak, but Tersh shook his head.

"We talked about this," she said. She was stern, but Kareth heard a softness.

Kareth's hands clutched at the familiar leather, feeling the hard bones, the bones of his father and his father and on and on and on, though some of the older ones were so brittle he knew they'd shatter if he was too rough with them. He imagined some of these men might have lived the same time as Paref Neema had.

"Can't I just wear it today? Just to say… goodbye?" The word was surprisingly hard to say.

"The servants will see you. So long as you work in Imotah's stables, you can never wear it."

"Why can't I just turn it around, like we did before?" He'd asked this question before, and Tersh had answered before, a dozen times or so, and the exasperation in Tersh's eyes made it clear she was tired of having the same argument.

She answered all the same. "No stable boy wears a cloak."

"I'm not a stable boy, I'm a chief's son!" It was humiliating to serve another man, to clean up after an *animal*. His father never would have suffered something like this.

Tersh went down on her knees, looking at Kareth with dark eyes. "You will always be a chief's son, whether you wear a cloak or not, whether you clean after horses or starve on the street. Nothing in the future can ever change your past." Tersh reached out and put her hands on Kareth's, pulling the cloak away. "You will wear it again, when you stand before the Paref and speak for the gods you will wear it. Until then, you must keep it hidden.

"If you make a friend of Imotah, maybe you can see the Paref soon. No one is going to help you unless you help yourself first. Besides, you need to learn their language. No man in Mahat respects someone who cannot speak their tongue. If you want the Paref to heed you, he must respect you," Tersh spoke urgently, but Kareth was too bitter to respond.

"You must learn," she finally added.

Reluctantly, he rolled his cloak up, tying it into a small bundle so it looked like any other bedroll. He took the broach he had used to mend it, and put it on his belt as a buckle instead. When he came back he wouldn't return to this room but would go to the servant's quarters. He put his scratchy tunic on and stared around the lush room, at Paref Neema sitting by himself on a throne. Where had the woman Neema stared at so intently gone? He wanted to ask, but he knew he wouldn't like the answer.

They made their way out to the gardens, the sun just above the walls. It was always cool in the mornings, and he felt cold in his tunic and wished he had worn his cloak despite Tersh's warnings. The servants stared at Tersh as she walked by, some looking shocked or confused. A few looked at her with anger. Imotah saw them and smiled. Samaki was there with him, and six guards were standing with bridled horses, some of which had packs on, but the others only had a saddle for riding.

Kareth had never ridden a horse, and was frightened of doing so now, so he was slightly relieved when he realized there weren't enough horses for everyone assembled. Some people had to walk.

Samaki and Imotah were speaking loud enough for all to hear, and he could tell from their cadence and gestures they were saying some kind of formal farewell, though he couldn't pick out the words. Servants were lined up around them for the departure as well. Kareth couldn't stop playing with his belt, his fingers feeling too jittery to stay still. Instead they traced the woman's face on his buckle. He wished they would stop talking so they could move on.

When they finished, Samaki and Tiyharqu mounted up with the guards. It was all for show, Tersh had told Kareth. They didn't need guards for protection; it was just for Imotah and Samaki to seem more important than they really were. Kareth and Tersh followed behind on foot with a few more guards. The horses moved at a leisurely pace. Outside the gate a few members of the Afeth's crew joined them, having come from the inns. The rest of the crew would be waiting at the dock.

The streets were bare, save for a few people pushing carts here and there. They were most likely shopkeepers taking new wares to their stores or traders. Kareth hadn't left the grounds of Imotah's home since arriving, not caring to explore the city, but he now felt himself looking around and wondering what lay behind buildings and down alleys. There was an entire world around him he had been ignoring. This place would be his home until he finished his mission. Shouldn't he get to know it better?

"How many people do you think live here?" Kareth asked, not knowing what else to say.

"A thousand thousand," Tersh shrugged. "You don't see it here, but in the poorer parts of the city people live on top of each other. Houses built on houses, small rooms housing entire families."

"I thought you'd never been here before."

"I haven't, but all cities are much the same. The rich have palaces. The poor have hovels. These people live like heathens. Watch you don't fall into their ways. The gods would not forgive you."

He had no interest in their palaces or their hovels. The only bed he wanted was soft sand, the only roof the starry night. The only home he needed was the desert, and he would only tolerate this place until he could return there one day.

They soon saw the Afeth's two masts in the distance. They had left her at a dockyard at the end of the grand street, with a hundred or so ships mostly belonging to the lords in this area, but the Afeth stood out from among them. Other ships were more beautiful in their decoration with gold flakes and colourful paints and wooden statues carved along the gunwales of the gods of Mahat. Yet the Afeth was taller, sleeker, and longer than any of them, and there was a beauty about the simplicity of the red snake coiling around the ship from bow to stern.

He would miss the ship, Kareth realized suddenly with a pain. He had spent so long travelling on it that it had become a kind of home to him. He would miss leaning on the gunwale, staring out at the palm trees and they floated by, spotting tall white ibises or watching the fishermen with their nets in the early mornings, waving as they went by, shouting pleasantries. Tersh might come back one day, but would he ever see the Afeth again?

"I dreamed she would bring us here," Kareth said absentmindedly.

"Maybe you did," Tersh smiled.

The sadness and worry only increased. "I dreamed the beast would devour you, too." *Don't get on that ship*, he wanted to cry, but he knew Tersh wouldn't listen.

"The Rhagepe say sometimes dreams are hard to understand. The images they see are not a complete truth, but a... representation of the truth," Tersh seemed to be struggling to think of a way to explain her thoughts. "You saw birds carrying us, but the truth was a ship. You saw a beast devour me, but that doesn't mean it was the truth."

"Beast or no, being devoured can't be a good sign."

"Hm... maybe not, but I expect my journey to be long and hard. It may feel like a beast devouring me at times, but that doesn't make it literal."

They reached the Afeth and Samaki was shouting orders at his men before he even dismounted. The crew buzzed around the ship like bees, but the Whisperers stood still.

Sef walked up to them, a large smile on his face as he put his weathered hands on Kareth's small shoulder. "Be good, eh. Don't make any trouble," he winked at him.

"Thank you... for..." Kareth wasn't sure what the word was. Thank you for teaching me words. Thank you for pulling me from the water. Thank you for taking me from the jaws of that animal. Thank you for saving my life. Thank you for being my friend.

Sef merely nodded. "You're welcome boy." He smiled at Tersh. "He'll be fine." He walked away to leave the two to say goodbye.

A long silence settled between them as the final preparations and checks were made on the ship.

"How long will it take?" Kareth finally asked.

"To reach Matawe? Samaki says it will take ten days or so to reach Hattute."

"And then... will the chief there see you? Will he listen? How long until you come back this way?"

Tersh looked at him sadly. "You know I don't know the answer."

Kareth's eyes felt itchy. He wanted to cry then, just as he had wanted to when he had left his mother and his tribe by the foot of the mountain. He had been preparing himself for this moment, but still it hurt more than he expected. He couldn't think of what to say, and his mouth hung open looking for words.

"I will come back this way, when I am finished..." Tersh looked away, maybe wondering if it would be just as difficult to go before the king of the mountain as it was for Kareth to see the Paref. "We can travel back to the desert, together."

But her words had no weight to them, and it seemed like they floated away with the wind.

Tiyharqu, standing on the deck, smiled down at them and called out something in a friendly voice, but it made Tersh frown.

"We're leaving," she muttered.

"No, don't..." Kareth trailed off. "I've never been alone before."

"You're not alone. Make friends with Imotah. Make friends with the stable boys. Above all else, learn." She put her hands on Kareth's shoulders. "You are the son of a chief. You were chosen to speak for the Goddess of Life. You crossed the sea of sand and sailed up the Hiperu. You will speak to the Paref. You will make sure the gods are appeased. Dream of that, if you must dream of anything."

Kareth tried to say something back, but he couldn't think of any words, save for one: "Goodbye."

"Goodbye." Tersh turned and walked up the plank to the ship.

Men on the docks cast off the ropes, and as the ship began to drift away Tiyharqu gave an order and the oars came out, plunging into the dark water. The Afeth turned and began to pull away. Tersh walked to the stern of the ship, raising a hand in farewell.

"We were the first!" Tersh called out in a strong, clear voice.

"And we will be the last!" Kareth called back, but his voice cracked. He raised his hand in return, feeling for a moment like he could reach out and touch her, but the ship moved away. Tersh became smaller and smaller until Kareth could no longer make out the features of her face. He was going to stay until he lost sight of the ship, but he felt someone nudge his shoulder. He turned back and saw a guard standing there, motioning back the way they came. The other guards had already mounted the horses and were ready to go back to Imotah's estate.

He turned away from the water's edge, wiping away the tears from his cheeks, wondering when he had started crying, following the mounted guards. They rode faster on the way back and Kareth couldn't keep up with them at the pace he was walking, so he let them trot ahead, looking around the city. More people were out now, litters being carried by hunched-over men were going this way and that.

He let his feet lead the way without thinking of where he was going, and before long he was back at the walls of Imotah's home. He could see the guards dismounting by the stables. He knew that's where he had to go, but he suddenly felt lost. Was there someone he needed to speak to first? He walked through the gate, the guards giving him no more attention than they might to a stray dog.

A young girl, barely a woman, was walking across the garden towards him. He hardly saw her until she stood in front of him. She wore a simple white shift and a plain black braided wig. She wasn't too much older than him. She had a big nose and a small chin and he thought she looked rather funny. Yet her smile was kind and it made him feel better.

"You are Kareth?" She asked slowly, and he could understand her words well enough to nod. "Please come."

She motioned towards the main building and he followed. They did not go to the main entrance, but this time went to a small one to the left of the building. The door was down a few stairs. It was so small his head brushed against the top. He realized most people coming through here would have to stoop.

Unlike the grand halls with large windows and beautiful painted frescoes of Imotah's home, the servant's wing was narrow and dark, with slits instead of windows for light. There were more servants than Kareth had realized. There were so many that the halls here seemed flooded with people, all shoving past, carrying trays or tools, all looking as though they were working on some important task. The girl took him to a small room. The floor was sloped and there were drainage holes, and buckets full of water, and he realized this was a washing room.

"Off," she ordered with a smile, pointing at his tunic.

Kareth felt strangely self-confident as he undid the belt and took off his tunic. He had never worn clothes until coming to Nepata, that was true, but he wasn't used to having a girl stare at him with a strange half-smile on her face, as though he were there for her amusement. There were a few wooden stools in there and she pointed to one.

"Sit," she commanded again and he sat, as a rather rotund woman entered the room with a young boy in tow. Unlike the young girl, the large woman wore no wig, but wore coloured powder around her eyes on and her cheeks. Her head was wrapped in white linen, making her head look like a large painted egg. The young boy, who wore a simple tunic, was bald save for a single black tress of hair at the side of his head. He carried a basket.

Kareth was focused on the newcomers and hadn't noticed the young girl pick up a bucket of water and turn it over his head. Kareth sputtered and nearly fell backwards as the water splashed down on him. The girl giggled, placing the bucket on the ground as the boy and she grabbed something from the back. A second later they were scrubbing his skin with something rough that felt like a stone.

The rotund woman muttered something angrily as he tried to pull away. One look from her stony gaze was enough to make him stop struggling and sit still as the two others scrubbed away at him, both chuckling to themselves. Finally, with his skin red and tingling, they stopped and the woman pulled a large curved blade out of the basket. Kareth's eyes went wide in horror, and in his distraction the girl managed to overturn another bucket of water over his head.

"Stand," the woman ordered, and Kareth was obedient. He stood deathly still as they shaved the hair from his head. Tersh had told him they would, so he had been expecting that, but he was shocked when the woman moved down and began to shave the rest of him. There were few hairs to speak of, but she shaved them off all the same. Kareth felt strangely faint as the knife moved closer to his manhood, but the woman's hands were deft and not a single red mark was left in the blade's wake.

When they were finished, Kareth raised his head to feel his shaved scalp. It was smooth, and strange, and it was with an odd sense of disappointment that he realized they had left a little patch of hair on the side of his head.

They think of me as a child, he realized. Only children had tresses on their heads. But he had the mark of a man tattooed on his shoulder, and he felt indignant.

"No," he said, pointing to the hair they had left. "I man."

The girl giggled again and the woman's mouth cracked into a smile for the first time.

"Fine," she said, and took the knife to his head once more, shaving away the rest.

The girl picked up another bucket of water, but this time Kareth saw and took the bucket from her, emptying it over his own head. The boy handed him his tunic and belt and he dressed himself once more.

He wished he could see himself. He must look just like any other man from Mahat. If his tribe walked into the room that very moment, would they know him as a Whisperer, or would they think him as a stranger? The thought was oddly thrilling. *If I can look like them, I can act like them. If I can act like them, maybe the Paref will listen to me.*

The woman and boy left him alone with the girl, and she led him back into the narrow passages. She was speaking to him, but he could barely pick up anything she was saying, and he was too distracted to really listen. He was too busy trying to look down passages. He wondered where he would sleep and eat and all the other things. He soon realized they were going back the way they had come. As they went outside once more, Kareth was nearly blinded by the sunlight.

Across the gardens they walked to the stables. Kareth entered the place he had been dreading to see.

The stables were warm but smelled of manure, and damp oats and horses, all of it stifling Kareth's senses as he walked in. There were twenty horses kept in the stables. The stone floors were sloped with troughs at the end to catch the horses' urine and keep the stable as dry as possible, but still he knew it must be difficult to keep the floors clean every day. Each stall had a stone water basin and tethers and there were twice as many men and boys working the stables than horses living there.

The stable master, a lean hard man with leathery skin and a few missing teeth, was yelling at a stable boy who was unsuccessfully trying to force a horse into a stall as they entered. He saw them and started towards the entrance with an annoyed look on his face. Kareth couldn't help but instantly dislike the man. He wondered if the horses felt the same and if he had lost those teeth because one had kicked him. The girl said something and he knew she was introducing the man.

"Piye?" He asked, fairly certain that's what she said his name was.

Piye barked something in a gruff voice, but was only met with Kareth's blank stare. He spat, his expression only growing more annoyed, and grabbed a shovel from the wall, thrusting it towards him and pointing at another stable boy who was using a similar shovel to scoop horse dung into a bucket.

Kareth's face scrunched up in disgust, and without thinking he quickly – and rather forcefully, said, "No."

He was still looking at the poor stable boy when he felt the blow to his face. Piye struck him so hard he stumbled, and unable to get his balance back he fell to the ground, his face pulsating in pain. He felt his jaw in shock, wondering if Piye had knocked any of his own teeth out.

Piye yelled something at him, holding the shovel out again, and Kareth realized the girl had disappeared. He was shaking, and struggled to push himself back to his feet. Now he understood. Outside he was a chief's son. Outside he spoke for the Goddess of Life. Outside he was free and careless. In here he was nothing.

He took the shovel.

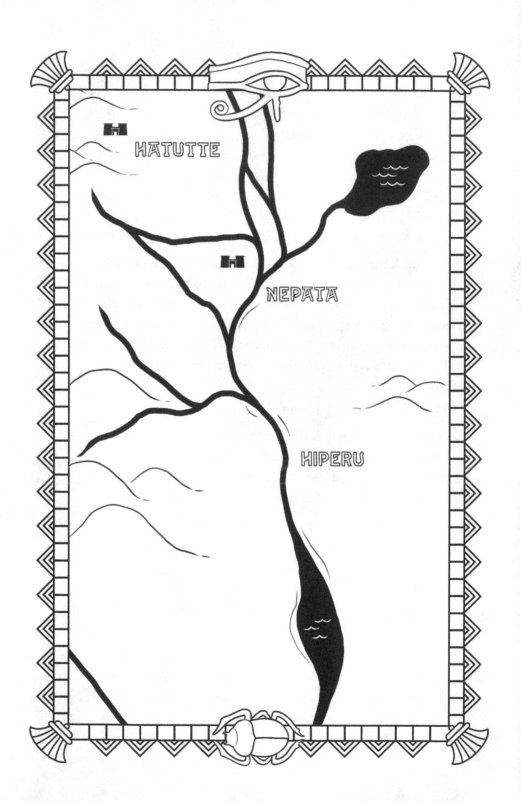

HATTUTE

BOTH KINGS WILL SEE YOU

The city was as much a part of the mountain as the rocks and trees that surrounded it. The great palace, the Hall of a Thousand Gods, was carved into the mountain itself. From this distance they could just make out the dark holes that served as windows into the cavernous halls. They said most of the rooms had been carved before Paref Amotefen had come to this place and decided to build the great city. Whether people, or the gods, or some other force had carved them, no one knew.

The walls surrounding the city were a semi-circle, meeting at the mountains. They were not nearly as high or as daunting as the walls of Nepata, but they were much thicker and built from dark stones. They made Samaki feel uneasy. All the buildings were made from that same dark mountain stone.

There was only one great gate they could see into the city, a gate on the northern side of the semicircle. Although the river they sailed up flowed from the city, the way was barred by walls and underwater grates. A large quay had several dozen ships docked there. They would have to walk into the city itself. A long line of people streamed into the gate, most of them merchants from the lands of Ethia and Kuroe, their skin the same as Tiyharqu's dark charcoal. This was the city where three great lands met; Mahat, Ethia, and Matawe, but for all that the city still paled next to the richness of Nepata.

The land around Hattute was rich and full of foliage. Hundreds of rivers flowed from the mountains here, eventually collecting to become the Hiperu river. Paref Amotefen had realized that this was the perfect place for a great city, just as the prince of Matawe who took it after Amotefen died realized it would be a city worthy of conquering. But neither of them had been realized that this city would be a cause of strife and war in the two hundred years that had followed its founding.

Tiyharqu was busy throwing ropes to young men by the wooden quays. The river here had been dug out to be wider, to moor the many boats that needed to dock. The reason for the single gate was plain enough. The city had been built to be impenetrable. Despite that fact, it had fallen more than once before. The walls never failed it, but the people manning them certainly did.

"Stay with the ship," Samaki nodded to Tiyharqu as the ropes were tied off and a plank was lowered on the quay. "The Go-man and I will get some carts for the tribute." Samaki motioned for Tersh to follow him.

"Why do you need my help getting a cart?" Tersh asked.

"I thought you might like to see the city a little," he smiled, but the truth was wrapped around Tersh's shoulders. "Leave your spear." He knew with a Whisperer at his side crowds would part to let them through. He wondered when the last time a Whisperer might have come to this city was. He didn't know, but he did know that every single man, woman, and child in that city had heard stories of the Whisperers and had grown up believing them to have otherworldly powers.

As they neared, Samaki could see that there weren't as many people trying to get into the city as he had thought, but the gates were so narrow that it took a considerable amount of time for merchants to get their carts through. Samaki, annoyed that he had been sent here in the first place, frustrated with his future dangling by the whimsy of a child with a crown, felt a confidence only the truly desperate understood. He ignored the looks the merchants gave as he passed and walked up to the gates. A few guards wearing boiled leather skins and half helms with nose guards stood at the gate holding long spears. They had wild dark hair coming from beneath their helmets and around their mouths were long moustaches and pointed beards. They looked at Samaki with bored expressions. And then they saw Tersh.

At first there was a look of confusion on the guards' faces, and then one of them leaned into another man's ear and whispered something urgent. Soon all the guards were talking excitedly. By the time Samaki reached them he couldn't help but smile at their wide eyes and chalky skin as the blood seemed to drain away from them.

"W-w-what do you want?" One of the guards stuttered in accented words of Mahat. In this part of the world, the crossroads between three lands, the tongue of Mahat was preferred. None of the guards could tear their eyes away from Tersh, who by this point looked fairly uncomfortable by the attention.

"Carts, perhaps three. We bring tribute for your glorious King, on behalf of the Paref, newly reborn in the great city of Nepata."

"Is she... She can't be... Can she?"

"Go-man? Rattlecloak?" Samaki asked, a gleam in his eye.

"I am a Whisperer," Tersh corrected in annoyance. "I am called Tersh Hal'Reekrah of the tribe Go'angrin."

One of the guards had already walked away and was yelling towards someone in the distance. Samaki saw with a pleased sense of satisfaction that a few guards in the distance were hurriedly hitching up three carts to some donkeys for their use.

"Clear the way!" Another guard started shouting at the merchants to vacate the area around the gate so the empty carts could quickly move through.

Tersh had moved away from the crowd, seemingly to ignore the stares, and instead looked toward the city. Samaki thought the buildings of Hattute were hardly impressive in height or width. They all looked rather similar, squat and small, but Samaki admired the order of it all. The city had been built on a grid, and everything was completely symmetrical. The main road from the gate to the walls surrounding the Hall of a Thousand Gods was wide, and lined with statues of leopards, each one taunt, as though it were about to pounce on the people walking down the middle of the street.

Finally the carts were through and Samaki and Tersh helped take them back to the Afeth. Tiyharqu laughed as she saw them approach. She stood on the quay now, surrounded by a few barrels and boxes, while the crew carried more things down the ramp from the hold.

"That was fast, Maki! We've barely started unloading!"

"Ship captains are well respected in these parts," he winked at his first mate, while Tersh sulked off to another part of the ship.

If he was honest with himself, Samaki would have admitted he was nervous to walk up to the Hall of a Thousand Gods, even with three carts full of tribute from the new Paref. He had never heard a kind story told of the warring kings. There was much treachery and death within these walls. He prayed he would be able to sell or trade the extra goods he had brought along the trip, but the dark city made him think he would be more than content to leave as soon as the goods and Tersh were delivered.

This was where the Whisperers had been slaughtered, their screams washing the streets of the city. There was a deep curse in this place, and he worried that the simple act of stepping through the gates would taint him. He wanted to get in and out as quickly as possible. He knew the guards would be eager to help if he had Tersh at his side. The fear of the Whisperers was deep in this city.

He pushed his foolish thoughts aside and picked ten of his crew to accompany him, the rest he left with Tiyharqu and the ship.

"I'll be back by this evening, and then we'll decide what to do with the rest of the goods," Samaki said as the men finished loading the carts.

"Sell it, surely?" Tiyharqu looked slightly confused.

"Hm... let us see how my audience with the king... or *kings*, goes."

Although Tersh hadn't removed her cloak or turned it inside out, she walked between the carts, as though trying to hide herself as they made their way into the city. Samaki had planned to wait in line this time, not feeling the same smugness he had earlier, but when the guards saw them approaching they ordered everyone aside and let them pass.

Word of the Whisperer's arrival must have spread quickly, because there seemed to be more people in the wide street, and they were all watching with keen eyes to find Tersh among them. A few children had climbed onto the leopard statues and were pointing excitedly. Tersh looked more and more like she wanted to fold into herself and disappear.

The inner walls were exact copies of the outer walls, save they were shorter. But their thickness and the gate was the same. Already the large wooden doors were being pushed open as they approached, and a man came forward. He must have been a captain of the guards, for his helm looked to be of better quality, and he wore a bronze badge clasping the leather cloak he wore.

He did not have the same look of fear on his face, but he stared at Tersh with something akin to uncertainty.

"You come on behalf of Paref Rama?" The guard asked, his speech nearly flawless. He had the same pointed beard on his chin and long moustache, but had pale hazel eyes. He seemed to be in his late thirties, grey hair speckling his beard.

"I do," Samaki stepped forward, and the captain finally looked away from Tersh.

The captain looked slightly surprised. "And you are?"

"I am the merchant, Samaki, a great favourite of the late Paref Rama. His son bid me to undertake the great honour of delivering tribute to your..." Samaki faltered a moment, not knowing if it would be insulting to say king or kings, so the word came out slightly choked and stuttered, "kings."

"Yes, both kings will see you," the man smiled, as though he understood the discomfort Samaki was feeling. "Your men can wait in the courtyard. Our guards will carry your tribute."

They entered into the courtyard and Samaki could finally appreciate the Hall of a Thousand Gods. There were a few large buildings in the courtyard, stables, a guardhouse, and such, but he felt a thrill when he saw the gate into the Hall. Four massive columns had been carved from the mountain, and above the columns stood statues of four men. Who the statues had originally been was unclear, but from the different colouring Samaki could tell the heads had been replaced. Their bodies were dressed in garbs of Mahat yet their heads wore helms of Matawe. Between the columns was the entrance into the Hall, sealed with large wooden doors intricately carved with battling figures. The doors began to open and into the Hall they went.

The entrance was a wide, high hallway that branched off into many different directions. Torches lined the walls. The guards who escorted them also carried torches to pierce the natural darkness inside the mountain. Samaki and Tersh walked side by side behind the captain, other guards following them in a long line with the tribute. After weaving their way through the dark hallways for some time, the narrow passageway opened into a large cavern. From the light of the many hanging torches and braziers it was clear to Samaki that the rounded hall had not been carved by man. There wasn't a single marking on the smooth walls. Unlike the city outside, there was no symmetry in here, the walls undulated like swelling waves and the fires cast shadows off the many bends.

The hall was almost empty of people, a few gruff looking men stood waiting for them. In the centre the kings sat on two large stone thrones. They were both young men, one of them perhaps a little less than thirty years old, and the other one maybe half his age.

"You are the emissaries from Paref Rama?" The older of the men asked. He had long wavy black hair, well groomed, and a long goatee. He wasn't fat, per se, but his waist seemed thick and his face rather full. The younger of the two was pale, his hair an earthy tone, and his narrow eyes seemed to be bright copper. He had a short wispy goatee, obviously a new addition to his young face.

"Paref Rama sent me, King..." Samaki trailed off, not sure which king he was.

"I am King Hatturigus, the sixth of my name, King Under the Mountain. This is my ward," he motioned towards the younger man. "King Over the Mountain, Laberne, the third of his name."

"And who sent the witch?" Hatturigus' eyes narrowed at the Whisperer.

Samaki was about to answer, but the Whisperer stepped forward before he had the chance to.

"The gods. I speak for the Goddess of Death."

The room became unnaturally silent. The only thing Samaki could hear was the crackle of the burning torches around him.

"It is a dark thing, to have a Whisperer seek you out," Hatturigus leaned forward in his chair, his face becoming shaded from the light.

"These are dark times," Tersh seemed to stand taller, raising her head, as though the Goddess really was giving her strength.

Samaki heard himself laugh awkwardly, trying to break the tension.

"Oh great kings, please accept this humble gift from the king of kings, Paref Rama."

Hatturigus snorted in derision, but waved forward the guards, who began to place the barrels and golden figures, the bales of wheat, and jewel encrusted bracelets, the beautiful bronze spears, and on, and on, until a small hill of treasure sat before the Mountain Kings.

"Well! This is very well," Hatturigus smiled. He leaned back in his great stone chair, a look of contentment on his face.

"Of course we shall send gifts in return, the finest gems cut from the mountain..." he droned on his a bored voice, clearly not too interested in the formalities of such an exchange.

"I am certain the generosity of you and your people will be greatly welcomed in Mahat."

"Tell us of this new Paref," the younger Laberne spoke up suddenly. He had the eagerness and curiosity of youth.

Samaki wasn't too sure what to say, but of course he knew the truth would not do. "He is the very image of this father." *If his father lost half his weight*, Samaki thought with a smirk. "His wisdom and kindness is unparalleled."

"How wonderful," Hatturigus waved a hand dismissively. "Thank you for your services, merchant. You will be given rooms while your ship is made ready for the return."

"Will you listen to what I have to say?" Tersh asked quickly, and Samaki felt a growing sense of annoyance. Couldn't the damn Go-man learn to hold her tongue?

"Of course," Hatturigus rose to his feet, "the words of a Whisperer must always be listened to, but not today. We must... retire. You shall be our guest as well."

Hatturigus motioned towards Laberne and together the two kings walked away from the thrones to an oblong entrance at the back of the room. Although Hatturigus had completely dismissed them, Laberne took a quick glance back before disappearing into the passageway. As they left, quiet conversation broke out with the others in the room, all of them ignoring Samaki and Tersh, far more interested in the treasures that had been set before the thrones.

"They will hear me, won't they?" Tersh asked, a look of concern on her face.

"Aye, they'll hear your words, they might even thank you for them, but I can't see what good it will do. Kings are proud men."

"If you thought my coming here was useless, why did you take me?"

"Why not?" Samaki shrugged as a guard moved towards them. "You wanted to come, and I like playing senet with you. We'll talk more in private," Samaki said in a low voice as the guard reached them.

"Come, I will show you your quarters."

They walked through the dark twisting paths of the Hall. Some of the paths were cut, their walls were straight with corners at perfect right angles, but most of them were clearly made naturally, the surfaces uneven and flowing. They eventually came to a large wooden door, torches on either side.

"King Hatturigus says you may take these chambers, that you may bring your servants and guards to stay as well – as many as will fit comfortably," the guard said, and with a bow of his head turned and left.

Samaki opened the door and at first could only see the dark, then he grabbed one of the torches hanging next to the doorway and entered. He found a few torches and began to light them. Tersh had followed his lead, grabbing the second torch and moving along the other side of the chamber.

The main chamber was massive, like a small throne room. There was a pit for a fire and lots of tables and chairs, there were several rooms surrounding them, one with eight beds in two rows piled on top of each other for guards or servants to sleep on, a few rooms with lavish furnishings, animal furs and large soft beds, and a few more rooms where food could be cooked or one could wash themself.

"It's a palace in a palace," Tersh said in awe.

"I can tell you haven't been too many palaces," Samaki laughed.

Tersh's face flushed slightly. "This would be the first..."

Samaki had almost taken it for granted how many times he had been inside palaces. He could barely remember the awe he had once felt, the fear of getting lost in the numerous halls and rooms. He could almost feel his father sneering at him from the afterlife.

"How grand my son has become."

"Listen, about the kings..." Samaki pushed the thought away and put the torch in a slot on the wall as he sat in one of the wooden chairs.

"What about them?" Tersh sat across the table from him.

"Maybe you'll convince them to throw away their traditions and become Whisperers in the mountain, I don't know. I do know you're a fairly good con woman," he chuckled.

"I don't want them to become Whisperers," Tersh started protesting. "They couldn't even if they wanted to."

"Whatever you say," Samaki picked up a flagon on the table, frowning as he realized it was empty. He set it down. "If they don't listen to you, and after meeting them I think that's the most likely course, then you shouldn't let that stop your journey."

"Well... thanks for the encouragement... I think," Tersh frowned.

"Hattute is nothing. Understand? The power of Matawe does not lie here; it lives in the city of Nesate. I don't know all the facts, that's true. But I do know there has been civil war in this place for two hundred years now. You've already met two of its kings, well there are more in Nesate, queens I believe. The stories are a little mixed."

Tersh nodded. "That is good to know, but I cannot fail here. I have to convince all of them. There is corruption in this place – evil. The old ways must be honoured, or this land and all the lands will drown in the gods' wrath."

"This land has... mixed feelings about Whisperers," Samaki said cautiously.

"I couldn't tell if they were looking at me with fear or reverence," Tersh said, furrowing her brow in obvious confusion.

"Both, most likely. Had you ever heard of this city before coming here?"

Tersh thought a moment. "Of course I knew there was a country in the mountains. I knew of the people of Matawe, I knew nothing of their cities or their civil wars though. Why?"

"The history of this city is a bloody one," Samaki leaned forward in his chair, feeling the darkness in the room moving in on them. "It was built by a Paref, Amotefen, the sixth and the last of his name. He rejected the gods of his people, and he hated the Whisperers. In that time thousands of Whisperers lived freely in Mahat, and Amotefen began to hunt them. He brought them here, to his great new city, and he killed them. It was not a quick death, either, he had them encased in bronze. They were alive, and it's said their screams echoed to every corner of this city."

Tersh had become completely still. She showed no emotion on her face, no sign of anger or sadness. Samaki wondered if he should stop, but he felt the Whisperer had a right to know.

"They say the slaughter forever cursed this place. There has been nothing but war and strife in these lands since. The people blame the Whisperers for this, and also fear them deeply. Here your people are known as the Whisperers of the Dead. You will find no love here."

Tersh continued to stare, barely breathing.

Samaki stared back at her, searching her dark eyes for a hint of what she was feeling.

When Tersh spoke, her voice was dry and distant. "Fear may suit my purposes just as well."

"Maybe..." Samaki nodded, standing up. He needed to go fetch Tiyharqu – and some damn wine.

"Samaki," Tersh looked him hard in the eye. "What happened to the Whisperers? To their bodies?"

"They were called living statues, and I believe the Paref lined a grand boulevard with them. I couldn't say if that's true."

Tersh was silent for a long moment after, never looking away. "The Whisperers did not curse them. They cursed themselves. And the gods will not forget."

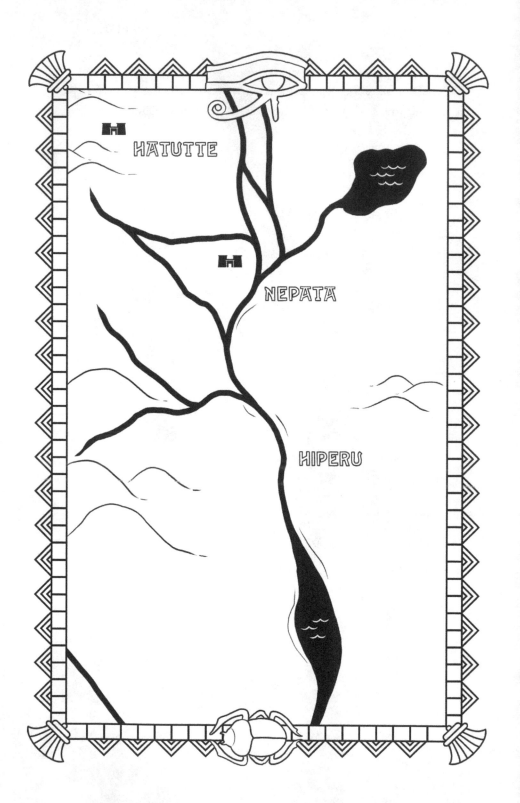

THE HALL OF A THOUSAND GODS

YOU DAMN US ALL

Tersh felt an uneasiness settle in her as the crew entered the chambers, getting comfortable, making fires in the pits and opening a cask of beer to celebrate their arrival. She sat along the wall of the main room, watching the men sing and laugh. Her talk with Samaki kept repeating itself in her head. Samaki didn't think she had a chance to succeed here. Surely it was because the kings seemed like they couldn't be reasoned with, but Tersh couldn't help but wonder if the fault lay with herself.

She remembered well the words the Rhagepe had told the three chosen messengers before they left, of the horrible prophesy they had witnessed, how the lands had been corrupted, how only their journey could calm the furry of the gods. She was so focused on getting to Hattute that she hadn't given much thought of what she would do once she got there. Kareth had tried to pry that information out of her a thousand times, and yet she had always been dismissive, telling herself that the Goddess would simply speak through them when the time came. Now she felt uncertain, and she thought maybe the people around her could read that on her face.

"Go-man, drink with us," Tiyharqu sat next to her, handing her a stone goblet brimming with cloudy beer.

"I don't really drink," Tersh said, taking the goblet anyway.

"Do your Goddesses not allow it?" Tiyharqu laughed, taking a large gulp of her own cup.

Tersh smiled. "I've never heard them speak evil of it," she set the goblet down, "it just doesn't agree with my stomach."

"Why do you look so pained?"

Tersh stared at her hands, her broken fingernails and the dirt caught in the creases of her dark skin. "Do you think the kings can be convinced to listen to me?"

"A king is just a man, and all men can be convinced, or persuaded, in the end," Tiyharqu finished her beer and grabbed Tersh's, taking a large swig.

"But do you think *I* can convince a king?" Tersh turned to face her.

"Convince them of what, anyway?" Tiyharqu raised an eyebrow.

"To follow the old ways."

"What old ways? Whose old ways?"

Tersh narrowed her eyes in frustration. "There is only one old way. Ours. We were the first, and-"

Tiyharqu started laughing, cutting her off. "I know, I know, and you will be the last, right? You don't think those kings will ask these same questions? Come Go-man, you've never met anyone more skeptical than a king. He will say his ways are the old ways. You think he'll just start walking around naked with his father's bones sewed to his cloak overnight?"

"They don't have to go naked," Tersh tried to calm herself down, balling her hands into fists, but she felt like something was about to burst open inside her. "It's not so literal as that! You people have turned the gods into entertainment, giving them stories and romances, turning them into characters! Those are not the gods! The gods are in the wind and the fire and the – the damn beer!" Tersh grabbed the goblet from Tiyharqu's hand and flung it across the room. Only then did she notice the entire room was staring at her. She looked back at the now bewildered Tiyharqu, her face flushed with heat.

"I'm sorry. I shouldn't have done that."

"Easy, Go-man," Tiyharqu clasped Tersh's shoulders with her large strong hands. "I am on your side, friend."

The rest of the room quickly grew bored of watching them and went back to their drinking, the sounds of celebration starting again in full force as though they had never stopped.

"Your passion is good, but your anger..." Tiyharqu laughed, drowning out all other sounds around them. "Keep that to yourself."

Tersh tried smiling, but her embarrassment crept in again. "I'll get you another drink."

Tersh quickly got up, searching for a full flagon, a few of the men teasing her as he walked past. "Don't spill the beer, don't you know that the gods are in there?" One man chuckled as he poured too quickly and some of the frothy liquid splashed onto the wooden table. Tersh ignored him, going to Tiyharqu, who had joined one of the songs. She handed the first mate the goblet – even though Tiyharqu had already found another one – and made her way into a smaller room.

There were eight beds, one on top of the other to save room. She climbed onto one on the top, fairly certain most of those men wouldn't be able to climb anything tonight. As she sat on the soft straw-filled mattress, it occurred to her that she had never slept on a bed before. Even in Imotah's home she had merely slept on some skins on the floor. She thought it would be softer, and perhaps the beds of kings were, but lying there under her cloak she would have rather been in the desert sand, Ka'rel, Ba'rek and Farek nestled up close to her. She closed her eyes, trying to push the thought of them away, Ba'rek singing as they walked through the desert, Farek laughing as he chased a scorpion, the smoothness of Ka'rel's mouth, his lips closing around her nipples and mouth. She could go back to them. She could get on the Afeth with Samaki and travel back to them. It would be so easy...

As she fell asleep, the only thing that weakened her resolve to do so was the simple thought of Ka'rel's bright eyes, looking up at her in disappointment. *"Why did you give up?"* He would ask. *"Why did you fail?"* And she could not fail...

✦   ✦   ✦   ✦   ✦

"Do you know why it is called the Hall of a Thousand Gods?" Hatturigus, King Under the Mountain, asked.

The throne room was packed full of people that day. It seemed all the lords wanted a chance to see the Whisperer in person. Everyone had to stand shoulder to shoulder, which seemed to suit them fine because they could not stop gossiping into each other's ears. Tersh found the people rather strange in appearance. They were much darker than those from Mahat or the Whisperers, and the men all had long goatees and long hair –no man seemed capable of growing hair on their cheeks. Their eyes looked much narrower too, their noses small and their brows less pronounced.

The only space left open was a small circle in front of the two seated kings, where Tersh stood by herself. Since she had left the sands of her home, she had never felt as alone or as much of an outsider as she did right then, but she tried to hide her uneasiness, standing straight, her nakedness practically shouting at the audience around her.

"Not really, no," Tersh finally replied, her voice sounding weak.

"We dedicated this mountain to all deities," Hatturigus' voice was strong and reached every corner of the room. "You see, my people do not reject others' gods, we welcome them, we worship them the same. We have all the names and faces of every god carved into the rocks around you. All are treated with the same respect. So, your gods are welcome here too."

Tersh could already feel her annoyance creeping back into her, but she found it easier to swallow back down than the night before.

"The gods are not mine, they do not belong to people," Tersh tried to make her voice just as loud and the King's, but it still sounded thin in comparison. "A thousand gods you say? Perhaps there are a thousand, or more, or less, that is not for us to know. Neither their names nor their faces matter," Tersh stopped herself from saying that it was because they had no names or faces, but she didn't want to be disrespectful. "All that matters is their anger. The gods are very, very angry. They are disappointed with us, and their fury will wipe the land clean if we do not appease them."

"Ah yes, we have heard of the great wave," Hatturigus smiled. "But we live in the mountains, no wave can reach us here."

The crowded room laughed softly and Tersh could feel her face turning red.

"It was a great tragedy," Laberne finally spoke up. Tersh had begun to think the younger king would remain silent the entire time.

"Yes," Hatturigus interjected, looking slightly annoyed with his ward, "but it is a tragedy of Mahat. It has no bearing on us. The gods are clearly not displeased with us."

"The gods have more than one way to destroy us," Tersh warned.

"I'm getting impatient," Hatturigus motioned over a servant holding a copper platter next to him, grabbing a large piece of meat and stuffing his mouth full of it. "What exactly is it you need to tell us?"

Tersh could see the half-chewed meat moving around his tongue and frowned. "The Rhagepe saw a terrible vision."

"The raw gehpee?" Laberne asked.

"The sand witches," Hatturigus shrugged, grabbing another piece of meat.

Tersh ground her teeth to keep from shouting. "The Rhagepe are our holy women. The gods speak to them, and they share the gods' messages with us. They are the true whisperers."

Hatturigus laughed. "And why whisper, eh? If the gods spoke to me I'd be sure to yell so everybody could hear!"

Again, the crowd tittered their approval of his joke and Tersh could feel her nails digging into the palm of her hand. Why did everyone have to take things so literally? "They say..." she cleared her throat, and for the first time her voice seemed loud enough to fill the room, "the words of the gods are too powerful. To speak them louder than a whisper would be enough to shatter a man. You must *respect* the words of the gods."

"So what was this vision?"

"The gods will drown the world, as they did a thousand thousand years ago, long before your people existed, when there were only the Whisperers. Since then the Whisperers have been careful to heed the gods. To stay to the old ways, but it isn't enough. Your kingdom is at war with itself, a beast devouring its own tail. The gods are furious, and they will make sure everyone knows!"

"War is common, and often justified. Gods delight in the wards of men. Their disappointment, as you put it, has nothing to do with us. Take your words elsewhere."

"You don't understand. All will be held accountable," she turned away from Hatturigus, looking around the room. "The greatest lords and the poorest of babes. All will suffer! The gods don't care for our borders or speech. All will be punished!"

Behind her, she heard Hatturigus begin to laugh, and soon the entire room erupted. She looked around in disbelief, finally facing Hatturigus again.

Hatturigus frowned, mocking her seriousness. "Such angry gods you have. Perhaps you should worship someone nicer, we have a thousand gods for you to consider," he trailed off into loud laughter.

Laberne looked slightly uncomfortable, but was chuckling as well.

Tersh went to her knees, bowing her head down, holding out her arms. The laughter died down, everyone looking uneasy, probably thinking she was planning some horrid curse.

"I pledge my life to you, great kings, if you will only consider what I have said. Turn away from your thousand false gods and embrace the old ways. End the war in your land and turn away from evil deeds. Help me save all of us."

"Enough. I've been far too patient with you, but I've had enough now. You say we must end the war? Fear not, the war will end as soon as Laberne, the rightful King Over the Mountain, sits on the throne of Nesate. Your think your gods will destroy us all unless we all change our ways? Bah, it's impossible! You cannot change the colour of blood and you cannot change men's hearts, and I will not suffer any fool who believes that they can. You have the grace of my hospitality, because you amuse me, but that is all. Now leave, before I change my mind and have you thrown out of my city, Whisperer or not."

Tersh felt cold. The stones she knelt on seemed like they were frozen. She had never felt such coldness. There is no warmth in the mountain, she thought, pushing herself up with weak arms. She stood, but felt like a breeze might easily push her down again.

"Please, you damn us all," she spoke, but her words were barely a whisper, and Hatturigus either didn't hear, or simply chose to ignore her. The kings started speaking with each other, and all those who were watching followed their example and began to speak in loud voices. The noise seemed to drown out her thoughts. She barely heard Samaki, who had made his way to her side.

"Come Go-man," Samaki urged her with a soft voice, taking hold of her arm.

"No, I..." *I cannot fail...*

"It is finished. They will not hear you now," Samaki pulled again and this time Tersh followed, as though someone else were controlling her feet. The crowd parted to let them through, recoiling as though they feared to touch the Whisperer, and perhaps that was true.

"Remember what I told you yesterday," Samaki said once they were in the hallway.

"I cannot leave here until I get through to them," Tersh shook her head.

"They are never going to give in to your ideas."

"They aren't *my* ideas!" Tersh pulled away angrily.

"Why do you look at me like this?" Samaki looked genuinely hurt. "I am not your enemy!"

"Why do I need enemies or allies? Why is this a battle? Why can't people just listen?"

Samaki suddenly began laughing, and Tersh felt an urge to hit him.

He calmed himself down, leaning against the wall for support, trying to supress his laughter. "I'm sorry, I'm sorry. I'm not laughing at you. It's just, I'm fairly certain everyone in the world asks themselves that question. If there was an answer, I doubt very much the gods would have needed to send you in the first place."

Tersh leaned against the wall herself, feeling her anger drain away.

"I really did think I could make them see sense."

"I don't mean to make you any angrier," Samaki took a deep breath, his laughter fading away completely. "But if you think those kings will ever see sense, you must not have any yourself."

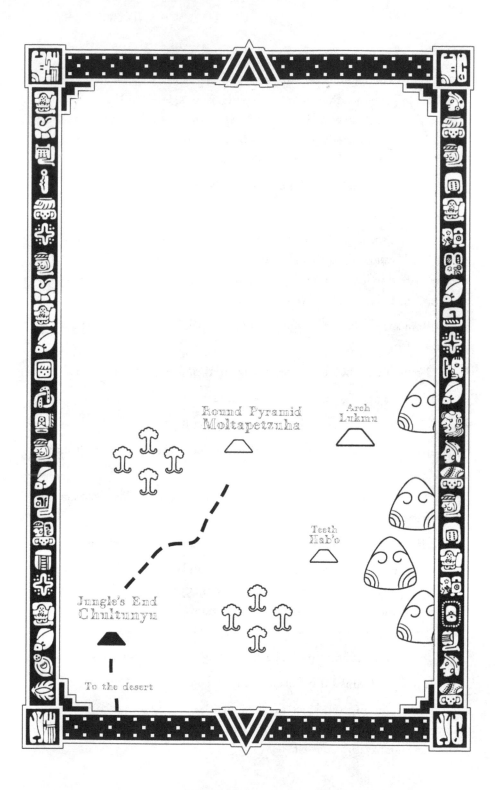

Round Pyramid
Moltapetzuha

Arch
Lukmu

Teeth
Hab'o

Jungle's End
Chultunyu

To the desert

MOLTAPETZUHA

READING IS A NOBLE PURSUIT

The huun had the texture of cloth, but felt smooth like skin. Sha'di knew it was made from trees, but was unsure how exactly. These documents were long, folded together so although they looked like only one page, if you unfolded one completely it would wrap around the room they were kept in. Tanuk had called them katytz, scrolls made from huun. Both sides were covered in their square hieroglyphs and large pictures depicted what the words spoke of – which was good for Sha'di since he couldn't read anything on the page.

They had arrived at Moltapetzuha, Round Pyramid, two nights ago. As the name suggested their pyramid did not have four sides like Chultunyu's had, but was rounded, like a cone with the top chopped off. Instead of red, it had been painted the same colour as the jungle. Everything blended in with the leaves around them here. The dye on the people's skin and the ornaments they put in their hair. It was their sacred colour. It allowed them to disappear in the jungle, so when they approached Sha'di thought at first he was seeing spirits move between the trees.

Aletz, he had remembered the word Belam had taught him.

As they travelled there Tanuk had explained everything he knew about Moltapetzuha to Sha'di. How it was the oldest of all the pyramids, and as such had the most complete written record of their people's history. Sha'di wasn't so interested in the pyramid. As far as he could tell any man could pile stones on each other, but writing interested him a great deal. Turning sound into images seemed impossible. The Rhagepe came close with their symbols, but those only represented an idea. Hieroglyphs could tell entire stories.

Tanuk encouraged him to read the katytz and see for himself that their people were without a doubt the oldest. That was all well and good, but Sha'di didn't know how to read. Still, he had eagerly asked to see them.

First, they had had to meet the Moltapetzuhuitl, the Chief of Round Pyramid.

Up the spiral ramp they went to the modest stone house that stood atop the pyramid. Although it was round and a different colour, outside the entrance was the same bloody altar, staining the calm leafy colour in a rusty red. The chakatl here, aside from being keener on bright foliage rather than red, seemed the exact same to Sha'di, chubby men ornamented in jewels and precious metals, with the strange elongated skulls. Their chief was an older man, and his introduction was long and boring.

"Moltapetzuha-na-chib'atl... who carries his brother's standard in his stead... He who has lived the longest... He who keeps the legends..." Xupama prattled on while Sha'di barely listened. He wanted to take out Nnenne's lure and get her to fly around the room, scaring the chakatl. The thought made him smile and Nnenne stirred with impatience on his shoulder, as though she were thinking the same thing.

Tanuk and his younger brother Tenok were invited to stay in one of the largest stone houses at the base of the pyramid and Tanuk invited Sha'di to stay with them. The stone house had three modest rooms, an eating and cooking room, and two rooms for sleeping – one for the masters and the other for their servants. It was cosy with three people sharing one room, but it was nice to have a roof over their heads and soft dry furs to sleep on.

The second day, as promised, Tanuk brought him to the katytz room.

"I came here once as a child," Tanuk explained, holding a torch as they entered a door at the base of the pyramid and descended into the depths. "These rooms were built before even the pyramid was."

Sha'di nodded. He could understand most of what Tanuk said these days, provided Tanuk spoke slowly and didn't use unfamiliar words. In Moltapetzuha he spoke exclusively in katan. The chaktan here was different from what was spoken in Chultunyu. Few words were shared between the common people of different pyramids and the accent was even more strange. Only the chakatl spoke katan.

The stairs leading down were narrow and incredibly steep. They had been used so many times and had been worn down so much they barely resembled steps and several times Sha'di almost slipped and fell into Tanuk. Still, it was cool down there and the farther they went the dryer and nicer it became. Sha'di was tempted to ask if he could sleep in the katytz room while they stayed there.

"Can you teach me?" Sha'di asked, his eyes eagerly looking over every hieroglyph, trying to see if he could make sense of them on their own.

"Well, I'm sure I could try..." Tanuk stood over his shoulder, and pointed to the first hieroglyph on the page. "It's easy once you get the basics. Each hieroglyph is a word or sentence or a name, made up from the glyphs inside it. Some glyphs are sounds, and others are words."

Sha'di felt like he was going cross-eyed staring at the numerous incomprehensible glyphs. "Oh yes... *so* easy."

Each of the hieroglyphs were made up of anywhere from two to five smaller images, all of them rounded. There were many circles and swirling lines. Some were pictures of faces or animals while others must have been symbolic. There seemed to be no set shape for each glyph. Most had a rounded square shape, but some were long and thin, and others circles or half circles. Each hieroglyph was of the uniform shape and size of a rounded square. The one Tanuk pointed to had the head of a lizard on the top left, followed by an elongated half circle with dots and swirls inside it. Beneath it was a face with corn in the hair and a bright red long shape that looked like two wings attached to a small round body, perhaps a bird.

"You start on the top left, then the top right," Tanuk's finger followed the hieroglyphs as he spoke, pointing now to one with an emerald and grey bird, then the face, "then the bottom left and then the bottom right. You go until you finish the columns, and then back to the top and the next two columns."

"So... I must learn sound each picture make?"

"Right, exactly."

"Can you write 'Sha'di'?" He knew they couldn't pronounce his name exactly, it always came out sounding like 'Xa'ti'.

"Hm... well, not exactly, but," Tanuk grabbed a lose piece of huun, and a small thin stick next to it, that had been sharpened into a point. There were many coloured inks on the table, but he dipped it only into the black. "'Xa' would be a jaguar," he drew a jaguar face in a rectangle on top, "and 'ti' is..." he smiled, switching inks and drawing the red bird from before, "there. Now you know two sounds."

"I try?"

"Sure," Tanuk handed him the writing tool, and on the same piece of huun he tried to copy Tanuk's hieroglyph, but his own looked childish in comparison. He frowned to himself.

"Not good."

"Don't worry. The shape or look is not that important. So long as you get the aspects of the glyph."

It was true, even comparing the red bird Tanuk drew of the one in the katytz it was completely different, save in colour and the fact that it was a bird. But the fact that every time he read a hieroglyph it might look completely different made his head spin.

"Yes, look," he pointed to the red bird. "In the katytz they've drawn the wings as four feathers on either side of a round body, I drew one feather on either side, but it's the idea that matters. So long as you have two long shapes on either side of a small shape. If you add dots for example, then it's different."

"Hm... this was bad idea." He sighed. Nnenne gave a short squawk of encouragement.

"Your bird's right, reading is a noble pursuit," Tanuk smiled.

"Joke?" Sha'di was fairly certain he had never heard Tanuk even attempt humour before, but Tanuk suddenly seemed more interested in the open katytz on the table and didn't answer. "So... how many sounds for pictures?"

"Hm," Tanuk furrowed his brow. "I'm not sure. A few hundred."

"Oh great," Sha'di replied in his own tongue, rolling his eyes.

"Don't worry," Tanuk smiled again. "I'll get Xupama to write them all out for you."

"Thank you..." he looked at the picture on the page, a man dancing, though his face was that of some kind of dog. He wore the same ornate headdress and skirts Sha'di had seen on some of the chakatl, though his headdress was almost as tall as he was and his body looked impossibly contorted in its crazed dance. "What this story?"

"Ah, that's Huhukotl, the trickster. He can change form, and likes to prank the gods and humans alike. This story..." his eyes scanned the words for a moment. "Ah yes, the story of Huhukotl and Tzochketza,"

"And... they are?" Sha'di leaned back and Tanuk took a seat next to him.

"Sometimes Huhukotl appears in the form of a human, other times as a coyote. Tzochketza is the goddess of love, the most beautiful of all the gods, even overshadowing her twin sister in radiance."

"Can you read it?" Sha'di felt embarrassed asking. He felt like a child asking his father to tell him a story.

Tanuk looked at him kindly. "Of course," he turned to look at the katytz and began to read. "Huhukotl was determined to woo Tzochketza from the first moment he gazed upon her beauty. His heart did rend after their first meeting when they were forced to part. Tzochketza, however, cared nothing for the trickster god." Tanuk unfolded another page, a picture in the middle showed a god – who must have been Tzochketza – turning away from the pleading Huhukotl, who was on his knees holding out a basket of food.

"Huhukotl disguised himself as a coyote and snuck into hundreds of forest gardens, climbing over the low stone walls and making away with their crops, and offering the sweet corn and ripe squash and fiery chilli peppers to her. At her feet he planted trees of mammee apples, pineapple, vanilla and avocado. He fooled dogs and turkeys to come to grand feasts he was holding, only to butcher the animals and present the meat to his love. But always Tzochketza would turn away, her face up to the sky in disapproval."

"He should have wooed Whisperer. We never say no for food," Sha'di laughed.

"Much time would have been spared, I'm sure, and much sorrow," Tanuk grinned, unfolding the next page, this time the picture showed Tzochketza within a small room, and Huhukotl crouching beneath the window. "Growing frustrated, Huhukotl planned to trick her into a lover's tryst. Huhukotl hid himself outside of Tzochketza's pyramid and, imitating the voice of Tzochpili, Tzochketza's beloved sister, Huhukotl cried out.

"'Come sister, quick! Let me in and shelter me from the rain!' But Tzochketza looked to the window and replied: 'Come now, the sun is out, there is no rain today.' 'No, it rains, dear sister. Reach your hand out of the window and feel it!' Tzochketza then reached out of her window and Huhukotl spat upon it. 'Ah!' cried she. 'It does rain! Come in quick, sister!'"

"I felt rain. No someone can be tricked by that. He should have thrown water," Sha'di interjected.

"Those who are easily fooled, tend to want to be fooled," Tanuk said, unfolding the next page, where Huhukotl stood in another crazy stance, reaching for a large antean flying above him. "Huhukotl burst into the pyramid, ready to claim his prize, but upon seeing him Tzochketza turned into a great white antean and flew from the pyramid, safely out of reach. However, when Huhukotl had spat on Tzochketza, she became with child-"

"Wait, wait, wait. What?" Sha'di laughed.

"Yes, I suppose it is a little strange. But they are gods, after all," Tanuk said thoughtfully.

Sha'di couldn't help but think of Nnenne, the woman he had left behind. What would she have said about that story? If he had told her all this time he could have just been spitting on her hand to give her babies.

"*Sure, but sex is more fun,*" he could imagine her winking, and the thought made him smile for a moment. Then Nnenne the bird rustled her feathers and he felt the distance between them.

"A bird is a poor replacement for a lover," he sighed, whispering in his own tongue.

"Sorry?" Tanuk asked, leaning in. He had the look of a man who didn't appreciate people leaving him out of a conversation. Sometimes when the younger prince Tenok came to Sha'di to practice speaking the Whisperer's tongue, Tanuk would get that look on his face. It was a mix of annoyance and exasperation.

"You believe this happen? This truth?" Sha'di leaned forward.

"I know *this* happened," Tanuk pushed the katytz aside.

"How you know?"

"Because what happened next. You see, you cannot wrong a god the way you can wrong a man. And you certainly cannot wrong a woman in such a way."

"So Zech... Tzoch...ketza was angry?" The room almost seemed colder as Tanuk leaned over him.

"We nuktatl," *old lords*, "have a saying. The only wrath worse than a woman's is a god's. The wrath of a female god would be... most terrible."

Sha'di laughed nervously. Nnenne would have liked that saying. But Tanuk did not smile, he was not making a joke.

"So what Zach... What she do?"

"Nothing. Her anger and fury grew inside of her with her child. Her womb filled with malice and hatred and the child became an entity of fire and suffering," Tanuk was no longer reading from the katytz, he was staring Sha'di directly in his eyes, holding his gaze like a cobra about to strike. "At that time, my people lived in the greatest kingdom man has never known. They said our pyramids not only reached over the trees, but cut the very sky. The gods and men would meet atop the pyramids and share their wealth and knowledge. It was paradise..."

"... And then... she had baby?"

"She did not give birth to the child, it burst from her uncontrollably. Fire rained onto my people, the rivers turned to conflagrations, the sky was ash, the trees became bonfires. Those who survived the inferno fled to the ends of the jungle, and had to rebuild the once great kingdom we had, but without the gods at our side, our pyramids now are just pale imitations of what we were once capable of."

"That how Chultunyu was made?"

"That's how all the nuktatl came to be."

Sha'di shook his head. "But why punish Petzuhallpa? Why not trickster god?"

"We cannot understand how the gods work. Are not your gods now willing to punish everyone for the sins of some? Do not the gods in your people's stories do such things?"

"The gods... no. They have no stories," Sha'di shrugged. "The Rhagepe think it wrong to make stories for gods. They teach gods are strange as wind or sun."

"You think the sun is strange?" Tanuk looked like he might laugh.

"No, I..." He waved his hand in the air, as though trying to pull a word out of it. "I don't know right word."

"Well, gods are strange, that much is true. But to them, I suppose we are very strange," Tanuk began folding the katytz up again. "Who can say why and when the gods punish us."

"Um... Story over?" Sha'di asked.

"Well, there is more of course, but it's getting late. We'll be feasting in the pyramid tonight and it would be rude to arrive after the wrestling matches," Tanuk stood up.

"*Did* she punish trickster god?" Sha'di got up as well, stretching out his body as he stood.

"Oh yes, she cut of his penis and planted it in her forest garden."

Sha'di's eyes widened. "That..." Sha'di shuddered, his hand cupping protectively around his own penis.

Tanuk nodded. "It is a little extreme, true. But sometimes the extreme must be done. It turned out well, it grew into a daughter. So she had a son of fire and a daughter of earth."

"The extreme..." Sha'di could still remember the day they left Chultunyu. The extremes they went through then to ensure their journey would be safe. They wouldn't stay here forever. Soon they would leave again... and...

They reached the exit and began climbing the stairs. "Tanuk... when we leave. Will priests do... that again? Sacrifice?"

Tanuk stopped, but didn't look back. "It would be the... proper thing to do."

"Proper?" The word almost made him angry. How could anyone think it was proper to murder a child?

The chib'atl turned his head slightly; his eyes were kind. "Your gods told you to leave your home and travel here. Our gods tell us to sacrifice our lives to sate them. Your gods tell you we must follow your ways, or they will wash the life from the face of the earth. We cannot understand how the gods work."

"But..."

Tanuk held up his hand to silence him. "But we can agree on one thing: The gods must be heeded."

The gods of the jungle were indeed heeded as they left Moltapetzuha. Once more they stood in front of the bloody alter at the top of the pyramid, though this time the blood stains stood out against the jungle-coloured stone, impossible to ignore. Everything else was the same as before, they waited at the top as the five priests made their way up the ramp, these priests wore dark vine coloured tunics, but the same silver bands with topaz adorned their foreheads. There was no dye upon their skin, their heads had no hint of hair, and again the last priest wore the large headdress of turquoise feathers and a skirt made from the same plumage.

Xupama translated for him once more, but Sha'di didn't listen. His focus was on the young man standing ready by the altar. He had met his father just before the ceremony began, one of the chakatl. He had had a strange mixture of pride and sadness on his face as he spoke to Tanuk.

"He is my youngest son. He asked me for this honour, I..." he hadn't been able to finish, but Tanuk had told him how his son had brought honour and the god's favour on his family for generations to come.

The young man, perhaps the same age as Sha'di himself, had a stony face of resolution. Sha'di wished he could walk over and ask him how exactly it was one mentally prepared themselves to face death, but all he could do was stare at him and try to read his expressionless face.

And then the moment came. The young man stepped forward. The four priests held his limbs, leaning him back over the altar. He was gritting his teeth, Sha'di could tell, as the priest brought his knife down across his stomach, just under his ribs, cutting open the flesh, red trickles of blood beginning to run down his otherwise untouched skin. He had been ready for this moment, he had asked for it, but even so he still screamed in pain as the priest lunged his hand into the man's stomach, and pulled out the dark, pulsating, red heart.

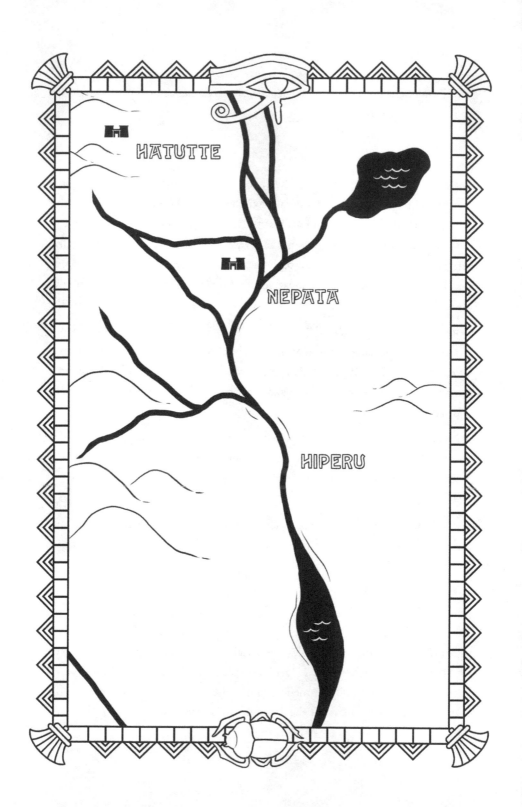

NEPATA

TRAPPED IN HIMSELF

"*Above all else, learn.*"

Tersh's words to Kareth as they parted on the dock had etched themselves into his mind, like the hieroglyphs on the building walls. *Learn.* The word tasted bitter to him. *Learn,* he muttered to himself every morning as he woke with the sun. And learn he did. By the end of the first day working in the stables he understood the words for water and horse and oats, and that he dare not look confused by the orders Piye was shouting at him. He learned to watch the other stable boys and mimic what they did. By the end of the second day he had learned the names of the horses, of which ones would bite and kick, and which ones would nuzzle your face with their soft noses and let you feed them oats from your hand.

"*Learn.*"

The word screamed in his mind as he felt the stick strike his thigh. This was not the first time he has been beaten by Piye. The stable master was always angry. And he would find any excuse to hit you on the ear. It was so hard that sometimes you couldn't hear properly for the rest of the day. His anger would burst from him if you were too slow, or too weak to carry something, or looked too sleepy in the morning, or just if he wanted to.

Kareth had broken a vase, just a small ceramic container. He had been filling one of the horse's troughs, and had slipped and broken it. Piye seemed to reach him from the shadows. Stepping out and grabbing his ear, yanking it so hard he thought for a moment it had been ripped from his head. Then the stable master had dragged him outside, throwing him to the ground and striking him with one of the horse crops over and over. The other stable boys watched on with gleaming eyes. He knew they would have laughed, but if they did Piye was just as likely to turn on them next.

Working in the stables wasn't terrible because of Piye, or because of the smell and the biting horses – in fact he quite liked the horses. It was truly unbearable because the other stable hands were cold to him, barely speaking to him. The only friends he made those first few days were the mares.

Ten of the horses, massive stallions, were chariot horses. The biggest of them were fierce black ones that made Kareth feel nervous to be around. Their names were Horem and Meheb, and they were Imotah's favourites, apparently. There were six other stallions, smaller than the chariot horses, and they were used for leisure riding. They were more gentle. Finally there were four mares, they were the same colour as the great sea of sand he had once called his home. He liked brushing them, gazing at the contours of their shoulders and haunches, remembering the sand dunes he had once played in.

At night he would return to the servants' quarters. The servants all slept within the main building, but on a lower level near the kitchens. Those who worked in the stables had the smallest rooms, three or four sharing with each other. Kareth was given his own room, though he could barely stretch out in it. It was smaller than the horse stalls he cleaned every day, and he imagined it hadn't been meant as a room in the first place, probably just a small storage space they weren't using at the moment.

At first he felt annoyed. He would listen to the other boys whispering and laughing softly to each other as he drifted off to sleep. He felt envious, and he felt alone. A few nights he would feel tears in his eyes, and he would bury his face into his cloak, breathing in the musty scent of leather and his people.

Kareth dared not wear his cloak on Imotah's property, and kept it in his room, draping it over the scratchy hay to give him some comfort at night. Everyone had warned him that he would have enough trouble if they found out he was a

Whisperer; wearing his cloak would only encourage someone to steal it or worse. It was better left in his room, hidden from eyes. It pained Kareth to leave it every morning, but he knew he had no choice. He had to live with these people, even if their ways were strange.

Learning the language at that point became his only goal. Suddenly understanding their words was the one thing protecting him from most of Piye's swift anger. He started mimicking the other stable boys. As they chatted in the stalls next to him or in the small common room for their morning and evening meals, he would repeat everything they said under his breath, keeping a careful eye on their lips. At night he would just repeat songs he knew, or commands Piye had shouted. As the days accumulated and a turn of the moon passed, their words and sentences began to make sense. He began to connect the sounds and actions with thoughts. He began to understand the conversations he was eavesdropping on.

Although he understood more and more every day, he still had no one to speak to. It wouldn't have mattered if they knew he was a Whisperer, he realized. They had no love of foreigners here. They would stand up from a table if he sat next to him. They would turn away if they saw him coming. No one was cruel to him. No one made faces. In fact, other than Piye, usually people would smile at him, but it was always a distant, uncaring smile.

"Master Piye!" A small voice cut through the crowd gathered around watching Kareth getting beaten in the dirt. Kareth lifted his face, caked with mud and tears to see a young girl walk through the boys. She was taller than most of them, though far thinner and of lighter skin. She looked very delicate next to the gruff crowd.

Piye spat into the dirt, standing up straight and lowering his crop. Looking clearly annoyed by the interruption. "What? I'm busy!"

"Forgive me, master," she nodded her head in respect. Kareth recognized her then. All the servant girls wore the same simple white shift and a plain black braided wig. But he recognized her big nose and small chin, and most of all her smile. The first time he has seen her, when she had helped to wash and shave him, he had thought she looked rather funny, but now he couldn't help think she looked like one of those graceful white ibis birds he had seen along the shores of the Nepata. "Mistress Ankhet has asked for him."

"Him?" Piye snarled, showing off the gaps in his teeth.

"Yes," she stared at him, a small smile on her narrow lips. Kareth had never seen anyone look so directly at Piye before, and for a moment was afraid the stable master might lash out at her too, but instead Piye just spat again.

"Take him. I am done with him for today anyway," Piye turned towards the stable boys who had gathered to watch. "Get back to work you lazy sods! Who said you could have a break!" He kicked at the nearest one who just managed to dodge and they all ran back into the stables.

Kareth started pushing himself up, his legs burning. For a moment he wasn't entirely certain if he could stand.

"Are you all right?" The girl kneeled next to him, for the first time her face showed concern.

"I'm fine," he said, wincing. She took his arm and helped him to stand. He looked down and was surprised to see that despite the fact that he felt like his thighs had been cut with knives, there was not a drop of blood. Obviously Piye was well practiced at beating the boys, while leaving them able to work.

She leaned in close, and he was taken aback by the smell of perfume on her. He was so used to smelling horseshit all day, but she smelled like lily, myrrh, and cinnamon. He leaned back, suddenly self-aware that she might think he stunk, but she showed no signs of disgust.

"Mistress Ankhet doesn't really need you, I just can't stand crotchety old Piye hurting anyone."

"Will you get in trouble?" Kareth asked, worried.

Her face brightened. "Wow, you're speaking much better these days!"

Kareth's face felt warm. He knew he still had a thick accent, but he tried his best to correct it. "Well, I, uh, practice lot – a lot."

She nodded enthusiastically. "That's great! We better go. I can find something for you to do in the kitchens for today. You'll have to wash first," she laughed softly. The same laugh she had when she had helped to cut his hair before.

"Um... your name. What is it?" Kareth asked as they walked across the wide promenade to the main house.

"Oh, Tahye," she said. "I forgot to introduce myself, I guess."

He was taken aback for a moment. Tahye was the name of the oldest of the mares, she was the gentlest horse in the stable and for that reason his favourite. He would spend the most care when brushing her down, making sure she had a glossy coat before moving on to the next horse. He wondered if the lords of Mahat saw servants the same as pets.

"I'm Kareth, son of Resh," he had long ago stopped telling the name of his tribe, hiding his identity as a Whisperer.

"Oh, I know," she smiled.

He couldn't help but look at her body out of the side of his eyes. He'd started to notice girls a lot more recently. There was something distracting about the curves beneath the shifts they wore. Tahye was still at that awkward stage between girl and woman, her face had the full cheeks of youth, but her limbs were long, with just the hint of breasts on her chest. The hypnotic smell of her perfume made Kareth swallow hard.

"Um, so, you're a kitchen girl?" He asked, trying to focus on his sandaled feet instead of her body.

"I usually serve in the manor, but that takes me to the kitchen more often than not. I like the kitchens better. There's always the smell of something delicious cooking, and I like the energy. And sometimes Mistress Ankhet lets us have the leftovers after a banquet, and..." she trailed off, seeing the look of confusion on Kareth's face. "Sorry, am I talking too fast?"

"Uh, maybe, but it's okay."

They entered and Kareth went to the washing room to get rid of the stench of the stables. He washed there every evening with the other stable hands, almost always hiding in the corner. It was nice to have the room to himself for once. He splashed a bucket of cold water over his head, gasping as the water hit the welts on his thighs. Bleeding or not, they still stung intensely. He strained his neck to see the back of his legs, the ugly red marks seeming to swell as he looked at them.

"Does it hurt very much? Do you need something for the pain?" Tahye asked, her concerned face popping through the doorway.

Kareth nearly fell over, turning way, his hands instinctively covering his crotch. He wondered where that shame of being naked in front of a woman came from.

Kareth tried to laugh his embarrassment off. "Uh... do you have coriander?"

"Coriander? I'll ask," she disappeared and Kareth grabbed his tunic from a hook along the wall, throwing it over himself before she came back. He was just clasping his belt with the silver buckle as she walked into the room, her arms so full of bottles and bowls it looked like she might drop one any second. "Do you need fresh coriander, or oil, or dried and crushed?"

"Um... oil... maybe."

She brought her bundle of jars over, placing them not too gently on the floor, looking through the labels of hieroglyphs he couldn't read. He felt a twinge of jealousy as he watched her eyes scan the symbols.

"Ah, here we go," she handed him a small thin ceramic bottle. He popped off the topper. The strong smell of coriander, a mix of spicy and sweet, nearly overwhelmed him. "Do you need help rubbing it on?"

He had a sudden thought of Tahye on her knees behind him, her thin fingers covered in oil, rubbing the soothing coriander into the skin of the thighs. He nearly fell over his own feet trying to back up, and hurriedly calling out, "No, no, no, no, no – no thank you!" He turned away from her, afraid she'd see the flush creeping onto his face.

Kareth poured some of the oil onto his hand, awkwardly leaning back to rub the red welts he could just make out. The feeling of relief was so quick he actually sighed. Wherever the oil went, a cold tingling began to spread. When he was finally finished he wiped his hand onto his tunic and handed the bottle back to Tahye.

"Here," Tahye handed him a cloth, "you might want to clean your hands a little better. Coriander doesn't taste bad, but they might wonder upstairs if the bakers have changed their recipes. Who taught you to use it as a medicine?"

"Thanks," Kareth wiped at his hands and fingers until only the faint scent remained, then rinsed them for good measure in the water. Before Tersh had left, she had taught him a few important words like the names of herbs, in case he ever needed to ask for medicine. "Many women in my..." *tribe*, he wanted to say, but couldn't, "village use it."

"One of the lake villages?"

He nodded. He knew he had to make up some kind of backstory to account for the fact that he wasn't from Mahat. He had decided to tell people – if they asked – that he had come from one of the lake villages he and Tersh had passed through before entering Mahat. At the very least he could remember enough about them that his story wouldn't be entirely dubious. "Sometimes they boil it and rub on you, or drink." He shrugged.

They started walking to the kitchens, Kareth helping Tahye to carry the coriander jars. The kitchens were always alive with the fire of the ovens. The servants who worked here did not wear wigs, even Tahye had removed hers while he washed. The boys were content to leave their heads bald, but the women all wore white linens wrapped around their scalps.

"Are you two going to play or prepare that bread?" Mistress Ankhet yelled at them from across the room, but unlike Piye there was no lash to her words. In fact, she seemed more amused than anything. She was the woman who had helped shave and wash him the day he started working in the stables. She was quite old, her back slightly hunched, and she was rather chubby. Many of the kitchen servants had a little extra weight to them. He assumed they freely helped themselves to extra food.

"Yes, mistress! He just needed a little aid," Tahye called back, putting the other jars and bowls away as he took a seat at one of the large wooden tables. He held his breath as he sat down, his thighs still throbbing.

Tahye sat down next to him, pointing to a pile of little balls of dough on a wooden tray. She took one of the balls and flattened it into a small circle with her knuckles. Then with a dull knife she cut it into the shape of a crescent moon. "Tomorrow's bread. We get the dough ready now so all the bakers need to do in the morning is put them into the oven."

He wasn't fond of bread. He never ate it before coming to Mahat. It was dry, and bland. However, it did fill your stomach nicely, and he enjoyed using it to dip in sauces and wrap fish or whatever vegetables they could get into an easily managed meal.

"Why don't the bakers do it?" Kareth asked, grabbing one of the soft balls and trying to squish it flat. It had a lot less give than Tahye made it seem.

"The bakers need to get up before the sun. It's good to help them."

Kareth shrugged. "Oh." Anything was better than cleaning up after horses.

"I hope you're not letting Piye get to you. I know he can be unbearable, but the worst thing is when you let a man break you." She gave him an encouraging smile.

"He doesn't–" he made a sharp intake of breath as he shifted on the wooden bench. Kareth started imagining the dough was Piye's head before he squished it. "He doesn't... bother me. Not... really."

"Sorry?" Tahye looked up in confusion.

"Piye. He doesn't bother me."

"Oh... well good," she smiled.

"He reminds me of story – a story. The Chief Trapped In Himself."

"What's that?" Tahye leaned in a little, clearly interested.

"My grandmother told me... many times." He hadn't thought of his grandmother in a long time. She had died before his father had. She had seemed fine, but one morning she simply did not wake up. "*She has gone back to the earth,*" his father had told him. He had missed her for a long time. He wanted to hear her stories, feel her warm embrace. Then his father had died and her memory had been eclipsed in his mind.

"Can you tell me?" Her smile was wide.

He felt himself grin at the attention she was giving him.

"There was a chief. He was strong and fought well, but unkind. He wanted power. He wanted all knowledge. He wanted to help only himself. One day he went to the..." he furrowed his brow, trying to think of what he could call the Rhagepe. "Um... I don't know the word. Someone who answers a chief's questions?"

"Like a tzati? A councillor?" She cocked her head to the side.

Kareth nodded. "Yeah, like that. He asked a councillor. There were three. One knew about life. One knew about death. One knew about rebirth. He asked the councillor for life for the secrets of the desert. She told him go to the desert. She told him find two scorpions. She told him put the stingers in his eyes. The chief went to the desert. The chief found two pale scorpions. Their stingers were as big as his nose. He stabbed his eyes with the stingers. Suddenly, he was blind. He screamed in pain. He had to go back to the... uh, village.

"He knew he needed to go east. He waited until morning. He felt the heat on his face and walked towards it. His hearing was better now. He could hear lizards move in the sand. He could throw his spear and hit them. He skinned them, with his teeth and fingernails. Twenty days he lived in the desert. Every day he was stronger. He could hear the water under the sand. He could dig deep into the dark to drink the springs.

"He returned to the councillor. He was angry. He wanted kill her. '*Why did you trick me?*' He screamed, but she laughed. '*Now you know the secrets of desert.*' It was true. He traded his sight for the secrets. He was happy.

"Next he went to the councillor of death. He wanted everyone to love him. She told him to take her fire knife and cut out his tongue. He took her fire knife-"

"What's a fire knife?" Tahye interrupted him.

"Oh... it – it's made from black stone. Very sharp. Very magic... magical."

"Sorry, go on."

"He took her fire knife, and cut out his tongue. All his words became... um," he made a low moaning sound.

Tahye giggled softly. "Groans?"

"Yes, groans. He groans, all day. Everyone who sees him loves him. There's no... respect. They feel pity. They love him with pity."

"That's very sad," she frowned.

"Maybe," Kareth shrugged. "He felt sad. He went to the last councillor."

"Rebirth?"

"Yes. He asks rebirth to give him bliss. 'Please take away my pain,' he asks."

"I thought he couldn't speak," Tahye said with a teasing lilt to her voice.

Kareth rolled his eyes. "It's a story. Maybe she understood his groans? The Rha... councillors of my people hear things." *Like the gods*, he thought.

"So... she says she'll help?" Tahye tossed another piece of flattened bread on a wooden tray, this one in the shape of a fish.

"Yes, she tells him to go back into the desert. She tells him kill a snake. She tells him eat the snake. She tells him take the bones of the snake. She tells him stab his ears with the bones..."

"... And?"

"And he did all this. He went to the desert. He killed the snake. He ate the snake. He stabbed his ears with the bones."

Tahye leaned forward. "... And?"

"And there was silence. And there was peace."

"So he just spent the rest of his life in silence?"

"Trapped In Himself."

She furrowed her brow, as though trying to decide if she liked the story or not.

"If you want only for yourself, you'll have only yourself," he flattened another piece of dough, trying to shape it into a turtle, but on second glance it looked more like a palm leaf. "Piye will end up only with himself. Anyway, he'll probably scare a horse one day and get a hoof to the head. I dreamed it..."

"A dream? I see all sorts of things in dreams."

"But sometimes my dreams come true," The thought made him smile. He had dreamt about that happening a few nights ago and had been happy for the first time since Tersh had left, though the feeling had only lasted until he joined the others for his morning bread. If only he *did* have visions like the Rhagepe.

She laughed, obviously not believing him. "Don't worry so much about dreams, just focus on the dough. Nice cactus."

"It's a..." he nearly corrected her, then smiled. "Yes, thank you."

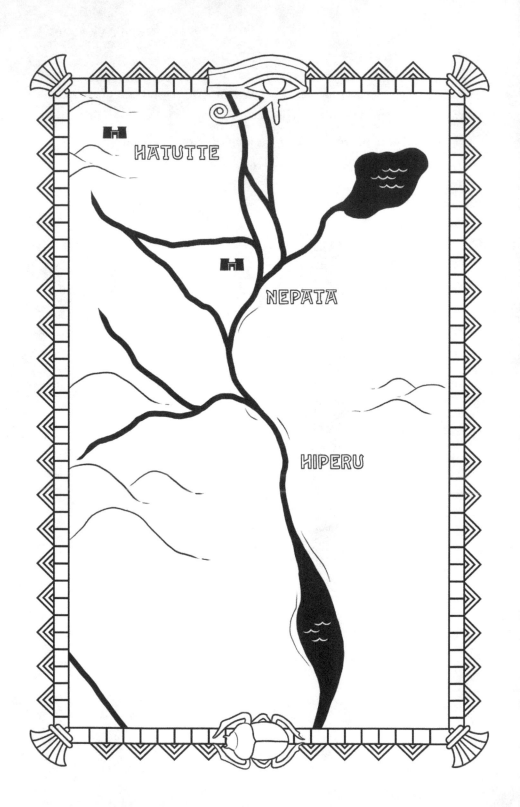

HATTUTE

I NEED NOT FEAR THEIR CURSE

Every day Tersh asked for another audience with the kings, a private one this time. She hated how she had been treated like some entertainment before, some exotic toy to bemuse them. She walked through the stone halls, wanting everyone to see her presence, to remember the one who spoke for the gods was still among them. She practiced over and over what she would say in her head. She would not plead next time. She would not get overly emotional. She would let the words of the Goddess of Death flow through her. If death could not convince them, nothing could.

Her requests went unanswered, either because they were ignored or simply not delivered. She grew more anxious each passing day. Samaki was already making plans to set sail back down the Hiperu. The captain had sold all the wares he had brought with him and had bartered several more things to sell. The merchandise of Hattute mostly consistent of wool, or copper from their mines, but their prize export was precious jewels. Still, most of what Samaki chose were weapons.

"The two things men need most are food and weapons. Hattute has no food to spare, but they have more weapons than soldiers," Samaki had said as he oversaw the packing of his ship's hold.

Food and weapons. It seemed a cynical thought to Tersh, but she couldn't deny it. If a land had no food, they needed weapons to get some. If a land had unlimited food, they needed weapons to protect it. The Whisperers were not a warfaring people, but even they always kept weapons on hand.

Watching Samaki make preparations to leave made it all the clearer to her that she was running out of options. A part of her was still tempted to return with Samaki, to leave these fools to perish in the mountains, but she feared the consequences of that action. She could try to stay and convince the kings, but as the days continued to pass that thought felt more and more futile. So the other option was to take the pass up the mountain, to the city called Nesate, where the queens, and the cause of the civil war, resided. But even that option wasn't available to her.

The weather had changed since coming to the foot of the mountains. At first it was just a strange chill in the west wind. Tersh had felt cold before, the nights in the desert could freeze you to the bone, but with a fire and a warm body next to you it was easy to deal with. This cold stabbed at her. Her cloak did nothing to protect her, and she felt herself shivering all the time.

"This is nothing," Tiyharqu had laughed. "A little wind. In the mountains they have snow enough to bury entire cities."

Samaki was determined to leave before the snow. Snow. It was a new word for Tersh. Rain was a rare thing in the desert, but it was something she was familiar enough with, especially from her childhood in the Sea Mahat. But snow? When the winds grew so cold the rain itself froze. Apparently it only happened high, out of reach of the Hattute. The higher you went the colder it became. When it happened the streams stopped flowing into the Hiperu, and the waters became so shallow a ship would become grounded.

The captain had given her a tunic and a set of woollen boots to help keep her warm. She appreciated the gesture, but even that felt like not enough. Winter was coming, and until it passed, the mountain pass would be closed to her.

"Return to Napata with us," Samaki offered. "Come back in the spring."

"I doubt any other ship will bring me back," Tersh had frowned.

"I'm sure you can trick some other poor captain into taking you," Samaki grinned.

"I'm not sure there are any other captains as gullible as you." Tersh couldn't help but grin herself, and Samaki had laughed.

And then came a day when the ship's hold was full and Samaki was ready to set sail. The days were crisp with cold wind, but with the sun out it was still warm enough for Tersh to manage. Tersh asked if it would get much colder as the mountains above them froze.

"Take the coins, Tersh," Samaki offered the modest purse once more as they walked towards the quay. There was a lot of activity at the docks, since the Afeth was not the only ship trying to leave before the water levels dropped too much. They could just make out the Afeth among all the other ships where Tiyharqu was taking a roll call of the crew. She stuck out, being the largest ship there.

"I've done nothing to deserve it," Tersh said, uncomfortable with taking charity. She tried to give Samaki some of the jewels she still carried with her, but Samaki refused that.

"You've beat me at senet so many times I'm sure you deserve this and more," Samaki held the purse out to her once again.

"I have enough to trade, I don't need your silver."

"It's mostly copper," Samaki winked. "These coins hold no meaning in Mahat. They're useless to me there. Anyway, your treasure will serve you well enough, but men who realize you carry it with you may try to take it. Better to use coins, to avoid being cheated. The men here are cold, just like their winters."

"I thought you said no one would hurt a Whisperer here."

"They fear Go-men here, that's true, but they fear starving more. I tell you, this country is sick, and the winds and the wars starve them into doing terrible things if they have the chance."

Tersh hesitated a moment longer, before reaching out and taking the bag. It was light, probably just enough coin to make it through the winter. "Thank you," she muttered, slipping it into the opening of the skins she carried. "Will you check on Kareth when you're in Nepata?"

"I'll try to see him," Samaki said.

Tersh shot him a concerned look.

Samaki sighed and added, "I will make sure to enquire about his well-being, and I'll make sure he knows you arrived here safely.

"Don't worry about the boy," an older sailor walked past carrying a large vase. It was Sef, the man who had saved Kareth from the river when he had fallen overboard.

Tersh looked away. Maybe she should return to Nepata, just to watch over the boy. She shouldn't have left him so soon, and she wasn't much use here. Surely she could find another ship back here come spring... *No*, she shook her head. She couldn't give in like that. She needed to be strong, for Kareth, for herself... for her family. She knew if she left now she wouldn't stop until she was back in the arms of her family.

"Will you ever return this way?" Tersh asked, hopefully.

Samaki was quiet a moment before answering. "I can't honestly say I will. This country is not ideal for a merchant like myself. I never truly know where my next port will be, but it's always possible. Hopefully, you'll take my advice and the next time I come here you'll be in Nesate."

"I can't imagine I'll have better luck with them," Tersh muttered glumly.

"Kings and queens, it makes no difference. Rulers are all the same. They all want to hear how wonderful and important they are. If you make them believe they're the only thing standing in the way of the wrath of the gods, they might listen just to make themselves that much more important," Samaki grinned.

They boarded the ship, and Tersh stayed on the wooden pier, watching the young sailors unfurl the sails and helping to untie the leads, to break away from shore. Samaki called out to her one last time, a spear held in two hands. He tossed it down to Tersh, who caught it smoothly in both her hands. Feeling the wood on her palm reminded her of the journey through the sea of sand with Kareth. She hadn't thought much of the spear Ka'rel had given her since joining the Afeth. It somehow seemed heavier than it had before.

"Watch your back, Go-man!" Samaki said, with a final wave and a laugh.

She imagined Kareth must have felt the same way, watching the Afeth start to drift away, being left alone in a foreign land he knew nothing about. The fear she felt was so palpable that she could taste it, a bitter stinging taste. Her throat seemed dry. She wanted to call out to them, but she didn't know if it was to say farewell one last time, or beg them to take her. She remained silent, unmoving, watching the ship disappear, her vision blurring over for a moment.

When she knew they were far enough that even her shouts wouldn't reach them, she felt a strange sense of relief. The choice had been robbed from her, and now she would have to stay. Now she would have to follow the path the gods had made for her. She would stay the winter here, trying to convince the kings to hear her. Come spring, her goal completed or not, she would head higher into the mountains to see the queens in Nesate.

It felt good to finally know what needed to be done, even if it wasn't what she wanted to do.

She turned back to the city, noting that the sun was hanging low in the sky. The gates would close at nightfall, and she knew spending her night out here in the cold would be more than she could handle. As she walked she let the butt of the spear fall on the ground, using it much like a walking stick.

People had been staring at her wide-eyed since she came here, but for some reason she noticed it more now. When she had been with Samaki or the others she could ignore it well enough, or simply hide from view behind one of the crew, but now being alone the stares seemed all the more intense. Whether it was hatred or fear or both, she couldn't honestly tell, but she despised it.

The guards let her pass through the city gates without problem, their eyes following her. When this city was being built by the men of Mahat, a thousand Whisperers had been slaughtered, bronzed alive, cursing this city for all time. They looked at her as though she carried the curse on her back, as though if they came too close or gave her any problems they might catch it. It made her feel as though her cloak were a shield protecting her.

She felt like she was lost in a dream as she walked back to the palace. She felt like she was floating through the streets, so disconnected from everything that she couldn't even feel the ground beneath her feet.

The damn boots, she smiled at the thought, looking down at the boots Samaki had given her. *They cut me off from the earth.*

When she reached the second gate, leading to the Hall of a Thousand Gods, the guards did not step back to let her pass, but instead looked at her with uneasy glances.

"You cannot pass," one of the guards managed to say through a thick accent. It was obvious he couldn't really speak the tongue of Mahat, but had simply learned a few sentences to help with his post.

"Why not? What's going on?" Tersh asked, feeling a sudden unease. There were a few people, servants and guards, walking just beyond the gate, within earshot, but obviously trying to avert their glances.

The guards looked at each other, one of them shrugging ever so slightly, as if indicating that he couldn't understand what she was saying either.

"Is it my spear?" She pointed to her spear with her free hand. It was true she hadn't tried to enter their halls armed before. It might be making the guards overly cautious. "I can leave the spear with you. I don't need it inside."

There was a pause, the guard looking more distressed. "You cannot pass," the guard repeated, shaking his head, his eyes looked more frightened than intimidating. Tersh felt like she could have just pushed past them and they wouldn't have done anything to stop her.

There was no point in trying to rush past them though. She tightened her grip on her skins. She had enough to trade and pay for another place to stay. There was nothing left for her there. If the kings would not see her, they damned their people, but she could go on to Nesate and then return again to this place. Perhaps if she had success in Nesate, convincing these fools would be easier.

She turned away, not sure where to go, but just decided to take whatever road she came upon. She took a bridge over the wide river that ran from the palace to the docks outside the walls. The city was closing down. Stalls were packing up their wares and shops were locking their doors for the night. The streets were mostly empty, only a few people here and there making their way home, most likely. The only noise she really heard came from the alehouses and inns. She needed to find one that would let her stay. She would have better luck, she realized, if she turned her cloak inside-out.

Tersh stopped to do just that, when she noticed that the street she was on ended in a large gate. It seemed out of place for a neighbourhood that the rich did not inhabit. The gate was massive, at least as tall as the buildings around it, either side of the entrance heralded by large statues of men. They held their arms out, their hands up, as though warning them not to enter this place.

There was just enough light left in the sky to catch a glimpse of what was through the gates, and Tersh was curious. She walked the rest of the way, finding it odd that such imposing gates had nothing blocking the entrance, neither door nor fence. Anyone could walk through, yet the street beyond was completely deserted. She came to the entrance, standing between the statues, but not daring to walk through them. The atmosphere seemed to change around her, a colder wind blew out, and she shivered as she saw what the walls surrounded.

It was a road. Three times as wide as the one she stood on, but the same road nonetheless. She turned around, looking back the way she came. The road led straight back to the Hall of a Thousand Gods. This road must have been a twin of the grand avenue lined with leopard statues, but while that one remained pristine and exquisite, this one had been abandoned to shop owners and innkeepers who needed more space, building onto the road, shrinking it to its current size, all save for this one portion which had been walled off and remained untouched.

She looked back through the gate, to the statues that lined the avenue. The other avenue had been lined with stone statues, but this one was lined with bronze ones. She couldn't make out what the figures were at first. They seemed twisted, each one completely different from its neighbour. She didn't need to guess what they were. She knew. The last rays of sun just barely glinted off what had once been the heads of a thousand Whisperers.

Tersh shivered, taking a step through and walking up to the closest of the statues. The man had been standing, his arms had been stretched away from his body, his legs spread apart. His face must have been looking up, for now his head seemed to crumple backwards. She could just make out the pained expression on his face, his teeth gritted, his eyes closed tightly, but the rest of the details of his face were obscured by the glops of hardened bronze. They must have poured the liquid metal over his head.

The air seemed to catch in her throat. She looked at the next one. This man had his arms and legs bound tightly together. Tersh could still see the chains wrapped around his body. He hadn't been completely covered in bronze though.

His head had lolled forward, and where his face had once been, the bronze had not entirely covered, and she could just make out the smoothness of his skull.

"I wouldn't touch that. No, not I." The voice was calm, but had a certain command to it.

Tersh pulled back her hand. She hadn't even realized she had been reaching for the Whisperer, and turned around.

"Why not?" The last rays of light disappearing behind the buildings, but she could still make out the figure in the fading dusk. His hair was shoulder-length, sandy-black, and his chin had a shaggy light beard. She couldn't make out his eyes so well, but they seemed dark whatever they were.

"Do you know why the gates have no door?" the man asked softly.

"It is not a forbidden place?" Tersh shrugged to appear unconcerned. She suddenly wished she were not standing within the gates anymore, but did not want to look like she feared standing among the dead of her own people.

"It is a forbidden place," the man smiled, like he was telling a joke. "We need no door here, because every man, every woman, every child, knows this place cursed. They know only someone wishing to die comes here."

"I am a Whisperer. I need not fear their curse."

"No? Then why you look desperate to leave this place?"

Tersh realized she was still shivering, and started walking towards the gate, trying to keep as much distance from the man as possible. "I am merely too cold to continue standing here."

"Ah, you need place to rest?" The man reached out, not grabbing her, but touching her shoulder to stop her.

Tersh shrugged away the touch, but stopped walking.

"Do you know of an inn?"

"One that would wish for a Whisperer of the Dead to stay under roof? There's no such inn at these parts. No, I'm sure every inn you visit will tell you that 'oh so sorry,' all their rooms are filled this evening."

Tersh took off her cloak in one swift motion, then folded it up and placed it into her skins. She was instantly colder, and she hated having to hide it away. The thought suddenly occurred to her that she could take some of her skins and stitch them over the bones, but she doubted she had enough skins to spare.

"Why, you don't look a Whisperer at all now," the man said positively, but Tersh couldn't tell if he was being serious.

"Goodnight. May the gods walk with you," Tersh nodded, continuing on her way.

"Wait, wait," the man followed. "My name's Arzaia. What's yours, friend?"

"I am called Tersh Hal'Reekrah of the tribe Go'angrin," Tersh tried walking faster, but Arzaia seemed to easily match her pace.

"That's quite long name. Is it all right if I call you Tersh?"

"How is it you speak the tongue of Mahat so well?" Tersh asked, wondering if this man was a merchant. She may have liked Samaki, but most merchants were interested in profit only and would take advantage of any situation they thought might benefit them.

"I often travelled there when younger. My father was a priest, and so I learned their tongue."

"Your father was a priest? And what are you?" Tersh looked at the clothes he wore, a simple wool cloak, a hide tunic and leggings. The man wasn't poor, but he didn't look like well off.

"I work in the inn. I find weary travellers like yourself, help them find beds," he pointed down a street, motioning them to follow.

Tersh looked down the avenue. It seemed wide and had many inns along it. She was suddenly weary the man might be trying to take her to a small alley to rob her, so she kept her distance as they turned down the road.

"Your family's inn?" Tersh asked.

"No, no. My father was priest. I found work in the inn after I decided following the gods was not a path for me. Come, here." He stopped by a building.

There was light and noise coming from inside, which made Tersh certain that it wasn't an empty building, but did nothing to allay the thought that it was filled with men hoping to ambush her. She hesitated.

"I don't have much to trade," Tersh said.

"We make good price for you, friend," he motioned again, perhaps a tad too eagerly.

"No, I think I'll stay elsewhere," she took a step back.

In the same moment Arzaia reached out to grab her and shouted a word in his own tongue. Tersh couldn't understand it, but just then the door to the inn was thrown open and from it five men holding knives – and one a short sword – came out and rushed towards her.

Tersh barely had time to raise her spear to block the sword coming down on her. It imbedded itself into the wooden shaft, but luckily the spear held. Still, in another breath the others would be on her. She seemed aware of every single movement around her. One man's arm being raised, another muttering some kind of curse-word, Arzaia slinking off into the surrounding shadows, the sword being yanked out of her spear so it could be used to come at her again.

She put one leg back, crouching down. She had never turned a blade on a person, but the motion seemed natural as she aimed the head of the spear at his sternum. The man's arms were raised; there was nothing to stop the blade from slipping into his soft flesh. She heard the man grunt, felt the spear stick into him, just as a knife came down on her left arm.

Tersh cried out in pain, losing her grip on her spear and stumbling back. Someone grabbed the sword from the fallen man, who crumpled to the street, blood gurgling out of his mouth as he moaned in pain. Tersh stumbled back, four armed men coming at her, with no way to defend herself against them all.

I speak for the Goddess of Death, she thought to herself. *I cannot die here.*

The man closest to her, whose knife was a hand's length from plunging into her chest, suddenly called out in agony, falling to his knees. Tersh first saw the bronze spear in his side, then the man who held it. All attention turned to this stranger. The three still standing turned to the newcomer, now aiming their attacks at him.

The stranger pulled the spear out, chucking it swiftly towards the man farthest from him. Before the spear hit he was already pulling a sword from the belt at his side. He slashed at one man's belly, and as he folded over, clutching at his guts to keep them from spilling onto the street, he stabbed the next man in the throat – just as the spear hit the man, easily sliding into his ribs, and throwing him onto his back.

Everything went still. Some of the men on the ground were still groaning in pain, but it was clear from their injuries they would be dead soon. The man with the sword in his neck stood a moment longer, his eyes open wide in shock. His arm came up to grab the blade but went limp before he could reach it. He collapsed onto the street next to his fellow cutthroats.

Tersh scrambled to grab her spear, jerking it out of the now dead man. She swivelled around to aim at this newcomer, but the man was paying no attention to Tersh. He was wiping his bloody sword on one of the dead men's clothes, before putting it back into his belt.

He muttered something, then spat on their bodies, before walking over to retrieve his own spear.

Tersh felt her body relax, and became aware of how fast her heart was beating, and how heavily she was breathing. "Who... who are you," she asked in the tongue of Mahat, hoping the man could understand.

The stranger regarded Tersh a moment, and the Whisperer got a good look at him. His hair was a lighter colour than most of his people had, perhaps brightened by the sun, and she thought he had sandy eyes, it was hard to tell. From the few grey hairs speckling his beard Tersh guessed he had seen around three full cycles.

"Are you a soldier?" Tersh asked, but the man wore no insignia or helmet.

He laughed softly. "... I was a soldier." He answered slowly, perhaps not sure if he could trust the Whisperer.

"I am called..." her voice seemed weak. She stood to her full height – which was still shorter than this man – and cleared her throat. "I am called Tersh Hal'Reekrah of the tribe Go'angrin."

"Well, Tersh Hal'Reekrah. My name is Tuthalya, and I suggest you go home to your tribe. These streets are no place for a Whisperer of the Dead."

"Of the Gods," Tersh was quick to correct him.

Tuthalya grinned. "I'm sure..." he turned to walk away.

"What of these men?" Tersh looked around, all five were dead now, Arzaia still nowhere to be seen.

"They're another man's mess to clean. You best leave before they're found though. People here won't take kindly to a Rattlecloak having killed them, even if they were scum."

Tersh looked at the first man who had fallen. The man she had killed with barely a second thought. Shouldn't she feel more... something? Shouldn't she just feel more? She felt nothing for the dead man, except perhaps relief that she wasn't the one lying on the street in a pool of blood.

"I've... never killed a man before," then Tersh looked up at Tuthalya in surprise. "How did you know I was a Whisperer?"

The man chuckled. "Everyone knows who you are. Even if they didn't see you with your cloak. Your hair and face, you're a ruby in a sea of diamonds. Everyone knows there's a Whisperer walking among them. You don't look like anyone from Mahat; you certainly don't look like one from Ethia. So you must be the Whisperer everyone is talking about. Why do you think I saved your life?"

"You fear my blood on your streets?"

"This city was built of the bones of your people, its walls were mortared with your blood, and it has been cursed ever since. This land needs no more curses. You're right, I was a soldier once, but this land only takes," his laugh turned into a sigh. "There's nothing here for me. I'm leaving, going back to my family's home in the mountains."

"Nesate?" Tersh turned in the direction the mountains must have been, though they were hidden in darkness.

"No, far closer. After the winter, when the pass has cleared, I will leave here. Until then, I need no more curses. So, I say again, go home. Leave us be."

"Is there an inn that will take me?"

Tuthalya laughed. "No. There is no inn. There is no one."

The ex-soldier continued to walk, and Tersh let him go. She turned and left as well, going back the way she had come. No, there was no inn and no one to care for her. There was still one place for her though. The gate soon loomed in front of her again. There was only one place for a Whisperer in this city.

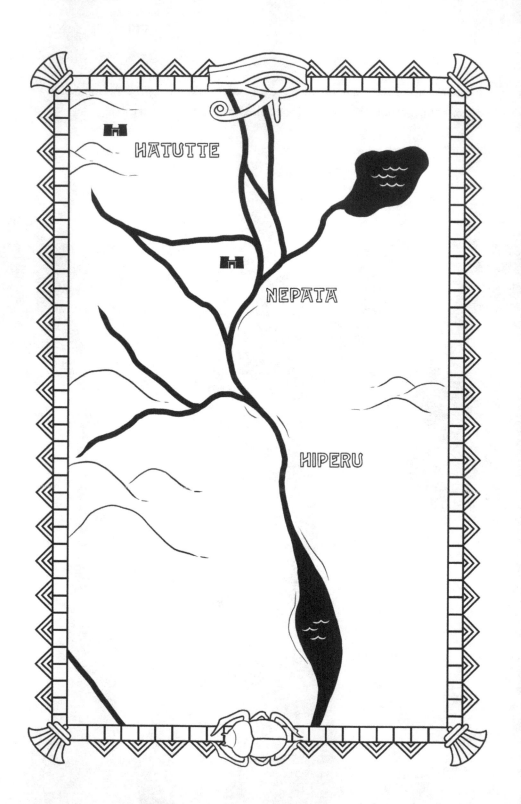

NEPATA

THE STREETS ARE FILLED WITH PEOPLE

The journey south along the Hiperu river was blissfully swift. The Afeth followed the current, and if the winds were right they could unfurl their sails to double their speed. Samaki was eager to return, eager to get his affairs sorted, to pay his debts and plan his next move.

The bright limestone walls of Nepata were a welcome sight. The west gate they entered was identical to the south gate that led back to the Sea Mahat. The only difference was in the statues on either side of the gate. They held the same pose, one foot forward, an arm across their chest holding a sword as though ready to meet any enemy. The only difference was that these two statues depicted the god Anmur who had the head of a leopard and Ha'alat who had the head of a scorpion. These were gods who loved war and battle.

The guards stationed atop the wall made little notice of them or any of the other ships entering. Samaki couldn't help but feel unease as he looked at the thick wooden and bronze gates that always remained open. His time in Hattute had left him feeling uneasy. Those kings, especially Hatturigus, looked restless on their thrones. For now maybe they were preoccupied with their own civil war, but what if the Go-man was right? What if that flood was only the beginning? Nepata would need to start watching their gates a little closer.

They entered the canals, heading towards the same inn they had stayed at last time. Samaki stayed there whenever he could. He was friends with the innkeeper, Pawura, and always received a good price from the man.

Samaki didn't want to call on the services of any of the tzati or royals again. He was worried they might learn of his 'favour' for the new Paref and ask for one of their own. He just wanted to leave this city as soon as possible and head back towards the Sephian Islands. However, he had promised Tersh he would tell the boy she'd arrive in Hattute safely, and he might be able to get some help from Imotah before heading back towards the Sea Mahat.

For the briefest of moments, he thought it might be nice to stop at his old village, to see his father again, but then he remembered.

"You look distracted, Maki," Tiyharqu said, slapping him hard on the shoulder. "Tonight we will have drinks and women. You aren't happy?"

Tiyharqu laughed, but Samaki nodded towards the streets they could make out through the buildings.

"Doesn't something seem different to you?" Samaki asked.

Tiyharqu squinted to get a good look at the people. It seemed like the population on the streets had doubled since the last time they had been there. Most of them seemed aimless, and they wore rags – though that was being generous with how shabby they looked.

"Where do you think they've come from?" Tiyharqu asked, her voice seeming slightly less jovial than before.

"The south. Where else?"

They arrived at the inn soon after, mooring along the courtyard of the inn. The same guards as before met them and Samaki threw a leather purse down to them.

"Tell Pawura I have thirsty men who need a roof over their heads," Samaki gave his best smile.

"Aye, there are many thirsty men these days," the guard pulled open the purse, peeking inside before slipping it into his dark tunic. "How long do you intend to stay?"

"It's hard to say. I have merchandise to sell and buy before I can move on. It could be one or two months."

The guard stepped back, waving them down.

"If you can keep paying, the inn keeper will keep feeding you. You can make arrangements with him inside," he turned, his attention being taken by a small dingy trying to dock next to them.

✦ ✦ ✦ ✦ ✦

It was still high afternoon, so Samaki decided to pay the tzati a visit. Sef was anxious to see how Kareth was doing and followed his captain. They hired a small reed boat to carry them to the tzati's estate. Luckily, the guards at the gate still recognized Samaki, and he was let in to the lush gardens.

"Tahye!" the guard yelled towards a young servant girl who was rushing towards to stables with a bowl of hot water. "Please inform the great and noble Tzati Imotah that Captain Samaki here has come to pay him a visit."

The girl looked frantic. There was a lot of activity near the stables. She dutifully handed water to another man standing there and rushed over to the gate. Samaki looked at the crowd, trying to spot Kareth, but didn't see him.

"I think Imotah said he'd put Kareth to work there," he nodded to Sef.

"I think I'll go have a look then." Sef grinned and headed over to the crowd while Samaki followed the girl towards the house.

"What's going on there?"

"There's been, ah, an accident," the girl flushed, speeding up her walk. Although she wasn't complaining, Samaki could tell she was obviously busy and annoyed that she had to add yet another task to her plate.

"I hope everyone is all right."

"Yes, it's just the—" she clenched her mouth shut, as though she had been about to say something very rude, then took a deep breath and continued in a calmer voice: "The stable master was injured last night."

"I'm sorry to hear that..." Samaki couldn't quite remember the stable master, though he'd seen him the day they had left. He seemed to recall that he was a grizzled man. "I hope he recovers soon."

"Of course," Tahye wore a strained smile.

They walked through the main entrance, into the dark cool hall.

"Please wait here," Tahye bowed her head and then rushed through a doorway. Samaki waited a long while, staring back out through the window at the people near the stables.

"Ah! Welcome back, captain."

Samaki turned and smiled as he saw Imotah standing in the open doorway Tahye had disappeared through.

"Tzati," the two came towards each other and clasped arms. "How are you?"

"Fantastic, all things considered," the tzati smiled wide and led him through into the room. There were golden chairs seated around a pool of water.

"What things?"

"My fool of a stable master got himself kicked in the head by one of my prize stallions... again. A little too much drink. And worse, the streets are filled with people, but none of them have anything to trade," Imotah shrugged. "I hope you've brought something of value back from Hattute."

"Silver and copper and all the rest."

"Fabulous," Imotah gave one of his famous smiles. "Come, have a seat. We'll talk over some honey beer – the good vintage," Imotah clapped his hands and a young boy who'd been standing in the corner raced out of the room.

He motioned to one of the golden chairs, and Samaki sat.

Samaki laughed. "Of course."

Almost instantly the boy came back with two silver cups and a pitcher brimming over with bittersweet beer on a tray. He kneeled between the two chairs, holding the tray out and acting as a table while Imotah took the other seat. "A toast, to your silver."

They held their cups up, nodding at each other, taking a long sip at the same time.

"Ah," Samaki put his cup down on the tray, looking at the boy uneasily. The boy made no effort to get up and move.

"They've been trickling in for months now, ever since the end of Ahken. Those who had ships were the first to arrive, but now those who made the journey on foot are joining them," Imotah finished his cup.

"On foot?" Samaki grimaced. "They must be desperate."

"They are. The flood waters receded but left the soil rich in salt. They couldn't grow food and they couldn't pay their taxes. Most of them abandoned their farms rather than face their keti's punishment. If they stayed, they would starve, so they came here."

"But with nothing to trade..." Samaki looked into his cup, the liquid bubbling silently.

"They starve here. Every day I see a body floating down the river. They should have gone to the lake villages instead of coming here." Imotah lifted the pitcher, refilling both their cups.

"I'm sure some did," Samaki shrugged, still staring at his cup, but not drinking. "These are dark times, Imotah."

"Dark times, ha," Imotah took another sip, holding the cup to his lips, lost in thought for a moment. "These people have come for food, but if they want food they need to work, only there aren't enough jobs for all of them. So most will die... and when they die, their bodies will rot on the streets, and then will come pestilence and disease. *Those* will be the dark times."

"This isn't the end of Mahat." Samaki felt like he was saying that to himself instead of to Imotah.

Imotah put his empty cup back on the tray. "I've seen famine before, of course. A few failed crops here and there, but the entire Sea Mahat ravaged? I have no idea what that will do to this land," he shrugged. "Then again. The waters have receded, and the land will bloom again eventually. Things will get better. They always do."

Samaki picked up his cup, unable to voice his thoughts, but feeling in his heart that things would not be getting better this time.

The inn was about half an hour away on foot. Samaki and Tiyharqu made their way there on muddy streets after the skies had opened to unleash a torrent of rain. Rain was rare in the Mountain Mahat. In the swamps of the Sea Mahat it rained all the time, but here it always took him by surprise. It maybe rained once a year, but when it did... He tried wiping the water from his eyes, but it was futile. He felt like he had been thrown into the Hiperu. Tiyharqu was smiling though, opening her mouth to catch drops. Rain was always a joyous occasion for Tiyharqu.

By the time they made it to the inn, the rain had stopped but they were wet through to their bones. Samaki opened the door and stepped into the warm room, a puddle of water forming around his feet. A few men sitting in the large low-ceiling room gave a chuckle when they saw him and Tiyharqu, but most were more interested in the musicians playing in the back, of the beer on their tables. There was singing drowning out most of the sounds around them.

They approached the smiling innkeeper, a large man with a clear love for gold, judging from the excessive jewellery he wore.

"Did you have a late-night swim?" He asked with a loud booming voice.

Samaki just frowned, he didn't feel like exchanging pleasantries with the man. "I'm here to meet a man by the name of Weneg."

"Weneg?" The innkeeper scrunched his face up, as he tried to think of the name or face.

Samaki sighed. He hadn't wanted to come here in the first place. He had been hoping to trade with the usual merchants he dealt with in the past, but the usual merchants seemed to have disappeared. Everything had been displaced by the wave, and he had spent the last few days making new contacts. It was just like restarting from the young marshman's son he had once been. His hold was full of wares he couldn't barter or trade yet. Imotah had convinced him to come and meet this Weneg person. Imotah seemed confident that Weneg could set them up with a buyer for their weapons. "What can I get you? Bread and beer?"

Samaki nodded, taking a seat. "Yes, yes, fine."

"You sit, I'll ask around for Weneg," Tiyharqu offered.

Samaki had a feeling she just wanted to move closer to the musicians and enjoy the music.

"Come back when you find him," Samaki grunted.

He sat down, scanning the faces in the room, the mix of skin shades, men and women from a dozen different places, all come together for a common cause, food and drink – and entertainment, of course. Some weren't content with merely singing. They jumped up next to the musicians and began to dance.

He had expected Imotah to ask for something in return for telling Samaki about Weneg, but he had feigned some nicety about how he was thankful towards Samaki for bringing Kareth into his service. Imotah said that he owed Samaki a small – ever so small – favour. Apparently Kareth was doing well. Sef had rejoined him as he'd left to tell him he'd seen the lad, that he'd put on weight. Kareth was working in the kitchens and could have a half-decent conversation in a real language now.

A cup of beer and flat bread came. Samaki tore off chunks, dipping it into the beer, absentmindedly chewing as he wondered how long he would have to wait. He heard the raised voices, but thought nothing of them at first, not until the other sounds in the room began to die away, as attention turned towards the fight that was breaking out.

"If you have nothing to give, you can't eat!" The innkeeper bellowed at a young man, skinny and dirty, though he still looked strong enough to be a threat. He had just come in, and his rags were as wet and muddy as Samaki was.

"Let me work for it. I can clean the–" The man was taller than the innkeeper, and although his voice sounded desperate, he leaned forward as though he meant to attack.

"I don't need your filthy hands to clean my inn! This is not a place for the flotsam of that damn wave."

The man looked like he was about to speak again. His hand was squeezed into a tight fist. But instead of striking, he turned and stomped out the door, leaving a trail of mud behind him. Samaki looked down at his bread, it seemed hard and tasteless to him. He pushed it away, as the innkeeper started laughing.

"Let's drive out the rats with music," he called out, and the singing resumed as though nothing had happened.

"The gods should have drowned them all," the man next to Samaki muttered to his companion. Their shaved heads glistened as their heads bobbed with laughter.

"I don't know," his companion smiled. "I liked their women. They tasted salty."

"They tasted like marshlands and looked like fish too. The gods were right to wipe them away, to leave more space for real men."

"Real men?" Samaki gripped his cup. "I see no real men here."

They looked over at Samaki, glaring at his interruption. "Maybe you should stop looking at your reflection in your beer."

Samaki looked at his beer, the murky white colour, solids floating near the top. It was like staring at the waters that had churned up soil, carrying bits of debris and corpses after the wave had crashed against the land.

"You wouldn't laugh if you had seen it, if you had been there," he took a sip of his beer, the sweet honey soothing his throat.

"Bah," one of the men spat. "You're from the Sea Mahat? You should go back. We can't feed you bastards."

"You're not feeding anyone," he looked them over. They obviously weren't merchants, they wore nothing of value, and their clothes were basically rags. They were sailors, most likely. "You're not farmers, or fishermen. Most of them were, though. Fields of wheat and barley are gone. They'll starve to death first, but you'll follow soon after."

"Is that a threat?" One of the men clenched his teeth.

Samaki laughed quietly. "I don't feel like teaching you ignorant whore sons a lesson."

"What did you say?" One of the men stood up in anger, his companion put his hand on his arm, not holding him back, but warning him to be cautious.

"I'm sorry. Obviously my words were too hard for you to understand. I said you are stupid, and your mother has fucked every sailor from Sareeb to Hattute."

The man lunged at Samaki, who had just enough time to grab his cup and smash it into the man's face. They went sprawling to the ground, the man falling on top of him, clutching his face in pain, blood spurting from between his fingers. Samaki kicked him off, just as his companion grabbed Samaki by the vest, his other hand connecting with Samaki's cheek.

Samaki tried to stand up and move away, but he lost his balance, and felt the fist hit his face again, this time hitting his ear. The world suddenly became muffled and dull. He couldn't seem to focus on the man holding onto him, his eyes swam over the sea of faces. He saw the dark figure emerge from the crowd, like a shadow cast from a lit torch. She reached them, grabbing onto the man assaulting Samaki, pulling him off and throwing him to the ground.

Tiyharqu had lost her usual smile as she grabbed Samaki's arm and helped him to stand. "What are you doing?"

"Teaching him a lesson," Samaki smiled, his face already becoming swollen. "Watch out!"

The man was on his feet again, he was charging at Tiyharqu, who turned and with one vicious punch to his neck sent the man sprawling onto the ground. He made a gurgling sound, but didn't try to get back up. The man with the bleeding face had pulled out a knife. A jagged cut was on the bridge of his nose, his mouth and chin covered in blood.

"Come here you scum!" he screamed, spitting blood as he raised the knife.

Tiyharqu dodged the knife, crouching low and punching the man in the side, once, twice, and then a third time in the stomach. He groaned as he fell, doubled over and clutching himself in pain. Samaki's hearing slowly returned to normal.

"Get out! Get out!" The innkeeper was screaming.

"For the mess," Samaki muttered, taking off one of his jewelled rings and throwing it onto the table next to his unfinished bread.

They turned and left, and innkeeper's angry screaming followed them out into the night.

"What in the world are you thinking, Maki?" Tiyharqu let loose when the inn was out of sight. They walked fast, the rain having died down to barely a drizzle, in case either of those men got up and tried to follow them, or had any friends who might have seen what happened. "We need business partners, not enemies!"

"They attacked me!" Samaki returned, though his cheek ached from the movement. It would be a while before he would be able to speak without pain.

"Yes, and I am certain you did nothing to provoke them!"

Samaki looked down at the road, gritting his teeth. "They were fools."

"You're the only fool I seem to deal with."

They slowed their pace, the danger seemed to be behind them.

"... I'm sorry. I was in a bad mood. I wasn't thinking," Samaki muttered.

"Well, now I'm in a bad mood," Tiyharqu said, but already her voice was returning to normal. If there was one thing Samaki knew about Tiyharqu, it was that it was impossible for the woman to stay angry, no matter how justified she was.

"We'll have to find this Weneg another way," Samaki said.

"Unless that was Weneg's face you cut open," Tiyharqu shrugged.

"Then we'll find another dealer to trade with," Samaki smiled, and Tiyharqu couldn't help but join as well, her bright smile seeming to light up the dark road.

"Maybe let me do the talking next time."

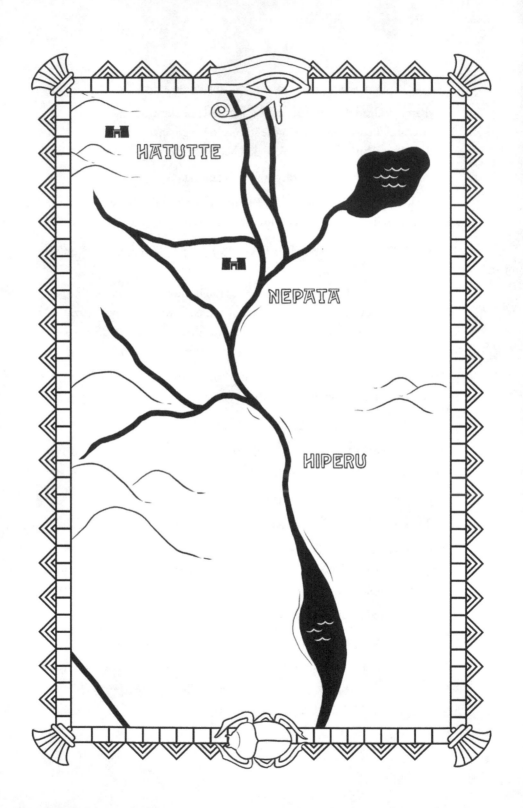

THE PALACE OF THE RISING SUN

I AM THE SPEAKER OF THE GODDESS OF LIFE

Kareth had never seen so much food before, had never even suspected this much food could exist. The preparations for the banquet had started days ago and the coronation was still two days away. He had been sent to the Palace of the Rising Sun, the home of the Paref, with Mistress Ankhet at her request.

"You have a talent for spices," she had remarked with a smile, though whether or not that was true, he had no idea. He was just happy to leave the stables for good.

Animals, grains, fruits and vegetables had been flowing into the palace for days. The courtyard outside the kitchens was packed, and Kareth couldn't help but stare with wide, hungry eyes, until Mistress Ankhet would give him a rather strong pat on the head and tell him to get back to grinding the grain into flour on the large stone slab.

The servant's side of the palace looked no different than Imotah's home. The last time he had seen the palace he had sailed in on the river and been able to peak at the beautiful lush gardens, but this time he walked in through the back. There was no massive stone plaza here, no grand entrance guarded by tall black obelisks. Here there was just a low stone entrance to a large dirt courtyard and a labyrinth of catacombs filled with kitchens and cleaning rooms and crowded quarters. As tzati of the royal court, Imotah had sent his personal cooks and servants to help prepare for the great coronation feast of the young Paref Rama, and sometimes it was hard to move through the halls without bumping into someone.

Unfortunately, the one person he wanted to bump into, the one person he was desperate to talk to, never seemed to be around. Tahye had come to the palace with them, but was whisked away by some task, and he had yet to see her re-emerge from the kitchens.

Tahye didn't even look at Kareth anymore, not since Piye had had his accident. It hadn't been the first time Piye had ended up with a hoof to his head, but this time he didn't recover. He had been alive for days, his eyes wide open, his breathing steady, if not laboured, but despite all the salves and prayers he received, Piye died.

Kareth had been nowhere near the stables at the time. He hadn't even seen Piye after he had been injured. Everything he knew he learned from listening to the stable boys' gossip, but suddenly no one would look him in the eye. Whereas before there was a general disdain for him, now there was something else. Fear? Awe? He had no idea what had caused it, not until he saw Tahye afterwards. He had called out to her, and she had quickly turned and scurried away. She had looked frightened.

It was only later in the day he remembered the dream he had told her about.

"He'll probably scare a horse one day and get a hoof to the head."

He felt a shiver run down his body, the hand of the Goddess of Life caressing his spine. Tersh hadn't believed he was receiving visions from the gods, but here was another one come true. So small and innocuous, and yet exactly how it had happened in his dream. Still, he wished he hadn't told Tahye about it. He hadn't made it happen, yet she and the other young servants looked at him like he had.

He tried to focus on work in the palace, but even that seemed impossible. He kept imagining that somehow he would be called into the main building, and through a series of events finally find his way in front of the Paref. Maybe Imotah would summon him to speak to the great leader, or perhaps that young princess he had met, Harami, would see him from a distance and call on him. Every moment in his mind something occurred that would finally bring him to the end of his mission, but until then he was busy with the tasks Mistress Ankhet had given him.

A few of the goats in a pen next to him were becoming interested in his grains. He tried to move away from them, but that only brought him closer to the pen of hogs on his other side. He wished they would just slaughter the animals already to give them more room to work. The majority of that would only be done the day before the celebration, and he wasn't exactly looking forward to cooking straight through the night and the next day to make sure all the dishes were ready for the evening.

A fisherman entered through the gate carrying a basket. He was one of a dozen who came every hour carrying a basket full of fish or wild birds he'd caught to offer to the Paref. They were carried down into the deepest cellars which were cool and dry. There they were placed in piles of salt to keep them. Earlier a fisherman had come with a maseh, one of those large animals that had nearly killed Kareth when he had fallen overboard. This one had been about as long as Kareth was, which didn't sound very imposing, but even dead it had caused quite a commotion with the younger servants crowding around, poking at its still open eyes. It was in one of the cellars as well, being cut into dry strips rubbed in anise. He had been promised one by Mistress Ankhet, if he managed to get his chores done early.

"Why are you nice to me?" Kareth had asked Ankhet the night after they came to the palace. He had been given a cup full of beer and was feeling warm and dizzy, otherwise he never would have asked the question.

"What along this great river are you asking? I'm nice to everybody," she had replied curtly.

"No one is nice to me," Kareth had shrugged.

"Hm, this is about that dream nonsense, isn't it?" Ankhet sighed.

"Tahye spoke, err, told you?"

"I doubt that girl told anyone, but *you* told her in a kitchen full of servants, and gossip travels fast in these parts," she had laughed, a deep belly-laugh. "People can be too superstitious in times like these."

"Time like these?" the sentence was unfamiliar to Kareth.

"The time between a Paref's death and a new Paref's coronation can be very stressful, spiritually. People see spirits around every corner."

"You don't?" he asked meekly.

Again she had laughed, louder this time. "I've wished a lot worse fates on Piye, and I'm sure I've dreamed of them to. You had the misfortune of telling a room full of on-edge people about a dream that resembled an event that happened a few days later. And those eyes, like the silver on a king's crown." She had stared at his eyes long enough to make him feel uneasy. "No one here has seen eyes like those. It's easy to think you otherworldly. However, it wasn't the first time Piye was struck in the head by a horse. It's all a silly coincidence, and soon everyone will forget."

A part of him was happy to accept it was all a coincidence, if it meant he could talk to Tahye again, but a much stronger part of him felt offense at the very notion. It *wasn't* a coincidence. The Goddess of Life had felt his distress and had sent him a vision. Still, one thing became clear after speaking to Mistress Ankhet. Most people would rather not be confronted with the power of the gods. It was too frightening.

"Kareth!" Mistress Ankhet was waving at him from the doorway to the kitchens. "Come inside, I want your opinion on something!"

Kareth hurriedly put the mill stone aside and scrambled to his feet. Mistress Ankhet was nowhere near as scary as Piye had been, but she still had no qualms about boxing anyone's ears if they were too slow. He scampered into the room, lit by the thin windows and the large ovens. The smell of honeyed bread mixed with dates permeated the air. There were a dozen or so people forming dough into breads of various shapes and sizes, most mimicking the image of animals, or other interesting designs that had no apparent meaning to him, but some looked like the hieroglyphs he saw on the walls everywhere.

"Taste this," Mistress Ankhet shoved a small bowl into his face, a mix of spices. He dipped his finger in and then touched it to his tongue. It was stronger than he expected, and his face twisted into discomfort.

"Bad?"

"Not bad," he coughed. "Just too much."

"Hm, I can't seem to replicate the recipe you taught me," she muttered in annoyance, turning back to a wood table covered in jars of spices and bundles of dried herbs.

He hadn't really taught her the recipe. Before the accident with Piye, when Tahye was still talking to him, he had told her about some of the different foods he had eaten growing up among his people. She had been curious, so Kareth had set about trying to make one of the spice mixtures his mother had often used when cooking. The spices were hard to come by for Whisperers, but his mother loved them so much it was always the first thing she looked for when they traded with merchants. He had fallen asleep at the table as he tried to recreate it, and Mistress Ankhet had found him the morning after. She wasn't angry, she had simply tasted it and remarked that it would taste good on oryx. He had only made it that one time, enough times to make her think he had a talent for spices.

He pulled a stool next to the table, looking at everything laid out on the table and trying to remember what he had mixed the last time, he started smelling the jars, tasting the powders, chewing on a bit of herb here and there, trying to remember the tastes of his youth, the freshness of mint, the tang of mustard seeds, the tingling of cinnamon, the vague sweetness of safflower. It was strange, Zera hadn't even left Orope yet, but already his childhood with the Whisperers felt like a different life.

The loud sound of shattered pottery didn't distract him from his task, but the panicked shouts that followed made everyone turn away and wonder what had happened. A few people ran down the hall. No further noises came, and most people turned back to their work and conversation, but Kareth's curiosity had gripped him and he got up to find out what had happened.

"Put him on the table!" Mistress Ankhet sounded distressed, and that in itself made Kareth uneasy.

"No, get him out of my kitchens!" another woman shouted.

Kareth peeked into the storeroom. Mistress Ankhet was motioning to three men carrying another to the table in the centre of the room, while another woman looked on in annoyance. One of them swiped his arm over the table, pushing the few jars off and crashing them to the floor, spilling the beer they contained.

"What are you fools doing!?!" It was Mistress Baketwernal, or Baket as everyone called her. She was a shrill old woman, thin, but with sagging skin that seemed to move independently beneath her shift. "Take him outside before you break anything else!"

"He needs help before he's moved anymore," Mistress Ankhet said in annoyance.

"You're the tzati's kitchen maid. You have no authority here!" Baket screeched, the man lying on the table moaning as the others tried to comfort him.

Kareth looked at the man who was clearly in pain. At first he didn't see anything wrong with him. He lay there, clearly dazed. There was no blood, nothing wrong with his head or chest or arms. It wasn't until he looked at the man's legs that he noticed something unusual. Everything below his left knee looked... off. The shape of it wasn't quite right, and the colour of it seemed to be darkening with bruises as he stared.

"What happened?" Kareth asked, stepping into the room. Baket and Ankhet were still arguing, but one of the men looked at him.

"One of the carts collapsed as we were unloading it. It crushed his leg," he spoke with worry seeded on his brow.

"Kareth, be gone with you, coriander isn't going to help this boy," Mistress Ankhet waved him away.

"No, not coriander, but..." he struggled to think of the word. He wasn't sure if anyone had taught it to him, certainly he hadn't seen a scorpion since coming here, so he'd never had the chance to ask about it.

"But what?"

"What are you asking some dirty little boy for? A priest is coming, he'll be able to help," Baket snarled.

"I don't know the word. They have tails," he lifted up his arm as though it were the tail of a scorpion, his fingers pinched together like the stinger. He whipped it back and forth, trying to mimic the motion of the little sand beasts. "Poison tails. And big..." he opened and closed his hands fast like the scorpion's claws.

"A nawse?" one of the men asked.

"Maybe? Some, their poisons make good medicine. You have some?" Kareth asked quickly, the man's moaning was becoming stronger, he was coming back to his senses.

"Do you have any in the storerooms?" Ankhet turned to Baket.

"Some," she turned up her nose. "For the feast."

"Get them," Ankhet ordered one of the men, who turned and ran from the room.

"Those are for the Paref!" Baket cried in disbelief.

"I'm sure you have more than enough to spare!" Ankhet roared, and Baket seemed to shrink a little.

"I will make sure you are punished for this," Baket said, then turned and left, bumping into Kareth on purpose as she exited.

"Are you in trouble?" Kareth didn't want the one person who was nice to him suffer on his behalf.

"Ha, unlikely. She is a hippo that one, loud and violent, but so long as you don't stand between her and the water she's harmless," Ankhet smiled to herself, letting out a small chuckle as the man from before rushed back, followed by two young boys, all of them carrying baskets.

"Which ones?" The man asked, opening them all.

Kareth took a step back in surprise. He thought they would all be dead, but the baskets were alive with crawling scorpions. There were three distinct scorpions, one kind in each basket.

"Not those, close that one," Kareth pointed to a basket full of small pale scorpions. Their claws were tiny, but their stingers massive and full of deadly venom. When he was still alive, his father had never been uneasy around anything, except for those scorpions.

Kareth looked at the other two baskets, feeling uncertain. They were both a similar dark colour, though one had a red stripe running down its back. He couldn't remember which ones they might be – or if these scorpions were the right ones at all. He'd only seen the Rhagepe use scorpion venom a handful of times, and only once did they have to kill the scorpions first, usually they had several stingers on hand for such an occasion. The man groaned, muttering something Kareth couldn't understand, and he pointed to the scorpions with the red stripe, whose stingers were slightly smaller.

"Those. We need two," he reached into the basket quickly, grabbing one in each hand by the stingers. One of his favourite childhood games was catching scorpions with his friends, and he couldn't help but be amused by the wide-eyed look on the servants' faces as he grabbed two without hesitating.

He crouched down on the ground. "Sorry, little sand beasts," he spoke in his own tongue as he ripped the stingers off. The scorpions squirmed to get away, but once the stingers were gone and they were back on the ground they went still, completely pacified.

"You have a...?" He mimicked the motion of using a mortar and pestle, the word slipping from his mind as he turned to look about at the still surprised faces.

"Go," Ankhet nodded to one of the boys, who quickly closed his basket and scampered off, only to return a moment later with a small stone bowl and pestle, usually reserved for crushed herbs.

"Mistress," Kareth put the stingers in the bowl and began to crush them. He looked at Ankhet and smiled, "coriander can help. Oil."

"You heard him," Ankhet looked at one of the servants again with exasperation.

The man on the table was becoming frantic with pain, his groans and mutterings were becoming shouts and crying.

"Do you mean to have him drink it?" Ankhet said, clearly not liking the idea.

"No, that is death," the boy had returned with a bottle of coriander oil, and Kareth mixed them together. "I need..." he started to rip his tunic, pulling off long strips.

"Wait," Ankhet said, grabbing a bolt of linen from one of the shelves. Her and the other men helped to tear them up and hand them to Kareth. "These are clean."

Kareth soaked them in his mixture a moment. He looked at the man squirming on the table like the scorpions had done a moment ago. "Some of you need to hold him down, another, lift up his leg."

In the time that he'd been working, the leg had become a swollen sickly mass. It made Kareth uneasy just to look at it. As one of the men grabbed the leg to lift it the man screamed, the scream of a thousand night terrors lashing out at once. Kareth was frightened, watching the man fight against those holding him down, those trying to help him.

"I am the speaker of the Goddess of Life," he whispered to himself, taking a step forward. "I was chosen to walk this path for the gods. I have their power in my skin, in my blood, in my bones."

He started wrapping the soaked linens around the man's leg, starting at the foot, which was by far the most disfigured, and slowly moving up to his knees, all the while taking time to soak more bandages, talking to himself, reminding himself that the man was in pain now only so he could be healed later.

"I am the speaker of the Goddess of Life. We were the first, and we will be the last," he finished, nodding to the man holding his leg, who gently set it back on the table and stepped back.

The man had already started struggling less. His eyes rolled back and his screams turned back into dull moans. From the tingling sensation in his fingers Kareth could already tell it was working. The venom would numb the feeling in his leg, and the coriander would help with the pain a little. For how long, he had no way of guessing, and it certainly wouldn't heal him, but he wouldn't suffer as much waiting for the priest to arrive.

"I need... water," Kareth said, turning quickly, walking as fast as he could without running to the courtyard. He went to the well, the feeling in his fingers disappearing quickly. Luckily a man was at the well, filling a vase full of water. Kareth didn't think he'd be able to grip the rope himself.

"What are you doing?" The man looked down in annoyance as Kareth knocked over the vase, letting the stream of water run over his hands

"Sorry," Kareth muttered, washing his hands as vigorously as he could.

"Let him! Get him more water while you're at it," Ankhet called out, having followed him back into the daylight.

The feeling wasn't coming back to his hands, but it wasn't getting any worse at the very least. For all he knew he had paralyzed some feeling in his fingers for good, and the thought made him sit heavily in the sand, staring at his hands with worry.

"Looks like you have more than just a talent for spices," Ankhet said in a friendly voice, but she wasn't smiling.

"I watched the Rhagepe. I was... interested," Kareth said absent-mindedly. "And Tersh, she taught me some..."

"When they... visited your village, by the lake?" Ankhet asked, a sharpness in her voice, reminding him they weren't alone.

"... Yes. The sand witches traded, sometimes..." Kareth nodded up at her as the man next to them gave Kareth another vase of water.

The man spat. "Damn the sand witches," he muttered, and walked away.

"Kareth. Are you awake?" Mistress Ankhet stood in the doorway to his small room.

He wasn't. He had only just drifted off to sleep. He'd been dreaming that he was walking through a place dense with trees, and hiding among them was one of the statues of leopards he often saw in the streets, only this one was alive and hunting him. He pushed himself up, trying to look fully awake.

They returned to Imotah's villa every day after sunset and would return to the palace just as the sun was beginning to peak over the horizon. Kareth was already curled up, sleep heavily weighing him down, but the sound of her voice brought him back.

He was wearing a new tunic, fresh and white. Ankhet had made sure he was given a new one right away, and a new belt made of plaited reeds. The thought that he would ever own nice clothing had never occurred to him when he still lived among his people, and it was surprising to him how proud he had felt to put the tunic on in front of the jealous stable boys.

"Yes, Mistress Ankhet."

"Don't get up, I'll join you," she said, then sat down, letting out a deep breath as she did so. "Oh Kareth, these bones are old, this body is old. I am old, and fat," she laughed, "but I still have my wits." She reached into a pouch on her belt and handed him a dried strip of maseh. "I believe you were promised this."

With a grin, Kareth reached out and grabbed the salted meat.

"Tell me true, Kareth." Her face had lost its smile.

"Tell what?" Kareth asked uneasily.

"Who are you?"

"I'm Kareth, from the lake villages."

"*Kareth*," her voice had that warning sharpness again. "*Who* are you?"

"... I am Kareth Al'Resh," he whispered now, but his voice was stronger than before, "of the tribe Gorikin."

"Go-man," she practically hissed.

"Gogepe. Whisperer of Gods. I speak for the Goddess of Life."

"You are a child."

"I am not–"

"Hush," she held up her hand. "I speak now, and I need no gods to give me voice. There are some in this land who will fear you for what you are, who will curse you, who will hurt you, or kill you. You can't go around saying that word you have for sand witches. I am not the only person who recognizes it. Where is your mind, boy?"

"I'm sorry," he looked down at his feet. He felt like he was back in the desert, being yelled at by his mother for throwing rocks at the girls.

"Don't be sorry, be smart. What you did today was good, and I hope you can help someone else again one day soon, but that's only going to happen if you're smart. Understand?"

"Yes," he looked her in the eyes, his silver eyes seemed to shine in the dark, reflecting themselves in her sandy eyes. *Learn.* Tersh seemed to be yelling at him from a distant place.

"Now," she smiled mischievously. "Can I see it?"

"See what?" Kareth furrowed his brow.

"Your rattlecloak."

"It's the cloak of my father's father's father, not rattlecloak," he muttered in annoyance, but got up and lifted it from the hay all the same, unrolling it and turning the leather around so she could see the rows and rows of bones stitched to the cloak.

Her lips parted, as though she meant to say something, her hand reached up, but didn't dare touch it. "Kareth," she managed to speak. "Please be careful. If you think a few people hearing about your dream has tipped over your world, imagine what would happen if they heard you speaking of sand witches – not to mention all that muttering you did as you helped that poor boy. People notice. People speak."

Kareth's throat felt dry. "Is he going to be fine? The boy? Did the priest come?"

"He..." she smiled sadly, too sadly. "He won't live the night," she put a heavy hand on his shoulder, "but at least he won't suffer through his last moments here."

She walked away, and the room seemed colder in her absence.

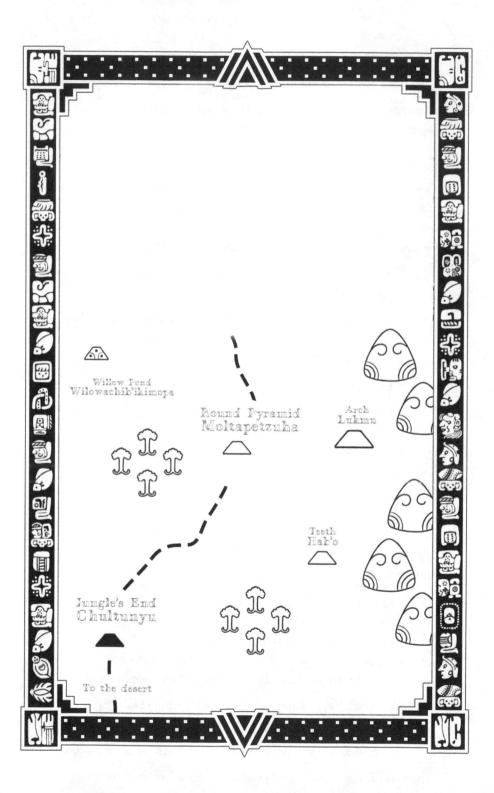

Willow Pond
Wilowachib'ikimopa

Round Pyramid
Moltapetzuha

Arch
Lukmu

Teeth
Hab'o

Jungle's End
Chultunyu

To the desert

THE JUNGLE

IT HAS ONLY JUST BEGUN

When Sha'di dreamed now, he walked through a sea of faces. He saw the faces of his tribe, some of them with the same bright red hair he himself had. They would smile and cheer him on. "Speaker of Rebirth! Speaker of Rebirth!" Nnenne would reach out for him, but before their hands could touch her fingers lengthened into feathers. She would transform into a falcon and circle above him as he continued his journey.

He saw the faces of the three Rhagepe who had chosen him to go on this journey, those gnarled women with their shocking white hair and silver eyes. Their skin was like the leather cloaks they wore on their back and their nails as sharp as the fire daggers they used in their ceremony. They would point at him, blood dripping from their nails. "The wrath of the gods is being brought down on us," they would whisper, accusatory. "We must go to the kingdoms and demand they heed the gods or else the world shall be swallowed by water a second time."

He would walk by Tetchtok and the other men who had led him into the jungle, past the laughing children who used to watch the falcon Nnenne do tricks for them by the river in Chultunyu, though now each one had the same bloody wound on their sternum as the others who had been sacrificed. He would see Tanuk's serious face, next to his younger brother's smiling one. He would see Xupama's disapproving gaze, and the determined stare of the young man sacrificed atop the round pyramid at Moltapetzuha.

All the faces would greet him as he walked towards the Rhagepe's temple, where now always, always, the burning woman would greet him with a blistering embrace.

Sha'di would always wake up before the sunrise, feeling cold in the muggy heat. He would feed Nnenne before finding any food for himself. Sometimes he would look at the falcon, remembering seeing the woman he loved transforming in his dream. They shared a name, couldn't they also share a mind? Could Nnenne Hal'Sharag of the tribe Gonnamdi hear the words spoken to Nnenne the falcon? He would say a few pleasantries to Belam and the men he had come to call friends, but usually he avoided any real conversation with them. He didn't want to add to the parade of faces that haunted him every night.

He had been shocked by how often it rained when he had first come here. Sometimes it had been such a downpour it felt like he was wading through a river. Yet that experience paled in comparison to how often it rained now. It was a continual stream of misery. Now when someone announced that it had stopped raining, what they really meant was that it had started to drizzle.

When once they had walked through the jungle with a kind of jovial atmosphere, now everyone was quiet and always looked straight ahead. Nnenne no longer sat on Sha'di's shoulder. Instead he carried her shivering in his arms, trying to cover her with his cloak. Her wings were so waterlogged she could not fly at all. She merely flapped them uselessly when she felt aggravated. They slept under tarps, and while that kept the water from falling on them, nothing stopped the streams of water flowing on the ground beneath them as they tried to sleep. It wasn't all that surprising to Sha'di that he now preferred the feeling of burning in his dreams to the perpetual damp and wet he was forced to endure upon waking.

Tanuk had shrugged when Sha'di had asked him why it was raining so much. "Now is the time of rain." He said it so matter-of-factly, like it didn't bother him at all. Admittedly, Tanuk never looked like anything bothered him. His younger brother, on the other hand, expressed what he was certain everyone was thinking on the inside.

"Curse the rain!" he muttered every once in a while, wringing the sling he always carried in frustration. It would make Sha'di smile to himself. *Yes, curse the rain.* The mere sentiment would be blasphemy to his people, but he didn't care.

He wasn't with his people. He was with the Petzuhallpa, and they hated the rain and now so did he.

It had been two turns of the moon since they had left Moltapetzuha, and no one could say when they would reach their next stop, the pyramid of Chub'al. Apparently, it never took the same amount of time to travel between two places, because the jungle was always growing over their paths, and the way they walked would change.

"There used to be roads, large and well-kept, but those days are long gone. We keep to our own now," Tanuk had told him one night. Sha'di would occasionally join the brothers in their tent for dinner. He enjoyed the meetings mostly because it meant he could be out of the rain for a while, giving Nnenne a chance to dry herself by a fire, but it was also nice to learn more about the Grey Mist.

Tanuk couldn't tell him how long ago those roads existed, or why they had stopped using them, or even if they had really existed at all. While going through the katytz together in Moltapetzuha, Sha'di had learned from Tanuk that for a long time the Petzuhallpa only lived in the south of the jungle, but then something changed and they began to move north. The roads disappeared, and the huitl of places like Chultunyu and Moltapetzuha became known as the nuktatl, the old lords.

Sha'di tried to imagine the jungle with large roads cut into it, wondering how much faster it would have been to go from one pyramid to the other without having to chop your way through it and stop because the foliage proved too thick. It was laborious and frustrating to have to find a way to go around without losing their bearings. He asked Belam about it one time, but the young warrior had shrugged and asked what they needed roads for anyway.

"There's less rain today, don't you think?" Sha'di said, ironically, holding his hand out and feeling the torrents of water falling.

Tanuk smiled at the Whisperer. "Yes, a very dry day... compared to yesterday."

His younger brother, Tenok, was shivering uncontrollably. Sha'di imagined it was out of discomfort more than feeling chilled, merely from the fact that the rain was reasonably warm. If håe wasn't so wet, he would have quite liked this temperature. It was far nicer than the intense humidity he had dealt with when first coming to the Grey Mist.

Tenok's teeth chattered. "I was a fool to leave Chultunyu. I was always dry in Chultunyu."

"It doesn't rain so hard in Chultunyu?" Sha'di asked, readjusting his cloak to keep Nnenne dry in the crook of his arm.

"Oh, it rains like this," Tanuk nodded, "but there we had a roof over our heads. Here, the canopy does not do as good a job, I think."

"Does it last long?"

"Oh," Tanuk smiled grimly, "it has only just begun."

"I should have stayed in Chultunyu. I'd be in the hall right now, playing with the little ones, laughing at the chakatl trying to keep their feathers dry as they climbed the ramp." Tenok chuckled through the click-clack of his teeth.

It wasn't hard to imagine. Xupama had been quite the sight over the last few days, attempting to keep his grand feathered headdress from wilting, but still trying to keep it on his head as much as possible.

"Soon our dear Xupama will be asking to join you under my cloak," Sha'di had remarked to Nnenne.

Sha'di smiled at Tanuk, but his face seemed to have darkened. The little ones, his younger brother had said. Sha'di realized the importance those words had for Tanuk. The little ones, his sons.

"Are they... they come to Chipetzuha?" Sha'di asked, searching for the right words, hoping not to offend.

"My sons?" Tanuk looked at him, frowning. "Yes, it is the path all the nuktatl must take. My father travelled there, his father before him, and so on since Chipetzuha was first built."

"Why go there? It's not an easyâ path to take," Sha'di looked around, nodding towards the procession of people struggling through the dense jungle and rain,

"There's *no* path to take," Tenok shivered.

"We are the Petzuhallpa. Our place is together, the huitl ruling together, living under the protection of the gods, and their blessing is at Chi-"

Tanuk was thrown to the ground before Sha'di, and it took the Whisperer a moment to see the large feline that had tackled Tanuk into the tangled undergrowth, and far longer to hear the gurgling noises coming from Tanuk's mouth as the black beast's jaw clamped onto his throat, red blood being washed away by the clear water as quickly as it spurted. It took a lifetime to see everything that was happening in front of him, but that lifetime ended as he blinked, and suddenly the world exploded into motion.

Someone knocked Sha'di down in an effort to reach Tanuk. Sha'di could hear wild screaming around him. He turned, pushing himself up. Nnenne was free of his cloak, flapping wildly and trying to fly away, but her wings so waterlogged she could barely lift herself off the ground.

The beast dropped Tanuk, and his brother was instantly at his side, grabbing his arm, shaking him and screaming his name, but Tanuk remained motionless, his eyes wide, the white of them nearly blinding to Sha'di.

A warrior jumped at the animal, brandishing his yaxha, the black jagged rocks sticking out of the wooden sword glinted in the rain. The beast batted the weapon away with one paw, and with the other paw opened the man's stomach, shedding his intestines onto the jungle floor. Sha'di saw the man screaming and flailing as he fell to the ground, but more importantly he saw the man's weapon lying in a puddle.

Sha'di had always been a good tracker, but hunting was never in his blood. He picked up the surprisingly heavy yaxha. The balance of a weapon felt unnatural in his hands. He didn't know what he should do, except run forward and fight.

The beast was looking around wildly as two well-aimed clay balls hit it in its square head, its ears going back in anger. It bared its teeth as it roared at its attacker – and found Tenok. Tenok stood over his older brother as a lion stands over her cubs when hunters have come upon them. There was a ferocity in his eyes Sha'di had never seen before, had never known Tenok had ever possessed. Tenok was quickly loading another shot into his sling, but the beast was moving too fast, it would reach Tenok and open him up just as easily as it had the man at Sha'di's feet.

Sha'di screamed and brought down the yaxha. The jagged stones dug into the wet black fur near its tail, ripping a bright red hole into its left flank. It roared, a high-pitched wail, as it swung around. The weapon was ripped from Sha'di's hands and he took a step back in fear. He fell as more warriors rushed to move in and fight.

It lunged at the nearest standing man, jumping over Sha'di, who could not help but be awed by the grace and silence of the creature as it flew through the air, crashing into the man. The man only just managed to bring his arm up, and the beast's long teeth tore into his flesh as two other warriors slashed down at it with yaxha, cutting at its back. It was clearly mortally wounded, but it turned to attack again.

It saw Sha'di. Its yellow eyes locked onto him. He tried to back up, slipping on the mud, and a spear sailed over Sha'di and planted itself into the cat's throat, causing it to finally collapse to the ground, dead.

Sha'di turned his head to see who threw the spear, and was shocked to see a woman standing between two trees. She had no paint on her skin, unlike every other person in the jungle he'd met. She wore a simple leather shift around her hips, the rest of her lean body laid bare and gleaming in the rain. Her hair was cropped short, a curved bone of some sort was pierced through the septum of her nose, and around her neck she wore a necklace made of beads and claws. The rest of her body was covered in leather straps, each one holding one or more small pouches. She was young, but her dark narrowed eyes looked far older.

The commotion around them was dying down. The man whose stomach had been slashed was still alive and moaning, a few men clutched at his wound, trying to soothe him with words, since there was nothing else they could do as he slowly died. Everyone else, injured or no, was looking at the prone body of Tanuk. The noise of the rain seemed to drown out Tenok crying over his older brother.

Even then Sha'di could not really understand that Tanuk was dead, that their conversation would never be finished. Tenok continued to sob loudly, unashamed to clutch at his brother's clothes and beg him to come back. Sha'di felt a sudden pain in his chest, remembering a day when he had kneeled next to the cold body of his father, his mother taking his father's Ancestral Cloak and placing it on his own shoulders, but he had barely felt the weight, only wanting his father's eyes to open. They had taken him to the Matahe Sea, and there given his body to the salty waters.

The bones they had kept.

"Who was he?" the woman asked, breaking the trance everyone had found themselves in.

"Chultuyu-na-chib'atl," Xupama's voice seemed to boom over all of them, "who carried his father's standard in his stead. He who was Nuktatl. He who was Chultunyatl. He who Guarded the Passage. He who Heard the Whisperers."

Sha'di pushed himself to his feet, feeling Xupama's eyes burn into him. *He was taking me to Chipetzuha*, he tried to say, but his voice was gone. *He was only here, because of me.* Instead he turned to the woman, who looked calmly at the group of men openly mourning.

"His name was Tanuk," Sha'di said, his voice was barely audible over the pounding water.

"Petzuhallpa don't belong in the jungle," she said, slowly walking to the beast and pulling her spear out of its throat. She paused, turned her head towards Tenok, her eyes softening slightly. "I'm sorry I don't kill it sooner. Two days, I tracked it."

"You brought it to us!" Xupama pointed accusingly.

She wiped the spear on the ground, getting rid of the last vestiges of blood. "No one brings the jaguar. I followed it. It attacked. I killed it."

Sha'di looked at the beast, the jaguar, finally recognizing it for what it was. He had seen many pelts of the sometimes gold, sometimes black, spotted beast. He had heard the name countless times, but this was the first time seeing it as it had lived. He could still see it leaping over him, its muscles rippling under its black fur, its claws extended to strike its prey.

"Leave her alone," Tenok cleared his throat, struggling to contain his emotions. He glared at the interpreter.

"Look at her, she is Ilotz'ai!" Xupama looked incredulous, but no one was paying him attention anymore.

The woman took a black knife hanging from one of the leather straps at her waist, and crouched next to the jaguar.

"Don't touch that!" Tenok screamed, instantly on his feet.

She turned towards him, her eyebrows going up. "It is my kill."

Xupama looked aghast. "Show your respect! He is Chultunyu-na-chib'atl now. He who–"

"Shut up!" Tenok snapped, and Xupama looked away indignantly. "That... *thing* k–" Tenok swallowed hard, unable to say the word for a moment, "killed my brother. I am no chib'atl, that title goes to... Koyo, his son..." Tenok looked to the ground, perhaps realizing for the first time that Tanuk's sons would never be able to join their father at Chipetzuha.

"What your name?" the woman stood up.

"Tenok," the young man managed to whisper.

"Tenok. I am Qayset. It is my kill... but," she held her arm out, the fire knife in her hand. It looked the exact same as the knives of the Rhagepe, as the knife Sha'di himself carried, "the skin is yours."

In one motion Tenok took the knife and stepped to the jaguar's corpse, and with fury cut into its still warm flesh.

Sha'di had seen enough animals skinned not to be shocked by Tenok's arm covered with blood as he separated the black skin from the pink meat underneath. The rain had seemed to die down, barely a drizzle making it through the leaves, and the jungle around them seemed to brighten. What shocked Sha'di was when the warriors with them took flint knives and began to cut into Tanuk and the other dead man's body.

"The flesh will rot before we can reach Chub'al," Xupama had explained in the Whisperers' tongue, seeing the expression of shock on Sha'di's face. Xupama sounded unusually serene. "Rotting flesh brings the insects, and the insects bring the bad air, that rots the mind. The bones are all we will bring with us."

Sha'di watched, wide eyed, as they cut and scraped and slowly began to make a pile of the dead chib'atl's bones. Tenok, quite purposefully, was keeping all his attention on skinning the jaguar. Qayset stood over Tenok, nodding in approval, crouching down once in a while to help cut through a particularly difficult part.

When they had finished taking off the pelt, Tenok and a small group of men helped to clean it. They had tied sticks into a crude square and spread the leather pelt out on it, making the beast look twice as large as it had been in life. They shaved its underside with flint knifes, scraping away any remaining blood and fat. They stitched back together the cuts in the pelt and rubbed it with salts and other cures to keep it from rotting with everything else.

Qayset went to work on the corpse, cutting off its flanks into cuts of meat, wrapping them in large leaves and tying it with vines. She piled these next to her, wiping the sweat away from her brow, only to leave a smear of blood. He thought the red suited her, made her look like she belonged among the men covered in red dye surrounding her.

The flesh they cut away from Tanuk's corpse was bundled just the same, but instead of being piled up, they were carried with great reverence to a fire pit that was being built. They were having a hard time finding dry wood, having to dig to locate any at all, but the pyre was growing steadily, and soon they would have enough to burn the flesh and organs.

When they had freed all the flesh from Tanuk's skull, Sha'di was absolutely transfixed by it. He had seen many skulls in his life, but this one was shaped oddly. Sha'di had already seen that the heads of the chakatl were oddly elongated, but he assumed it was by some trick of the hair, or something to do with their fat, but now he saw the skulls themselves were long. Xupama had claimed more than once that they were gods, but this was the first proof he had seen that maybe they weren't as human as he had assumed.

"You're uncoloured, but not the same as me."

Sha'di hadn't even noticed that Qayset had finished and was now standing next to him.

"I don't know... what 'uncoloured' is," Sha'di struggled to use the high tongue, it was still a little difficult for him to follow people when they spoke too fast, and was shocked that she spoke katan since he had assumed she was a commoner by the way Xupama had treated her.

"The Petzuhallpa bathe in dye to worship piles of rocks. My people are not Petzuhallpa, we are the jungle, and the jungle is us," she smiled.

"You speak their words," Sha'di countered.

"You too," she laughed. "I learned, as you did. So what – who – are you?"

"I am Sha'di Al'Sha'di, of the tribe Gonnamdi. I was sent by my people, the Gogepe, to speak for the Goddess of Rebirth, to warn the Petzuhallpa that the gods are angry and need to be appeased," he had been practicing how to say that in katan for when he finally reached Chipetzuha and made his case to their great allpa. He had felt pride with how smooth it had sounded when Tanuk was patiently helping him, but now the words sounded stiff, unconvincing.

Qayset blinked, "oh."

Sha'di looked back to the pyre. They had finished arranging the wrapped parcels on it, and the men had begun to gather.

"The gods are very angry," he whispered in his own tongue. Wondering why the gods would take Tanuk from them, wondering if it was punishment for the chib'atl, or for those who followed him. Or could it be the gods had just wanted to amuse themselves?

"You travel to Chipetzuha," she was not asking.

"You know?" he asked, surprised.

She raised her eyebrows as though it was the most obvious thing in the jungle. "Petzuhallpa leave their rock piles to go there. They hate the jungle, hacking and crashing through my home," she grinned. "We know the secret ways. We do not share them with the Petzuhallpa. I could fly there now, fast as anteans."

"Can you take me?"

"No," she shook her head gently. "I will help though... reaching Chub'al... A debt is owed."

They had started to light the funeral fire, but the kindling wouldn't catch, still too wet. Everyone, even Tenok, had gathered around the pyre now, waiting. Sha'di turned back to Qayset, pointing to the fire knife sheathed on one of her belts.

"Can I use?" he pointed, taking his own out from his skins. "For fire," he motioned.

She hesitated a moment, then took it out, flipping it in the air and catching it by its blade, handing him the knife handle-first. "Be quick."

He took it and walked through the crowd, crouching down next to the pyre, looking at the small parcels wrapped in leaves that only that morning had been a man, a brother, a father... a friend. He fought the urge to reach out and touch one, wishing he could clasp hands with him once more. He struck the knives together twice before the kindling finally caught. More kindling was thrown in until the fire grew large and hot enough for the pyre to catch. He stepped back, the smell of smoked meat quickly filling Sha'di's nostrils. The darkness of the jungle was moving in on them, trying to overcome them.

It only burned until the rains started again, and then nothing could reignite the flames.

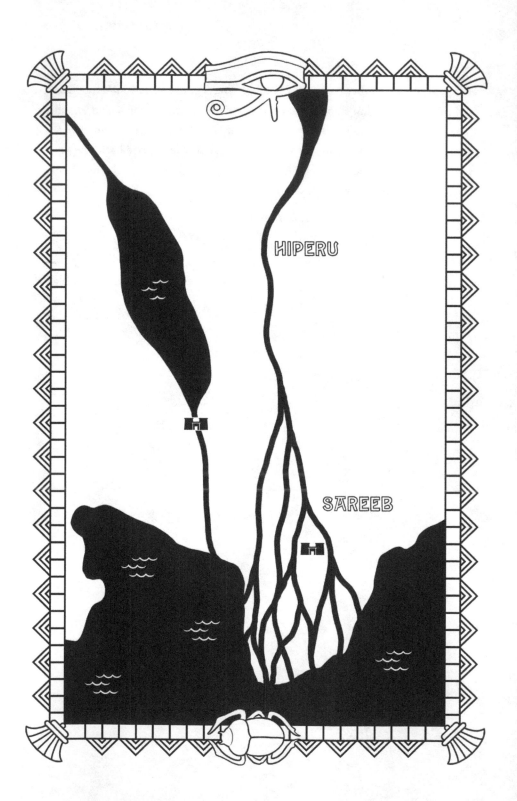

FROM THE GOLDEN TEMPLE TO THE AZURE SEA

IF YOU'RE NOT HAPPY WITH WHAT YOU HAVE NOW

The entire city was celebrating. From the highest tzati and priests of Mahat, to the poorest street vendors. Kings had travelled to see this, as well as peasants. There wasn't a single person left indoors. All were out on the streets, or on their ships, all eyes pointing towards the Golden Temple. Only those prominent in the Paref's court were allowed to enter the grounds of the palaces and temple, so all others filled every available space outside.

Samaki had been invited to the Golden Temple by Paref Rama himself. A great honour, as everyone kept reminding him. After he returned to the palace to tell the Paref of the successful delivery of his tribute, and finalize the sale of the wine the boy had promised he would honour, the Paref had informed him that for his loyalty and the love his father had shown the merchant, he would be allowed to stand within the walls of the Golden Temple during his coronation.

Of course Samaki had bowed and graciously accepted, but in truth he was annoyed. Normally such an invitation would have filled him with pride, given him something to attempt to brag about to his father, but all he wanted to do was leave this land, and this delayed him even further. Even loading up his ship's hold with all the silver and jewels brought nothing but a grimace to his face. He used to love the sight of more treasure than he knew what to do with, but as a merchant it didn't take long to realize those riches would soon be gone. Gone to buy new cargo, to pay sailors and debts with innkeepers, docking fees, and the grain he needed to feed his crew and pay taxes. He looked at that treasure being loaded onto his ship now, and only saw within the chest countless ledgers of accounting.

"What good is gold?" His father used to chuckle when Samaki raved about how well his merchant business was doing. *"If your ship capsizes, gold won't keep you afloat."*

And when the wave came, father, Samaki frowned to himself now, *your bitter words did nothing to save you from drowning.*

Tiyharqu was happy enough for the both of them, though. That morning she had spent a long time picking out her best embroidered silk vest, her finest gold and ruby chains, her thickest silver rings. On her head she wore a fine white wig, silver thread running through the braids. Samaki had laughed when he saw his friend wearing the thing, but Tiyharqu only laughed louder.

"I want to honour your people's customs, and your people have very... unique customs," her laughter echoed around the room.

It was true though, everyone was wearing their most interesting wigs. Silver wigs and topaz wigs, wine and coral, every single colour imaginable, all fettered with silver or gold and jewelled coronets. Usually wigs were simple black or earthen, but this was a day that called for special consideration. Even the poorest people in the streets wore their best wigs, though theirs were made from dyed linens and painted beads.

Still, Samaki had no desire to wear a wig. He wore his finest silk vest and pants, his jewelled necklaces, rings and bracelets, just as Tiyharqu had, but his head he left bald and shining in the bright sunlight. They rode borrowed horses to the palace, the canals filled with so many ships even early in the morning, that to try to navigate the Afeth into the palace grounds would have proven impossible.

The Golden Temple was directly to the north of the two palaces. It was a large plaza, without any large proper buildings like the palaces, but instead filled with statues and columns. It was laid out as a long rectangle, surrounded by tall gold and silver painted walls. Guarding the entrance at one end were statues of the first Paref Rama and his High Wife Khaferti, twice the size of normal men, their bodies adorned with rich gems.

They took small golden boats across the river from the palaces, following the largest ship, where the high priest and the young Rama were being carried. The next ship in the procession held the Paref's young wife Merneith and her father, King Utarna, quickly followed by the King of the Mountain Mahat's boat. They both wore the same silver nemes, but on the brow of the Mountain Mahat King was the head of an eagle and on the Sea Mahat King's was a golden face wearing a feathered hat. It was obvious from his rower's exhaustion that the Mountain King was trying to keep pace with the other king's boat, to prove that they were equal. All others followed in no particular order. Everyone was drinking and eating sweet melons and almonds as they lounged on the water, slowly following, enjoying each other's company.

When they reached the golden quays, they entered between the tall statues, a line of priests chanting, calling to their gods, pronouncing that here the Paref Rama, reborn in his son, was entering the temple to take his rightful place among them, as a living god. Samaki felt like the sight of gold would make him sick for the next month.

As they walked through the entrance, Samaki noticed that the crowd had settled into murmuring. They were entering a sacred place, and all felt the need without being told, to show respect.

"When does the proper feast begin?" Tiyharqu leaned over to whisper into Samaki's ear.

Samaki playfully elbowed his friend in the ribs. "You don't need any more feasts."

Tiyharqu slapped her round stomach. "I must replenish my strength at every occasion," she winked.

There were three sections to the temple. The first was filled with pillars as tall as four men, each one so large it would take six men holding hands to circle one completely. They were so close together a man could stretch his arms out and touch two across from each other. There were almost two hundred of them, creating the feeling that one was entering a forest with no exit. Each was identical, save for the ones that created the main aisle that the Paref now walked. Those were twice the height as the others, and it was only these columns that could be seen from outside the walls of the complex. Samaki felt like a child looking up at them, and he – and many others in the procession – felt the need to stop and look up in amazement.

Once past the columns they entered the next part of the temple. This section had no structures save for statues along the walls, each representing a different god, here the head of a jackal, there the head of a snake, each one holding the crook and flail of a Paref in arms crossing their chests. In the centre of the area was a large pool of clear water, surrounded by lush flowers and trees, a beautiful garden dedicated to the gods.

Beyond this was the third part of the complex, separated from the garden by another wall, with another gate protected by the statues of the first Paref Rama and his wife again. Through these walls Samaki could not enter. Only the royal families and the priests could enter the inner sanctum of the gods. Instead he waited with the others, while servants wearing sheer tunics, giving a hint of the pretty bodies underneath, served dates and other precious fruits in golden bowls.

Everyone strained to listen to the words being bellowed by the priest inside the inner sanctum.

"Come as you will, god among men, the pantheon awaits you!"

Samaki could hear the faint words over the rustling of nearby bodies, clearing of throats and quiet coughs.

"I can't hear a damn thing," Tiyharqu muttered, taking another handful of dates and stuffing them into her mouth with loud sucking sounds.

"What a mystery," Samaki rolled his eyes.

"... am your god... Your Paref... the gods by my side..." The young Paref was speaking now. His voice was, unsurprisingly, far weaker than the bellowing priest's had been.

After a few moments of straining, Samaki gave up on trying to listen. "He'll emerge from the inner sanctum, we'll cheer, then after he shows himself to the people we'll get you to your feast," Samaki smiled, taking a cup of wine being offered by a passing serving girl. His wine, he realized after taking a sip of the savoury red liquid, the wine he had brought here from the Sephian Islands.

When he had first set sail as a merchant, this was the kind of life he had imagined for himself, this was the kind of life he would brag to his father about being able to have.

"Haven't you ever wanted more from life?" Samaki had pleaded with his father to understand.

"If you're not happy with what you have now, you never will be." His father had dismissed him, focussing instead on mending the fishing net in his hand as he sat on the dirt of his adobe hut.

"How can you be happy with only fish and mud?" Samaki had wanted to scream at his father, to shake the senseless old man. Instead he had only dismissed his words. Of course he wasn't happy with the life he had as a child. It was no life. Looking around now at the temple filled with lords draped in jewels and gold, drinking beer and wine out of silver cups, surrounded by supple young women he could take aside and have his way with if he desired it – *this* was life.

He frowned as he thought the words – or was it the wine? – tasted bitter in his mouth. Yes, this was the life he had dreamed of, but even in death his father was laughing at him.

"If you're not happy with what you have now, you never will be," he muttered to himself, standing in a golden temple.

He had managed to make good relations with this new Paref, he had secured a hold full of goods that he knew he could easily sell anywhere. He would soon have accrued more than enough to buy some land, a nice villa, perhaps on one of the smaller Sephian isles. He could marry a woman, have a brood of sons, continue to sail the Middle Sea. He would have everything he had ever wanted when he set off on the Afeth. Yet all he could do was frown.

◆   ◆   ◆   ◆   ◆

After the Paref emerged from the inner sanctum, they had returned to their ships, first going along the canals, past cheering crowds of people, all wishing to see their Paref and his wife. Soon their faces would be on a dozen statues and a thousand murals, but to see them in the flesh was a treat, which they would tell their children and their children with great pride.

It was nightfall by the time they returned to the Palace of the Rising Sun. It wasn't long before Samaki was so full of food and wine that he felt like he would be sick, but still course after course of food marched past them. Roasted mutton, fried crocodile, boiled hedgehog soup, more fish dishes than Samaki even knew existed, but which he was sure his father would have been able to name every one of.

Tiyharqu was making a fool of herself, joining the dancing girls who wore nothing save a silk belt around their waist and weights tied to the ends of their hair, making their hair fly as they twirled. They laughed good-naturedly at Tiyharqu and Samaki couldn't help but laugh as well. The more he drank, the more he enjoyed himself.

He didn't remember leaving the palace, or returning to Pawura's inn. Yet when he awoke it was well into midday and his head felt like it was trapped between two stones being pressed together. He looked around the dark room, the straw strewn on the floor, the cracked water pitcher in the corner, the coarseness of the linen sheets. This was his life, not the life he had peeked at the night before. He sighed, pushing himself to sit up, fighting against the wave of dizziness that swept over him, wondering what it would feel like to have a wave take you and drag you down.

Samaki struggled to his feet, still wearing the same clothes as the day before as he walked into the harsh sunlight.

"It lives!" A friendly voice called out.

Samaki looked over and saw Pawura by the well, fetching some water from the well and filling some pitchers. He was an older man, bone thin with a face wrinkled by years of laughter. Only his bald head remained smooth.

"I didn't think I'd see you again until the evening meal," Pawura laughed, his leathery face crinkling up like parchment left in the sun too long.

"And rob you of my company? Never," Samaki had to clear his throat, his voice was hoarse and his mouth felt sticky. "Where's Harqu?"

"Still walking with the gods, I imagine. You returned alone," Pawura shrugged, bringing up a jug of water and dumping it into one of the pitchers.

"When you see her, send her my way. We need to start planning our departure," Samaki turned towards his ship.

"Leaving so soon?" Pawura called over to him.

"I've already stayed too long!" Samaki called back, not slowing down as he walked up the ramp to his silent ship.

Samaki was not surprised to see that there was no activity on the canal around him. It seemed like the entire city was still asleep. He was regretting now telling his crew to report before sundown the day after the coronation. He doubted everyone who had signed on would be able-bodied enough to show up, but he felt uneasy, restless. He needed to leave, sail back to Serepty, and get back into his usual shipping routes.

He opened the hatch and descended into the hold, grabbing the manifest that lay rolled up next to the ladder. He had already gone over it a dozen times, but he did so again, just to feel like he was accomplishing something. He sat down to rest halfway through it, his headache only becoming worse instead of going away.

His fingers traced over the feeling of coarse papyrus, and he wondered for a moment about where it had come from. This sheet could very well have been made from the reeds his father had collected every day. His father's deft fingers might have helped cut and shaped the sheet that was now pressed between his own. He breathed in the smell, the dryness, the hint of sweet, the smell of his father. He must have fallen asleep, because he awoke to Tiyharqu nudging his shoulder.

"Maki, the crew is starting to arrive," his first mate said.

Samaki's head still felt like a dull throb, but otherwise he felt fine, and with Tiyharqu's hand, got to his feet.

"Make ready to sail, we leave at nightfall."

"Yes, captain," Tiyharqu smiled, taking on the role of first mate once again.

The crew looked haggard, some still looked drunk, others as though they hadn't slept at all, one of them was leaning over the side of the canal, emptying his stomach into the low water.

Samaki had a list of all their names, and he ticked each one off as he greeted the crew. About half of them had arrived, but there was still plenty of time before sundown.

Sef arrived not long after, him and a handful of other older men who had been sailing on the Afeth almost as long as Samaki had been.

"Welcome back," Samaki nodded to each one with a wide smile on his face.

They nodded at each other, then Sef and the others climbed up to the ship.

He looked at the city, wondering when they would return again. Samaki had never really worked on a terribly strict schedule. It was harder to plan too far ahead, because there was always a worry that something would go wrong with the shipment, or you might not get what you were expecting, or you could only trade for goods that your next planned port wouldn't be interested in, forcing you to change your tactics. Still, he knew he would return to Nepata. He hoped that by then all the trouble from the flood would have passed.

"The gods are angry," he whispered to himself, squinting up at the sun, wondering what they had planned for him next.

They left just as the sun was beginning to disappear behind the mountains. Iason and a few of the crew were muttering their annoyance at having to leave at sunset. He couldn't blame them. It was a strange time to set off on a journey. It made him feel like he was escaping from some danger. He had decided they would take shifts to keep going through the night. Most of the rowers could sleep, since they were using the current to move. They just needed someone to man the rudder, and two or four oars in motion to ensure they didn't go off course.

"It is good to be on the water," Tiyharqu smiled. She always looked more at ease on the ship, her high energy settling down.

"I don't know why we ever go on shore, to be honest," Samaki smiled back, but Tiyharqu met him with a knowing gaze.

"Yes, you do," was all she said, turning away to take a deep breath and look at the murky waters of the Hiperu.

"A month from now, we'll be tying the Afeth to the docks of Serepty, and we will have our fill of women and wine," Samaki said wistfully.

"Uh," Tiyharqu frowned, the colour of her skin seemingly to pale a moment. "Don't say wine."

"Ha, this time tomorrow you will be wishing I had kept a few wine barrels for you."

"Tomorrow is none of my concern. Today is the only time you should be focussing on," Tiyharqu folded her arms.

"In that, my friend, you may be on to something quite profound."

"I am always profound," Tiyharqu laughed.

Samaki felt he had to laugh with her.

"You'll find nothing in Serepty, my dearest Samaki," Hamota frowned, taking a seat at the fine marble table. It was obviously new, like most of the things set out in Hamota's small, but richly furnished home.

They were in Sareeb once more, the first place they had been able to moor the Afeth since entering the Sea Mahat. The waters had indeed receded, but nothing about the Mahat was the same as the one they had left. The villages north of Sareeb were under heavy guard, to protect the unsullied farmland from those who had been displaced. Bowmen guarded spiked ditches and half-built walls along the river. It had been King Utarna's last decree to ensure the remaining crops in the Sea Mahat were properly distributed – namely into his own stores.

He already knew the villages south of Sareeb were all gone, washed away as if they had never existed. Thankfully the marshes and swamps had been relatively untouched, and marshmen were already starting to rebuild. Crude huts once more grew on the banks, but far less than had existed before, and the no one had attempted to till the farmlands. They would be left until the Nepata overflowed its banks soon, in the time of flooding, Anken. Life could blossom there once more. Even then, there was fear that there might not be enough farmers to grow the crops.

"Have you personally heard word from Serepty, or is this all hearsay, Hamota?" Samaki pressed the merchant for more information, staring down at him from next to the table, not wanting to sit.

He had come to Hamota to restock their stores before setting out across the Middle Sea. Hamota wanted them to take their time making arrangements, but Samaki just wanted to trade and be gone the next day. He hadn't expected this when he had mentioned he sailed next to the Sephian Islands.

"Many of their ships came this way, not long after the great flood. They said they had come north because the south had been destroyed. When they saw it was the same for us, they left. I've no idea where they've gone. There's nothing west, so they must be sailing to the east. The point is, Serepty was flooded just as badly as we were."

"Caemaan," Tiyharqu nodded in one of the seats, happily drinking the wine Hamota had offered, the same the merchant had won from Samaki the last time they had met. There were many places to the east, but Caemaan was the only one worth mentioning. Caemaan was the gateway to the east, and therefore the gateway to all its richness. Bolts of silk, ornately carved jade, mystical medicines that could cure any ailment, all came through Caemaan before reaching the Middle Sea.

"Tell me, how are things in the north?" Hamota asked, his hand reaching out for his cup, but not taking a sip. "Most of the ships leaving Sareeb head north, as though only in the Paref's bosom can they be saved."

Samaki shrugged. "Perhaps they are right. Perhaps only the gods can save us."

"The power to save us, the power to destroy us," Hamota shrugged, bringing his cup to his mouth, taking a long inhale before taking a sip, the red tinting his lips a shade darker. "It is all the same to those who wield it."

◆   ◆   ◆   ◆   ◆

"What now?" Tiyharqu asked as they walked back through the streets of Sareeb to their ship. The damage that had been done to the great city was barely noticeable. The people had been busy, repairing the city. New houses lined the narrow streets, made from fresh cut limestone and sandstone mixed with salvageable materials from the destroyed buildings. Still, there was evidence of the destruction. The obelisk that had tumbled in front of the palace had disappeared. A new one had yet to replace it.

Samaki wondered if Serepty had managed to recover like this. He was trying to reconcile this idea with the memories he had of Serepty. He could picture the shining gypsum palace, a jewel set in the lush forest of the mountainside, and the perfectly symmetrical vineyards, with their dark red grapes, dipped in dew, hanging from their vines. Was it all gone? Had the palace been washed away? Had the vineyards dried up? Had the grapes rotted on the ground? They had neither the wealth nor the manpower to rebuild at the same speed as Sareeb. Serepty would be the same as the land south of here, abandoned and unfertile.

"If Serepty is anything like the Sea Mahat, we cannot trade there," Samaki finally said.

"Then where can we go? Back to Hattute?" Tiyharqu asked in exasperation.

"You said it. Caemaan," Samaki winked at her, turning the corner and walking along the muddy riverside.

"And what if Caemaan is like all the rest? What if every great city along the Middle Sea was cracked and poisoned like here and Serepty?" Tiyharqu followed him.

"You heard what Hamota said. Serepty is gone, and going back is not an option. We will go to Caemaan."

"You know the journey there is treacherous," Tiyharqu warned. "The storms on that route are sudden – and terrible."

"And what about the storms in the north? The homeless and starving? The sick and diseased? The unrest? A great storm is coming to this land, all of Mahat,"

Samaki stopped, looking along the shore. From the river he could see most of the sprawling city. Sareeb, for all its rebuilding, was still crowded with those who had lost everything in the flood, though perhaps half as many as now roamed the streets of Nepata.

"We face dangerous waters then no matter where we sail." Tiyharqu shrugged, looking defeated.

"Nothing can sink this ship." Samaki laughed, continuing their walk, making out the Afeth's mast above all the others in the distance.

With the crew back on board, Samaki stood at the bow.

"Men, we make way for the lands of Caemaan, and the treasures therein!"

"What about Serepty?" one of the men closest to Samaki asked.

"By now I'm sure most of you have heard rumours. Serepty is no more, or if it exists at all, it is a pale image of what it once was."

There was murmuring about the men. Perhaps they had heard rumours of Serepty, but they had also heard the tales of ships being lost as they tried to make way to Caemaan. Everyone knew the safest way was by land from the Sephian Sea. Samaki could see the fear on their faces and stepped forward.

"Come men! This is the strongest ship that ever sailed on the Middle Sea and Hiperu. This ship rode the wave! You saw it," he pointed to Sef and his group of men, "and you over there," he pointed to another set of familiar faces. "This is the ship the gods chose to spare! This is the largest ship of her kind, strong and swift," he patted Tiyharqu on the shoulder, always standing strong at his side. "You built a marvel, the jewel of the Middle Sea, the ship of the god Afeth! We celebrate chaos, because we were born for it! We cannot be brought down by chaos, because we celebrate it!"

Tiyharqu was shaking her head in bewilderment, but the men seemed taken by Samaki's words, beginning to cheer as he ended every sentence, pumping their fists in the air as he did.

"We can sail to Caemaan! We can fill our hold with silks and jewels! We can enjoy their dancing girls! We can drink their sweet honey beer! The only thing that can stop us," he looked Tiyharqu in the eyes, "is our unwillingness to go on! To Caemaan!"

They took hold of their oars earnestly now, rowing in time, digging deep, and moving with a sudden swiftness. Samaki smiled at his crew, and held back the turmoil he felt. The choice had been taken from him. He was a senet piece, waiting for the sticks to tell him where to move.

To be continued in

Pekari – the Azure Fish

GOGEPE GLOSSARY

Dage	'Why'
Di	'Follower'
Hat	'Place'
Hothome	'Touch'
Iru	Modifies a verb into the present tense.
Karlai	'Fat'
Kin	'Craftsman'
Ko	'This'
Kreesh	'Vision'
Mahe	'Burial'
Mo	Signifies the verb that follows is modifying the noun that precedes it.
Morikah	'Man'
Nnam	'Sun'
Pema	'Silver'
Ri	'Spear'
Temech	'Me' or 'I'
Tharlaum	'Awaken'
Thenu	'Ugly'

For more information about the characters, locations and cultures of this world, visit: http://whisperpedia.wikia.com/

ACKNOWLEDGEMENTS

You wouldn't be reading this book if it wasn't for Lara Helmling deciding to take a chance on this not a quite fantasy, not quite a historical fiction novel. Gayle West, and everyone at Morgan James Publishing, helped edit and shape this novel into what it's become.

My mother, whom I dedicated this novel to, and my step-father Wally cannot be thanked enough. They supported and encouraged me while I edited the book. Their patience and kindness is a blessing I never deserved, and will be eternally grateful for.

The maps would still be barely legible pencil sketches if it were for the incredibly talented Sheharzad Arshad who helped turn them into little works of ancient art.

Thanks to Jack Howitzer and John Hodson, friends who were kind and gracious enough to read (and reread, many times) the first few chapters. Without your feedback, I think the beginning of this novel would read like a drunk National Geographic article.

And finally, I want to thank Noel, who helped me stick with it and do my best to try and get published, especially when I was about to give up. Te amo, peluchissimo.

This book could not have been finished without reading countless history books (and watching endless documentaries on YouTube) over the years. I can't remember everything that lent itself to my interpretation of the Bronze Age, but a few that do stick out in my memory are: *Mysteries of the Oracles* by Philipp Vandenberg, *Ancient Egypt: Everyday Life in the Land of the Nile* by Bob Brier and Hoyt Hobbs, *The Oxford History of Ancient Egypt* by Ian Shaw, *Egyptian Myth: A Very Short Introduction* by Geraldine Pinch, but perhaps the greatest wells of inspiration were *The Iliad* by Homer and *The Histories* by Herodotus.

ABOUT THE AUTHOR

Guenevere Lee has spent a lifetime interested in the Bronze Age, devouring any book or documentary she could get her hands on, as well as inventing languages and drawing maps in her journals instead of listening in class. Inevitably the Bronze Age seeped into her journals, and the world of Orope began to form. Having lived and worked in Canada, England, and Japan, and travelled around the world, her experience with learning different cultures, religions and languages is the basis for the Whisperers' journey. She is currently editing *Pekari – the Azure Fish,* the sequel to the Whisperers of the Gods series.

https://gueneverelee.com/

Photo by: Rebecca Menard

CPSIA information can be obtained
at www.ICGtesting.com
Printed in the USA
JSHW011041130123
36236JS00001B/18